Princess Smile

Princess Smile

Princess Smile

adele royce

DAGMAR
MIURA
LOS ANGELES

Published by Dagmar Miura
Los Angeles
www.dagmarmiura.com

Princess Smile

Cover photo by Merrell Virgen

Author portrait by Laura Bravo Mertz for Solifoto

First published 2021

ISBN: 978-1-951130-72-5

For Mom and Grandma (the original Jane)
And for all my precious girlfriends

*In the memory of Rebecca Ellen Augustine, my beloved editor
and friend. Rest in peace, dear Becky. I will always miss your
gentle, inspiring way.*

PINK CARNATIONS ARE TERRIFICALLY maligned. Carnations in general are the ugly stepsister flower no one wants. But here I was, tolerating the perfumed bouquet on my desk—leftovers from a mediocre date on Bumble. Alan was his name. He donned a cheap, ill-fitting sports coat with khakis—loafers without socks. His hand trembled as he handed me the bouquet. He obviously had not bothered researching carnations—if only to discover that they are the plain Janes of the floral universe. Why did I bring them to the office? Because there was nothing else to remind me that a man, regardless of whether I would ever see him again, took the time to buy me something—anything.

Warren burst into my office, halting my masochistic blossom-pondering.

"Hi, Warren," I greeted him in my professional voice, straightening up in my chrome swivel chair, and grabbing a pen and notepad.

"Jane, our friends, the Henrys, are not happy with the retouching on the bus wrap," he said with a frustrated sigh.

"You mean *Rita* Henry?" He must have just hung up from a call with the aging entertainer. I also knew the retouched image he was referring to, which was slated to grace the side of a metro rapid bus.

"Let's meet Jeffrey in his office to discuss it," he said, ignoring my comment, and holding the door open for me.

I knew what I was in for. I had been working at Warren Mitchell & Associates advertising agency for four years and had navigated my way around the many clients' likes and dislikes, hot buttons, triggers—whatever you wanted to call them. I was an account director—a job tailor-made for those who had little creative talent, but lots of patience, tolerance, and the ability to maintain calm confidence in the middle of any confrontation.

My best friend, Marisa Silva, taught me about the art of remaining calm—at least on the outside. Being a reporter for a local news affiliate, her facial expression was tested on a regular basis. Only when the lights and cameras were off, could she drop the cold exterior and vent with me in a dark bar over vodka sodas.

As I followed Warren to the art department, I eyed the many offices in my area of the building to see who was in, out, arguing with clients, or just tapping away at their keyboards.

I noted that Anna, my biggest nemesis, was out of the office. *Perfect.* No dealing with her smug grin and scathing comments today. I also noted both Tara and Brooke, nemeses numbers two and three, respectively, were engaged in conference calls.

I rounded the corner, past the war room where several creatives were scribbling on white boards; ad concepts for a new client were spread out on the conference table.

I was now skittering down the hallway so I could keep up with Warren, who took long, quick strides when he was on a mission. I didn't want to miss a word about Rita Henry's latest complaints.

Jeffrey Vance, the creative director, had clued me in two years ago, when Warren handed me the keys to their account. They were a country music duo who had once been married. According to Jeffrey, Chance Henry loved to talk trash behind his female counterpart's back. He was gay with a full-time partner, though he kept it under wraps, so he wouldn't alienate his female fans.

Rita Henry was now married to the band's manager, David Kaufman, who made her his trophy. Rita suffered delusions that her target audience was comprised of twenty-something males who were all in love with her.

"Two of the most neurotic people in show business," I recalled Jeffrey telling me. "They have a huge budget and they've been with the agency forever. They were all the rage about three decades ago. Not so much now. But don't tell them that … they still consider themselves A-listers."

And his conclusion was: "If you can make Rita happy, you're way ahead of the rest of us."

Jeffrey's office was encased in glass, so you could always see when he was there and who he was with. Today, he had a full house. Warren forcefully pushed the glass door open. Jeffrey, surrounded by at least five creatives, didn't look up to see who it was.

I entered right behind Warren and caught everyone gathered around Jeffrey's colossal computer screen, snickering at the image of Rita's face, zoomed to 200 percent, and pointing out plastic surgery scars, moles, and other skin defects.

Warren was an attractive middle-aged man with a full head of salt-and-pepper hair and no apparent warmth. When I first came to work for him, I found him shallow and icy. He didn't want to hear about anyone's personal life or what his employees did after they left the office. He just wanted us to show up every day on time and be ready to jump when he needed something.

At first, I thought he was stoic and humorless but, over time, I understood he was just deeply cynical. He, like many of his peers, experienced the universal shit trenches and transient glory that comprised life in advertising and so he, understandably, had become bitter and jaded.

"Okay, guys," Warren said sternly, yet sounding exhausted, like he had been through these scenes too many times before. "The client's not happy with the retouching. I just got off the phone with Rita—she was on a tirade—says we're *trying* to make her look unattractive. The creatives had dispersed like frightened mice and were now lining Jeffrey's office walls to make room for the boss. I just trailed behind him.

"Jeffrey, pull up the original photo, so I can see it next to the one we've altered," he ordered.

Usually, Jeffrey had a supernatural ability to remain objective in these situations. Today, however, he pushed back. "Sorry, Warren, but I'm an ad guy, not a psychiatrist," he quipped, pulling up the two images for a side-by-side review. "She looks like a sixty-year-old bride of Frankenstein trying to look twenty. It's just not going to happen."

Jeffrey was thirty-something, a total smart ass, and like a brother to me. He was the only one in the agency who ever had my back. He wore stylish clothes, hip, horn-rimmed glasses, and his medium brown hair stuck up a bit on one side. I always had the urge to smooth it down with my hand.

Warren studied the two images. "Why don't you pull an image of her at twenty and piece her face together from that."

Jeffrey looked at him and said flatly, "I'm not a miracle-worker."

"Christ, Jeffrey," Warren erupted. "Fucking figure it out. That's what I pay you to do. Perform fucking miracles."

Wow, I thought to myself. Two F-bombs, one statement. It was clear Warren was now the one on a tirade, which rarely happened.

"And who do you think's paying for this work?" he continued. "That's right, the client," he finished before Jeffrey could respond.

Warren then looked up, scanning the room with a frown. "And I would advise the rest of you to think twice before you say or do anything to piss these people off … remember, clients are the reason you get a paycheck. Believe me, it could stop any time and, if it does, you'll be out looking for your next job. Got it? Now get back to work," he said, quickly regaining his cool composure before sauntering out.

Everyone looked down, backing away toward Jeffrey's

door like children who were just scolded by their father. And, as dysfunctional as it may sound, Warren was a little like a father-figure to everyone—especially to me.

I don't quite remember when I started to view Warren as the father I never had. He was the opposite of my real father, who left me when I was eight. Warren, a man who wore posh suits and Italian shoes, had a quiet, intense way of making you respect him, and an ability to sway people in the right direction by making them think it was their idea. Or he would just flat-out tell them what to do in a stentorian voice.

Somewhere, in my heart, was a seed of hope that Warren would fill the void left by my father. He knew nothing about me personally and seemed pleased with what I did professionally. And that was what life was all about … pleasing others.

Jeffrey glared up at me and interrupted my thoughts. I was the only one who had lingered in his office after Warren's visit.

"Jane, do you happen to know the time what's-her-face is coming in today?" he asked. I glanced at the appointment calendar on my smart phone and saw that Rita was scheduled to meet with Warren that afternoon.

"She'll be here at four. Do you need anything from me?" I inquired.

"Not unless you know any priests—I'd say we need an exorcism," he answered.

I laughed. "No. If you'll recall, I'm Jewish."

"I'd welcome a rabbi, too," he teased.

I CALLED AN EMERGENCY lunch meeting with Marisa. Of course, she stormed into the restaurant ten minutes late, frantically texting and juggling her bag and car keys.

"I'm sorry, Jane," Marisa said as she briefly looked up from her texting. "My producer just called me about a story, so I don't have a lot of time."

"That's okay," I said. "Who's the unlucky soul whose party's getting crashed today?"

"You're funny," she said, fumbling around in her bag for a phone charger and glancing around the room for a power outlet. This constant state of crisis, I would come to know well, was just Marisa's way.

"I'm starving," Marisa said as she skimmed the menu and motioned to the waitress to take our order so as not to waste one second.

"So, what's new in the wonderful world of advertising today?" Marisa asked in a forced pleasant tone. I had to get used to that voice, because she used it a lot when she was trying to generate a conversation. It was one of her reporter tactics.

"Don't ask," I said.

Marisa made a face. "Oh, come on, give it up—you're the one who called me."

"The usual," I answered. "The wonderful world of advertising would be awesome without the clients." We both chuckled.

I told Marisa the story of the Henrys while she devoured her lunch, and soon I had her almost choking with laughter. And while I didn't reveal the names of the clients in question, Marisa figured it out quickly.

"Don't worry," she said wiping her mouth in between bites. "You know our conversations are always off the record."

I realized this was not the smartest thing for me to do. After all, you didn't have to be a PR expert to know that nothing was ever off the record when it came to reporters. Marisa, a Puerto Rican who grew up in a tough Bronx neighborhood, made a living pulling lurid details out of people and sharing them with the world. It was her job to bludgeon people into giving up the story, and she was good at it. One of the reasons I still had a job was that I didn't blab office details. But she was my best friend, my only friend. I had no choice but to trust her.

Marisa shook her head. "What a train wreck Rita Henry is." As she said this, she waved down our waitress for the check. "Can't say I'm surprised. Always drama. Yet we seem to revel in it."

"Yeah, I know," I said, looking at my watch. "Feel my pain."

Marisa laughed, fished some cash out of her bag, and slapped it down on the table. She leaned over and whispered, "Princess smile." Marisa and I had coined the term to use as code for having a crap day but smiling like a princess to get through it.

Marisa got up abruptly. "I have to run now," she said, getting on her phone and hurrying out the door in pursuit of her next assignment.

I sat alone for another few minutes, pondering Marisa's words. There was no question about it: on some level, I did revel in the work drama, mostly because I didn't have much of a personal life. Sometimes I longed for stalkers like Marisa had, even though she was always complaining about them. Men chased her with a vengeance. When we were together, heads turned, both male and female. I longed for someone to give me that kind of attention. I rarely had dates and, if I ever did, there would never be a second one.

My earliest dating disaster happened when I was sixteen years old. Grandma allowed me to go to a concert with Asher from synagogue. The Strokes were playing at the Hollywood Palladium and his parents bought tickets for Asher and six of his buddies.

I remember standing with Asher and his loser friends through the show, because we wanted to be in the front row. When the crowd got thick and people started to shove each other to get to the front, I remember holding onto Asher for dear life, so I wouldn't get trampled. He picked me up and put me on his shoulders, and before I knew it, his hands were sliding up my thighs and around to my ass. I was wearing a nineties grunge outfit—plaid flannel shirt, cut-off jean shorts with tights underneath, and Doc Martins. I quickly slapped his hands and urged him to put me down.

After the concert, he told everyone I was easy and that he got his "money's worth" for the tickets. The worst thing was that everyone believed it. From then on, life was pure hell. One time, I was sitting in English class when Asher and his friends were in the back of the room laughing. When I turned back to see what they were laughing at, one of them remarked, "What are you looking at, fire-crotch?" This was followed by another round of laughter, and someone muttering, "Ask Asher about that," which made my face turn scarlet.

When I got home that day, I remember going straight to my room and locking the door. I cranked Nirvana's "Smells Like Teen Spirit" as loud as it would play, desperately trying to drown out what happened in class that day.

With the lights out, it's less dangerous, Kurt Cobain screamed in the background while I slumped down on my purple canopy bed and cried.

My final two years of school were spent in solitude as I had been branded an outcast and felt it necessary to fully become one. I skulked in the shadows with earphones plugged in to avoid actual conversations, and I became more inward with every passing day, withdrawing into my own lonely world.

"Would you like anything else?" the waitress broke into my depressing thought bubble.

"No, thank you," I replied, taking her hint, and rising to leave.

❧

TRAFFIC WAS RELATIVELY LIGHT as I drove toward the agency, which was in downtown Santa Monica, near Tongva Park, and not far from my apartment on Lincoln and Colorado.

When I arrived, Tara and Brooke, who looked exactly like Barbies, complete with long blonde hair, false smiles, and pale blue eyes, were in my office, seemingly snooping around.

"Can I help you?" I asked without attempting to hide the sarcasm in my voice.

They jolted in unison and turned toward me. I whiffed the faint scent of coconuts—Brooke's signature scent.

"Oh—hey Jane," Tara said, eyes wide like she didn't

expect me to bust her nosing around my office. "We were just looking for *LA Insider Magazine*. Have you seen it?"

Both Tara and Brooke always wore low-cut blouses and dresses that showed off their perky, perpetually tanned breasts. Today they looked like twins—they both wore Kelly green DVF wrap dresses. When they caught me eyeing their identical wardrobe selections, Brooke immediately piped up. "We didn't plan this," she said, waving her pointed finger between herself and Tara.

"I guess I didn't get the memo," I responded, side-stepping them and moving behind my desk. I shuffled through a stack of magazines, locating *LA Insider*, which had a photo of a crowd of well-dressed men and women on the cover. The headline read, "Special Edition: LA's Top 20 Entrepreneurs."

"Is this the one you're looking for?" I asked the green twins, who were now beaming at the publication.

"Yes—can we borrow it?" Brooke asked in a disingenuous saccharine tone usually reserved for clients. "Anna said *Craig Keller* is in this issue."

"Who's that?" I asked, naïvely.

Tara's eyes became round as saucers, and she drew in her chin. "Hello—he's only the hottest guy in town and he owns the biggest agency. You've never heard of Keller Whitman Group?" She was now glaring at me like I was a complete idiot.

Brooke stifled a giggle.

I did my best to recover. "Oh, yeah—that guy. Of course, I know who he is," I replied, thinking I needed to get out more. I had no idea who this man was, but he was obviously a big shot to Tara, Brooke, and Anna.

"We'll bring it right back," Tara said, snatching the magazine from my hands. The pair spun around and made a quick exit, somehow reminding me of the twins from *The Shining*.

❧

LATER, ALONE IN MY office, I prepared to leave for the evening. I turned off my computer and began gathering my things. I noticed the magazine had been returned to my desk. I picked it up and flipped through it.

"LA's Top 20 Entrepreneurs," was something *LA Insider* published once a year to distinguish the top young executives in the city. The executives were named in alphabetical order, and, out of sheer curiosity, I leafed through to the Ks. There was only one—Craig Axel Keller. I took one look at his photo and had to catch my breath. Tara was right. He was a total stunner—unbelievably sexy with glossy dark hair that was not too long and not too short. His eyes looked to be a translucent jade with lengthy eyelashes. But it was his smile that entranced me. He had the straightest, whitest teeth I'd ever seen. *This man could be a G.Q. model.* He wore a navy suit with a pale blue tie. The shot was from the waist up, but from what I could tell, he was extremely fit and trim. *So, this was what all the hype was about.* I studied his image for a few more minutes and, just as I was about to read the accompanying article, Anna poked her head into my office.

"Oh, I thought maybe you'd already left," she said, glancing at her watch as though *she* were my boss, not Warren. Anna wore a medium brown shiny bob that bounced from side-to-side when she walked. Unlike Tara, Anna never feigned respect for me—she spent her time either trying to sabotage my projects or making herself look good. She managed up well when Warren and Jeffrey were around. Her employees hated her.

I sighed. "I thought you were out of the office today."

She tossed her bob and gave me that smug grin. "No, just in meetings with Warren—you know, he relies on me for everything these days," she said, like it was something she didn't love—didn't *live for.*

"What do you need, Anna?" I drummed my fingers against my desk.

Her eyes darted to the magazine in my hand, and she let out a snide laugh. "Why, Jane Mercer—are *you* crushing on Craig Keller?"

I set the magazine down on my desk and felt my cheeks get hot. "I was just …"

"You were just *drooling*," she interrupted, now giggling wickedly. "Don't get any ideas—that guy is so far out of your league—he wouldn't pick you out of a crowd of two."

"That's it, Anna," I said pointing at the door. "Get out of my office."

She was laughing hysterically now. "He'd probably mistake you for the drapes," she continued.

"Get out, now," I commanded, rising from my swivel chair, heart now pounding.

She finally relented and left my office, her laughter fading the further away she walked.

As soon as she was gone, I shut my office door, locked it, and sat down again, alone with the magazine. I stared at the cover, shivering with humiliation that Anna had caught me ogling Craig Keller's image. I waited a few minutes, then thumbed to the page where his photo was and read his bio. He was thirty-six, ten full years older than me. He had graduated from Stanford University with honors and was managing partner of the most successful advertising agency in Los Angeles. There was a long list of awards and accomplishments as well as his involvement with certain charities where he sat on the board of directors. I read his quote. "Success is always finding new ways to do things, hiring the best talent, and inspiring them to reach their full potential. I only hire people who are smarter than me. I never settle for anything but the best."

My eyes moved to the photo again. I sighed, closed the magazine, and stashed it in my messenger bag. I got up and walked to the door, where a full-length mirror hung. Anna's nasty comments echoed in my mind—how he wouldn't pick me out in a crowd of two and would mistake me for the drapes. I examined myself from head to toe, dissecting my features. I observed my long auburn hair, big almond-shaped green eyes—I had always been told my eyes were my best feature. My nose and mouth were sort of average—lips not too big nor too thin. At least my teeth were straight. Grandma and Grandpa had taken care of that with braces. After a sufficient analysis of my face, I started on my body.

I wore smart clothes because they were my passion, but the drapes comment lingered in my mind. I turned to the side to examine my figure. At least I was slender. But there was something about my lack of confidence that made me invisible.

Anna was right. A man like Craig Keller—or any man, for that matter, would never notice me.

S ATURDAY AFTERNOONS WERE FOR napping—especially after a night out with Marisa. Today, I didn't even bother getting out of bed and transporting myself to the couch. I considered that a form of getting up. Instead, I rolled over, grabbed the TV remote and flipped on some tragic reality show about brides getting jilted at the altar.

I examined the clock and realized I was close to missing my window to call my grandparents. They required me to call them at the same time each week. I sighed.

I was raised by my grandparents. When I was around two, my drug-addled mother left my father for another man and moved to Australia, never to be heard from again. My father, Aaron Mercer, a career Naval officer, was almost always at sea, so I was left with a live-in nanny, Petra. Although my father wrote long letters to me late at night when he was drunk and lonely, my only memories of him were dark and depressing. He ended up leaving me when I was eight, to be raised by my paternal grandparents, Bruce and Barbara Mercer.

My grandparents were well-intentioned but annoyingly out of touch with the modern world. Grandpa was a retired history professor at Cal State and was always on me about something. I saw shades of my father's asshole tendencies in Grandpa, although at least he didn't drink excessively. But he hated my job—acted as if it were a joke—something I fell into because I had no other plan.

A slight hangover began kicking in along with substantial guilt, so I decided to get the call over with. I grabbed my cell phone from the nightstand, but clumsily let it slip from my grasp. I reluctantly managed to roll myself over, grab the phone off the floor and dial their landline.

"What's the matter? Were you out late last night? You're not still sleeping, are you? Are you still coming for dinner this evening?" Grandma's obnoxiously loud voice blasted into my ear.

"Yes, I'm coming, Grandma," I answered sleepily.

"Why don't you bring Marisa?"

"Who?" I asked pretending not to understand. Marisa had only met my grandparents once or twice. That was on purpose. Knowing how nosy and overbearing they were, I tried to keep them at a distance.

"You know darned well who, young lady. When are we going to see Marisa again?"

"Grandma, she's probably busy tonight."

"Of course, she is. Busy with work I suppose just like all you girls these days. Would you at least ask her? We haven't seen you for two months."

She was not going to let this go. "Okay. I'll ask."

"Really? Good. I'll make extra helpings."

I would owe Marisa big time. That is, if she said 'yes.'

❧

AFTER AN ABNORMALLY TRAFFIC-FREE cruise down the 405 to Los Alamitos, Marisa and I arrived promptly at 7 p.m. to find Grandma busily putting together a pupu platter, as she called it.

The house was your average suburban California home built in the seventies but never updated, so it was like entering a time-warp. My room was exactly how it was when I moved out, except for the absence of posters of Oasis, Killers, and Green Day. Grandma had the room repainted, but the white eyelet curtains and purple paisley bedspread had been left excruciatingly intact.

The rest of the house had pretty much stayed the same since my childhood. The shag carpet was dark brown, and in desperate need of replacing. The furniture was old, worn and a mixture of unfashionable colors. Grandma always kept the lights down—probably to hide the condition of the furniture.

"Welcome, girls. Tonight's theme is Oriental," she said gleefully as she greeted us, glass of pink box wine in hand, grey-blonde hair piled high into a beehive and multiple layers of bangle bracelets and chains clanking and chiming as she moved around. "Would either of you like a Mai-Tai?"

"Grandma, I think you're supposed to say Asian, not Oriental," I said feeling my first pang of embarrassment after giving her a hug and kiss and re-introducing her to Marisa, who was on her best non-cursing behavior.

"Huh?" Grandma shrugged her shoulders at me. "I don't know what you're talking about."

"And since when do Asians drink Mai-Tais?" I continued to needle her.

"They do at Trader Vic's, wisenheimer. You were too young to remember, but that's where we always took you for Asian food," she said, exaggerating the word 'Asian' for my benefit.

"Grandma, I think that's Polynesian. There's a difference."

Again, I glanced at Marisa to gauge whether she was offended. I had told her many times that my grandparents were anachronisms, so she shouldn't have been surprised.

"If you're serving Asian food, then it should be something served in an Asian country, like Chinese, Japanese, or Thai cuisines, for example." I couldn't help but patronize. I was constantly annoyed at her failure to recognize that politically incorrect references were hardly amusing to anyone who entered the work force after 1960.

"I'd love a Mai-Tai, Mrs. Mercer." Marisa jumped in quickly, flashing Grandma a princess smile and handing her a bouquet of pink tea roses.

"Oh, call me Barbara," she said, accepting the flowers and shooing me away with her hand. "These are lovely." She was holding the bouquet next to her pink two-piece sweatsuit. "Look—they match my outfit," she commented with a hearty laugh. "And don't listen to Jane—she's always *meshuga*." As she said this, she pointed her index finger at her temple and made air circles for emphasis. Grandma always threw in a little Yiddish to keep it real. "Ever since she got that job, you know, working for that fancy-pants boss guy, it's been nothing but sass out of her mouth," she said to Marisa as though I weren't in the room.

"I can hear you, Grandma." I decided it was in my best interest to change the subject. "Make that two Mai-Tais, please. Where's Grandpa?"

"He went to get ice. He'll be back in a jiffy. Jane, make yourself useful and put some records on, light some candles, you know, jazz up the place a bit," Grandma barked over her shoulder as she disappeared into the kitchen via double 'saloon doors'.

"You know, Marisa, you don't have to drink a Mai-Tai," I said, while sifting through the music selections in their huge wooden console. "I'll make you whatever you want. Just don't drink the wine unless you want a headache tomorrow."

Marisa was busy marveling at the authentic, orange-colored spaghetti-bowl lamp with the base lit up, making it look like a big, sparkling ball of fire.

"This place is awesome" Marisa commented. "Where did they get all this retro stuff?"

"I hate to spoil your fantasy, but it's not retro to them," I said. "They had it during the first cycle of popularity."

"These things would cost a fortune in West Hollywood."

"Well, maybe you can convince them to give you some of it," I said. "I've been trying for years to get that lamp, but they don't want to part with it. It's not that they know it's cool or anything. It has a function."

I heard Grandpa entering through the garage. He appeared wearing an old faded blue bowling shirt with cargo pants. He had a slender frame with a slightly distended mid-section. His white hair, though receding, was worn too long and jutted out at the ends in all directions. He looked sort of like Albert Einstein but without the mustache.

"Hey, Gramps." I jumped up to help him carry in the ice. "I hear we're having a Tiki party tonight," I said in a smart-alecky tone as I put my arms around his neck and kissed his cheek.

"Oh?" he asked, refraining from kissing me back. "I don't know what that is. Tiki, did you say?"

"Well, neither does Grandma, but that's what we're having. Grandpa, you remember my friend, Marisa."

Marisa went to shake Grandpa's hand. "Nice to see you again, Mr. Mercer," she said politely. "Jane always says such nice things about you."

I had explained many times to Marisa how Grandpa and I weren't exactly chummy, so I knew she was trying to score points for me.

"Call me Bruce," he said holding out his hand. "Glad to see you again. Are you in the ad business, too?" Although Grandpa had been introduced to Marisa in the past, his memory occasionally failed him on the details.

"Oh no, I'm a news reporter," she said, knowing that would also score high on Grandpa's regimented list of acceptable professions.

Grandpa's face lit up with admiration. "I'll bet that's an interesting job. I want to hear all about it."

At that moment, Grandma burst into the room balancing a drink tray and the appetizer platter, with a lit cigarette in her mouth. "Bruce, help me with this stuff, will you?" she managed to utter between inhalations.

As far back as I could remember, Grandma smoked, and she was always trying to quit. As she got older, she insisted it kept her weight down. "You'll be the thinnest woman in the graveyard," Grandpa always warned. I had long ago stopped talking about it.

Grandpa got up and took the platter.

"Food looks great, Barb," he said. "We were just talking about Marisa's career as a news reporter."

"Oh, I know, Bruce—I see her on TV every day." Grandma said, shooting him an annoyed glance, like he should have remembered what Marisa did for a living.

While we noshed on the appetizers, Grandma and Grandpa pumped Marisa for details about her job, what it's like to be on TV, and how she coped with the stress.

I sank deeper in their baby-blue crushed velvet Lazy Boy sofa and took a huge gulp of my Mai-Tai. I couldn't understand how, in five minutes, Marisa had become a superstar with my grandparents, and no one even bothered to ask about how my job was going. I knew they considered what I did frivolous, but it wouldn't hurt to get an ounce of support here and there.

By the time dinner was ready, I had already sucked down two Mai-Tais and was getting a third. The stuff wasn't half bad. I wondered what Grandma put in it. Of course, I located a gallon-sized jug of syrupy mix and two bottles of rum. I quickly poured an extra stiff one and returned to the family room.

Dinner was some beef dish with sauce served over Grandma's attempt at fried rice. Grandma was not that great a cook, unless it was from a box, but was especially awful when she strayed a bit too far from her normal meat-and-potatoes safety net.

Over dinner, with Doris Day playing on the turntable, the attention finally turned to me.

"How's the boy situation these days?" Grandma asked with a mischievous little grin.

Great. "Not seeing anyone," I murmured before shoving a heaping fork-full of rice in my mouth, so I could have the excuse of chewing rather than talking.

"You girls are too focused on your careers," Grandpa remarked. "When your grandmother and I met, we never even discussed work. It was a given that I would earn the money and Barb would make the home nice. It was simple."

I looked at Marisa. *Here we go.*

"Well, you see, Grandpa, things really aren't that simple now," I explained slowly, like I was talking to a child. "Not only do we women have to support ourselves, but we also deal with the dating world which, in case you don't know, has also become a lot more complicated than it was in the days when you were dating Grandma."

"Pshaw," he dismissed me. "You girls make it complicated by trying to compete with men. You're scaring them off. If you'd just relax and act like a girl sometimes, you'd have all the dates you want."

I thought Marisa might choke for a second, but she maintained a neutral expression, likely well-executed due to regular Botox injections.

"Bruce, leave her alone," Grandma scolded, acting irritated, even though it was she who brought up the sore subject. "We didn't raise her to be a shrinking violet. Things are a lot different now and you can't blame the girls for wanting careers."

While Grandpa and Grandma began an old, tired debate, I excused myself and signaled Marisa to come with me.

"Where are you girls going?" Grandma intoned just before making another point to Grandpa about the importance of feminism, which she always spoke of as though it were a new concept. "We have dessert coming."

I gave her the international smoking hand gesture. "We'll be right back."

As Marisa and I walked out, I heard Grandpa ask, "Since when does she smoke?" and Grandma answer, "*Oy,* Bruce, you're driving her to smoke with all this crap about acting more like a girl ..."

"Oh my God, can you believe them?" I cried as soon as we hit the back porch, which was right off the kitchen. I grabbed the pack of cigarettes from the counter on the way out and lit up a smoke by the fire pit. Grandpa was right. I rarely smoked, mostly because I didn't want to get hooked like Grandma but, at that moment, I had to. I just couldn't take another minute of their foolish banter.

Marisa laughed. "They're hilarious." Then she saw the look on my face and added, "Aw, they're just old-fashioned, Jane. Give them a break."

"Easy for you to say. You didn't grow up with them." I took a long drag on my cigarette, inhaling deeply. "They have no idea what they're talking about—they don't even know about Match, Bumble, and Tinder or any of the other online dating apps."

"Are you still doing that?" Marisa asked, crinkling her nose as she grabbed a cigarette out of Grandma's pack and set it between her lips. I held the lighter up for her.

"I don't have a choice, now, do I?" I answered, smoke streaming out of my nostrils. "I can't date people from work, I'm always at work, and I don't want to meet guys at bars."

"Maybe you should join some groups," Marisa suggested. "There are lots of groups—find one with a shared interest—like politics, for example—at least you'll know on the front end what you *won't* be arguing about."

We sat smoking in silence for the next few minutes. Maybe Marissa was right. Maybe I should try to join some extracurricular groups. I tried to think of interests and all I could come up with was fashion—which I doubt would snag me a heterosexual male. I lit another cigarette with the one I had—a real class move. My thoughts suddenly went back to the magazine and Craig Keller's photo.

"Marisa, have you ever met Craig Keller?" I asked, thinking that with Marisa's job, she had to have run into him at least once.

Marisa's eyes lit up. "Oh my god, Jane, I've been trying to get an interview with him for years—he's really tough to get a hold of—he's worse than a celebrity." She took another drag of her cigarette. "What made you think of *him*?"

"Oh, I don't know. I just saw a picture of him in *L.A. Insider Magazine*. He's *so* gorgeous."

"Girls," Grandma called from the back door. "Come back inside, will you? We have baked Alaskas for dessert."

"Be right there," Marisa and I chimed in unison. It was

the end of my Craig Keller inquiry, but I was still thinking about him.

"I'm pretty buzzed," I told Marisa as we stomped out our cigarettes. I felt myself stagger a bit as we walked back through the kitchen. "Are you okay to drive us home?"

Marisa nodded. "Of course—I only had one of those drinks—you really tied one on."

"Did you just use a pun?" I asked giggling and swatting her on the arm.

As we were leaving, Grandma gave us both a hug and said to me, "Don't pay any attention to Grandpa, honey. He just wants the best for you. I do too."

As soon as we were in the car and Marisa was pulling out of the neighborhood, I leaned over to look at myself in the side view mirror. I did this whenever I was in a car, whether driver or passenger. It was an obsessive habit I had had ever since high school. I couldn't help but think about Grandpa's comments about how I didn't have a boyfriend. I wondered why, at age 26, I never had a real boyfriend. At least I wasn't still a virgin—I'd had a few sexual encounters—mostly forgettable. When I was twenty, I had a one-night stand with a drunken barfly who was much older than me. I figured if he were sober, he never would have gone for me at all. I remembered waking up in a strange apartment next to a disheveled slab, covered in bed linens. All I could hear was muffled snoring. I noiselessly stole out of the apartment without leaving a note, praying he wouldn't remember my name or face—I was sure we had not exchanged phone numbers. My stomach lurched at the memory.

"We're here," said Marisa, snapping me back to reality. We had been silent the entire ride from my grandparents' house, and I didn't even realize it. "Are you okay?" she asked.

"Marisa, do you think I'm attractive?" I sounded meek and vulnerable.

"What?" Marisa looked puzzled.

"Be honest."

"Oh Jane." She rolled her eyes. "Do you think I'd hang

out with you if you weren't?"

"No, seriously, Marisa, *please* be honest."

Marisa shook her head and stared at the steering wheel. "Man, you sure have some issues tonight, Jane. Must have been those three Mai-Tais you guzzled."

"I'm not getting out of this car until you tell me," I said, looking her right in the eye.

She let out a high-pitched laugh but looked away. Her long dark hair flew in the direction of her head as she pretended to investigate the driver's side rear view mirror. "What's wrong with you?"

"Come on, Marisa. Tell me the truth. I'm plain—*plain Jane*, right? I flipped the interior car light on and turned to the side, so she could inspect my face. "Well?" I asked impatiently when she remained silent.

"Oh my god, Jane—you're gorgeous. *You're* the only one who doesn't think so. You have the most beautiful green eyes, perfect skin, and shiny hair. Your figure is to die for—I don't know what you want me to say."

"All I know is I never get dates and I've never had a boyfriend. But you ... you seem to have men clamoring to hook up. What's *wrong* with me?"

Marisa gave me an empathetic look. "Jane, I really think you're being hard on yourself. I get stalkers because I'm on TV every day."

"What if I had some work done?" I asked. "You know, Botox and fillers—the stuff that *you* get done. Would I be prettier then?"

Marisa shook her head. "That *stuff* is expensive, you know. And it's addictive—you must keep doing it to maintain—well, you know, a certain look. Plus, you're naturally beautiful—you don't need any of it." Marisa let out a deep sigh. "I just do it because I have to—there's always someone younger, prettier, smarter—ready to take my place."

I turned to look Marisa in the eye. It was the first time I'd ever heard her vulnerable. "Does that really worry *you*?" I asked, in awe that Marisa could possibly be that insecure herself.

"I'm human, Jane. And I work in an industry that is super competitive—in a city filled with attractive, superficial people. But you're not on camera all the time—and besides—you're twenty-six—I'm older than you."

"Oh, right, Marisa, you're only thirty." I looked in the car mirror again, turning my face from side to side.

"Jane," Marisa said gently. "If you're going to spend a bunch of money, I'd go to a therapist and figure out why you think you're unattractive."

LATER THAT NIGHT, I couldn't resist engaging in my favorite masochistic pastime—getting out the hand mirror and gazing into the side that made my face look at least five times its normal size. I would sit and dissect my features, trying to figure out where I needed the most work.

I closely resembled my mother—the one who abandoned my father—and he always resented me for it. When he was home for any length of time, he spent his days drinking and drawing me into his emotional wreckage. I was around seven years old, and my features were burgeoning into my mother's.

"You weren't blessed with beauty, Jane," he had said after giving me the once over in disgust. "You'd better work hard at being good at something because your looks will get you nowhere."

Those words and different versions of them infiltrated my thoughts until I was thoroughly convinced that I was born a misfit, unloved and unwanted by anyone.

Often in the face of my father's drunken outbursts, Petra the nanny would pull me into her ample bosom to comfort me. She was a large blonde woman in her late-forties and had grown up on a farm in the Midwest. "Now, Jane, don't you listen to him," she would always say. "His mind's not right. You're a beautiful little girl, you know that?"

As much as I wanted to believe Petra, I never did. Even my name was plain. *Jane*. Really? My parents could have been a little more creative. Over the years, I tried to position it as artsy and minimalist. But deep down, I knew it was still just Jane.

During the rare times my father was sober, he would bring home presents from his world travels—little leather bracelets and pendants, hand-made by natives of some small foreign town. I never wanted the presents. I only wanted him to love me, which he was incapable of doing.

One time he even took me to Disneyland, which wasn't exactly fun. It only skirted the periphery of fun because I knew that once we were home—once he was able to self-medicate with a bottle of vodka—he would berate me for existing. Sometimes, I would purposely make my facial expression so benign that he couldn't possibly get angry and explode. It never worked; I still looked like my mother; I was still ugly in his eyes.

There had to be a way to reinvent myself with a make-over. People did it all the time—with clothes, hairstyles, and makeup. But I wanted something more—something that would make me as glamorous as Marisa. I had a few thousand dollars in my savings account, and a credit card with a $10,000 limit. That was it. I would find a med spa the next day and make an appointment.

Three

THE WORK WEEK WAS hectic because we were sitting for three days in focus groups. Tara was supposed to be spearheading the groups; however, she got stuck in a snowstorm in Vermont while visiting her family and ordered me at the last minute to cover for her.

"Just sit there and don't say anything," she commanded on the phone from her 'family estate.' "If they ask you a question, defer to Jeffrey. And take good notes for me so I know what's going on. Don't mess this up for me, okay, Jane?" Her voice contained a veiled threat.

"You know what, Tara?" I replied haughtily. "It's not my first focus group, and I'll handle things the way Warren would want me to." That stopped her in her tracks.

She said, "fine," in a huff and hung up.

I sped to meet Jeffrey and two of his creatives at the Studio City facility. I parked my red Jetta in the garage, made my way to the elevator and pressed floor 5. Once I stepped out of the elevator, I found Jeffrey in the hallway, carrying a cup of coffee, and scarfing a pastry from the continental breakfast setup outside the research room.

"Glad you could make it," Jeffrey scoffed, still chewing, as I strode in balancing my laptop, bag, and client files while teetering on four-inch Louboutins. I had found them for a steal while scouring local consignment stores and was excited to debut them at work.

"I didn't know I was coming until a half hour ago," I shot back. "Where is everybody?"

Jeffrey nodded in the direction of the room. "They've already started assembling; at least ten people representing the client plus the agency and moderators, so it's a full house. You'd better get some coffee and food because this is going to be a long one," he said, lobbing the rest of his pastry into the trash and opening the door for me. "After you."

Great. We're going to be packed like sardines for three days, eating junk food and watching simpletons discuss our work. The subject was a series of new ad concepts for The Henrys. We presented five options, narrowed it to three, and the client couldn't decide which one they wanted. Rita favored a sort of film noir approach, which had her prominently featured while Chance hovered in the background. Of course, Chance disagreed, requesting a design in which they were featured equally. The agency favored the third option, which was a marquee with their names in lights and silhouettes of the two performers in the background. It was the type of homerun ad that would score us an Addy, the holy grail of advertising awards.

We recommended a focus group, so they could test out the campaigns among their core customers and make the decision afterward.

The room was dim and indeed full as we entered. Jeffrey led the way to our seats. Bags of Skittles, "snack-size" candy bars, and Chex Mix were scattered all over the tables. Focus groups were always the same in terms of setup, with movie theater-style chairs and long tables facing a glass barrier that enabled us to watch the group on the other side and listen to their discussion, almost like stalking people except they knew they were being watched. They were being paid for it.

I spotted Johann, one of our copywriters, and Sam from the art department, seated way in the back and up high. The two looked like they were barely out of high school but were well into their twenties. I had nick-named the duo 'the toddlers', which Jeffrey thought was brilliant. They wore faded jeans, black T-shirts displaying obtuse symbols, Converse All Stars, and drab-colored hoodies. Johann, a smallish Nordic-looking blond, had ridden his motorcycle to the facility so his heavily gelled-up hair looked unruly. Sam, a Pacific Islander with mild acne scars, appeared bored as he sat creating Animojis on his iPhone, snickering, and texting them to Johann.

"Did you hear that?" Jeffrey whispered. "The guy in the red shirt just said he doesn't like our preferred tagline."

Johann spoke first. "He's some middle-aged bro from bum-fuck Iowa so he doesn't get it."

I turned my attention to the red-shirted Iowan in question on the other side of the glass. He was stirring controversy among the other group members, and they started to agree with him.

"That guy's taking over the group," Sam growled. "Now they're going to pick the ad we hate."

"We don't hate it, Sam," I chided. "We designed it and gave it to the client knowing it could be favored."

Jeffrey nodded. "And we still have two more groups to sit through so let's not give up yet."

The toddlers sulked while tearing into some Skittles. I stole a quick glance at my watch. Not even an hour had passed. I sighed, opened my laptop, and settled in for the long haul.

By Friday, I felt like a prisoner ready to be freed for the weekend. Not only was each focus group day like watching paint dry, but I also had to deal with the incessant emails and phone calls from Tara, who had nothing better to do than harass me with questions and commentary.

At 5 p.m. on the dot, I was back at the office gathering my things and about to make a run for it when my phone rang. It was Jeffrey. "Hey, Jane. Can you stop by my office? Warren's here and wants to talk to us."

Crap. What now? I was only occasionally summoned to an in-person meeting with Warren. Full of consternation,

I pulled a compact out of my purse and examined my face, turning in different angles. Then, I grabbed a pen and notepad and headed down the hall to Jeffrey's office.

Warren was sitting across from Jeffrey's desk. He swirled around in his chair to face me, smiling pleasantly. "Jane, I hear you were a super star this week filling in for Tara."

"Oh, it was my pleasure, Warren. Happy to do it," I responded, smiling from ear-to-ear. My eyes met Jeffrey's as he gave me the 'I'm about to puke' gesture from behind Warren's back.

He pulled a stack of tickets out of his pocket and fanned them on Jeffrey's desk. "The team deserves a fun weekend," he said. "I have tickets to the game tomorrow, Dodgers-Cardinals. Great seats. I bought them for Caroline, the boys, and some of their friends, but we're going out of town, so please take the group."

Jeffrey's eyes met mine for a second before we both smiled graciously at Warren. "That's great. Thanks, Warren," Jeffrey said to break the silence.

"Yes, that's very generous," I chimed in with a full princess smile.

Warren handed off the tickets to Jeffrey. "No thanks necessary. You guys deserve a reward. I gave tickets to Veronica, too, so you'll probably see her there."

Veronica Scarsdale was Warren's executive admin, AKA the agency police. She was always observing potential violations and reporting them back to Warren.

As soon as he had gone, Jeffrey shot me a look. "Don't take this the wrong way but I don't fancy spending my Saturday with you and the toddlers."

"Oh, and you think I want to spend my Saturday at a baseball game? You know I can't stand sports," I complained. "I was planning to spend the weekend on the couch with Netflix and a bottle of wine."

"Come on, Jane. A cute single girl like you staying home all weekend? I don't believe that for one minute," Jeffrey said in his smooth, charming pitch voice, obviously trying to butter me up. There was no way Jeffrey thought I was even remotely cute. He treated me like a little sister most of the time. "Why don't you ask one of your admirers to go in my place?" he asked.

"I don't have admirers and, if I did, I wouldn't take them to a baseball game," I responded stubbornly.

"Well, with Veronica there taking attendance, one of us needs to show," Jeffrey insisted. I felt him getting ready to pull rank. Instead, he backed up a bit, pulled in his chin and looked at me with a puzzled expression. "You look ... different," he said, studying my face like it was an ad concept. "Did you do something with your hair?"

"Not really," I shrugged, moving my face so that I was staring down at my shoes.

"Jane?" Jeffrey was waving his hand over my eyes. "Did you hear me?"

"I have an idea." I said this before he could venture any further about the changes to my face. "What if you go for the first half of the game and I go for the second half? That way, you can get out early and I don't have to get up early."

Jeffrey stopped staring at my face in his funny sort of fascinated way long enough to consider my proposition.

"It's a win-win," I added. "Veronica will report back that we were both there."

"Nice pitch," he said finally. "Sorry for the bad pun. Okay, deal."

AT HOME THAT NIGHT, I thought about Jeffrey's questions about my new look. It had been two weeks since I had been to the med spa. The clinic was offering a deal on several procedures, and, despite Marisa's protests, I decided I needed both Botox and fillers. The doctor was Latina, speaking in broken English. She first suggested contouring by injecting filler in my cheekbones and jaw. The doctor convinced me that my nose could be perfected with a little filler at the tip to make it tilt upwards. With the slight change to the shape of my nose, the doctor suggested filler in my chin to balance my profile. Botox between my brows would temporarily prevent frown lines, and if applied around my eyes, would prevent crow's feet. While she was at work on my face, I had her inject lip filler, so they appeared full and pouty. *Just like that.* I went home broke, and thrilled.

No one questioned me. And no one, except Grandma, even noticed I had the work done. It was hard to pull one over on Grandma. At least she had the decency to take me aside without Grandpa around.

"Jane, what did you do to your face?" she demanded as soon as we were alone.

"What do *you* think, Grandma?"

"I know, but why? You didn't like the face you were born with?"

"It's none of your business, Grandma, but now that you ask, no. I didn't like it. In fact, I hated it."

"What, exactly, did you do?" She asked, shaking her head.

"Why do you care? It's my face, not yours," I said stubbornly.

"What about your lips? You look like one of those actresses who's had too much work," Grandma scorned. "It's that place, isn't it? That job. Did that boss of yours tell you to do it?"

I shut my eyes and took a deep breath before saying, "Grandma, I did it for myself. I'm happy with my decision. I don't want to talk about it anymore."

Grandma just glared at me for a moment and walked away muttering, "I guess what's done is done ... a damned shame if you ask me."

She never mentioned it again and, miraculously, didn't tell Grandpa.

THE NEXT DAY, AFTER battling horrible traffic on the I-10 freeway for an hour, I arrived late to Dodger stadium to relieve Jeffrey of his shift.

He was sitting with one of his twin girls. She had on

navy shorts and a pin-striped button-down shirt with an army jacket. A Greek fishing cap sat smartly on her little head. *Jesus, this guy even dressed his kids cool.* The place smelled sweet stale, like cinnamon sugar mixed with bitter ale.

"Hey, Jane," Jeffrey greeted me, immediately standing up and shuffling past to make way for my seat. Peanut shells crunched underneath his feet. As he passed, he said, "This is Mandy. Mandy, say hello to Jane." The miniature style maven shook my hand, then said, "Daddy, can we get out of here now? This place sucks."

"Yeah," I said, looking down at her. "I know what you mean. Where's Veronica?" I inquired to Jeffrey.

"She's a no-show," he replied, pushing his glasses towards his forehead.

I grimaced. "You mean I got out of bed for this and she's not even here? Talk about a waste of a good shower," I whined.

Jeffrey laughed and passed me a twenty-dollar bill. "Here, get a hot dog and a drink. The toddlers are at least two beers in." He winked as he fled out of the aisle with Mandy in tow.

I sat down in the far seat and placed my purse on the empty seat between Johann and me. Sam was on the other side shoving fistfuls of popcorn in his mouth and washing it down with beer. They both threw me the peace sign. Oh well, I thought. At least it's a nice day and the sun is out. I might as well get a hot dog and a beer.

It took only half a beer before I got bored and began checking out the crowd. An attractive couple had taken the seats next to me, and I caught the eye of the guy who was sitting closest to me. He had sandy blond hair, large hazel eyes, and a genuine smile. I decided, after a full Budweiser, that he was my exact type. A pretty woman sat next to him looking barely amused, checking her cell phone every few minutes.

The guy kept glancing at me as though he wanted to say something, so I smiled and said hello.

"Hi, I'm Derek," he said, giving me a casual wave.

"Jane," I replied, smiling even wider and returning his wave.

I quickly hit it off with Derek as we shared a feeling of contempt for our own names.

"It's just Derek," he lamented. "Not even a good spelling. It's short for nothing and you can't shorten it." I nodded empathetically and offered to buy them a round of beers.

As I sat next to him, suddenly ecstatic to be at the game, I learned that Derek grew up in Portland where nineties grunge rock originated. This intrigued me, given my own love for that era. His all-time favorite band was Nirvana and, like me, he couldn't stand its later incarnation, the Foo Fighters. Derek was a musician himself—a violinist—and taught lower-division music classes at USC by day, performing in an orchestra most weekend nights.

Stella was an architect working at a fancy firm downtown. She was tall and thin with light blonde hair. She didn't seem to be jealous or possessive at all while I monopolized her boyfriend throughout the entire game.

I was attracted to Derek and, while not completely certain, thought he liked me. He was boyishly handsome, and we easily engaged in conversation. It felt like I had known him for years. Derek had this endearing way of lowering his eyes shyly while speaking, only occasionally shooting me a sideways glance with a smile that somehow melted me. By the end of the game, all I wanted was to hang out with Derek. I handed Derek and Stella each my business card with the hope of getting Derek's phone number.

Unfortunately, Stella was the only one with a card on her.

"I'll send you an email with my information," he said apologetically while getting up and putting his arm around Stella. "Great talking to you, Jane."

We said our goodbyes and parted ways.

Crap. I'll never see Derek again. I didn't even get his last name. It's probably just as well. *Why would he want me when he had Stella?* No. I needed to forget our little *meet cute* and move on.

Four

I LOUNGED ON THE COUCH Sunday with my laptop reading online news headlines and considering a gym visit. My phone bleeped and there was a text—from Derek!

"Hi, Jane. It's Derek Lowell. Nice meeting you yesterday. Stay in touch."

My heart skipped a beat. *Derek Lowell*—such a strong name. *Does he like me? Why would he send me a text on a Sunday if he didn't like me?*

I just had to call Marisa. "Hey, I met a guy yesterday at the game."

"Really?" At a baseball game?" Marisa sounded interested. "Tell me about him."

I explained how we met and about Stella and the text from Derek this morning.

"So, you met a guy you like but he already has a girlfriend and he's flirting with you right in front of her?" Marisa asked. The suspicion in her voice was unmistakable. "Sounds like a real prize to me."

I ignored her sarcasm. "Do you think that note is flirting? Let me read it to you again."

"*Puh-lease*, Jane. Of course, he's flirting. No guy goes out of his way to send a text on a Sunday morning unless he's thinking about you in *that* way," she said. "But why would you care when he's not even available?"

"He's not available for now, but what if they break up? They didn't seem too interested in each other."

"Then you'll be rebound chick," she retorted. "I'm just looking out for you, Jane. You have to be selective."

"Marisa, I can't really afford to be selective—it's not like I ever meet anyone interesting." I couldn't help but see, as usual, there was some truth to her assumptions. I was experiencing the giddiness of feeling attractive and noticed a significant difference in the attention I was getting post-injections. And I liked it.

❧

THREE WEEKS AFTER WE met, Derek called to tell me Stella had dumped him. "Oh, no," I said with false concern.

"It sucks." He sounded genuinely hurt. "We were together a year and I felt like everything was going great. We were getting serious. She really punched me in the heart."

"I'm sorry," I lied. "Did she give you a reason?"

"She says I'm immature and unfocused. Says I work all the time but don't have any real money. She needs someone who's more ambitious, someone who has a big house, a nice car … luxury, I guess."

"Are you okay with all that?" I asked, thinking he was being way too honest with me, too soon. I instinctively glanced around my tiny apartment and realized we shared the same socioeconomic status. I wasn't so sure that was a good thing.

"Not really," he replied distantly. "I'm not sure why I called … I just … let's talk after I've had a chance to process all this."

❧

ABOUT TWO WEEKS LATER, Derek called and asked to have dinner with me. It was First Friday in Venice and we hit the food trucks—not exactly the most exclusive or romantic type of date, but I was ecstatic to have a date. Once I saw Derek again, I remembered why I was initially attracted. He was so boy-next-door cute in his white button-down shirt and pale grey sweater vest. He seemed to be in good spirits. And that night, over Korean Barbecue at the Kogi Truck, he told me Stella had been secretly dating another guy for the past three months. The new guy was an 'entrepreneur,' and bought her expensive clothes and jewelry.

"I guess I've never been that type of guy—you know, the type who wants all that fancy stuff," he explained. "How about you?"

I had to think about that. Yes, I wanted nice things. I coveted them at times—it's just that I had not yet arrived in life. I wasn't sure how to answer because I didn't want to turn him off by revealing that mine and Stella's desires were similar. My mind drifted to the magazine image of Craig Keller and that the term 'entrepreneur' had been attached to his name. I chose not to respond.

After a glass of wine, we discovered we were kindred spirits when it came to music, and we talked for hours about bands, singer-songwriters, and new artists. I felt like the vibe was right and we were really bonding.

When the check came, Derek asked me to pay half—which somehow turned me off. Still, this was a guy in my age group who seemed to like spending time with me. I decided to give him a break on the check thing. After all, as a modern career woman, wasn't I supposed to pay my own way? I was so out of the loop on dating, I had no idea what was customary and what wasn't. I should have asked Marisa, I thought ruefully.

I went home feeling like our date had gone well—yet somehow like I was a bit of a fraud. I grew up poor—Grandma and Grandpa always put food on our table, but I often longed for a lifestyle that included luxury—longed to be one of those women everyone noticed. Grandpa always told me I needed to come to grips with my own ordinariness, but I somehow couldn't. Just knowing there was a possibility I might have everything I wanted someday kept me hopeful.

I caught myself wondering if I were shallow to feel that way.

Derek called the next morning and wanted to meet again. In fact, from that day on, we met at least once a week for dinner, each paid our half of the check, and called each other almost every day. Even so, I didn't know where we stood. I got butterflies in my stomach and sweaty palms whenever I was in his presence, but he only seemed interested in being a friend.

One night we decided to see Beck at the Hollywood Bowl. There we were, seated on the lawn with our brie round, baguette, and Chardonnay, getting ready for the concert to start, when Derek suddenly looked aghast. "She's here," he said, staring over my shoulder. "I don't believe it."

I turned and saw Stella with a guy. She had on a tea-length silky midnight-blue dress that looked sort of like a slip, hugging her every curve. Her hair was straight, flowing down her back. She looked chic. I scanned my own attire, a vintage Pretenders T-shirt and skinny jeans with red Converse All-Star sneakers. I couldn't help but think Stella was the *Ginger* and I was the *Mary Ann*.

Stella's new boyfriend appeared to be much older than Derek, deeply tanned, wearing an expensive checked sport coat over a linen shirt, designer jeans, and trendy boots. Lots of gold. His look screamed *uncool*.

Then I saw the look on Derek's face. "That guy doesn't even know who Beck is," he grumbled. "It must have been *her* choice."

"Yeah—he probably think's Beck is something on tap at the bar," I said, attempting to soften the blow.

"He looks old enough to be her father," Derek continued. "At least they won't be sitting with us in the cheap seats," he said gloomily, shaking his head. "She left me for that guy. It must be true love." He turned to me and raised his wine glass. "Here's to finding true love."

"Or finding truth," I said, trying to sound confident and philosophical, instead of destroyed at the thought that he could still be in love with Stella and not at all interested in the person who was sitting beside him. It's not like we were on a date, but I still felt the sting of Marisa's words: *rebound chick*.

The night wore on and I started to relax and forget about Stella. Soon we were swaying to "Everybody's Gotta Learn Sometime," and Derek and I found each other's hands in the darkness of the open theater. We held hands through the rest of the concert, but when the lights went on, we couldn't even look at each other. It was beyond awkward. Outside the venue, Derek's eyes darted anxiously at me.

"Um, Jane," he stumbled over his words. "I'm not sure what happened in there …" his voice trailed off as he looked at me, embarrassed and apologetic.

I forced a smile but was totally shattered. My poor luck with men had me wondering if this guy was even remotely attracted, especially with the new-found facial enhancements. My ego could not take yet another rejection, even from this man, who told me from the beginning he only wanted to be friends.

We ended up at a coffee shop, where Derek poured his heart out about Stella and what she had meant to him. "I was really in love with her." He looked down and pretended to brush something off his jacket. "I introduced her to my family … thought maybe we would get married one day. I was saving for an engagement ring. I'm such an idiot." He folded his arms on the table in front of him, eyes lowered.

I could do nothing except nod and listen to his painful story. I would never have thought a guy could be so vulnerable, especially in the presence of a female. Something about it made me uncomfortable—like I wanted him to be a little more in control—a bit more stoic and masculine. Again, I wondered if there were something wrong with me.

Regardless, I had to come to grips with the reality that Derek and I would only be friends; there would be no impending romance; and I had not finally found a boyfriend. I was still plain Jane, somewhat improved, but unwanted by any man.

As Derek and I went our separate ways that night, I felt deflated, as though someone had sucker-punched me, and I couldn't catch my breath.

UPON RETURNING HOME FROM the Derek debacle, I stood in front of my full-length mirror, turning all the lights to the brightest level, so they were glaring down on my body. I shed my clothes until I was completely naked and began the punitive dissection of each body part. I picked up my hair with both hands and held it atop my head, moving my gaze slowly to my shoulders, breasts and eventually my waist. I turned to view my rear end and thighs, sighing in disgust.

Again, the magazine with the photo of Craig Keller came to mind. I located it in my magazine rack, buried underneath a pile of Vogues and Elles, and sat, still naked on my bed to view his picture again. I fantasized about being dressed up and having dinner with him at an expensive restaurant, and I was positive he would never ask me to pay half of the check. I stared longingly at the photo—I had his face memorized by now, taking in the perfect symmetry—his eyes, nose, mouth, jawline—everything was perfect. But his teeth were the showstopper. I thought about what it would be like to kiss him—to have him kiss me back. I wondered what he smelled like, and I started to feel aroused. I lay on my back with the magazine open, face down, covering my chest, and I imagined it was really him, lying on top of me. I closed my eyes and pictured his light jade eyes peering into mine, his breath becoming labored as he slowly and gently entered me. I couldn't get him out of my mind for the rest of the night.

Five

To say I was a shopaholic would be an exaggerated understatement. And Warren had just given me a salary increase. He had called me into the office earlier that week to tell me what an incredible job I was doing. Then he wrote a number on a slip of paper and slid it across his desk.

"Does that make you happy?" he had asked.

I had glanced at the number, smiling, and nodding. And, even though the increase didn't comfortably support the numerous trips I made to Fred Segal and Neiman Marcus, I somehow justified it: I was in a high-profile job; I lived in Los Angeles; I was single and needed to attract dates—there were a million reasons I needed more clothes. The other things driving up my debt were the never-ending visits to Dr. Feelgood, as I had nicknamed her, at the med spa, to get yet another round of Botox and fillers to maintain my new look. The problem was that they didn't last—so I was continuously engaged in both a vicious and expensive cycle.

While squeezing into a tight Versace sheath in the Fred Segal dressing room, my phone rang. To my dismay, it was Anna. She had made it a point to avoid me altogether ever since the demeaning conversation regarding Craig Keller's photo, only giving me the occasional smug grin. But today, she took on an air of new-found congeniality.

"Hi, Jane. I wanted to see if you could join us for a little happy hour after work tomorrow. It's casual but feel free to bring a date."

"I'd love to," I beamed, suddenly feeling liked and important even though I had branded Anna a member of the despised Barbie trio years ago. It was unfathomable she might potentially become a friend. What frightened me most was that I secretly desired her friendship more than I would have liked to admit.

"Great, see you then."

The next night, I debuted my newly acquired treasures: navy Balenciaga wide-leg sailor pants paired with a pale grey silk blouse and snakeskin Fendi heels. I had put everything on my credit card with the justification that I had just been given a salary increase—a dangerous game I had skillfully mastered. I strutted into the restaurant feeling high on life.

And there they all were. The account team plus some stragglers from the art department, crowded around the bar, talking, and laughing. I caught a glimpse of Tara, tittering with some blond frat boy. I quickly assessed that everyone there had a date … except me.

Anna greeted me first, wearing a tight-fitting low-cut plum-colored dress, her freshly cut bob bouncing from side to side. "Hey, Jane, glad you could make it," she said, smiling to the point where I thought her face might crack. "Have you met my boyfriend, Dr. Moring?" A rather plain complacent-looking man with pale skin and a receding, mousy-brown hairline shook my hand.

"Call me Rob," he said.

"Nice to meet you, Rob." I said, smiling while doing a quick scan of the room, still marveling at all the couples, and needing a drink quickly.

Once Rob was out of earshot, Anna took a step closer and put her face right up to mine. I whiffed the pungent scent of wine on her breath as she whispered, "I know exactly what you're doing and don't think everyone else in the agency hasn't noticed, too."

I recoiled as she advanced again.

"We all know you got a raise, and we all know *how* you got it."

"I … I don't know what you're talking about," I said, finally realizing what she was not-so-subtly implying. "If you're saying I have a relationship with Warren beyond work, you're totally mistaken."

"Oh, I'm certain there was *work* involved," she snorted, adding, "And I'm sure that's why you've had so much *work* done. God, you're desperate." With that, she turned her back and returned to Rob, who looked bored and unhappy.

I shuddered and longed for Marisa to walk in at that very moment and save me; but, since she was not there, I settled for a vodka martini … with olives. I sipped my drink alone at the bar trying to shake off the disturbing conversation. My thoughts were zigzagging. Was Anna telling the truth? Did everyone in the agency think I had sex with Warren to get a raise? And Jeffrey … what about Jeffrey? Did he, too, think this low of me? He was my only real friend at the agency. At least that's what I thought.

I suddenly knew what I had to do, and fast. I stood up, handed the bartender a twenty-dollar bill and whirled around to locate the nearest exit. As I moved through the crowd quickly, I almost bumped into Brooke, who was just arriving. Her light blonde locks were crimped around her face, and she wore a hot pink strapless dress with no bra. She also appeared to be surgically attached to some young boy toy who didn't look old enough to be anywhere near a bar.

I fled to the parking lot and found my car, calling an emergency meeting with Marisa, who was miraculously available. We met at Finn McCool's on Main Street in Santa Monica, a far cry from the trendy restaurant I had just left, but a great place for cheap booze and live music. Marisa was not crazy about my choice of venue, but she nevertheless agreed to meet me.

I arrived at the noisy pub and got us a table in a spot

where we could hear the band, but where it wouldn't be too noisy to have a conversation. It smelled vaguely of stale beer, vomit and Pine Sol. Marisa showed up in a stunning black skirt suit and high leopard pumps. She arrived, walking fast, on her cell phone, seemingly harried and bitching at someone for not getting her an interview with some billionaire who had allegedly murdered his wife.

She smiled and gave me a hug while still talking on the phone. "Can you get me a vodka soda with lime?" She cupped the phone while mouthing the words. This was Marisa's diet drink—the only calories were from the booze. I ordered drinks while she continued, rolling her eyes like she was held captive by someone who talked incessantly.

"Jane," A male voice called. I looked up and there was Derek, smiling cheerfully. I realized this was exactly the type of place Derek would be on a Friday night—it was affordable and had live bands. He leaned over to kiss me on the cheek. He turned to face Marisa, who was just finishing her call.

"You Marisa?" he asked, grinning.

She gave him a tight-lipped once-over and answered, "Yes. And you are?"

"Derek, here." He held his hand out.

"Oh, you're the guy from the baseball game," Marisa commented, taking his hand, and quickly dropping it.

"Yes," he answered, glancing at me. "Jane's mentioned you a couple of times in passing."

"I guess you don't watch much TV," she replied, "But that's sort of refreshing." Marisa's foot was wagging back and forth at a frenzied pace, like she was impatient with Derek's sophomoric small talk.

Derek blushed. "Sorry. Of course, I should know who you are already. But you're right, I don't watch TV—I live my life in a bit of a music vacuum."

Marisa shot me a look and gave Derek a closed-mouth smile, which meant this was going to be work.

"Mind if I join you ladies?" he asked politely. My eyes met Marisa's and she gave me a casual shrug accompanied by an eyeroll. I nodded to Derek, and he took the chair next to me. "What's everyone having?" Derek asked.

"We've already ordered vodkas," I replied, pointing at the bar.

Derek signaled the cocktail server and ordered a beer. We had a few drinks, and everyone loosened up. Marisa dropped the cold reporter exterior within the first twenty minutes which meant she was at least comfortable. When Derek got up to use the bathroom, I had a moment alone with Marisa.

"Well?" I questioned. "What do you think of Derek?"

Marisa sipped her drink and sat back like she was a movie critic getting ready to give her analysis. "He's okay, I guess—seems smart enough and definitely cute. I don't get the impression he's gay. So, the big question is, why doesn't he want to date you?"

"He just wants to be *friends*," I said, using air quotes. "That's always how it is with me." I slouched in my chair. "Plus, I told you he and his girlfriend recently split. I suspect he's still in love with her and doesn't want to date for a while. Isn't that a good thing?"

"I suppose," Marisa said thoughtfully, eyes shifting upward as though she were working out a tough math problem. "General rule is six months of singlehood for every year invested. But the worse the relationship, the longer the rebound time."

She took a sip of her vodka soda. "The thing is—if he just wants to be friends, that's not likely to change. Guys are either interested or they're not. Trust me."

"Maybe I'm fine with being just friends," I said, a little defiantly. "He's not exactly my type anyway." I stirred my drink with a paper straw, feeling like Marisa was picking on me.

"Who *is* your type?" Marisa questioned with one eyebrow raised. She then leaned toward me, elbows on the table. "Who really *does* it for you, Jane?"

I immediately thought about Craig Keller, and the magazine that teased me every night and I felt my face flush.

Marisa would ridicule me for being so obsessed with a man I'd never met. "Oh, I don't know—someone with class—power, you know the type." I was about to say 'money', but I stopped myself. "Someone who wears a suit to work every day—an executive."

Marisa eyed me with a mysterious smile. "Then you're definitely barking up the wrong tree with this guy," she concluded.

I sighed, thinking I needed to change the subject. "You know what? I have bigger issues right now. Apparently, everyone at work thinks I'm sleeping with the boss."

"What? Who told you that?" she asked, straightening up in her chair, eyes narrowing.

"Anna-the-bitch from work." Marisa was aware of my nemesis. "Oh and, allegedly, they all know about my injections and think I'm a dateless, horrid single woman-viper."

Marisa laughed.

"It's not funny. My reputation's at stake."

"And you think no one has ever said that about me?" Marisa said. "You're smart, beautiful, and competent. Some people will be threatened and try to knock you down. Get used to it. It's part of the turf."

"But how am I supposed to go to work Monday and face everyone, knowing they don't take me seriously?"

"Fuck them," Marisa said with a wave of her hand. "They don't sign your paycheck. Warren's the only one who matters, and you've already won him over. You'll go to work Monday looking fabulous as always. Let them hate you even more."

As Marisa said this, Derek returned, interrupting our conversation.

I sat in quiet thought, watching Marisa and Derek interact. They appeared to be exact opposites, but they had more in common than one would think. Marisa was always so outwardly tough, so ready for a fight. She wouldn't have put up with the shit I had just endured without aggressively fighting back. Derek, who was mostly gentle and conflict-avoidant, stood up for himself in a quiet, confident manner. He would simply dismiss anyone who insulted his dignity.

The weak link was me. Why didn't I have that kind of *chutzpah*? *What was I afraid of? Despite the changes to my appearance, I still had low self-esteem. I still hated my face and body.* Marisa was right. I needed to forge ahead with confidence, but was I capable of doing that? I had to be. With the career I had chosen, there was simply no other path.

The band played a cover of Aerosmith's "Dream On," and I felt the numbing rhythm of the bass pulsating through my body. Listening to Derek and Marisa conversing with ease, I took a deep breath and settled into a sense of calm and gratitude. Somehow, through innumerable odds, I had found these two kindred souls who were far from perfect but who complemented my quirky personality and made me feel profoundly connected, a stark contrast to the earlier part of my evening with Anna and the others, where I felt exposed like a raw nerve.

"Isn't that the way," the lead singer crooned into the microphone, "Everybody's got the dues in life to pay ..."

ON A PARTICULARLY HAZY morning when I was already feeling bleary-eyed and downtrodden from yet another dateless weekend, Veronica called my office to let me know Anna backed out of attending a luncheon at the last minute. It was a women's networking thing and Warren needed another director to represent the agency.

I had been to these types of events before; I rarely enjoyed them because they disrupted the day and were almost always tedious. I was sure this event, which was at the Peninsula Hotel in Beverly Hills, would be no exception.

Upon arrival at the hotel, I checked in and received a nametag, which I promptly stashed in my bag because it would ruin the aesthetics of my outfit. My appointed table was full of the usual stiffs in skirt suits. The woman sitting to my right was tall, naturally blonde, and incredibly pretty in a New England old-money upper-crust sort of way—from what I could tell, that is. She wore large dark glasses.

Her look was polished, clean, and effortless. She had on a crisp white blouse, open to the collarbone, and an Hermès scarf tied just right. Her skirt flared perfectly: elegant, tailored, and clean-lined. Her medium-height spectator pumps were smart. She looked camera ready for an ad shoot promoting vacations in the Hamptons.

I put my hands to my own auburn hair that was smoothed in a low side pony which, before seeing this woman, I thought to be chic. I wore a vintage Mary Quant slate-blue mini-dress with a low-slung belt and simple white collar, and black tights with black patent leather Mary Janes. I had worn my eye-makeup a bit heavy-handed for a daytime event, but I was cultivating a sixties look.

I noticed 'Ms. Hamptons' was not talking to anyone at the table. Obviously aloof and uninterested in those around her, she looked down at her cell phone the whole time.

My stream of thoughts was interrupted by the emcee announcing it was time for the guest speaker, so I turned my attention to the stage. Someone named Katherine Blakely, who was president of some software company (I wasn't listening as I was still obsessing about the drone in the next seat), was invited to come forth. Wouldn't you know? Ms. Hamptons removed her sunglasses, stood up and walked, head held high like a ballerina with perfect posture, to the stage. Oh great, I thought. I couldn't wait to hear the pearls of wisdom she had to impart.

I couldn't have been more off base. What transpired was the most brilliant, articulate speech I had ever heard. I was riveted by this intelligent, poised, and graceful woman. I longed to be exactly like her.

When she returned to the table and sat down, I turned to her and smiled. "You're inspiring."

She just glared at me before pulling the pair of dark glasses out of her bag and covering her own once again. She finally responded, "That's very kind of you." Then she leaned over and whispered, "Would you happen to know anywhere around here I can get a drink? I would kill for a fucking Scotch. You're welcome to join me. What's your name?"

After I recovered from the flawless one dropping an F-bomb to a stranger, I glanced at my watch and realized it was only 3 p.m. I needed to get back to the office. "I'm Jane Mercer," I held out my hand.

"Good to meet you, Jane. I'm Katherine. But my friends

call me Kat." She still had the glasses on, but I detected a type of throaty sadness in her voice. She took my hand and lifted her glasses quickly. Her eyes were teary. "Look," she said. "It took everything for me to hold it together today. I just found out last night my husband is leaving me. We've been married ten years and …" She started to weep softly, right there in the event ballroom.

I hesitated. There were a million deadlines, and I simply could not be out of the office all day, especially with Anna lurking in the background, ready to pounce on any perceived transgression. I watched Kat's hands trembling as she searched her bag in vain for a valet ticket, obviously having given up on me. *What would Marisa do?* I asked myself, something I frequently did in difficult situations. I saw a crowd of women beginning to form around our table to get a chance to speak with Kat after her compelling presentation. It was like watching sharks surround a hapless bloody fish in the water.

"Let's get out of here now," I said in a loud whisper, standing and pulling her along with me out of the hotel and onto to the street, amid puzzled onlookers. One thing I learned early is that there are some days when one just shouldn't be at work. And for Kat, that day had come. Turmoil at home for women could be a career killer, because a crying jag, emotional outburst, or angry tantrum would always be remembered before all the incredible work victories earned. All it took was one time. I turned to Kat, "I know this place a few blocks away. Come with me."

Kat nodded trustingly as I took her hand and led her down the street in silence to Bar Noir on South Lasky Drive. It was empty, and I found a dark corner where we could speak candidly.

Over our first scotch and soda, I found out she was thirty-six, born and raised in a strict, well-off Catholic family in Cambridge, Massachusetts, had lots of brothers and sisters, went to Cape Cod every summer, graduated from Harvard. Kat moved to LA after graduation, fell in love, and got married.

After scotch and soda number two (Kat was on her

own at this point—I couldn't stand Scotch), I found out that Kat's husband, Jack, was a writer and that she was the breadwinner of the family; how hard she had worked to rise to the level she had in business; and the biggest surprise of all, how vulnerable she was.

"I've never felt so worthless," she blurted out at one point. "I thought Jack wanted me to be successful, so he could pursue his writing. I did everything humanly possible to keep us on track financially. Now he says he's in love with a younger woman with no education and no career." She hung her head in dismay, swirling her scotch with her index finger.

"Oh my, I'm so sorry, Kat," I said knowing at that moment it had been the right decision to get her to a bar quickly.

"Of course, now he wants to marry her. Total cliché, huh?"

"And he's a writer?" I asked, cringing at the thought.

"Romance novels." She held her face in her hands. "I thought I'd left the single life behind forever."

"Sorry … I wish I could help." I realized I was not helping. "Being single is really not that bad—I have good friends," I said optimistically. "Why don't you come to the next industry mixer with me, and I'll introduce you to some people?" Then, realizing that was probably the dumbest thing I could have said in the presence of this woman, who probably had her pick of top social events, I quickly retreated. "Sorry, I'm sure you already know everyone."

"That's sweet of you," Kat said patting my hand. "I have quite a mess at home to deal with first."

I nodded, and, at my insistence, we left Kat's car at the Peninsula valet, and I drove to her house, which was both sprawling and in Laurel Canyon. I was not surprised she lived there. Where else would she live?

The four-mile trip took an hour in rush-hour traffic and, by the time we arrived, it was almost dusk. The lights were on, and Jack's car was parked in front. It was a silver Jaguar with a vanity plate that said "Arrived." The house was of the Tudor variety, a ubiquitous style in LA's wealthiest neighborhoods.

"Your house looks like a storybook," I said wistfully, now curious as to what Jack was like and why he would want to leave Kat.

"Yeah, if you like Stephen King," she remarked, sighing deeply. I could tell her cocktail buzz must have worn off and harsh reality was setting in. The silhouette of a man appeared in the front window as Kat sniffed and lowered her eyes. I offered to walk her inside.

"No, thanks," she said. "It would only be awkward for you. I'll call you in a few days."

It was then I realized I hadn't given Kat my business card. I quickly located a card in the console and instinctively grabbed a pen from my bag, turned the card over, and wrote my home address and cell phone number.

"Here—in case you need anything." I handed the card to her.

"Thank you, Jane. Thanks for being there. I don't have many friends because I work so much. I don't know what I would have done today if I hadn't met you." We hugged, and I watched her disappear through the front door.

Drifting back toward Santa Monica, I felt heavy-hearted, as though I were the one breaking up. I couldn't imagine a ten-year marriage going down the toilet like that. I mean, how could he just walk away from the amazing life they must have? Did he just decide not to make it work? Marisa told me once that some relationships just end, with no real reason. But given I never had a long-term relationship, there was no way I could know for sure.

Jeffrey was now calling my cell phone. *Crap.* For the first time, I totally forgot about the office. "Hey, Jeffrey, what's up?"

"I was just checking on you," he said. "Anna told everyone you skipped out of work this afternoon."

Of course, she did. I felt my cheeks flush. Veronica must have blabbed.

"Jeffrey, I didn't *skip* out of work. I met a CEO who owns a big software company, and she wants to learn more about the agency," I said in a saucy voice, thinking it was better to be confident in my lies. "She might be putting out an RFP.

I don't want us to be late to the party, or worse, not invited."

It was a plausible story because a Request For Proposal could happen at any moment, and a decent portion of the business depended on winning them.

"You don't have to justify yourself to me," Jeffrey said. "I don't care if you spent the afternoon at the mall. I'm just giving you the heads-up that Anna's playing her usual games."

"I'll handle it," I said, drained and irritated that fighting someone as unworthy as Anna occupied so much of my time. "See you tomorrow."

THE NEXT MORNING, I spotted Anna walking down the hallway toward me with Warren. She was barely keeping up with his brisk pace by taking lots of tiny steps in her stilettos, all the while chattering endlessly. Warren just stared straight ahead, not breaking stride, nor responding verbally to Anna.

When they both saw me, Anna smiled viciously. *Uh oh. She's going to nail me in front of Warren for taking yesterday afternoon off to rescue Kat.*

I gave a princess smile along with a confident "Good morning."

"Well, look who it is," Anna sneered, "Our new business ambassador."

Before I could open my mouth, Warren cut in. "Jane, just the person I want to see," he said in a tone I had come to recognize as both stern and open-ended, so I was never quite sure of his intention. "Speaking of new business," he said, "We just landed a big client and I'd like you to head up the account."

He put his arm through mine and walked me into his office, leaving Anna standing in the hallway, open-mouthed.

"That's exciting," I said, glancing back at Anna as she stormed off in the other direction.

Warren and I sat on the red couch, and he called Veronica, who promptly thrust her head in. "Will you please get Jeffrey in here?" Warren barked. She nodded dutifully and bustled out. Warren got up and walked to his desk to get his tablet. placing it on the coffee table while taking a seat close to me on the couch. Warren always smelled serious—clean and sharp, like wrapping paper.

Jeffrey appeared in the doorway, wearing a lavender button-down shirt and black jeans. The rims of his glasses matched his lavender shirt. "You called?" he asked Warren.

"Yes, Jeffrey. I need to brief you and Jane about a client." Jeffrey pulled over a chair and sat next to Warren, so we could all see the tablet. "Now, I'm going to show you the website, and then I need your honest opinions," Warren prefaced.

"The client is opening a show at the Regal Oasis Casino and Resort in Las Vegas. It's dinner theater with magic, acrobats, and live animals," he said.

Jeffrey and I nodded.

"It's called 'Le Panda Magnifique,' Warren continued. "The producer's name is Frédéric Guerrant. He's originally from a small town in the south of France, but he now lives in Paris where he has had a resident show for the past nine years. The live animals are trained pandas from Beijing, and the performers are all young people, dressed and made up to look panda-like. The show opens in a few months, so we need to get cracking on the spec work. He can't use the Paris ads because they won't resonate with people who visit Las Vegas. He needs something original."

I stole a glance at Jeffrey, but his eyes were lowered as he typed something into his phone.

Warren brought up the website, so we could review footage. What we saw was a short, heavyset, bald guy (must be Frédéric) appear on stage in a puff of bright green smoke. He wore a top hat and tuxedo. He said something in French, and we surmised that it was an introduction to the show. Then came the dancing panda-performers, who looked extremely young, male, and female, dressed in pink tutus with their faces painted black and white. They danced down a catwalk that spilled into the audience, who looked to be chic young Parisians sipping champagne and nibbling canapés.

Warren fast-forwarded it to the part where Frédéric

returned to the stage, this time in a red bejeweled cape, still with the top hat, waving his hand as a puff of purple smoke produced two live pandas. They did tricks with Frédéric while the panda trapeze artists swung from the rafters. There was something odd about the pandas but, since I'd never seen an actual panda up close, I was hardly an authority on the subject. Warren stopped the show footage and turned to Jeffrey and me.

"Well?" Warren said. "What are your initial thoughts?"

"Can we change the name?" Jeffrey questioned, a disgusted look on his face.

"Maybe." Warren turned his focus to me. "What else?"

"Well, from what I know of the Regal Oasis, this show seems a little down market." The Regal Oasis Casino and Resort was one of the most high-end resorts on the Las Vegas Strip—I had been twice and was mesmerized both times by its glitz and glamour.

"Yes, I know," Warren admitted, cocking his head to the side. "I thought the same thing. There are a lot of agencies bidding on this account and the owner of the Regal Oasis happens to be a family friend of one of our biggest competitors."

"Really?" Jeffrey asked with curiosity. "Which one?"

Warren waved away Jeffrey's question as though swatting a fly. "It doesn't matter. They have a huge budget and want an LA-based agency to *create* their US brand. Jane, I want you and Jeffrey to lead the account pitch. You two need to do more research and review the scope of work. I want the creative brief ASAP: five concepts by Tuesday. We'll end up with three for the client."

"We'll do our best," Jeffrey responded. "I mean, they're hardly *Cirque Du Soleil.* They have no brand, so this is going to be an up-hill climb."

Warren looked like he wanted to strangle Jeffrey. "You'll do more than your best," he replied gravely. "I mean it, Jeffrey. You need to put the big guns on this one. We *have* to win this business."

Jeffrey straightened in his chair and glared at Warren.

"But you already said there's a competitor out there with an inside connection—why should we give them brilliant work and have this mysterious competitor just turn around and use it?"

I nodded, thinking this happened all the time. We would present something a potential client loved but instead of hiring us, they would have the agency they preferred take the same concept and change it slightly.

Warren's jaw had tightened. "Jeffrey, this is not up for negotiation—now get cracking on the work—come on—chop-chop."

We both jolted out of our seats, hurried out of Warren's office and headed to Jeffrey's, shutting the door.

"Good god, what's gotten into Warren?" I queried as soon as we were alone. "He just seems so serious and desperate."

Jeffrey scratched his head. "I don't know—I guess because there's a lot of money at stake. But that's always the case. I'm wondering more about which competitive agency is in bed with the casino owner."

I began wringing my hands. "I've never represented a Las Vegas client—especially a show with live animals."

"Aren't pandas an endangered species?" Jeffrey questioned. "How are these nut-wads legally using live pandas in a stage show in America, anyway? Who are we going to put on this account?"

I twirled a lock of my hair in my fingers, wracking my brain. "How about Fiona?"

"No way," Jeffrey answered, pursing his lips and shaking his head. "Fiona's an animal activist with no sense of humor. I wouldn't be surprised if she showed up opening night picketing."

"I'll leave that to you, then," I said, inching my way toward the door. "Whoever's going to be on the team needs to get up to speed fast. You heard what Warren said—about *bringing in the big guns.*"

"Let me think about it," he said shaking his head and muttering, "Fucking pandas."

"Fucking *dancing* pandas," I added, before opening the

door. "I'll work on the brief over the weekend."

"Yeah, good luck with that," he called as I exited.

Luck, I thought as I walked to my office, was something we were going to need in great abundance for this client, I could just feel it. This "big-budget" client was an unknown quantity and Warren was counting on me to make them successful. I was terrified of letting him down—would rather die than fail him. I equated Warren's approval with my own self-worth; without the one, the other could never exist.

Seven

*F*RIDAY NIGHT WAS DEDICATED to pondering the pandas. I sat at my kitchen counter and watched the entire video from start to finish. Then, I began researching pandas in general, so I could write an intelligent creative brief.

I happened upon Frédéric Guerrant's bio and found out that he was raised near the Pyrenees in the South of France. He had moved to Paris in the late nineties where he came up with the idea of the show. All the entertainers were recruited in the Netherlands and brought to Paris. He supposedly got the pandas legally in China and had a license to travel with them in Europe. I couldn't help but feel sorry for the poor pandas and wondered how badly they were abused. I never understood why people put animals into entertainment. It just seemed cruel.

I was soon bored of researching pandas and decided to research someone much more interesting: Craig Keller. I had grown tired of the magazine photo and found the internet to be a much richer resource to stalk the man I could only dream of. I was fascinated by him. I typed in Craig Keller, Advertising, and a flood of photos and news articles came up immediately. It was like having a box of chocolates put in front of you and not being able to decide which to stuff in your mouth first.

I clicked on his LinkedIn profile to start. A very professional-looking photo came up of Craig in a navy suit with a yellow tie and the words Craig A. Keller, Founder and Managing Partner, Keller Whitman Group, listed underneath the photo. There was no way for people to connect with him or even send him a message—you could only follow him. It was the same on Facebook. He had so many followers that he was considered a public figure, and there was only basic information.

I went back to Google and clicked on images. There, photo after photo popped up of him at parties, events, and speaking engagements. He always looked so tall and handsome—always photographed with beautiful blondes, some of whom were well-known actresses or celebrities.

I took a break from my 'research,' to find something to eat. Upon opening the fridge, I spotted a wedge of blue cheese, a container of Greek olives I had bought a couple of weeks earlier at Farmer's Market, several open bottles of wine, and two Heinekens. I took out the cheese, olives, and a bottle of French Chablis. It's no wonder I never had a date. *Who would want to date a woman whose refrigerator contents resembled this?* It should be filled with fruits and vegetables—the ingredients to prepare an actual meal. But I never learned how to cook.

Grandma was calling. This would be the topper for my Friday evening. "Hello, Grandma."

"What's cookin', Pigeon?" she crowed. Pigeon was a nickname Grandma adopted from the old Disney movie *Lady and the Tramp*. She only called me this when she had already downed at least one glass of boxed pink wine.

"Well, Grandma, the problem is, nothing's cooking. I have no food," I responded in an accusatory tone, like it was her fault for not raising me to be a skilled chef.

"What was that Pigeon?" When Grandma didn't want to acknowledge something, she pretended to be hard of hearing. "Anyway, where are your friends tonight? Are you going somewhere fun?"

"No, Grandma, not tonight." I poured a glass of wine and popped a piece of moldy cheese in my mouth.

"Well, I called to tell you that the Feldmans were over earlier for Shabbat, and they were saying that their son, Julian, is working for a big law firm downtown and just made partner. Do you remember Julian? You met him at Cousin Abi's Bat Mitzvah about ten years ago."

"No, Grandma," I said, suddenly very tired. I knew where this conversation was going. "I don't remember." I was sure he was some beast from synagogue I had tried to avoid. I sat back and closed my eyes, feeling a headache coming on.

"Well," she continued, naturally not getting the hint, "they said Julian hasn't met that special someone yet and would love to take you to dinner. I showed them your picture and they said you've grown up to be a beautiful young lady."

I was silent. All I could think of was a dreary night out with yet another dull, blind date. I'd been on these dates many times before. It was always a bunch of boring small talk over an expensive dinner, after which I would ghost the person or vice versa. "Grandma, I don't need a blind date and, if I do, I'll find my own," I said, annoyed.

"Now, Jane," I heard Grandpa pipe up sternly. He had been eavesdropping on the extension, the dirty rat. "You're not getting any younger and, if you don't mind my saying, you're not doing a great job of finding dates. All I ever hear you talk about is work and shopping. Before you know it, you'll be too old to have a family and then what will you have? A bunch of clothes that don't fit and an empty life."

"Bruce!" Grandma scolded. "How long have you been listening? I'm trying to have a private talk with my grand-daughter, and I don't appreciate you butting in," I heard Grandma take a long drag of her cigarette and blow smoke into the receiver. "And besides, Jane's clothes will always fit because she doesn't eat enough."

"Are you guys finished now?" I asked. "Because I really do have to go. Have a good night." I hung up the phone while they were still bickering. My face was hot, and I felt tears welling up. Grandpa was always so critical of me. *Would that ever change?* Why is it that they never understood that all I wanted was to be accepted as I was, to know that they were proud of me? *How difficult was that?*

I went to the bathroom and turned on the light, leaning into the mirror to inspect my face, turning from side to side to see it from every angle. *You're not getting any younger* trilled in my mind. *Jesus, is 26 considered old?* No matter what I had done to improve my appearance, my father's hateful words still threaded my unconscious. I made a serious face and then smiled, inspecting my teeth closely. They seemed a little stained. I needed Crest White Strips. It was also time for another trip to Dr. Feelgood for a much-needed touchup. I resolved to make an appointment Monday. Once satisfied that I had picked myself apart without mercy, I texted Marisa, praying that she would somehow pull me out of my miserable dateless funk.

But her response indicated that even Marisa was out on a date purportedly having fun. I knew it was time to call it a night. I took a long, hot shower and went to bed with my main man Weez curled up next to me.

MONDAY MORNING, I SAT in the office dazed from my shitty weekend, gulping down a latte. I had procrastinated writing the panda brief until late Sunday. I had emailed it to Warren and Jeffrey last night with a note asking if we could discuss it in the morning. I never heard back from Marisa, so she must have been preoccupied with her new man. I hoped this one was not an asshole, for all our sakes.

Jeffrey popped his head in the office. "Hey, how was your weekend?" he grinned, obviously having had a different experience from mine.

"It was lovely, thanks," I said, giving him my best princess smile. "Did you see the brief?"

"Sure did," he answered. "I thought it was spot-on. Especially the target audience. How did you pull that one off?"

"It was easy," I said with a casual wave of the hand. My

office line rang, and it was Veronica. "Jane are you in there with Jeffrey?"

"Yes," I answered.

"Warren wants to see you both in his office," she said in her secretarial monotone.

"Right away," I said, signaling to Jeffrey and grabbing copies of the creative brief.

When we arrived, I observed Veronica's polished desk, which was completely clear except for a phone, computer, and a white bud vase, which held a single fresh red rose. Veronica was an attractive African American woman in her mid-fifties. She had worked for Warren for at least ten years and was staunchly loyal to him. She had no personal photos nor the usual trinkets one might find on someone's desk. But I always wondered about one item: a small, free-standing gold plaque on the credenza to her right that read *One shoe can change your life … —Cinderella.* She was unmarried, so perhaps she was in some way waiting for her prince charming to arrive. That was probably the only thing we had in common, I thought wryly.

She made us wait while she finished a memo, clacking away at her keyboard with French manicured, acrylic nails. When she finally looked up, she had a bored expression. "You can just go on in there—he's waiting."

Warren was in his serious mode; I could tell by his posture and the fact that he didn't look up as we approached. He was finishing a call and staring at his computer intently. Warren's grey eyes were focused and his mouth a straight line, as though his teeth were clenched in frustration. "I don't care," he barked tersely into the receiver. He barely glanced in our direction and waved us to sit in the chairs opposite his desk. Warren shifted in his chair. "No, I want it by five today. Period," he snarled at the poor soul on the other end of the line and hung up. This side of Warren always came as a reminder that, no matter the kind words or pats on the back he ferreted out on occasion, we could still be on the receiving end of one of his lashings. He turned to us with his jaw still tight. "Let's talk about the brief."

I started rambling about my thought process regarding the pandas, but Warren cut me off impatiently. "I've read it. Direction's good. Jeffrey, who are you putting on the account?"

"I was thinking Sam and Johann for this one," he said. "I've already sent them the brief to chew on. They're young, bold, and up on the whole panda phenomenon. It's big among young Asian LGBTs and the eighteen-to-thirty-five hipster crowd, which ties in with everything Jane says in her brief. We'll have initial concepts to show you in a couple of days."

Naturally, the toddlers were 'up on the whole panda phenomenon.' *How did they find out about stuff like that?* "Sam and Johann are perfect for this one," I commented.

"Then I'll count on concepts by Wednesday at noon," Warren ordered in his dismissive manner, while putting his phone on speaker and speed-dialing his next victim.

Whew. We were done. I ran back to my office and found a message from Marisa waiting; we made plans for dinner later in the week.

❖

AT FRITTO MISTO, AN Italian restaurant, Marisa was flying high. In fact, I'd not seen her so happy since her last relationship, which did not end well.

"He's awesome," Marisa announced, glowing. "Total stunner, intelligent, exciting, fun—he has it all."

"Okay, slow down," I said, reaching for the breadbasket and grabbing a crusty roll. "Where did you meet him and when? What's his name?"

"I met him a few months ago during a studio interview," she answered, not going for the bread herself. Marisa rarely ate carbs unless she was having her period. She said they made her look puffy on camera—called it 'carb-face syndrome'. "His name is Drew, Drew Parkhill. He's totally loaded, a philanthropist raising money for a large non-profit. Old money. From England. Splitting his time between LA and London."

I was peeling the crust off the bread and taking tiny nibbles without butter. It was the only way I would eat carbs—sort of like not eating them—only getting a taste, even though I wanted to devour the whole basket. "When do I get to meet him?"

She shrugged. "I'm never sure when he's free."

"Let's go to the *LA Insider Magazine* party this weekend and you can invite him. Derek mentioned getting an outing together anyway and I want you to meet my friend Kat. She's going through a nasty divorce so maybe your newfound love vibes will rub off on all of us."

We made plans with the group to meet on Friday night. It was perfect timing because we were presenting initial panda concepts to the client Friday afternoon and, if everything went well, I would be in a celebratory mood.

Eight

WARREN APPROVED THREE FINAL panda ad concepts that would be presented to the client. He put us all through hell to get to those final concepts—the toddlers were moaning and groaning, threatening to quit if they had to make more changes.

That afternoon, we met with Frédéric and his agent, Philippe. Frédéric looked exactly like he did in the show, minus the heavy makeup and, upon close inspection, his skin was marred with deep acne scars. He wore a baggy sweater over jeans and a Kangol hat to cover his baldness. Mirrored aviators concealed his eyes and he smelled like stale cigarettes and bad cologne.

In contrast, Philippe was tall with light blond hair which he wore in a bun close to the top of his head. His piercing blue eyes peered out from heavy lids, and it was obvious he had not shaved for a couple of days. He had the darkest circles under his eyes, a deep crimson violet like he had either been beat up by thugs or had not slept for weeks. There was something profoundly creepy about him, about both him and Frédéric.

Warren greeted them and, as Jeffrey presented, both Frenchmen sat quiet and motionless, Philippe with his arms crossed at his chest. Warren interjected commentary here and there but the two had no reaction, either negative or positive.

"Gentlemen," Warren said after Jeffrey concluded. "Please share your thoughts on our spec work."

Frédéric and Philippe looked at each other. "*Un instant, s'il vous plaît*," Philippe addressed us, which I was able to translate into *wait*. The two proceeded to dialogue with passion in French as we sat there. All I could make out was the word 'panda' here and there.

"*Messieurs et mademoiselle*," Philippe said finally in broken English, "we thank you for your work, but we cannot decide at this time. Please give us the weekend and we will give a decision Monday?"

Jeffrey looked unsatisfied and intent upon nailing an answer. "Is there a direction you're leaning toward?" he pressed. "Because if there is, we should discuss it now and get the creative team working on revisions."

The two Frenchmen shot each other a look and shook their heads.

Jeffrey was about to say something when Warren cut him off like a court judge, adjourning the meeting. "That's great, gentlemen," he said. "We look forward to hearing from you Monday."

As Warren said this, he got up to accompany them to the door and the rest of us followed. We all shook hands with the Frenchmen but, when I reached Philippe, he kissed my hand instead, saying "*Au revoir, mademoiselle.*"

I knew from seeing enough French films that *au revoir* meant 'goodbye'. "*Au revoir*," I managed to stammer in horrible French.

Philippe smiled, and I noticed his teeth were badly discolored, probably from coffee and cigarettes. I wasn't sure if it was the tawdry nature of the two Frenchmen or the way Philippe put his lips on my hand, but I felt in dire need of a shower.

It was going on five and I couldn't wait to get home and freshen up for my big night out. Marisa had VIP passes to the event at the Shangri-La Hotel's outdoor courtyard promoting *LA Insider Magazine's* tenth anniversary. Kat and Derek were coming, and we were to meet Drew for the first time. Anyone and everyone in the entertainment, advertising, and PR industries would be in attendance and, after being cooped up all week in the office, I was in the mood for fun.

I LEFT THE AGENCY in a rare state of worry-free bliss with spare time to stop for a quick walk around Neiman Marcus on the way home. *Why not reward myself with a bit of retail therapy?* I could debut it tonight at the party. I often engaged in an internal debate every time I splurged. And somehow, any buyer's remorse would disappear, at least until the bill arrived, which now sat around twenty-eight thousand dollars. But the harder I worked, the more I wanted the clothes; they somehow pacified me.

This afternoon's decadence was a pale blue Chanel shift dress that went perfectly with the nude Manolo Blahnik pumps which I had been waiting for an opportunity to debut. The two items alone added another five thousand dollars to my credit card balance.

And new fashion was not the only thing I was debuting that evening. The day before, I took the afternoon off and headed to the hair salon, leaving as a blonde. The tedious process amounted to hours of stripping, lifting, bleaching, and conditioning so that my auburn locks were slowly lightened to a pale blonde, a look that made me instantly glamorous. At work, Anna mistook me for Brooke from behind. When I turned around, she made a face and snickered, "Oh, it's you." Warren acted as though he didn't notice. Jeffrey just said 'nice hair' in his deadpan way and moved on. I had yet to hear what my real friends thought; I was about to find out.

WHEN I WALTZED INTO the Shangri-La in my newly acquired duds, long blonde locks gleaming, I immediately spotted Derek and Marisa ensconced in black and white striped leather lounge chairs near the fire pit. The Shangri-La was an old thirties deco hotel right on the ocean in Santa Monica. It had been restored and transformed into an expensive, trendy boutique joint for the beautiful and chic. The party was in the hotel's courtyard, a multi-level outdoor haven sporting lush landscaping, a well-manicured garden, and an old-school rectangular swimming pool. The pool, which was an elevated centerpiece, was surrounded by a teak deck. Tall, curtained cabanas with striped awnings rimmed the pool area, and every corner glowed with candlelight, lending a sexy, sophisticated air to the place. The house DJ was spinning an Avicii tune as I shouldered my way toward Marisa and Derek.

"Hi, gorgeous," Derek said, standing and giving me a kiss on the cheek. "Wow look at you," he said, backing up to have a better look. It was the first time he looked at me that way since I'd met him.

"You like?" I asked, smiling, and tossing my hair.

"Jane, oh my god, what did you do?" Marisa blurted, eyes bulging.

"Just something different. You don't like it?" I asked, smoothing it on one side with my hand.

"No, that's not it. It's beautiful. It's just that you're a *blonde*." Marisa made a funny face. "What made you do it?"

I shrugged. "I don't know, just needed a change, I guess."

"You could have asked my opinion before you made such a drastic move," Marisa snorted, as though I had set out to cause her grief. I rolled my eyes and shook my head.

Derek was obviously uncomfortable to be caught in such a distinctly female conversation. "Who wants a cocktail?" he asked brightly.

We moved to the bar and ordered champagne, which they served in plastic flutes.

"Where's Drew?" I asked Marisa as soon as our drinks were served. "Don't tell me he's not coming."

"Working late," Marisa replied, glancing at her phone like she might be missing a text. "He'll be here later. Where's the divorcée you told me about?"

At that moment, I noticed a stunning blonde on the other side of the bar snaking her way through the crowd. It was Kat in a black leather jacket. As she got closer, I saw her white silk camisole underneath the jacket, tight black jeans, and strappy emerald Gianvito Rossi heels. She held a small matching emerald clutch. Her makeup was much heavier, with dark smoky eyes and pale lipstick. She was breathtaking. *How could any man leave this exquisite woman?*

"Here she is," I announced, waving to Kat.

I thought Marisa was going to fall out of her chair. "That's your friend?" Marisa asked, dumbstruck. "You didn't tell me it was Katherine Blakely! She's one of the most influential women in the city."

"Hi, Jane," Kat greeted me, leaning over for a hug. She smelled good, too, like clean hair and expensive French perfume. "I *love* your hair," she commented, taking chunks of my blonde hair, and running her hands through them. If Kat liked my hair, I didn't care what anyone else thought.

Derek was next in line to meet Kat. As I watched them shake hands, I wondered if Derek might be attracted to her. This was something I instinctively did whenever I saw Derek talk to other women and it bothered me—he was not my boyfriend. Still, I watched for his reaction to Kat, who was movie star beautiful, as far as I was concerned.

Marisa immediately put out her hand and introduced herself. "I'm Marisa Silva. It's such a pleasure to meet you, Katherine," Marisa pronounced with deference, like she was in the presence of the Queen.

"Yes, of course." Kat smiled and shook her hand. "You interviewed me for a story a long time ago."

"I did?" Marisa looked embarrassed. "I hope I was nice to you," she remarked, clearly trying to remember when she possibly could have interviewed Katherine Blakely.

"You did your job," Kat replied with a placid expression. "I had just started my company and you asked how I planned to survive in a male-dominated industry."

Judging from Marisa's reaction, the memory must have come back to her. "Oh yes," she responded. "That was you.

Well, I guess you showed me." Marisa gave her a fake smile.

"Almost a decade later, here I am." Kat laughed. "It's nice to see you again."

While Marisa and Kat reminisced about their careers in the early days, the bar started to fill up with more beautiful LA people. I excused myself to walk around. Every ad agency in town had representation here. I made my way toward the pool where a crowd was building, as cameras flashed. The evening air was cool and crisp, and the moon was full, hanging bright and low. There was obviously a celebrity in one of the private cabanas, so I headed in that direction to see who it was and felt one of my stiletto heels get stuck in the teak floorboards. That was it. I tripped and fell in my new Chanel, champagne spilling everywhere, purse and contents flying. My foot had come out of the shoe, which stayed stuck between the floorboards.

Horrified, I quickly tried to recover my shoe. The dim candlelight was not helping in my quest. It was dark, and I could barely see anything. After tugging on the shoe several times, it finally came free. I crawled around on all fours to find my bag and gather its contents, as a man's deep voice offered, "May I help you?"

I looked up and, with the light of the shining moon, recognized Craig Keller of the fabled Keller Whitman Group. He was holding out his hand. Trembling, I accepted it and he helped me up. I clutched my shoe and thought about all the hours I had spent researching him over time. I had seen so many pictures of him, it made no sense to see him in person. He had become an unattainable computer-generated myth—he might as well have been a cartoon character.

"Are you okay?" he asked. He was even more magnificent up close, with his gleaming white teeth, light eyes, and dark hair. But there was something else about him—something the photos couldn't begin to capture—it was a charisma of sorts—an aura of charm.

"Yes, thank you," I answered, straightening, and brushing off my dress, which was wet and sticky with champagne and dirt from the teak deck. "I'm sure that looked inelegant."

"On the contrary," he replied with a warm smile, "You pulled it off with grace." Before I could respond, he continued. "Have we met? I'm Craig Keller."

"Yes, Mr. Keller, of course. I know who you are," I responded, feeling disheveled and self-conscious—especially since he was dressed in an impeccable grey pinstriped suit with a white shirt and dark crimson silk tie. "It's a pleasure to meet you. I'm Jane Mercer." I longed to make a run for it and find a bathroom and mirror.

"Call me Craig," he said, again, with the smile. I couldn't help but feel intimidated—I was talking to *Craig Keller*, one of the most sought-after men in town—one of LA's preeminent ad men, his agency a juggernaut in the industry. Though I had never actually seen him in person, he felt oddly familiar to me from all the cyber-stalking. He was like a movie star—wildly successful—and I was now standing before him in a stained Chanel dress holding one Manolo Blahnik.

"May I?" he asked, eyes on my shoe. Without waiting for a response, he gently took the shoe out of my hand and knelt; he placed my hand on his shoulder for balance, lifted my foot and slid the shoe back on. I thought my heart might stop.

Then he stood, drew himself to his full height and smiled. "I already know who you are, too," he added slyly. "I've been following your career. Word about is that you're Warren Mitchell's protégé."

"Oh? Is that what people say?" I asked. I had absolutely no idea I even *had* a reputation let alone one of being Warren's protégé.

"He'd better be treating you right or someone might come along and steal you away," he remarked casually, yet with a certain shrewdness.

I felt my face burning. This made absolutely no sense. "Oh? Warren, um, he treats me fine," I stammered, trying to think of something clever to say but failing.

Craig Keller looked both charmed and amused. "You lost your drink, you know," he observed, looking down at my hands. "I'll get you a fresh one. Wait here," he said, and sauntered over to the bar while I stared after him in disbelief.

"Nice move," someone behind me blurted and I immediately snapped out of my dream state. It was Anna. Naturally, she would have to be an eyewitness to my embarrassing fall.

"I mean, you couldn't have landed at a worse angle," she jeered.

"Right, I planned it that way."

"You should have seen yourself." Anna was now laughing her mean-spirited laugh. "Too bad I didn't get video. It would have been fun to play back in the next staff meeting."

"Yeah, well next time I'll give you a heads-up, so you can have your camera ready," I muttered, furious at myself for being so clumsy.

"How do you know Craig Keller?" she prodded, looking like a hawk.

"I literally just met him," I answered.

"Really?" she asked with that insipid smile. "Are you trying to get a new boyfriend or a new job? I've heard he's quite the ladies' man, even though he's married."

That took me by surprise. Craig Keller was *married*.

Anna raised her eyebrows like I was doing something naughty. "Hear he likes blondes, too. Maybe that's why you dyed your hair?"

"Like I said, I just met him five minutes ago." I tried to keep my voice calm. She had this way of rattling me.

"Just don't let Warren catch you talking to him," she continued in a flip tone. "He might get the wrong idea."

Before I could say anything, Anna's boyfriend du jour, who looked thoroughly irritated that she had dumped him somewhere to come harass me, interrupted. *There is a God.*

"You just left me there," he complained, grabbing Anna by the arm, and leading her away, grumbling, "I've been looking all over for you."

She was out of sight by the time Craig Keller returned with two champagnes. "I'm sorry it took so long. There's a bit of a crowd." He handed me one of the drinks.

I accepted it nervously and we clicked plastic flutes.

"Cheers," I said with a smile.

"Salut," he returned, putting his hand in his suit jacket, and pulling out a business card. "Call me for lunch sometime," he suggested as he handed it to me. "I'd love to talk to you about some of the things our agency is doing. You never know what the future holds."

"Um … sure," I replied, feeling awkward. We shook hands.

"Oh, and be careful of the pool deck, Jane," he cautioned. "I'd hate to have to pick you up twice in one night." He winked before walking away.

I suddenly felt drunk even though I hadn't had one full drink. I quickly found the ladies' room to examine my face and stained dress. I was so engrossed in cleaning myself up that I almost didn't notice Marisa in the corner alone with her head down, texting. "Hey, I didn't even see you," I called.

Marisa looked up, evidently crestfallen. "He's not coming."

My mouth flew open. "Drew stood you up?"

"He says he's not feeling well—he's staying home. I offered to go over there and bring him soup or something, but he said he likes to be alone when he's sick."

"I wouldn't let you go anyway," I protested, shaking my head in disgust. "I'm sorry, Marisa, but that's poor form. He knows how important tonight is."

Marisa stared at me for a minute like she couldn't decide whether to be angry at him or at me. But when her look went from sadness to a scowl, I knew which way she was headed.

"What happened to Kat and Derek?" I asked.

"Kat was talking to some guys I didn't recognize," Marisa answered. "I'm not sure about Derek."

"You wouldn't believe who I just ran into," I said excitedly, while scanning the ladies' room and bobbing my head under the stalls to make sure we were alone. Once I was certain the coast was clear, I told Marisa the story of me falling in front of Craig Keller.

"Wow, Jane, that's crazy," she exclaimed, brightening

slightly at the thought that my predicament might be a little worse than hers. "What's he *like*? Is he as hot as he looks in all the pictures?"

"Oh, God, yes," I said, giggling like a schoolgirl. "He has the most amazing eyes and these insane long lashes. No man has the right to look that good."

"It's no wonder he has women crawling all over him," Marisa remarked. "Every picture I see, he's with a different blonde. But it's never his wife."

"I had no idea he was married, until *Anna-the-bitch* just informed me," I said, recalling how sexy and carefree Craig acted—as if there wasn't someone waiting for him at home.

"Yuck," Marisa said, making a face. "Why is *Anna-the-bitch* even here?" She removed a compact from her handbag, opened it, and began dabbing at her face. "But she's right—Craig Keller's married to a beautiful ex-model—he has two kids, too, I've heard. Do you think he was hitting on you?" Her eyes twinkled with mischief in the candle-lit bathroom.

"Nah, no way," I said, dismissing the comment with a chuckle. "It wasn't like that at all. He just made me feel so … important, knowing my name and everything."

"He knows who *you* are?" Marisa's eyes widened. "*How?* She immediately looked remorseful and added, "I didn't mean it to sound like that—it's just, well, it's *Craig Keller* we're talking about."

Three women in skin-tight bandage dresses and high heels burst in, chattering gaily, and smelling pungently of vodka, perfume, and hairspray. Our conversation abruptly shut down. Marisa and I made our way back toward the bar and, miraculously, spotted a row of empty seats. Kat appeared out of nowhere and joined us.

"This place is great," Kat said, sounding exhilarated. "I forgot how much fun it is to flirt. To hell with Jack. I'm so over it."

Marisa and I shot each other a look. It's not that I wasn't happy to see Kat having a good time with everything going on in her life but there was no way she was over Jack so quickly. She was putting on a major front.

"At least you're having better luck than we are," I responded, smiling. "I just fell in my new Chanel in front of an advertising magnate and Marisa just got stood up by prince charming."

"Oh no. I'm sorry." Kat changed her tune quickly. "Are you guys okay?" she asked.

"I'll live," Marisa replied. "He did have a valid excuse, I guess." It was clear that Marisa was reluctant to go off publicly in front of a woman she'd just met and so deeply admired.

"And what about you? How did you fall and in front of which magnate?" Kat asked me.

"Craig Keller," I answered. "And it wasn't just a fall. It was more like a splat."

Kat's eyes bulged, and her smile disappeared.

"I do have to say, though, he was a total gentleman," I added. "He helped me up, bought me a drink, and implied that he wants to *hire* me."

"Be careful," Kat warned, eyes scanning the immediate area like she was afraid of being overheard.

"Do you *know* him?" I was again reminded that Kat didn't travel in the same circles as we did.

Kat paused and then responded, "I know enough."

"So why should I be careful?" I asked, suddenly fascinated to hear the story of this powerful bad guy who made such a show of being chivalrous to this damsel in distress. "You *have* to tell me."

Kat shook her head. "Not now. Not here." She got up and grabbed her green clutch. "Ladies, this was fun, but I have to go home. I forgot I'm the only one taking care of Joyce." Joyce was Kat's Irish Setter, named after James Joyce.

"What? The night's just begun. Stay a little longer," I urged.

"I'd love to, but I really have to go. You girls stay and have fun. I promise next time, I'll close it down with you." She blew a kiss and exited hurriedly.

I could not help but think that Kat wanted to leave because of what I told her. "Why do you think she reacted that way when I mentioned Craig Keller?" I asked Marisa.

She blinked at me. "Maybe she had a bad business deal with him."

"But why wouldn't she just say that? It seems odd that she just left so abruptly." This was going to drive me crazy. I looked around for Derek and, instead, saw Craig Keller a few feet away, talking to a group of beautiful people. A rush of adrenaline shot through me. I motioned subtly to Marisa.

"Yum," Marisa mouthed and took a sip of her champagne. And, before I knew it, Craig was standing next to me, leaning into the bar, ordering a drink. I felt Marisa nudge my leg with hers.

"Hello, again," he said to me, smiling broadly. I observed his unusually straight, white teeth and noticed his canines were a little longer than the rest, giving him extra sex appeal. "Glad to see you upright. Having a good time?"

I felt my face flush and suddenly became tongue-tied. "Um, yes, having a great time." *What a lame-ass response.*

Marisa jumped in to save me. "Mr. Keller, I don't believe we've met," she said extending her hand. "I'm Marisa Silva, KVLA News."

His glance momentarily strayed to Marisa. "Hello, Marisa," he said, shaking her hand casually.

"I've been reading about you for so long, I feel like I know you," she gushed while searching her bag for a business card.

"Don't believe a word of it," he responded, gazing intently at me again. I felt like my heart was going to stop. There was something about this man that unnerved me like no one else. I almost wished he would turn his attention elsewhere and end the agony I felt in his presence.

"So, you two up to no good this evening?" As he uttered this line, the bartender handed him a drink. It looked like Scotch or Bourbon—one of the brown liquors.

"Always," Marisa returned playfully, handing him her card. Craig accepted the card but didn't offer his. "I would love to interview you some time," she said. "You know, get your take on advertising and how it's changed in recent years with the emphasis so much on digital marketing."

I just stood back and watched Marisa work Craig like he was anyone else she wanted to get on her show. She was not a bit intimidated by his fame, fortune, or good looks.

"Maybe some time," he replied to Marisa, then turned to me. "Jane knows where to find me."

Just then, a man I recognized as Ewan Blade, lead guitarist of the British heavy metal band, Brave Harlots, approached our group. He was at least six inches shorter than Craig, with long, wavy red hair and cerulean blue eyes. Marisa shifted her acquisitive scrutiny quickly from Craig to Ewan, who was not classically attractive, but infinitely cool in his motorcycle jacket and shredded jeans.

"Jane and Marisa, meet my client, Ewan Blade," Craig introduced.

Ewan shook each of our hands. "Nice to meet you both," he greeted us in his British accent.

Of course, it was Craig's client. Brave Harlots were a world-famous band with millions of fans. Those were the types of clients Keller Whitman Group acquired as opposed to the French panda brigade at Warren's agency.

He turned back to Craig, "Listen, man, I'm going to run—meet you at the office tomorrow."

"One o' clock," Craig responded. "See you then."

Marisa, wanting to seize the opportunity to exit the party with a rock star, immediately jumped off her bar stool, "I didn't realize it was so late," she said to me, then directly to Craig, "It was great meeting you. Have fun." She gave me a mischievous smile before running after Ewan.

Damn! Marisa thinks she's doing me a favor. Little did she know I was terrified to be alone in this man's presence. He was so out of my league, as Anna had pointed out a long time ago.

"I actually have to go soon myself," I declared, standing up and grabbing my bag.

"Oh, come on, stay and talk to me for a few minutes," he insisted, giving me a seductive slow blink with those light eyes. "I don't bite." As he said this, he sat down and motioned for me to do the same. "Do you live far from here?"

I shook my head. "Not far at all. Lincoln Boulevard near Colorado," I said, instantly feeling like a dope. *He doesn't care at which cross streets my lowly apartment sits.* I imagined him in a mansion like Kat's.

"Ah, so close to your office," he replied. "Your boss must love that. Easier for you to work long hours."

"I suppose so," I answered, thinking that Warren probably had no clue how far away I lived and couldn't care less anyway. I showed up every day and that's all he cared to know.

"He must have you very busy," he commented, not taking his eyes off mine even for one moment.

I was so awestruck by Craig Keller, I barely noticed Derek lingering not too far from us. He was by himself. I pretended not to see him, but he approached us anyway. "I was worried about you," he said, putting his arm around me and looking askance at Craig. "Didn't you get my texts?"

"Derek Lowell, this is Craig Keller," I announced enthusiastically, not answering his question but knowing damned well I was getting texts and ignoring them. Derek didn't bother shaking Craig's hand and just nodded in his direction. Craig stared back blankly, as though Derek were too ordinary for him to acknowledge.

"I think I'm going to head out," Derek mentioned to me. "I'm not feeling great."

"That's too bad. I hope you feel better." For whatever reason, Derek was reluctant to leave me with Craig. He just stood there, not budging.

"Will you excuse us for a minute?" I asked Craig, who shrugged as I got up and pulled Derek a few feet away. "What's wrong with you?" I asked as soon as we were out of earshot.

"Nothing. I just don't trust that guy." He wore a frown and his lips curled like he smelled something awful. "I don't think you should be alone with him."

"Derek!" My tone conveyed exasperation. "Have you lost your mind? You don't know anything about him."

"Well, neither do you. Plus, you've been drinking, and I think you should just call it a night," he said in a self-righteous tone.

"Wait—are you my father?" I demanded in disbelief. "Are you going to ground me and take away my driving privileges, too?"

"Jane, I'm just trying …"

"You're a buzz kill," I hissed, cutting him off. "I'll talk to you later, okay?" Without waiting for a response, I turned to find Craig who, in my absence, had attracted the attention of a pretty photographer and was being asked for a photo.

I waited patiently as he smiled for the camera. Viewing him from a few feet away, I again noticed his height—he had to be around six foot five—with broad shoulders and a trim waist. His green eyes sparkled with each flash of the camera. I remembered reading that he was around thirty-six years old. He looked grown up but still youthful—mature, yet approachable. I was unable to take my eyes off him.

When the photographer finished and seemed satisfied with the photos, she thanked Craig and walked away. Craig looked around, caught my eye, and waved for me to return.

"Sorry about that," I said as I approached.

"Who was that guy?" he asked with an air of amusement, again giving me the slow blink.

"A friend," I answered. "That's all."

"Well, Ms. Mercer, I'm not finished with you yet, but I do have to go." He took my hand confidently and added, "I do hope you'll call me." As he said this, he looked me directly in the eye, with *those* eyes, then turned and disappeared into the crowd.

I drove home with a sense of giddiness and exhilaration, going over the details of the evening in my mind as I sailed down Pico Boulevard with all the windows open, basking in the magic and energy of the evening. A litany of questions flooded my mind. *How did Craig Keller know my name? Was he really interested in hiring me? Or was it something else?* I couldn't imagine a man like him being attracted to me. I thought about the way Anna said, 'ladies' man'; Marisa's comment about him always being seen with a different blonde even though married with children; Kat's cryptic comments and immediate disappearance upon hearing his name, and then Derek's bizarre distrust. None of it mattered. I was full of an intense thrill that I couldn't remember ever feeling. Being with Craig Keller felt like wearing an expensive, impossibly rare gemstone but having to give it back at the end of the evening. I wanted desperately to possess it. In fact, I wanted to freeze this night in my memory, so it never ended.

Somehow, I made it home, despite not having paid attention to where I was going the entire way. As I entered my apartment and turned on the lights, the place took on a whole new brilliance. It felt like a palace and in it lived the luckiest girl on earth, a beautiful princess, like Cinderella, plucked by the hand of fate and placed before the most handsome prince in the land.

By the next morning, my pillow was imprinted with several of the previous evening's makeup hues. I went in the bathroom to brush my teeth and got a glimpse in the mirror. What I saw was disturbing. My eye makeup had drizzled down my cheeks in a pattern approximating the makeup worn by David Bowie during his Ziggy Stardust phase. My thoughts went to last night and all the strange occurrences. I grabbed my handbag, sifted through its contents, and there it was: a card bearing the words, "Craig A. Keller, Managing Partner." Then the events of the evening came flooding back to me, like a recent storm.

Grandma and Grandpa's number popped up on my phone. I didn't feel like dealing with them now, but I answered the phone. "Hello."

"Hi, Sweet-pea," Grandma chirped into my ear. The sound of her voice felt like someone drove a lead pipe into my brain.

"Hi, Grandma," I responded in a throaty, desperately-in-need-of-a-cup-of-coffee voice.

"You sound like you just got up. Late night?"

"That's because I did just get up," I grumbled. "Yes, I was out with some friends at a party."

"Well, Bubala, I called to remind you that we're set for dinner at Mastro's tonight with the Feldmans. They're bringing Julian," she added with a giggle. "I can't wait for you two to meet again now that you're both all grown up."

Crap! When and how did I possibly agree to such an event? Grandma must have tricked me into saying yes when I was busy and not paying attention. *Damn her!* I hobbled to the kitchen and started rummaging through my cabinets, urgently searching for a clean coffee mug.

Grandma plowed on with her monologue. "Now, honey, we have reservations for 7:30, so please don't be late. That place is pricey, and we are the Feldmans' guests, so I want to make sure you're there on time."

I sighed into the phone, saying nothing, as I finally located a clean mug and a K-cup. *Fabulous.*

"Jane? Hello? Are you there?" she started clicking the receiver, like they did in old movies. The funnier thing was that she was using a phone on which that move was still possible.

"I'm here, Grandma," I muttered as my coffee brewed, feeling like I had been beaten down and there was no use protesting.

"Okay, good. What are you wearing?"

"Grandma, I'll be there on time and, rest assured, I'll be wearing something appropriate." I winced at the thought of wasting a great outfit on this occasion.

"Okay, sweetie. But please, nothing too tight or low-cut. You know, Julian is a good Jewish boy, and I don't want him to get the wrong idea, you in advertising and all."

Oy, did this woman ever stop?

"I know you girls are always into the latest trends," she continued to hammer the point, "but could you please do me a favor and drop it down a notch just for tonight?" She was completely oblivious as to how annoying this conversation was to me.

"Grandma, you know I love you dearly, but you needn't school me on what to wear to a restaurant in Beverly Hills," I interjected. "In fact, I should be the one schooling about ninety-nine percent of the clientele at that place."

"Jane, honey, are you angry?" Grandma asked, sounding wounded. "I was just trying to help."

"Sorry, Grandma." At this point, I just wanted to get off the phone. "I'll see you tonight."

I hung up quickly. She was exasperating at times like this. It was truly the last thing I wanted to do on a Saturday night, especially after the excitement of the prior evening. At least Mastro's was a nice place. I would have to make the best of it.

THAT NIGHT, I GOT to the restaurant a little early, so I could get a quick drink at the bar before everyone arrived. I had selected a simple black Diane Von Furstenberg tunic dress with three-quarter sleeves and bateau neckline ensuring, as Grandma requested, no cleavage would see the light of day. I paired it with camel suede boots and a leopard scarf.

I grabbed a spot at the bar and ordered a vodka on the rocks with olives. Better to go heavy on the first drink in private so as not to look like a complete drunk in front of the ultra-conservative Feldman family. I wondered whether this rationale was at all normal. Regardless, I bellied up to the bar with hard-earned expertise.

The bar was busy, and I was scrunched in between a slightly overweight guy with black hair and glasses and a woman who displayed her way-too-big boob job stuffed into a shiny red corset dress.

I sipped my drink and noted Marisa was calling my cell phone. I had forgotten to call her and do a post-mortem on last night, like we usually did. I answered right away. "I can only talk for a minute." I leaned away from the guy next to me, whose pudgy arm was pushing against my waist. He reeked of garlic, and Chaps. I shot a disgusted look at him and took a gulp of my vodka. "I was roped into dinner with my grandparents and some geek they want to set me up with."

"That sucks," Marisa commented. "You have to tell me what happened with Craig Keller after I left last night."

"Oh, my god, Marisa! Isn't he a stunner?"

"He has to be one of the best-looking men I've ever seen," Marisa agreed. "And that's a real statement, coming from me."

"I still can't believe he knew who I was," I exclaimed, taking another long sip of vodka. "What about you? Did you talk to Ewan Blade?"

"Yes, and he agreed to do an interview next time he's in town," she answered. "He's such a sweet guy—so unlike your typical rock star."

"You and your Brits." I giggled.

"What about you? How did you leave it with Mr. Gorgeous last night?" Marisa was hungry for details.

I stuffed one of the olives into my mouth and washed it down with more vodka before responding. "He said I should call him for lunch, but you know I'm sort of nervous," I told her, chewing into the phone. "What if someone from the office hears about it?" My mind went back to Anna and her comments about how I should 'be careful.'

"Oh, come on, Jane, don't be so paranoid. Lunch is no big deal. You owe it to yourself to see what he wants. What if he offers you a job? If you worked for him, you'd see him every single day," Marisa elaborated wistfully. "I don't know if I could handle that. Could *you?*"

"Not sure. I mean, I know he's married and everything, but I really want to see him again. He's just … *so* amazing. The last thing he said was that he was *not finished with me*—what do you think he meant by that?"

Marisa was in silent awe. "I think that means he wants to see you again—*soon.*"

"Should I? I mean, how could any woman resist him?" The sight of my grandparents entering the restaurant stopped me in my salacious tracks. "I have to go now," I abruptly cut off Marisa. I laid some cash on the bar, put my phone in my purse, and shot down the rest of the vodka. I was feeling pleasantly buzzed and ready to get through the evening as I jumped off the bar stool, grateful to get away from both overweight smelly man and big boob chick.

Grandma greeted me with a big hug and kiss while Grandpa smiled uncomfortably. "How's my pigeon?" Grandma cackled, smiling until she noticed my hair. Her nose wrinkled up like she smelled something foul. "What did you do to your hair? Bruce, look at Jane's hair. What did you go and do that for? It makes you look cheap," Grandma scolded, still glaring at my hair like it was an ugly hat. "We'll talk about it later. The Feldmans are parking and they said Julian is already at the bar."

"Hi, Julian, over here!" she called. Before I knew what had happened, the heavy guy at the bar was standing in front of me.

Holy shit! This couldn't be happening. I felt my face redden as I rifled through my thoughts trying to remember exactly what I had said to Marisa on the phone, positive he must have heard every word, all that stuff about Craig Keller. I just wanted to dash to the nearest exit and run for my life.

"Jane," Grandma shouted to me, interrupting my mental anguish. "Say hello to Julian, will you please?"

I smiled sheepishly and held my hand out to him. "Nice to meet you," I managed to sputter out. He stared at my hand coldly, like I had a strange tropical disease.

"Hello," he mumbled, barely taking my hand, and letting it go immediately.

Luckily, Julian's parents walked in, and the hugging and kissing began, ending the awkward silence. We sat down in a quiet corner of the restaurant, and I was made to sit across from Julian. The waitress came quickly for our drink order. I ordered white wine.

"No more martinis?" Julian hissed, eyeing me with distaste. I couldn't even hate the guy because I so deserved the abuse.

"Nope, all good," I responded casually, so as not to draw Grandma's attention. I had to make sure she remained clueless about what had transpired at the bar.

"Jane, tell us what you're up to these days," Mrs. Feldman yelled across the table.

Julian gave me a look that seemed to say, 'I can't wait to hear this.'

I ignored him and leaned toward the other end of the table. "I'm in the advertising business and I work with a variety of clients," I responded in my professional voice. "It's interesting work. Every day is something new."

"I'll bet," Julian muttered under his breath, audible only to me.

I sighed and sipped my wine, trying to ignore Grandma's concerned stare. She must have read the body language between Julian and me. She quickly turned her attention to Mrs. Feldman, who had resorted to reading the menu aloud to relieve the tension. This was going to be a long night.

My mind drifted back to Craig Keller, with his light green eyes and dark hair. Marisa was right, I needed to find out what he wanted. I thought about the secret Pinterest board I'd created just for him. It was secret because I didn't want my friends, or anyone, for that matter, to know how obsessed I was with him. But the board included at least 300 photos of Craig in various poses. But there was still so much I wanted to know. Maybe if I slipped away now for a few minutes, no one would notice. Anything to get out of this horrible dinner.

"Miss, may I take your order please?" The waitress was peering at me over her note pad, like some restaurant cop.

"Sure." I hadn't even looked at the menu. "Do you have salmon?"

"Yes, it's grilled, and served with our special mango chutney, wild rice, and green ..."

"I'll have that," I asserted hastily, not even waiting for her to finish. "Excuse me," I announced to the table, rising to my feet. "I have to go to the ladies' room."

I strode back to the lounge area and found a chair in the back. I took out my phone and pulled up my private Pinterest board first, scrolling through the numerous images and remembering his every move the previous evening. Just seeing his magnificent face made me feel different—almost magical—like I was floating. After about ten minutes of obsessing over photos of Craig, I felt a tap on my shoulder. It was Julian standing there awkwardly, interrupting my cyber-stalking.

"Hey, I know you don't want to be here, but I thought you'd at least stay for your grandparents' sake," he said.

I stood up and faced him squarely, folding my arms over my chest, sighing heavily. "You're right, I don't want to be here. You see, my grandparents have set me up before without even asking. They don't think much of what I do for a living and want me to get married as soon as possible. I had no idea that was you sitting next to me in the bar earlier. Otherwise, I would have been more respectful. I'm sorry if I offended you. It certainly was not the intention."

"That's okay, you're not my type anyway," he said, unattractive face twisting into a snub. "I don't care to get involved with a promiscuous woman who drinks too much, talks all kinds of trash, and dates married men."

My mouth dropped open as he dealt that blow. "Great, well, then I guess we're on the same page," I exploded, grabbing my bag, and attempting to sidestep Julian. But he held his arm out to stop me.

"Wait," he said, face softening slightly. "I'm sorry, really, I am. That was rude." Even though I was stung by his comment, I stood still to hear what this boor would have to say for himself. He gulped and proceeded slowly. "The truth is, I have the same problem with my parents. I can relate. I hope you don't think I'm too much of a jerk. I just saw the disgusted look in your eye as soon as you sat down at the bar. Then when I realized you were supposed to be my date, I—well—I knew it wasn't going to happen. Please accept my apology and come back to the table. I promise to be congenial for the remainder of dinner."

I took a deep breath and considered the situation. If I left, Grandma and Grandpa would never let me hear the end of it. If I stayed, I might have to hear more sarcasm from Julian … or maybe not. He did sound sincere. I supposed there was no reason why I shouldn't go back and act like nothing happened. "Apology accepted," I finally uttered.

"I'm sorry to hear you have the same issue with your parents. Maybe we can just be friends?" I half-expected him to tell me, 'I have enough friends, bitch.'

"I'd love that," Julian said grinning, revealing a row of crooked teeth. "Let's start over. I'm Julian."

"Nice to meet you, Julian. I'm Jane."

We shook hands. His handshake felt warm this time. We exchanged phone numbers and went back to the table laughing.

The rest of the evening sailed by. Once my guard was down, I found Julian to be a decent guy. I was happy to have a comrade in the whole fiasco. I believed both Julian's parents and my grandparents were satisfied that they had staged a coup. Their single misfits were getting along smashingly. Grandpa even hugged and kissed me when we said goodbye.

On my way home, Derek called. I was suddenly reminded of last night's drama and his erratic behavior. "Hello, Derek," I greeted him cautiously.

"Hi, Jane, am I calling at a bad time?" he asked. I could hear a faint air of remorse in his voice.

"Not at all," I replied. "Just had dinner with my grandparents and their friends, and I'm on my way home."

"Did you hear that new Glass Animals song?" He spoke with feigned optimism.

"Yes, a couple of times," I answered. "Not sure I like it yet, though. Do you?"

"The lyrics are a little weird for my taste but I'm liking the vocals, sort of breathy."

I wanted to believe that good old Derek was back, but he sounded like he was trying too hard. "Did you go out tonight?" I asked, just to change the subject.

"Nah, we were performing at El Camino College. Besides, I had a big enough dose of the singles scene last night."

"Speaking of last night, what got into you anyway?" I queried.

"I don't know." He sounded relieved that I brought it up first. "I didn't have anything against that guy. I was just concerned … about you," he faltered.

"It's okay, Derek." I preferred to move away from the topic. "It's forgotten." I glanced at my sideview mirror and changed lanes.

"No, seriously, sometimes I think you're, like, my sister or something and I get protective." I slammed on the breaks because traffic inexplicably came to a complete stop. His *sister?* Was he serious? I was not at all thrilled to hear that comment. I didn't know how I expected him to see me, but 'sister' was not the preferred option. "Anyway, I hope you can forgive me," he concluded.

"Forget it, Derek," I urged, fighting the stop and go traffic.

"Did you have fun last night?" he asked casually. "I mean, are you going to see him again?"

"Who?" I asked innocently, glancing up at a freeway LED screen that read, "Disabled Vehicle in Right Lane." *Of course.*

"The guy you were talking to at the bar. How do you know him, anyway?"

"He runs an ad agency and, for whatever reason, heard my name in passing." I was trying to downplay the whole thing, but Derek wouldn't let it go.

"So, you're going to see him again?"

"I'm not sure," I responded, trying to keep my voice indifferent. "I might run into him again sometime. I mean, we do work in the same industry."

It was only quasi-true, but what was I supposed to say? *He may want to hire me, but all I can think about is loosening that dark crimson silk tie and tearing his clothes off, like an expensive gift, to see what heavenly treasures lie underneath.* Sometimes, it's better to say nothing.

"Oh," was all he said.

I could tell he was still thinking but I couldn't bear the thought of another comparison to Derek's immediate (or extended) family, so I made an excuse to get off the phone.

Early Sunday morning, I was on a fresh mission to educate myself about Craig Keller. *How was it that I didn't even know he was married?* I thought back to our encounter and he certainly didn't act like a married man. I made coffee and got on my laptop with the thought that I would scour the internet until I had absorbed every scrap of intel on him.

I went to the Wikipedia entry first. Craig Axel Keller, born September 28, 1980, raised in the San Francisco Bay area. His father was a well-known criminal trial lawyer named Donovan C. Keller, and his mother was a published poet named Julia Keller.

Craig graduated from Stanford University with honors, married when he was twenty-six. His wife's name was Alessandra, and she was Italian born. They met in Paris, where she was a runway model. One interview with Craig revealed that it was "love at first sight," and he "took her home with him to California," where they immediately married.

Upon searching images of Alessandra Keller, I only found a handful of photos. She was an exotic dark-haired beauty, with large, expressive brown eyes, olive skin that was California-tanned, and a long, aquiline nose. Her lips were full, and she wore red lipstick with little other makeup. I was only able to find one picture of Alessandra and Craig together. They were at a society gala and Craig wore a tux; his wife, a simple, off-the-shoulder black gown. She was bedecked in diamonds. What struck me was that Craig had his arm around Alessandra, but she seemed to be straining to keep them apart. While his breezy smile and careless confidence came through loud and clear, so did his wife's discomfort.

They had two children, a boy named Axel, age six; and a girl named Anabel, age four. I searched in vain to find photos of them. I pictured Craig in the hospital room while his wife was in labor, him changing diapers, and driving with a car seat in his vehicle. It was not an easy image to conjure. He just didn't seem like the type to be bogged down with a wife and kids. I could only envision Craig Keller's outward image, that of a playboy who exuded power, money, and sex appeal.

It wasn't until late afternoon that I realized I had been

so deeply engrossed in stalking Craig Keller on the internet that I hadn't showered, changed, or done anything else all day. When I finally settled into bed for the evening, my mind was consumed with thoughts of him: wondering how in the world he could be interested in me ... for *anything*? I resolved to find out.

Ten

WARREN CALLED AN UNEXPECTED meeting Monday morning with Jeffrey and me to review Frédéric's feedback on the panda concepts. Evidently, he didn't 'love' our work and was not ready to move forward with any of the concepts we presented. He also hinted that he might not hire our agency at all.

"They found our work boring and safe," Warren said while rummaging through his duffle bag, searching for a protein bar. As I watched Warren, I thought about Craig Keller, and wondered if they knew each other. They had so much in common but seemed so vastly different in personality. Warren had a serious affect that permeated everything he said and did. I could not picture Warren brazenly trying to recruit a young woman at an industry party.

"They said the concepts are too obvious, not clever enough to grab anyone's attention," Warren continued, finally pulling a Clif Bar from his gym bag.

Jeffrey reacted as though it were a personal affront. "What do they mean, 'too obvious'?" he asked with irritation in his voice. "We're giving them what they need to sell tickets in a new market. This is Las Vegas, not Paris, and the show is quirky. We need to make sure people know exactly what they're getting, especially at their elevated ticket prices. Once we've established who they are, we can get cute with the advertising—that's just 'Branding 101'."

Warren looked unmoved. "Well, they aren't buying it, so you need to have your minions come up with an alternative," he said, before unwrapping his Clif Bar and taking a bite out of it. "I don't want to lose this account to a competitor because the art department is lazy."

"Sam and Johann are out of ideas," Jeffrey responded sullenly. "I'll have to put another creative team on it just to come up with something fresh."

"Whatever you do, I need to see it by Wednesday," Warren demanded, still chewing.

We got up to walk out of the office, but Warren called me back, nodding silently to dismiss Jeffrey. "Jane, I want to talk to you," he requested. "Close the door, please."

"Sure," I answered, scanning his walls for a mirror, and neurotically drawing my hair behind my ears.

"I guess you made quite the impression Friday," he began, motioning for me to sit on the red couch. He wasn't smiling.

"Oh?" I asked, feeling my feet fidget.

"Yes," Warren added with an admiring, yet calculating gleam in his eye. "I'm starting to rethink our approach."

"Approach to what?" I asked. *What in the world is he talking about now?*

"Philippe could not stop praising you after our meeting Friday," Warren explained. "He found you charming, even called me to reiterate how excited he is to work with you."

"Really," I said, breathing a sigh of relief, but also wondering what Philippe was so excited about. My portion of the presentation was the briefest. "That's nice to hear, especially since I can't speak a word of French."

Warren gave me a false smile, and then straightened up in his chair, looking serious again. "Jane, he mentioned having lunch to get to know you better in the event they like our work and decide to hire us." He paused, searching my face to gauge my reaction. "How do you feel about that?" Warren was obviously making sure he was covered from a human resources standpoint in the event I got raped and stuffed in a trunk by the Frenchman.

"I guess that would be okay," I replied, not having the guts to say no to Warren. "I mean, I would do it for any other potential client." We both knew this was different, especially Warren, who would do anything to acquire this client—he made that clear from day one.

"Excellent." Warren concluded with a smile. "I'll set it up. I really need you to convince this client that we're the right agency to be handling their account, based on the revenue at stake."

I blinked at him nervously, not really understanding what he was asking me to do.

"Thanks, Jane. You're a real team player," he added before I could say anything.

I returned to my office, feeling vaguely like a prostitute, and sat at my desk trying to figure out why I had such a problem with the word *no*. Neither Marisa nor Kat would have agreed to such a lunch. They would be appalled that I had.

To assuage my disgust over having been cajoled into playing decoy, I pulled up my secret Craig Keller Pinterest board and started scrolling through the images, just absorbing his phenomenal beauty, and trying to remember the sound of his voice. It was deep, clear, and articulate, like a voice over model or actor for a fancy car ad. I wondered what it would be like to work for him—to see him and talk to him every day, like Marisa said. I smiled at the thought and didn't even hear Jeffrey enter my office.

"Jane, can we talk new panda concepts for a minute?"

I was so unnerved; I dropped my phone with a photo of Craig Keller facing upward. I dove to get it before Jeffrey, who was already kneeling. "I've got it," I cried, snapping up the phone and putting it face down on my desk. It was clear I was hiding something, but Jeffrey seemed too preoccupied with other things to notice.

"You know, Warren's counting on you to get these guys to hire us and sign off on one of our concepts," he cautioned. "I've never seen him so nervous about acquiring one account. They have a lot of money, and we have a lot to lose if we don't get them on board."

"What are you implying, Jeffrey?" I was feeling queasy that everything seemed to be riding on my art of persuasion.

"I'm just saying," he continued. "This is a whale, and we need to make sure we spear it. From the meeting and our initial concepts, it looks like they're not impressed. It's your job to change their mind."

"I'll do my best," I said, wringing my hands.

"I'm afraid you'll have to do more than that." Then he gave me a rueful look and exited my office.

I sat there wondering what just hit me. Not only did Warren suggest that my influence on Philippe was imperative to getting the account, but Jeffrey made a special trip to reiterate my importance in the matter. I wondered what Philippe expected of me at this point.

I got up, shut the office door, and pulled Craig's business card out of my bag. It was already dog-eared with the number of times I had turned it over in my hand, marveling at the black letters on metallic bronze: Craig A. Keller, Managing Partner. I ran my fingers over the logo, on which the letters KWG were emblazoned, shiny and raised. I took a deep breath, picked up the phone and dialed his office number, heart pounding, one ring, two rings, three, and then a woman's voice.

"Keller Whitman Group, how may I direct your call?"

Right then, I saw Warren's name flashing across my phone screen like an ominous banner, and I hung up to take his call. "Yes, Warren," I said, breathlessly.

"Jane, this is Veronica." Veronica had a habit of calling from Warren's office when he wasn't there so that people were sure to pick up the phone, rather than let it go to voicemail if they saw her name. I was guilty of sending her calls to voicemail myself.

"Hi, Veronica."

"Jane," Veronica said in her steady monotone. "I'm confirming you're meeting Philippe Barineau for lunch Thursday, 12:30, at Il Grano."

"Yes, fine, thank you." *Let the pimping out of Jane Mercer begin.* A pang of revulsion shot through my stomach.

When I hung up the phone, I was alone with Craig Keller's card again, which felt almost like being alone with him. I pressed it against my lips and decided to try him once more. This time, there were four rings and then a woman's voice. "Keller Whitman Group, how may I direct your call?"

"Craig Keller's office, please," I requested cautiously.

"Hold for one moment while I transfer you."

I heard the phone ring several times before another woman answered. "Craig Keller's office. This is Simone. How may I help you?"

"Yes, hello, Simone. My name is Jane Mercer and I'm calling to speak to Craig Keller."

"Mr. Keller is not available right now. May I leave him a message?"

"Yes, please. I met him at an event Friday night. He asked me to call him and set up lunch."

The woman was silent. "I see," she replied finally. "What is your phone number?" Simone's tone had changed, as if she thought I were in some way illegitimate. I gave her my cell phone number. "I'll give him the message."

I hung up feeling oddly like I had done something wrong. Maybe she had already taken many messages, just like mine, that day. Maybe there was nothing special about our encounter after all. Maybe he made a habit of singling out young women with no intention of following through.

By WEDNESDAY AFTERNOON, I still had not received a return call from Craig Keller and was beginning to feel the sting of rejection. I called Marisa to analyze the situation and she answered in a gruff voice.

"You sound awful. What's going on?" I asked.

She sighed into the phone. "Just dealing with yet another crazy jerk. I swear sometimes I wish I had chosen a different career."

"Have you heard from Drew?" I asked, thinking he must

be the one causing Marisa's pessimism.

"Not a word," Marisa snapped.

"Have you tried calling *him*?"

"Hell, no! I'm still upset about last weekend. And why do I have to call *him*? *He's* the one who made a date and didn't show."

"The man was sick," I reasoned. "It's not like he stood you up without letting you know."

"Never mind." Marisa sounded annoyed. "What's going on with you?"

"Well, I finally got up the nerve to call Craig Keller. That was Monday and I haven't heard back yet."

"Well, it's only been two days. He's probably busy."

"Yeah, I know, but I still feel like an idiot. Do you think he forgot about me?"

"Jane, the man runs a Fortune 500 company. Give him time before you start second-guessing."

"But what if he just does this type of thing all the time?" I asked, the hideous feeling of dismissal sweeping over me again.

"It's possible, but why are you worried about it?"

"I don't know," I responded, mind momentarily returning to the tone in the receptionist's voice.

"Jane, you have to stop overthinking everything. You'll hear back from him soon. And if you don't, then fuck him. You have nothing to lose."

'Yeah, I guess you're right. It's not like I was looking for a new job anyway."

"You should always be looking for a new job," Marisa shot back. "I have to go."

❤

I IMMERSED MYSELF IN work for the rest of the day until I had successfully gone through most of my emails, calls, and files. As I put things away on my desk and got ready to leave for the night, I spotted Craig Keller's business card under a heap of papers. I realized, with regret, that he still hadn't called.

I picked up the card and read his name, trying to remember exactly what we talked about the night we met. That was when I remembered Kat and her extreme reaction upon hearing his name—and that I hadn't talked to her since that night. I picked up the phone, dialed her number, and she answered right away. "Where are you right now?" I asked, rising from my chair, still staring at Craig's card.

"Just leaving work."

"Would you be able to meet somewhere for a drink?"

"I have to run home and feed Joyce." Her voice sounded harried. "Want to meet there?"

"I'll be there as soon as I can."

When I arrived at Kat's house, she was pulling into her garage. I realized that the last time I was at her house was the day I had met her. I wondered how everything was going with Jack and the divorce.

"Hey," she greeted me, giving me a hug and kiss, which immediately relaxed me. Kat looked chic in a glen plaid coat dress and high black boots. She wore her hair in a loose bun under a dark red beret. I watched her turning on the lights in the house and chattering about work. Joyce came bounding over to me, wagging his tail and sniffing around while I patted his head. This was the first time I had been inside her home, and it was effortlessly elegant, combining rustic warmth and modern style with an oversized red shag rug and distressed black leather chairs on dark wood floors. *Why did Jack ever want to leave her and their home together?* I couldn't imagine a more beautiful place to inspire a writer's creativity.

Kat opened a bottle of Pinot Noir, poured it into two glasses, and handed me one without even asking. "So, Jane," she began, "talk to me."

"How are things with you and Jack?" I asked, thinking I should focus on her drama while trying to find an appropriate time to probe her about Craig Keller.

"Completely awkward," she said. "You know he takes his new girlfriend everywhere now, and it's so humiliating. I actually ran into them last week at The Bungalow and suffered the indignity of watching them take the table where he and I used to sit and watch the sunset."

"Oh no," I groaned.

"Yes, well, at least it looks like the divorce is going to be final before Christmas, so I guess that will be my present." She smiled through clenched teeth.

"Are you okay?" I asked, examining her blue eyes for tears. There were none.

She nodded. "There are some things in life that are just out of our control. The damage has been done. There's no going back now."

I still had a hard time understanding what could have possibly gone wrong in their marriage—what drove Jack to cheat on Kat. "Well, if the divorce is final at Christmas, then we should plan to do something fabulous at New Year's," I proposed optimistically.

She gave me a maternal, closed-mouthed smile as though I were a naïve idiot. "We'll see. Tell me about you. You look sort of down."

"Just a few issues at work." I surveyed Kat's place and settled my eyes on a modern impressionist painting on her wall. "That's a beautiful painting," I remarked.

"Thank you—it was a gift from a—friend. What issues at work?" she asked, eyebrows furrowed, and face shaded in concern.

My eyes were still on the painting. "Must be *some* friend—is it an original?"

Kat sighed with her eyes cast down at her lap. "I believe it is—Claude Monet," she said. "Now tell me what's going on at work."

I tore my eyes from the painting and looked Kat in the eye. "I'm working with a difficult client is all. I'm sure it will turn out fine." I wanted to change the subject to the real reason I was there.

"Are you hungry?" she suddenly asked.

"Yes—starving."

Kat went to the kitchen to find us some nosh. As she rummaged through her pantry, she called to me casually,

"So, whatever happened with Craig Keller? Did he ever call you?"

"No," I shouted, racing over to the kitchen with sudden interest. I never thought she would bring him up first. "What do you *know* about him?"

"Oh, that's good he didn't contact you," she remarked, pulling out a tin of expensive French crackers. She then selected a couple of cheese wedges from her refrigerator and arranged them attractively on a tray with a silver cheese knife. She re-entered the living room with the tray and the wine bottle while I followed. She could be frustratingly cagey when it suited her.

"Marisa met him, too. We both think he's gorgeous." I was testing the waters. There was no way she could deny that.

She paused thoughtfully and ran her fingers through a few strands of her long blonde hair. "I guess that depends on what you consider gorgeous."

"What do you mean by that?" I asked. It seemed like Kat was playing some sort of game. Kat tossed her hair and pretended to inspect her manicure. "Kat, what do you know? Did he piss you off or something?" I was dying to hear what she thought.

There was a scarcely perceptible change in Kat's facial expression, almost like a horrendous memory came back to haunt her. But it was so brief, I barely caught it before she smiled and shook her head.

"You're not going to tell me, are you?" I leaned back in my chair.

"I just hope you avoid him. That's all I'll say on the subject." She put a cracker in her mouth and crunched it loudly, as if for emphasis.

After cheese and crackers and the rest of the wine, I knew it was time for me to get home. As I was leaving Kat's house, I turned to her one last time. "You know you can trust me, right?"

"Of course," she said, blinking her blue eyes at me. "What are you getting at, Jane?" Kat seemed like she might be getting impatient with my interrogation, but it didn't deter me.

"Are you *sure* there's nothing you want to tell me about Craig Keller?" I was now in Kat's doorway, and she began to edge the door closed, forcing me to back away.

"I'm sure, Jane. Now have a safe drive home tonight, okay? We'll talk soon." She gave me a hug and a kiss good-bye and shut the door. I heard her deadbolt clicking into place. I left her house feeling more curious than ever. *What was she hiding and why?*

I OVER-SLEPT THE NEXT morning and had no time to worry about outfit selection. I literally jumped in and out of the shower, pulled my hair into a side ponytail, slapped on the first dress and pair of pumps I saw in my closet and ran out the door, almost stepping on Weezer's tail. He meowed loudly in protest and scampered to an available windowsill. "Sorry, Weez—Mommy's late," I called to him as though he could understand.

Once at the office, I went straight to the break room to get a sorely needed cup of coffee and encountered Jeffrey and Warren conversing by the coffee pot. They stopped talking and glanced up as I approached.

"Good morning, Jane." Jeffrey smiled. "I was just telling Warren that you'll be previewing our new, improved concept with Philippe at lunch today—hopefully winning the business."

"Yes, that's right," I replied, princess smile in full effect.

"We're counting on you, Jane," Warren said. "Jeffrey, you'll want to prep Jane thoroughly, so she catches all the creative nuances."

"Absolutely," Jeffrey agreed.

As Warren left the break room, Jeffrey leaned into me. "We've got this nailed," he said confidently. "Just wait, he's going to love it."

And what he showed me had a lot of potential. It was the story of a couple out on a first date going to the show.

For the television spot, the plan was to follow the couple from the moment the man picks up his date to sitting in the theater's front-row seats, eating caviar, and drinking champagne, romancing each other. The couple was in the foreground while the camera cleverly captured a montage of show footage from the couple's point of view. It did what I had thought to be impossible: make the show look legitimate.

My eyes met Jeffrey's and he smiled. "I think they're going to be happy with this."

"Let's hope so," I said, while Jeffrey loaded everything onto my tablet.

He gave me a serious look. "They *have* to." There was that not-so-subtle threat again in Jeffrey's voice. "I don't care what you have to do, Jane. Do *not* leave the restaurant without getting Philippe's buy-in and winning the account."

I LEFT THE OFFICE to meet Philippe feeling my hands trembling on the steering wheel. Jeffrey and Warren were throwing me to the wolves. While I was battling the usual lunch traffic, Marisa called.

"Guess what?" she bellowed, causing me to lower the volume on my bluetooth. "Drew called yesterday, and we're having dinner tonight. You were right. He was sick that whole time and he's just now feeling better. He said he didn't want to bring me down by calling and complaining. Isn't that considerate?"

"That's one way of looking at it," I remarked. "Call me tonight and let me know how it goes."

"Hopefully, I won't be *available* to make calls," she responded with a smile in her voice.

IL GRANO WAS PACKED that day as I made my way toward the maître d'. I tried to get his attention but, out of the corner of my eye, I saw Philippe seated at a booth waving at me.

When I got to the table, he stood up and kissed my

hand in a grand gesture. "*Mademoiselle*, it is good to see you again," he purred. I sat down, feeling the stares of other lunch-goers. I wiped the wetness on my hand from his kiss on the skirt of my dress.

There were two chairs at the table, but he insisted I sit in the booth to his right, so that we were both facing the same direction. I preferred to sit across from him, so I could speak to him more directly, but I would just have to make do. "*Mademoiselle*, I apologize for being so forward," he began in his thick accent. "You see, we only just arrived here in LA, and it has been very difficult to know people."

"It's my pleasure." I gave him a princess smile. I had one thing on my mind and that was pushing the concept—pushing the agency—so they would hire us.

"*Merci beaucoup*, Jane," he said, grinning at me.

I felt like I had him in the palm of my hand already. We made awkward small talk. Philippe ordered a glass of champagne and pressed me to have one, too. I acquiesced but knew I would only take a small sip. I was on a mission.

Once we ordered food, I brought up the new concept. "After getting your feedback on our original concepts, we realized we need something that's sexy—like your show—something that will sell tickets in a competitive market. Why don't we look at the new concept? Then you can tell me your thoughts."

Philippe seemed irritated that I was disturbing our 'social time' with shop talk—as if there was any other reason for me to be there. I pulled the tablet out of my bag and set it up on our table, while Philippe eyed me with skepticism.

I started to give him the preamble of how we were positioning the show. He sat back and focused his piercing eyes on me—his dark circles appearing especially purple in the fluorescent restaurant rays. I could not tell whether he was buying my spiel or just wanting me to shut up, but I continued until it was time to unveil the new concept.

As I showed him the visuals, I read the copy, hoping he would get it without a lot of explanation. When finished, I smiled at him triumphantly. "Well? Isn't it perfect?"

The Frenchman looked unimpressed. "*Je ne sais pas*, Jane," he grunted shaking his head. "I don't think Frédéric will go for this."

We were interrupted by the waiter, who arrived with my chicken Caesar and Philippe's rigatoni. We silently watched as the plates were set before us. The waiter murmured, "*Bon appetit*," and left.

"Do *you* go for it?" I asked.

"It is okay. That is all." Philippe picked up his fork and took a bite of his pasta. "It looks like every other show ad in Paris. We are going to be in Las Vegas. We need to stand out."

"Do you have a specific idea in mind?" I asked, searching my brain for a way to get this stubborn fool to change his mind, Jeffrey's and Warren's pressure talk resounding in my mind like a persistent alarm.

"I want it to be clever, as you Americans say, tongue-in-cheek."

"But we need to establish your brand first," I explained, getting more desperate by the second. "It is after all a new entity being introduced to the Las Vegas market. Once we have the attention of the target audience, we can be glib with the messaging."

"U.S. ad agencies are all alike," Philippe grumbled with a frown. "You just want to make the deal—you never take the time to find out exactly what the client wants."

"Does that mean you're courting other agencies in town?" I asked, not knowing how to make this better. I was losing the battle and was deathly afraid of going back to Warren and Jeffrey empty handed.

"*D'accord*—not just here—New York, *aussi*," he answered coldly. "There are bigger and better agencies out there. We thought since your agency is one of the little ones, you might give us more personal attention. But it looks like you just want to shove your ideas down our necks and call it a day. That's not how it works with us."

I finished my champagne in one gulp and immediately needed another. This was becoming brutal. "Philippe," I said, looking as docile as I could without throwing up in my mouth. "I assure you; you'll get *nothing* but *personal* attention from us."

His countenance shifted to one of a hungry alley cat getting ready to close in on its prey. "How *personal?*" he responded with a lewd gleam in his eye. A few blond strands had escaped his bun on one side, touching his lips slightly. He crudely twisted his mouth to blow the hair out of the way.

"I'm just wondering if there's anything I can do to change your mind about our agency." After delivering this proposition, I pursed my recently plumped up lips seductively. And no matter how repulsed I felt inside, Warren's and Jeffrey's threats were scorched into my mind. My heart thumped in my chest.

Philippe leaned closer and whispered in an almost sadistic tone, "I don't know, *mademoiselle. You* tell me."

"We're going to need more champagne, you know," I suggested, anxiety deepening. I had no idea what I was getting myself into, but I knew, once it started, I couldn't go back.

Philippe then lowered his eyes to my breasts. "*D'accord.*" He signaled for the sommelier. As two more glasses of champagne were poured, I tried to figure out my next move.

"Here's what needs to happen," I began. "You take this concept back to Frédéric and convince him we are the *only* agency to introduce your brand to the U.S. Then, you have him sign off on the contract and scope of work, and we'll move forward with creative production." I gave a princess smile at the end of this statement.

Philippe suddenly laughed out loud, an evil laugh with his little pointed candy corn teeth showing. "*Mademoiselle,* you are … how do you say it? … a comic. It is not up to me. You see, I am only Frédéric's agent. He is the one who makes all the decisions."

"Yes, but he listens to you. He trusts your judgment," I offered, trying hard not to sound like I was begging, even though I was not above it at this point.

"That is true, *mademoiselle.* And he would also trust my judgment if I recommended not hiring your agency. But really the question is, what is *in it* for me?"

"I'm sure I can find some way to reward you for your assistance." As I said that last line, I scanned him from head-to-toe and gave him the most seductive smile I could conjure under the circumstances. The only way I could do it was by pretending Philippe was really Craig Keller—that it was he who was sitting next to me, with those crazy sexy eyes, asking what was in it for *him*.

He gave me a hard look. After what seemed like an eternity, he leaned toward me and said, "I'm sure we can arrange something, *mademoiselle*." As he said this, he pulled my hand under the table and set it on his crotch, which was already pulsating with an erection. Unable to hide my horror, I tried to yank my hand away, but he held onto my wrist with a vice grip.

"I—I didn't mean right now," I stammered. The waiter, unfortunately, was nowhere to be found and I began to panic. Although we were in broad daylight, the long black tablecloths hid what was going on under the table. "Not here—not in public."

"I want to make sure you're serious," Philippe hissed, leaning even closer and exhaling his boozy cigarette breath in my face. "Because, *mademoiselle*, if you're not serious, I will be very, *very* disappointed." As he delivered this threat, he twisted my hand around so that it felt like my wrist might crack. "Now do I have your word?" he demanded.

"Yes," I whispered, mouth dry and heart racing.

"Yes, *what*?"

"Yes, you have my word. Now will you please let go of me? You're hurting my hand!"

He released his grip slowly, eyes fixed on mine. Then he picked up his fork and proceeded to wolf down his pasta, intermittently sipping champagne and letting out a belch here and there.

I was so frightened I barely touched my salad. My eyes dashed around the restaurant. It appeared no one had noticed Philippe's aggressive behavior. The waiter suddenly reappeared with the check, which Philippe promptly handed to me with a gloating grin on his face. "If I am now the client, then Warren pays," he boasted with a sour look on his face.

Hands shaking, I sifted through my purse for my wallet and pulled out the company credit card. I could barely add up the tip, my mind was so jumbled. I dropped my pen and Philippe snickered at my clumsiness. As soon as the bill was paid, I grabbed my things and stood.

"Leaving so soon?" he taunted, tossing his napkin on his plate.

"I need to get back to the office now," I managed to utter with false confidence. My eyes were burning.

"Fine, *mademoiselle*," he dismissed me with a wave of his hand. "You will hear from me soon enough."

I scurried to my car and sped out of the Il Grano parking lot, finally free of Philippe. It was already 3 p.m. and I had somehow accomplished my mission. I had no idea how I was going to explain this to anyone, but one thing was for sure, I had no appetite to face Jeffrey.

When I returned to the agency, I stole into my office and quietly shut the door. I thought about the awful way Philippe spoke to me and felt sick again. I examined my wrist and noticed it was turning purple with finger-shaped bruises. *How the hell did I get into this mess anyway?*

Someone was now banging at my door. It had to be Jeffrey inquiring about my lunch. He must have been intent, too, because he just stormed in without waiting for me to say, 'Come in.'

"Well?" Jeffrey asked, shutting the door behind him. "What happened?"

"He likes the new concept," I answered, seething inside. "I think they're going to hire us."

"What? Really?" Jeffrey broke into a huge smile. "How did you do it?"

I took a deep breath. "Well, I just convinced him how great our agency is and … he … agreed." I was now weary as my mid-day alcohol buzz was waning.

"You mean just like that?" Jeffrey asked, eyebrows raised.

I shrugged with a princess smile. "Just like that."

"Jane, you're amazing. I don't know how you did it but thank you!" Jeffrey came around my desk, leaned down, and gave me a big hug. "You have no idea how good you are. Warren should promote you."

I smirked inwardly at the irony. In dire need of retail therapy, I left the office at six. I hit Fred Segal and bought a Nili Lotan slip dress, something trendy and expensive to offset my hideous day.

I deserved a burger at the cafe, since I had barely touched my food at lunch and, as usual, there was no food at home. As I sat ravenously chowing down on my burger, I heard a familiar voice somewhere in the vicinity. I didn't realize who it was until I looked up, burger juice streaming down my chin. It was Derek a couple of tables down. He was with a woman, presumably on a date. He caught my eye before I could make a move. He waved to me, so I grabbed a stack of napkins and attempted to wipe the mess off my face.

I smiled and waved back. He was summoning me to his table. The woman across from him look backward, following Derek's glance. From a distance, she looked painfully young. *Crap. I can't get out of this now. Why is it that I can't escape to have a sloppy burger in peace without running into someone I know?* I reluctantly gathered my purse and Fred Segal bag and trudged over to them.

"Hi, Jane," Derek said first, getting up to kiss me on the cheek, likely smelling leftover Kobe beef. "Meet my friend, Chelsea."

The woman smiled sweetly and held her hand out to me. She had fair, dewy skin and long shiny brown hair. She was impossibly thin and couldn't have been more than five feet tall, but she wore four-inch stilettos with a mini skirt and tight turtleneck. I could swear she was at least ten years younger than Derek, and this was obviously a date. "Nice to meet you, Chelsea," I said, giving her a princess smile and hoping I didn't have pieces of burger stuck in my teeth. I wanted to get the hell out of there but had no choice. I was stuck making fake conversation.

"Chelsea's a soloist with the Los Angeles Ballet Company," said Derek.

"Oh, so you're a ballerina," I responded without enthusiasm. "How wonderful for you."

Chelsea smiled as she shot an admiring glance in Derek's direction and tossed her long hair over one shoulder.

"She was originally my student at USC." He returned her smile. "And a very good one at that."

"So, you play violin in addition to dancing?" I asked, feeling like a whorish pariah in front of this innocent, waif-like beauty.

"Professor Lowell was my favorite," Chelsea gushed. "I couldn't help but work harder to get an 'A,' knowing what a perfectionist he is."

Professor Lowell? Was he dating a former student? How much more clichéd can you get? He should trade notes with Kat's ex. "Well, I have to be going." I tried to keep the displeasure in my voice at bay. "Have a nice evening." I turned to walk as fast as I could out of the restaurant.

"Hey, Jane, can we talk later this week?" Derek called after me. I pretended not to hear and spun outside the door to my car.

I GOT HOME AND took a hot bath. As I stepped in and lowered myself into the sudsy water, I felt dirty, both inside and out, and no amount of soap was going to wash it away. I sank as deeply into the tub as I did into my personal abyss of self-loathing. After the bath, I wrapped myself in a warm, fuzzy robe and snuggled up on the couch with some hot tea and Weez. I began to pet his soft coat and felt him purring. "Weez, why is life so complicated?" I asked him, continuing to run my hand along his striped fur. "Why do these things happen to me? What's *wrong* with me?" Weez suddenly turned his glowing pale blue eyes up at me and gave a loud meow that sounded more like a yelp or a complaint. "Totally agree," I answered, taking another sip of tea.

Marisa's call interrupted our deep conversation, but I let it go to voicemail. Then, feeling guilty for not answering, I dialed into voice mail and listened. "Hey—it's me. I have to talk to you." She sounded upset. *Oh, what now?* I was so tired of drama. I debated whether to call her back but knew what it felt like to get voicemail when you needed to talk.

I sighed and tapped her name on my phone. "What's up, Marisa?"

"Sorry—I know it's late, but I just had to tell you about my date with Drew."

"Oh?" I asked, wondering what the arrogant Brit had done to my friend now. "What happened?" I shifted my legs, so they were tucked underneath me.

"It's so weird, Jane, he took me to a lovely dinner at Lucques, we had a great conversation, wine, everything seemed to be going well. But then, I suggested we go back to my place, and he backed off. He wouldn't even kiss me good night. I mean, not in the way I wanted. What's wrong with me that he doesn't even want to kiss me?" Marisa implored. She sounded uncharacteristically insecure right now. "Am I unattractive? Do I need more Botox? What is it?"

I sighed. "Oh Marisa, you sound like me right now. Listen—there's nothing wrong with *you*. You're insane if you think there is. It's *him*. He should be chasing you. Promise me you won't call him."

"But Jane, I think I'm in love with him," she declared.

Uh oh. How could she possibly be in love with this clown?

"He just has this way," she added. "No guy has ever done that to me. I'm crazy about him—it's hard to explain."

I ran my hands over Weezer's coat again to calm myself. I felt a mat and glanced around the apartment for his brush. "Marisa, I think you should take a pill, go to bed, and try not to think of him. Please promise me you won't call him for the rest of the week."

"But I can't promise that." She sounded more vulnerable by the second.

"Please, Marisa, just wait until we've had a chance to

talk face-to-face," I pleaded, locating the cat brush, and then searching for Weez. He had already made his escape. *Cats always know when you are about to do something they don't like.*

She went silent for a minute. "Okay, I promise."

I GOT TO THE office early the next day, partially because the previous day was a total loss and partially because I woke up at 4 a.m. and couldn't get back to sleep.

As I went through the previous night's emails, my cell phone was ringing. It was Grandma. *Why the hell was she calling me this early?* I was about to send her to voicemail but realized something could be wrong. "Grandma?"

"Yes, honey. How are you today?"

"Um, I'm fine, Grandma. Is everything okay?" My voice rang with impatience.

"Yes, I want to start planning the holidays. You know, Thanksgiving's coming."

"Yes, I know, Grandma. It's in a few weeks—I'll be there like I always am." I began tapping my pen on the desk.

"Well, it's just that ..." She was beating around the bush. "You see, I want to invite the Feldmans, but I'm not sure how things are going with Julian. Have you seen each other since our dinner, honey?"

I threw my pen down and had to stop myself from groaning aloud. I let out an open-mouthed sigh. "Grandma, I'm pretty sure he has plans with his parents and extended family over the holidays."

"Oh. Well, I saw an awful lot of flirting that night!" she crowed.

I put my hand to my forehead and took a deep breath. "Grandma, we were just engaging in conversation because we don't know each other very well." I was in no mood for this nonsense.

"But that's why you must get to know each other, honey. Hasn't he called you for a date yet?"

Jeffrey suddenly appeared in my doorway.

"I have to go now," I told her.

"Jane, I think you may need to make the first move with Julian," she continued, ignoring what I said to pry further. "He's a shy person. Maybe you should call him."

"I'm at work now, so we'll have to discuss this later." My eyes met Jeffrey's and I made a face.

"Oh, okay. It's always about work with you. You're never going to find a man with that attitude," she added before hanging up. *So annoying.*

Jeffrey entered and closed the door. "Warren's ecstatic you were able to snare the panda show as a client," he announced with a grin. "The contract's being drawn up as we speak. When do you think they'll be able to sign off on the scope of work?"

"Soon," I responded, thinking it would only be a matter of time before I would be expected to 'make good' on my trade deal with Philippe. Then the memory of him twisting my hand and snarling flashed before me. There was no question about it. I would have to stall Jeffrey while I looked for a way out.

"How soon?" Jeffrey pushed. "Maybe you should call Philippe and give him a nudge."

The thought of speaking to Philippe again so soon made my skin crawl. "Let's give him until Monday," I suggested.

"Fair enough," he agreed. "But let me know the minute you hear from him."

I heard text rings going off every two seconds. It was Marisa begging me to meet her for lunch. She must be beside herself about Drew.

I acquiesced, and we met at Ammo on Melrose, a place I normally wouldn't go near because it was always teeming with advertising and PR vermin. But, since it was Marisa's favorite power lunch spot and she was having a bad week, I didn't object. When I arrived, Marisa was already there and not looking at her phone ... a first.

"Thanks for meeting me—you know it's an emergency or I would have waited until the weekend," she began, getting up to hug me. She was wearing a black wrap dress with flecks of purple, a color I never saw her in. With her New

York fashion sense, she always thumbed her nose at purple. Her hair was slicked back into a long ponytail.

"Okay, tell me you didn't call him." I slid into the booth across from her.

"I didn't. But he sent me a text this morning saying how beautiful I looked last night, and get this, how much he *wants* me."

I almost blurted an expletive because I could not believe what I was hearing. "Did you respond?"

"No, because I don't know what to say." she sounded vulnerable again.

The waitress interrupted to take our order. As soon as she was gone, I tried to reason with my friend. "Marisa, I know I haven't met this guy, but he sounds like a narcissistic sociopath. I can't believe you don't see it."

"That's not true," she protested, smoothing her ponytail with her hand. "We've been dating a while now and it only got weird the last couple of weeks."

"Then why hasn't he slept with you? What's he waiting for? It's not normal, Marisa." For someone so damned smart and aggressive, Marisa was acting like a sad, wilted flower. I just didn't get it.

"That's what I'm trying to figure out," Marisa argued. "He's sending mixed messages. What do you think I should do?"

"Dump him. Now. There's no way this is going to get better." The waitress had just delivered water and I took a small sip. Marisa started to tear up—another first. "Maybe we should just drop the subject for now," I suggested, scanning the restaurant. I wanted to make sure no one saw Marisa crying in public. I dug through my purse, found a tissue, and handed it to Marisa under the table. She accepted it.

"I couldn't agree more," she replied, voice quivering, dabbing at her eyes with the tissue.

Considering this lunch was supposed to be about Marisa's love life, we ate quickly and silently. Marisa even requested the bill, so she could pay her share and leave before me. As she stood and gathered her things, I watched her face closely. I just couldn't imagine her being so broken up over a guy.

"You know," she said with a pouty expression. "You could be a little more open-minded when it comes to Drew. You don't know what our relationship is about. No one really knows about anyone's relationship except the two people who are in it." With that, she left in a huff, muttering something about me not understanding true love. Maybe she was right—I was quite sure I had never been in love. But how could you be in love with someone who didn't love you? I finally wandered out of Ammo and found the valet station.

"Well, if it isn't Jane Mercer," a deep voice called. Startled, I looked up to see none other than Craig Keller. I felt the blood rush straight to my head.

"Mr. Keller. I didn't even see you. What are *you* doing here?" I quickly checked my outfit and breathed a sigh of relief—I had on a flattering, snug navy shift dress and red suede pumps. I was also carrying a navy Celine bag with red piping, a gorgeous accessory—one I still had not paid for.

"Having lunch, like you," he responded, eyes scanning my body in a seductive manner. "You seemed a million miles away just now. How are things with Warren? You bored yet?" He had a devilish grin on his insanely handsome face.

I laughed nervously. "Definitely not bored," I answered, truly meaning it. "Every day's a new adventure." I meant that, too.

"Is that why you haven't called me? Too busy having adventures?" He said, giving me the sexy slow blink and moving his body closer.

"Well," I began, trying not to sound too clingy, "I actually did call. I left a message. I just figured you were busy." I tossed my hair, relieved that I'd flat ironed it this morning.

Craig looked miffed for a split second before the easy smile returned. "Jane, I'm sorry. I didn't get the message. Not sure what happened there."

"Really, it's no big deal." I handed the valet attendant my ticket and turned back to Craig. If it were possible, he looked even better in the afternoon sunlight. His eyes were more of a sparkling light jade, his brown hair shiny with natural highlights when the sun hit it. His skin was slightly tanned, like he had recently spent time at the beach, and he wore an olive suit with a crisp white shirt underneath, the top two buttons open. His perfection gave me goosebumps.

"Are you off to some place fabulous?" he asked, lazily handing his ticket to the valet attendant. That was when I noticed his wedding ring for the first time, a simple platinum band with something etched into it.

"Just heading back to the office. I wish it were that fun." *Truer words were never spoken.*

"If you worked for me, you'd feel differently," he asserted. "In fact, why don't you come by the office next week? I'll show you around and you can see for yourself."

He appeared so cool standing there, with his casual smile and friendly gaze. But there was something intense about him. I could see how he must have a crazy power over women. There was no way I would refuse his invitation and he knew it. And, in the forefront of my mind was Frédéric and the pandas, along with the unspeakable situation with Philippe. Craig Keller suddenly shined with some benevolent force that was clearly my way out, my much-needed exit strategy from Warren Mitchell and Associates. "That sounds great." I finally said.

"Good," he responded. "I'll have someone call you to arrange a time."

The valet attendant pulled up in my car. I shook Craig's hand to say goodbye but instead he pulled me close to say something in my ear. A sexy, soapy scent floated into my nostrils. The closeness was so unexpected, it was almost daunting. "Don't worry, Jane. I'll be very discreet," he whispered.

"Yes, of course," I replied, realizing that I hadn't tipped the valet attendant yet. I reached into my bag and pulled out my wallet, but Craig stopped me.

"I got it," he said, slipping a twenty-dollar bill to the attendant, who looked especially pleased.

"Oh, thank you." I dropped my wallet back into my bag with an awkward thud.

He stepped back and looked with amusement at my red Jetta, which suddenly appeared to be a tattered jalopy before His Highness. "Cute car," he commented as I slid behind the wheel. I was sure this guy had a Jag or some rich man's vehicle. As I drove away, I saw a rakish black Bentley convertible in my rear-view mirror. *I was close.*

I made my way to the office and wanted badly to call Marisa to tell her who I had just run into but, after our conversation at lunch, I decided to just let her be for now. It's like my friend had taken a leave of absence and I was suddenly tasked with being the strong one … the caretaker, a role I was hardly comfortable with. I suddenly wished Drew would disappear fast. I knew it would mean Marisa's heart break, but he was causing so much chaos in her life … and mine, too, by taking her away from me. *That bastard!*

I desperately needed someone to talk to about my predicament with Philippe, so I would feel less isolated. But there was no one I could tell, and even if there were, they would lose all respect for me. I wouldn't blame them. I had this eerie, lonely feeling like something terrible was about to happen.

When I left the office that evening, I realized I had not a single plan for the weekend. I headed to Ralph's and stocked up on wine, cheese, bagged popcorn, Oreo cookies and trashy tabloid magazines, everything I would need for a weekend in front of the television, where Netflix awaited. When I finally arrived home, I turned off my cell phone, changed into pajamas, and plopped onto the sofa. And there I stayed, shut off from the outside world until Monday.

Twelve

*J*EFFREY HAD LEFT ME an urgent message when I arrived in the office. I walked down the hall toward his office but was interrupted by Veronica shouting from Warren's office. "Jane, I have Craig Keller's secretary on the phone. She said something about scheduling a meeting?"

Uh oh. Stay calm, Jane. Could Veronica have been louder or brasher? There's no way Warren didn't hear. I marched swiftly into her office and glanced over her shoulder into Warren's office. I was relieved to see he was not there. "Veronica, will you please transfer her to my office?" I smiled sweetly and tried to keep my voice from cracking. "I can't imagine why *they're* calling *me*."

I hightailed it back to my office and picked up the call. "Hello Jane, this is Simone, Craig Keller's administrative assistant," she said, completely ignorant of how much trouble she almost caused. "Mr. Keller would like you to visit the office around 6:30 this evening. Will you be able to make it?"

"Yes, of course," I responded without checking my calendar. "But Simone, will you please do me a big favor? Next time you call, please dial my cell phone. I need to be *very* discreet about my relationship with Mr. Keller."

There was total silence on the other side. Finally, Simone mumbled, "I see. Very well."

And she hung up. Just like the first time I spoke with this woman, I detected some sort of bizarre judgment. Regardless, I had a job interview with the managing partner at the top agency in the city. If I played my cards right, I would get a job offer within the next week and could tell Philippe to go pound sand. I felt a sense of relief. Just the thought of seeing Craig Keller in a few hours instantly changed my mood.

I observed my reflection in the full-length mirror behind my office door. I had chosen a simple grey, belted, sleeveless A-line dress by Versace. The hemline landed just above my knee. I had tall black leather Gucci boots and a skinny cardigan which covered the now purple-blue bruises on my left wrist. I wore my hair in a loose chignon bun. The overall look was professional, but not too overdone. Just as I began to dissect my face, inspect my pores, and check my makeup, Jeffrey entered.

"Oh, sorry, Jane, I should have knocked first." He looked embarrassed. "Did you hear from Philippe?"

"Not yet." I turned from the mirror to face him.

"Well, are you going to call him?" he pressed. "You said we would hear back today."

I shook my head. "No, I said to give it the weekend. If we don't have it in writing by end of day today, I'll rattle his cage." I pictured Philippe and felt my skin crawl again. Jeffrey's persistence was grating on my nerves to the point where I just wanted him to leave.

"Fine, but we really can't wait any longer," Jeffrey ordered sternly. "The scope of this project has me anxious about deadlines."

"Well, you're not the only one who's *anxious* about this project," I snapped and then muttered under my breath, "especially after *everything* I've been through."

Unfortunately, Jeffrey heard me. "What do you mean, 'everything you've been through'? Your job as account director is to manage the clients. You act like you're not getting paid."

"Yeah, well, I hope you come back as a girl in your next life, so you can see how much fun you've missed," I spat, bitterly.

"What are you trying to say?" Jeffrey asked, eyebrows knitted together.

I swallowed hard and stared at him, thinking, in my distress, I had already said too much. I could not confide in him. *Not ever.*

"You seem really freaked out right now," he remarked, looking genuinely concerned about me, like the big brother I never had, which made it difficult for me not to fall into his arms and cry my eyes out. "Is there anything I can do to help?" he asked. His tone had become gentle.

I shook my head stoically and smiled princess-style. "No, Jeffrey. Everything's fine."

He studied me for a minute, searching for some sign of what I was hiding, but I stood very still. I took a deep breath when he finally seemed to accept that I was not headed for a steep ledge, and he left my office.

Around 5:30, I started packing my things to get on the road to meet Craig. The route I needed to take to his downtown office was bound to be traffic hell at this hour. I stormed out the door to my car and spotted Warren in the parking lot, on his way back into the office. *Ugh.* This was the worst possible scenario. Not only was I leaving earlier than usual, but my boss was coming back to work late. I had the worst timing. Despite my attempts to pretend I didn't see him, he called out my name. "Jane, wait a minute."

I stopped and faced him.

"I want to talk to you," he said, now advancing toward me.

"Sure," I said trying hard to look casual.

"How's everything going?" he asked with a serious look on his face. He was wearing a dark charcoal suit and a pink tie. I was never too sure about pink on men, but Warren looked distinguished in the combination.

"Um … pretty good, I guess," I replied, eyes dashing around the parking lot.

"I heard your lunch with Philippe was a success," he complimented.

I just stared at him like an idiot. Of course, he was choosing this moment to put me on the spot—when I was late for a meeting with his biggest rival.

"That was great work, landing such a huge client and getting them to sign off on the concept without questions or changes," he continued. "In fact, I don't think I've ever had anyone else on the account team do that before."

"It was nothing, Warren." I felt my face turning red. "It's all Jeffrey—he's the one who nailed the creative."

"But you sold it to the client, Jane. You're responsible for keeping people in jobs. I didn't want to put more pressure on you but, without this client, I would have to lay off quite a few employees right before the holidays. Give yourself some credit—you've come a long way at this agency. I'm extremely pleased with your work."

I had never received this level of compliment from Warren, and it couldn't have come at a worse time. I watched the fine lines in his face as he spoke and remembered there was a time when I would have given anything in the world to hear him say exactly this. But instead of relishing the words, all I wanted was to break away from him. "Thank you, Warren."

He looked me straight in the eye but was silent. I thought the moment would never end. "Have a good evening, Jane." He turned and walked away.

I sighed with relief and then bolted to my car. Sure enough, there was bumper-to-bumper traffic. By the time I made it to the Keller-Whitman Group office building, I was frazzled. It was 6:35 and the only parking spaces in the half-empty garage displayed reserved signs. I kept rounding the corner for the next parking level, looking in vain for a space and getting more anxiety-ridden with every minute. I almost jumped when my cell phone rang. It was Derek. I answered, thinking he might be a welcome diversion until I located a space. "Jane Mercer."

"Is it really?" Derek asked. "I didn't think she existed anymore."

"I've been slightly busy, Derek. I only *work* in complete chaos." My tone was snippy.

"Hey, take it easy, Jane. I just called to see how you are. Is that okay?"

"I guess so. I'm fine. How are you?" I knew I sounded brusque, but I did nothing to soften my tone.

"Besides hurt that you never call me anymore, okay," he said. "I guess you're so busy dating that rich guy, you forgot your friends."

I remained silent because I had finally located a parking spot and was backing up, so the other car had room to exit the space.

"Are you still there?" he asked.

"I'm here. Speaking of dating, how's Chelsea lately?"

"She's fine," he replied. "But I'm not *dating* her or anything. We're just friends."

"You sure about that?" I jeered.

"Um, yeah, I'm pretty sure." He was chuckling softly like I was totally crazy to think he was dating Chelsea.

"She's so clearly impressed by you," I remarked, pulling into the spot slowly. "She tagged you in a Facebook post from your date the other night."

"Jane, I don't know what you're insinuating but I don't date my students, neither past nor present. We were having dinner and catching up—that's all."

I loved that he was getting indignant and felt myself wanting to cut him down even further. "I don't know, Derek, she looked pretty 'hot for teacher' to me," I taunted. His self-righteousness was making me sick. "Didn't you see her hashtags?" I recalled the photo of Chelsea and Derek, cheek-to-cheek with hashtag 'Finally' and hashtag 'Teacherspet.' I remembered feeling queasy at the sight.

"You're not listening, Jane. I said it's not like that."

"Oh, it's never *like that* with you, Derek. Hell, I'd have more respect if you just admitted you were doing her," I scoffed.

"What's *wrong* with you these days?"

"As long as I've known you, you're never into anyone.

You just want to be friends, right? Tell me, Derek, do you even *like* women? Or are you just a really good liar?" I had done it now. I had finally found the hot button and gotten Derek Lowell upset. I felt almost triumphant in my wickedness.

"Are you really doing this, Jane?" Derek's words were tinged with both pain and anger. "Because if you are, there are *some* things you can't take back."

"Yeah, well, I have to go now." I wasn't sure why I was being so mean to Derek but, for some reason, he rubbed me the wrong way every time I spoke to him lately. He was always so calm and collected—so stable and reliable. I couldn't figure out what our relationship amounted to anymore—he just didn't seem to fit in my life. I decided to put him out of my mind for now. I grabbed my purse, file folder containing my resume, notebook, and pen and made my way through the prison-like parking garage toward the building entrance. Once in the elevator, I realized it was already 6:45, and I hoped Craig Keller was not a stickler with time the way Warren was.

When I stepped out of the elevator into the office lobby, what I saw was spectacularly modern and sleek. Most advertising agencies had a contemporary appeal, but this one was on steroids.

The floors were gleaming white marble; the front desk and waiting area were backlit from floor to ceiling; the couches were pure white leather, accented with royal blue and lime green throw pillows; and fresh calla lilies in tall glass vases peeked out from every angle. A huge flat screen television sat to one side. The lobby was empty, and the overhead lights were turned off, casting an eerie glow.

I glanced at my phone. It was 6:51. I wasn't sure what to do so I sat down on one of the couches. It felt cold and hard. I began checking emails and scrolling through my Facebook, Instagram, and Twitter feeds.

That was when I heard high heels clicking down the hallway. A woman appeared. She looked in her mid-thirties with long, glossy black hair and lots of makeup, like she had gone apocalyptic at the makeup counter. She wore all black: dress, jacket, stockings, and five-inch heels. She did not smile.

"Are you Jane?" she inquired without visibly opening her full, shiny red lips.

"Yes," I replied.

"I'm Simone." I held out my hand, but she didn't shake it. Instead, she gave me the once over, pausing slightly at my boots with a faint indication of envy. "Follow me." She turned and strutted back down the hall, hips swishing from side to side, stopping at a door with a plaque that read 'Craig A. Keller.' She knocked.

"Yes," a voice from behind the door called.

Simone stood at the door and announced indifferently, "Your 6:30's here."

A moment later, Craig opened the door, appearing dashing in a navy-blue suit with no tie. His hair, which always appeared to be just the right length, looked a little windswept. His pinstriped shirt was unbuttoned a bit further than propriety dictated. One look at those intense green eyes and my heart skipped a beat. *Jesus, this man was sexy.*

"Jane, have you been waiting long?" he asked, giving me a lazy smile.

"No, Mr. Keller, only a few minutes." I shook his outstretched hand. "I apologize for being so late."

He obviously didn't care in the slightest about my tardiness. "Call me Craig," he requested, motioning for Simone to close the door. She shot him a look of contempt. "Thank you, Simone."

She immediately skulked out. *What an oddball that one is.*

Craig's office was decorated to the hilt in Eames-era furniture. His desk was all glass and the legs to it were tilted in on each side, sort of like a bow-legged woman in high heels. His chair was a swanky, mid-century modern white leather swivel with chrome. The chairs across from his desk were plush orange suede. Curtains to panoramic windows were flung open, displaying a breath-taking view of downtown. A full bar and lounge area were situated on the other side of his office, where a fireplace with an animal print rug lying at the hearth beckoned seductively. The whole place reeked of modern elitism.

I wasn't sure where to sit so I approached one of the orange suede chairs.

"It's after hours, Jane," he reminded me. "Let's have a drink." He motioned toward the white leather couches in the lounge and took off his suit jacket, hanging it gingerly on a wall hook. A mirror hung next to the wall hook, and I watched as he carefully fastened one of his shirt buttons and ran his hand over his hair. I was not sure where to sit; the furniture looked too pristine to be functional.

"What would you like?" he called as I settled into one of the white leather couches, carefully smoothing my skirt so that it didn't ride up my thighs and placing my notepad and file folder in my lap.

"I have vodka, wine, champagne, beer …"

"Water's fine, thank you," I responded shyly.

He laughed. "Oh, come on, Jane. Is Warren that much of a tight ass these days? Don't tell me he doesn't let you guys drink when you're working late."

"Maybe on special occasions," I offered slowly, thinking of the barely used bar at Warren Mitchell and Associates. "I mean, we *are* an ad agency."

Craig silently smiled at my comment while putting ice into two glasses. I looked around and noticed a large painting on the wall above the fireplace. It was of a woman lying on a horse, grasping it around the neck. She had long, red hair and wore a dress with a tutu. Her breasts were bare. Her look was solemn, and the background was blue with little shadowy circus characters floating in the background. Even though the woman in the painting was half-naked, not me, I felt exposed.

Craig handed me a drink and sat, right next to me. I awkwardly twisted my body to face him and crossed my legs, which I caught him eyeing.

"Salut," he said, clinking his glass against mine.

"Salut." I sipped the drink and tasted vodka. My eyes

widened slightly, and he smiled, showing those perfect, white teeth with the long canines.

"It's okay to loosen up in my office," he reassured, focusing his penetrating gaze on me. I felt the same way I did the night I fell in front of him at the party, like an insecure teenager in the presence of the hot football star.

"I brought my resume," I offered, pulling it from the file on my lap and handing it to Craig. He accepted it but didn't look at it; he placed it instead on the coffee table and set his drink on it, using it as a coaster.

"You like Marc Chagall?" he asked, casually gesturing toward the painting above the fireplace.

"I'm not very familiar with his works." I eyed the painting again. "But I like that one."

"The title translates to something like 'The Dancer at the Circus'," he explained. "I collect art and have several Chagalls throughout the office. If you're a good girl, I'll give you a little tour later."

A good girl? This was sounding less like a job interview with each passing minute. "What do you consider good?" I asked, feeling the warmth of the vodka in my stomach. He must have poured a strong one. It didn't taste like it was mixed with anything.

He lit up slightly at my comment, like he wasn't necessarily expecting it. "Oh, you'll know soon enough," he remarked, glancing down at my boots. Again, I was struck by the length and thickness of his eyelashes. On any other man, I might consider them girlish, but on Craig's face, juxtaposed with all his masculine features, they made him look fiercely sexual. "Tell me about you," he suggested, eyes fixed again on mine.

"What do you want to know?" I noticed he was not wearing his wedding ring tonight.

"Everything," he answered, taking a small swig of his drink, and resting his arm along the top of the couch, perilously close to my shoulder, eliciting a slight shiver.

It was then I realized I did nothing to prepare for this meeting and was not sure what to say. I guess I should have expected to get the 'where-do-you-see-yourself-in-five-years?' textbook question but this was not shaping up to be any average interview. There was no way he was expecting me to start listing my accomplishments at Warren's agency—not the way we were sitting nor the way he was looking at me. I began to feel confused, especially with the vodka taking effect.

"I—I'm not sure where to start," I stammered, looking down at my blank notepad. *What was he expecting me to say?*

Craig came to my rescue. "Jane," he said, letting his hand touch my shoulder gently. "Relax. This isn't an interview. I didn't invite you here to ask you questions about your work history. I know what you do and who you work with."

"Name someone."

"The Henrys, for example. How are *they* to work with?" he answered in rote fashion, like he had my career memorized.

I gulped my drink and felt it burn my throat. "Um, I guess they are, you know, sort of high maintenance," I began cautiously.

"From what I've heard, that's the understatement of the year," he remarked, laughing. "But good for you for not being negative about a client. I'll bet Rita's a piece of work."

"Let's just say she's very aware of the aging process," I answered.

"Well put." He laughed again. "How do you handle her?"

"It was a little challenging at first but, once I learned her hot buttons, I was able to navigate her personality. But honestly, Warren manages her more one-on-one. She prefers the boss's attention."

He nodded, looking as though he were processing the information. "Do they pay a monthly retainer, or do they have you guys work with a flat fee by project?" When he sensed my discomfort with this question, he quickly added, "I'm only trying to understand how big of a budget you've worked with in the past—just a ballpark figure—this is all strictly confidential."

"Retainer," I disclosed. "Somewhere around $150,000 a

month." I knew I shouldn't be quoting figures, but he gave me the feeling he was trustworthy. And, although I had never seen the Henrys' contract, I knew from the billable hours approximately what the agency was getting paid.

"Ah, okay. That's solid." He was looking at me thoughtfully. "So, Jane, tell me what you're passionate about."

I put my drink down and considered the question. *God, what was I supposed to say to that? Mr. Keller, I've never been passionate about anything in my life until I met you. Oh, maybe I was passionate about these boots that cost me a fortune, and which are still not paid for, but they are worth every penny because I saw the way you were looking at them and that kind of acknowledgement, coming from a man like you, is priceless. In fact, every single cent I've spent chasing fashion, facial injections, hair dye, and cosmetics is worth it at this moment because you think I'm attractive. What am I passionate about? Nothing, Mr. Keller. I hate my job and I owe sexual favors to a creepy client in return for his promise to retain our agency. Other than that, Sir, I've got nothing, so hit me with another question, one I can answer with superficial ad-speak. That's all I can really handle now.*

"You're being so quiet, Jane," Craig observed, suddenly snapping me out of my crazy thought bubble. I had been silent at least a full minute. "That wasn't meant to be a trick question," he said getting up for more drinks. The one I had was somehow empty, and I felt light-headed. But I didn't protest as I watched him make round two of the same strong cocktails.

"A woman as exceptional as you must have a lot of passions," he hinted, handing me another drink. I could feel my face turning red. He sat even closer this time. I must have seemed incoherent because I had absolutely nothing to say in response to his question, which felt inappropriately personal yet veiled under the guise of professionalism. Maybe that was his goal—to blur the lines between the two.

Thankfully, Craig's office phone rang so I could think of some sort of response that didn't reveal too much yet would satisfy his seemingly unmitigated craving for details about my life. It was all too clear that Craig Keller was more interested in me than I ever would have imagined. And I found myself wondering again what Kat was hiding about him. After a few rings, Craig stood up to look at the caller ID on one of his phones.

"Do you need to take that?" I asked, fidgeting in my chair.

"I'm sorry, Jane." He picked up the phone. His demeanor went from careless confidence to slight agitation. "I already told you," he uttered tersely into the receiver, eyes narrowing. "Yes, I know … no, I'm not … I'll call you from the car." He hung up, then looked up at me and smiled his relaxed smile again.

"I must be keeping you from something," I said, feeling like I needed to leave.

"You're not keeping me from anything," he denied. "So, what do they pay you over there?"

I hesitated before responding. "Not nearly enough."

He grinned. "No one thinks they get paid enough. Tell you what, whatever Warren's paying you, I'll give you thirty percent more in base salary, plus a performance bonus."

"That seems more than fair," I responded, thinking it was a huge chunk of change I hardly expected—that fleeing Philippe's crosshairs to the safety of Craig Keller was enough compensation.

"Think about it and get back to me." With that, he stood up and walked toward the wall hook where his jacket hung. "Now come with me," he ordered. "Take your drink." He grabbed his jacket and slid it back on, signaling me to follow him.

"Where are we going?" I asked, uncomfortably picking up my notepad and purse.

"Leave that stuff," he commanded. "No one's here. We're going to take a little tour." His face was filled with mischief.

I stood and advanced toward him, purposely leaving my drink on the table. He led the way through dimly lit hallways, passing dark vacant offices. I tried to read the name plates, alternately watching Craig's confident swagger directly in front of me. Benjamin Whitman, Steven Richards, Martin Strong—all men. When we got to the end of a long hallway, Craig took out his keys and opened the door to an office without a name plate. He turned on the lights and ushered me in. The inside was easily four times the size of my current office, completely emptied out except for a desk, chair, phone, and computer.

"If everything works out, this will be your office," he announced. "We'll do whatever you want in terms of decorating. You can choose what you like for the walls and furniture."

I walked slowly around the room and peeked out the blinds. It was a smaller snapshot of the same view Craig had in his office. There was a door in the corner behind the desk. "Where does that door lead?" I queried.

Craig sauntered to the door and opened it for me. "Bathroom and shower," he boasted. "We want our employees to like the place where they spend most of their lives."

I was dumbfounded, thinking that this office was close to the size of my apartment. I pictured myself bringing clients to meetings, feeling like a downtown LA big shot ad executive.

"I have something else to share with you, if you're ready," he suggested furtively.

I followed him to a room that was labeled, 'Art Library.' Again, he brought out his keys and opened the door. "After you," he said, holding the door open for me. I crossed the threshold and caught my breath.

"Wow."

He beamed at me with pride. He looked so handsome at that moment it was difficult for me to tear my eyes away from his face long enough to look at the paintings. Canned lights pointing at the artwork gave the gallery a romantic glow. Craig linked his arm through mine and led me from painting to painting, like we were on a date in Paris. With each one, he stopped and explained a little about it and where he acquired it. They were all Chagall originals. I just followed along in awe, hanging on his every word.

When we got to the last one, he stood behind me. "This one's my favorite. It's called "Lovers in the Red Sky.""

A woman stretched across the canvas, bare-breasted, wearing only a white skirt. A man clutched her from behind and they seemed to be bathing in red light. A bouquet of flowers was also floating, along with the shadowy circus animals in many of the other works on display. Again, I felt as exposed as the woman in the painting.

"I found this one in London when I was working on an ad campaign for an airline," he described. "I was so moved by it—it made me feel so, I don't know—hopeful? A little mysterious." His voice deepened as he moved closer behind me. "How does it make you feel?" I could smell his skin—the faint, divine scent of soap that I recalled from our valet encounter at Ammo. I felt the heat of his body and the consequent mind-numbing sexual tension.

"It ... it makes me feel ..." I mumbled dreamily, staring at the painting and inhaling Craig's scent. "It makes me feel like anything might happen—like maybe they'll come crashing to the ground—or maybe they'll emerge in a sea of light—something frightening or something beautiful."

I felt Craig's hands on my shoulders, caressing them softly. He moved his body so close that it was touching mine until we were in the exact same pose as the couple in the painting. I felt a shudder from head to toe, his lips on my skin, nibbling at the back of my neck, and I sank back into him. He slowly turned me around and pulled me close to him, looking into my eyes. "So, I guess we found what you're passionate about," he said in a soft, smooth voice.

"Yeah?" I breathed, feeling the heat of his lips about a quarter centimeter from mine. His breath smelled like cherry-flavored Jolly Rancher candies. He was moving his hands up and down my back, settling at my waist as he pulled me even closer. I panicked, and abruptly pushed him away.

"What's wrong?" He gave me a puzzled look, like it was standard practice to seduce a young associate prior to offering her a job, and as though I were the first person ever to question his advances.

"I—I'm sorry," I stuttered, the torture of humiliation setting in. "I can't—I didn't come here for this."

"Are you *sure*?" he asked, now amused.

I felt my cheeks flush. I thought about all the time I had spent stalking him on the internet, staring at his photo, imagining what it would be like to be in his world if only as a bit part player—a cameo in the sphere of his life. And here he was trying to kiss me—to give me exactly what I had fantasized about—and I pushed him away. *Why was I really here?*

"Come on," he said, taking my hand and pulling me closer to him, "don't be so narrow-minded."

"But that's not …" I faltered.

"It's not what? How the game's played?" He gave me the slow blink with those lashes.

I shook my head.

"No? According to whom?" he asked, taking a lock of my hair and running his fingers through it. I looked down at my feet in silence as he let the hair fall to my shoulder. "I don't follow rules, Jane. If you want to follow rules, stay with Warren. If you want to realize your potential, come with me. I have big plans for you. The door's open—you just need to enter."

I looked up at him; he towered over me, even while I was wearing four-inch heels. He didn't follow rules and that was what made him so exciting. The money and power were enough of an aphrodisiac; the looks and intelligence completed the package. The fact that he seemed to answer to no one made him, cruelly, almost God-like.

"But what would that make me?" I whispered.

"Successful." His voice had a matter-of-fact quality, and his expression was placid.

I stared at him in silence, trying to read more into his face. *What exactly was he offering?*

He smiled and shrugged. "Think about it."

I slowly nodded but said nothing. My thoughts were swimming.

"Let's go back to my office." He led me back down the hallway. Once we were in his office again, he went to the bar, pulled a bottle of water out of his refrigerator, and brought it to me. "Here," he said, handing me the bottle. "You okay to drive?"

I nodded, getting my purse, notepad, and file folder. My resume still sat on the coffee table, stained, and wrinkled from the condensation off Craig's glass, now dried into a round pucker, ink bleeding all around it, blending all the details listed on my *curriculum vitae*. So much for adhering to conventions, I thought wryly. I ventured toward the door and realized I had a long drive home and did not want to stop.

"Would you mind if I used the ladies' room?" I asked politely, once again aware that I was in the private office of LA's foremost ad executive.

"Of course," he replied. "It's right there." He pointed to a corner behind his desk.

I stepped into his private bathroom, turned on the light, and almost gasped at the elaborate layout. The walls were orange, and ornate silver fixtures and mirrors were everywhere. There was both a toilet and bidet, along with a walk-in rain shower. I hesitated to use the toilet as I realized there was a chance Craig would be able to hear me pee. I turned on the sink faucet so there would be no chance of that and quickly used his toilet.

Upon washing my hands in the sink, I noticed a ring sitting in the soap dish. I picked it up and examined it more closely. I recognized it to be Craig's wedding ring, the one I saw him wearing at Ammo. There appeared to be a Celtic symbol, resembling two interlocking ovals, sitting within a circle. It was engraved on the outside of the ring. I replaced it in the soap dish, dried my hands, and retouched my makeup, checking my face from each side.

I returned to find Craig leaning against the doorframe of his office texting someone. He looked up and smiled when I walked out. "All set?"

I nodded and we ventured back down the hallway toward the lobby. He stayed behind me, and I could feel his eyes on my body without even looking back. I was certain he was evaluating me.

"Let me walk you to your car," he insisted, pushing the

elevator button. "What floor?"

"Seven," I answered as the elevator door opened. We rode the elevator in silence as my thoughts raced. I stole a glance at Craig, who was staring absent-mindedly at the elevator reader. I thought about the ring he left in the soap dish and the call he received while we were in his office. It had to be his wife; I wondered about their relationship. If I were married to him, I wouldn't want him out of my sight. I would be beside myself with jealousy every time he worked late, especially given what 'working late' evidently meant to this man. I wondered if they had some sort of arrangement, that she knew at this very moment her husband's wedding ring sat in the soap dish of his office bathroom while he plied a young woman with drinks and expensive artwork. I wondered why she would stay with him. I suddenly felt sorry for his wife.

The elevator came to a halt, and we walked through the empty parking lot to my car. When we located it, I held out my hand to shake his. He grinned, taking my hand, and shaking it with exaggerated professionalism.

Then he leaned in, put his hand around the back of my neck in an oddly familiar way, pulled me close to him and whispered in my ear, "Don't take too much time thinking. I wouldn't want you to miss out on something great."

I backed away from him, so I could see his expression, which was not at all serious. Still, somehow, I knew he was not kidding. He didn't come across as the type of man who liked to wait—*for anything.*

I nodded, managing to get myself into my car, and, with trembling hands, drove away. I really needed to talk to someone but, for once, there was no one I could call. I knew I should call Kat, but she would interrogate me as to why I would have accepted an in-person meeting with Craig Keller in the first place. Marisa was too fragile right now and I didn't want to pile more drama upon her already over-burdened shoulders. Derek was out of the question for obvious reasons. So was anyone at work as well as my grandparents. Yet, something inside me wasn't interested in anyone's opinion. There was a sublime power in having caught the attention of Craig Keller, no matter how transient.

As I drove, I opened the car windows and cranked up the radio. I felt the cool November air, took a deep breath, and surveyed the evening sky, spread out in every direction with its infinite configuration of lights, street signs, houses, cars, traffic signals—and I suddenly felt a pang of exhilaration. *Is this what it's like to be an adult?*

Maybe life as a grown-up was really a never-ending series of decisions, not necessarily bad or good, black, or white. Maybe it was more fun to live in Craig Keller's world, where no one followed rules. But rules were the only things I ever knew, and one by one, I was shattering them, faster than I ever thought possible.

Thirteen

THE NEXT MORNING, I was back at the office dealing with the hundreds of emails that flooded in after I left the night before. Among the emails was one from Philippe which said, "Frédéric signed off on everything. Call me as soon as possible."

Under normal circumstances, this would have been good news. But this was only going to make Philippe more aggressive. *What was I going to do?* On the one hand, I had vile Philippe at my heels, threatening both my job and reputation. On the other hand, I had the omnipotent Craig Keller offering me—*what, really?* My mind went back to our encounter, and I felt a twinge of lust—the soapy smell of his body and the intimacy of his touch—like I was already his property. I shuddered. *What was it about that man that made me so crazy?* The image of his wedding ring in the soap dish still lingered in my mind, causing a knot in my stomach. When I got home from his office last night, I immediately searched Celtic symbols to understand what the etching represented: It turned out to be the Celtic symbol for family. I again wondered about his behavior.

Still, Craig Keller was offering me a life-changing amount of money. And it wasn't just that. There was the glamour of his agency—so many high-end accounts and brands I would represent.

I thought about Jeffrey and Warren. *Could I really leave them after four years?* They had been loyal to me. I wondered whether I would even be considering the offer from Craig Keller if I hadn't gotten myself into the dirty hijinks with Philippe. *What if I told Warren the truth? Would he protect me?*

Veronica's name was then flashing on the phone screen. "Good morning, Veronica." I put her on speakerphone.

"I have Philippe Barineau on the line for you," she said in her monotone.

I took a deep breath. Of course, Philippe was not going to let a day go by without reminding me of his power to make me follow through with what he thought I promised.

"Put him through," I said with dread.

"*Allo. C'est moi.*"

"Hello, Philippe." I smiled princess-style into the receiver. "How are you this morning?"

"*Mademoiselle*, did you get my email?"

"I did. Thank you."

"You know, it was a hard sell with Frédéric. He's still not convinced that this is the best way."

"What are you saying?" I asked, keeping my voice collected.

"He might change his mind," he replied gruffly. "About the concept and about your agency."

"I have your approval in writing, Philippe, so there's no going back now."

"*Oui, Mademoiselle,* that is exactly why I am calling," he said, breathing heavily into the phone. "We need to set a date for the payout."

I rolled my eyes at his bad English. Of course, he must have meant 'payment.'

"Right," I curtly responded, thinking I would have to decide about Craig Keller immediately.

"I am leaving for Paris tonight and will return next Friday."

I felt myself sigh in relief; I had more time to figure

things out. "Then meet me next Friday night, 8 p.m., at Chez Jay on Ocean Avenue in Santa Monica."

"You think I'm foolish enough to meet in public?" He was incredulous.

"We have to start somewhere, Philippe." A queasy feeling gurgled in my gut at the thought of him booking a cheap motel—or even worse, the thought of him knowing where I lived. "Tell you what," I suggested. "Let's go for a drink and decide from there." I made sure my voice had returned to the syrupy sweetness he responded to in such predictable fashion.

"*D'accord.* Don't be late, *mademoiselle*," he replied before hanging up.

LATER THAT DAY, JEFFREY was in my office lamenting upcoming ad deadlines, blissfully ignorant that I was sitting on a stick of dynamite with Philippe. I just pretended to be enthused, in the back of my mind obsessing about my next move with the Frenchman. His threat was clear. He could pull the entire project and give it to a competitor if I didn't keep my word. There was a lot of money at stake and Warren would fire me for sure if I was responsible for losing this client. There was no way I could avoid Philippe any longer.

Veronica entered right then lugging a spectacular bouquet of red tulips in a circular vase. She heaved it on my desk with a loud crack and shot me an annoyed look, huffing and puffing. Thick palm fronds were wound around and pressed against the inside of the vase so that it looked green in an organic way. There were at least three dozen flowers.

Jeffrey, who was busy texting, looked up. "New boyfriend?" he teased.

"No, of course not," I answered quickly. "I can't imagine who sent them."

"Ooh, this must be a good one. Your hands are shaking." His attention was focused on me.

"Never mind. Let's talk about the concept." The bouquet was so enormous, it blocked my view of Jeffrey. I tried to move it to the left, but it was so heavy, I struggled. Jeffrey immediately stood to help me lift the vase and place it behind my desk on a credenza.

"This one must have money," he commented, laughing.

"Jeffrey, please." I was desperate to get him out of my office.

"Well, aren't you even going to see who they're from?" Jeffrey baited, his eye on the white envelope tethered in the bouquet. I snatched it quickly and dropped it in my desk drawer. "Now I know you're hiding something—come on, Jane, who is it? Do I know him?" Jeffrey was now giggling.

Warren burst in and we both straightened up. "You guys sound like you're having too much fun in here," he commented looking from Jeffrey to me and back. He zeroed in on the bouquet. "Nice flowers, Jane. Did someone die, or do you have an admirer?"

When I didn't respond, he cleared his throat and changed the subject. "Do you have anything for me to review yet on those Kay Jeweler concepts?" he asked Jeffrey.

Jeffrey pushed his glasses toward his face and went into his serious mode with Warren. As soon as they left my office, I pulled the card out of my drawer and opened it: "Ms. Mercer, I'm not finished with you yet. CK."

Why on earth would he send these flowers to work? He must know how embarrassing and compromising it would be. *And what about keeping things discreet?*

Around 6 p.m., I packed my things, including the card from Craig, to make a clean getaway and saw Anna lingering in my doorway. "Leaving for the day?" she asked with that stupid fake-ass smile. She flipped her shiny brown bob.

"What do you need, Anna?"

"I was just looking for Jeffrey. I know he hangs out in here a lot."

I looked around my tiny office, shrugging my shoulders, "I don't see him."

Her glare was fixed on my flowers now. "That's an awfully big bouquet. What did you do to get those?"

"You'd be surprised." I stood, grabbed my things, turned

off my light and walked right around her through the door. "Good night."

I pretended to be on my cell phone as I flounced down the hallway, so no one could talk to me on my way out the door. I drifted home in total anxiety. By the time I entered my apartment, exhausted, I got a text from Marisa. "Can you talk?"

I called Marisa while she was doing a live shot. When she answered, I heard her yelling at someone, something about a white balance. "Yeah, hello" she shouted into the receiver, forgetting to adjust the tone of her voice from her previous interaction.

"Hey, it's me," I said. "Just calling you back."

"So, what the hell did you do to poor Derek?" She asked straightaway.

"What do you mean, *poor* Derek?"

"I ran into him today and asked if he'd heard from you," She explained. "He told me he'd rather not discuss you at all."

I sighed. "Well, I don't suppose I blame him. I sort of said some things that were, you know, not nice."

"Like what?"

The memory of me talking trash about Chelsea and implying he was gay came back to me. "Oh Marisa, it's no big deal. He's a big boy."

"Jane, Derek's extremely sensitive. He's an artist, you know. I think you should call him and apologize."

I went silent, thinking that Marisa was quick to take his side over mine. "Marisa it's just a little spat. I'm sure it'll blow over soon."

"To be honest, Jane, we're all a little worried about you," she said in a voice that reminded me of someone doing an intervention.

"Who's 'we'?"

"Your friends. Derek and Kat and I."

"You've been talking … to them … about me?" I pictured them gathering at some bar for a powwow about 'Jane's attitude.'

"Now, don't get upset. We're your friends. We care about

you." She sounded inordinately concerned which was even more infuriating.

"Look," I responded, trying to keep my voice calm. "I'm fine. I'll call Derek if that makes you feel better, but it's not going to be tonight."

"You know you can always talk to me, right, Jane? You can tell me anything."

"Of course," I lied.

A 213 area-code I didn't recognize popped up and I was looking for an excuse to end the conversation. "Oh, Marisa—forgive me—I have another call to take." Before she could respond, I accepted the incoming call. "Jane Mercer."

"Where … *are* you?" I could feel the hairs standing up on my neck. It was Craig Keller, calling from his private cell phone. He paused in a very seductive way between the words 'where' and 'are.'

"At home," I answered, heartbeat quickening.

"Are you alone?"

"Yes."

"Good. Do you like the flowers?"

"Yes," I responded, trying to sound casual, "but they were a little difficult to explain to my coworkers."

There was a long silence. "That's funny," he commented. "They weren't intended to go to your office. My apologies if I put you in an awkward situation."

How would that have been confused? The only address he had was my home address, which was on my resume. "It's okay, really. No harm done."

"So, Ms. Mercer, have you given our conversation any more thought?"

He must still be in his office, I mused, picturing him in his effortless button-down shirt and suit jacket, elegantly draped over his tall, lean frame. The image of us last night in the art library flashed before me again. Little did he know, I had given it nothing but thought. In fact, there was little else I could think of since I had met him. There was, of course, the money, the prestige, and the big office—but Craig Keller himself was what I really wanted. Just the sound of his voice made every apprehension melt away. In a short time, he had become a haven for me—a special gift from the universe packed neatly and tied up with a shiny red bow. I couldn't explain it, but I trusted him implicitly.

"Jane?" I heard Craig say, "Did I lose you?"

"No," I said finally. "Not in the slightest. I *have* given it quite a bit of thought and, well, I'm seriously considering your offer."

"That's fantastic, Jane." He sounded genuinely pleased.

"I know we have to shore up details for me to sign a formal contract," I said. "And I'll want to give Warren sufficient notice."

"Of course," he said with magnanimity. "I'll have a contract drawn up immediately. You can pick it up from my office anytime tomorrow and you can ask me anything you want Friday night over dinner. That is, if you're available."

"I'll make myself available," I responded, surprised but nevertheless delighted that he could get free on a Friday night. I just longed to see him in person again.

"I'll make a reservation for 7:30 somewhere in Santa Monica," he said. "Would you like me to pick you up?"

I glanced around my apartment in a panic. There was no way I could have Craig Keller see my place. He would be disgusted. From my cyberstalking, I knew he lived somewhere in Bel Air in a home valued at upwards of fifteen million dollars. "Oh no, that's not necessary. I'll probably be coming directly from work anyway," I fibbed.

"Okay then. I'll see you Friday. And Jane," he paused, "you have no idea what an excellent decision you're making."

And whether he was right or wrong, at least a decision had been made. I never felt so empowered in my life. I thought about Derek—poor Derek—with his sad little life of playing violin and teaching music, his ambivalence toward women, his compulsive frugality, and his wishy-washy ways. I couldn't believe there was once a time when I wanted to be with Derek. It felt so immature and silly now. There was something grown up about Craig Keller—something strong and impenetrable. He was a real man and

Derek was nothing but a boy. One thing was certain. If I was going to see Craig Friday night, I needed to get a new outfit. There was no doubt in my mind. I had to look perfect.

Fourteen

ONCENTRATING ON WORK THE next morning was futile. All I could think of was picking up my contract from Craig Keller's office and getting ready for the dinner in which I would seal the deal with Keller Whitman Group.

With Philippe out of the country and, effectively, out of my hair, I was able to leave the office with more regularity. Warren and Jeffrey seemed to be engaged in other things, so I blocked out time on my calendar to get out of the office early and grab the contract.

I sneaked out of work around 4 p.m. When I arrived at Keller Whitman Group and found my way to the now-familiar office suite, Simone was there, typing on her computer, shiny black hair hanging around her face, barely hiding her perpetually sullen expression. I couldn't imagine how Craig would keep her around—especially in the front office, with that attitude. Of course, she didn't look up when I walked in. "Excuse me, Simone, I'm here to pick up a packet from Mr. Keller," I said politely.

She didn't acknowledge me—she just robotically reached underneath her desk and handed me a puffy envelope that read, 'Ms. Jane Mercer.'

"Thank you," I responded, to which she simply nodded and went back to her typing. "Is Mr. Keller here now?"

"He's out of the office today," she grunted.

"Oh. Then, will you please let him know I stopped by to pick this up?" I wanted to get a reaction—any reaction from her.

"I'm sure he knows," she murmured and, for a split second, glanced up at me with a dour expression.

"Very well. I'll see you later." Again, there was no response, and I turned on my heel to leave. *What a hostile bitch.* I got in the car, turned on the interior light and tore open the envelope. There was a hand-written note on Craig's stationery, paperclipped to the front of the contract. It read, "Ms. Mercer, Looking forward to a long and successful relationship. See you Friday. CK."

My heart skipped a beat as I observed his handwriting. It was technically cursive but easy to read, like print. His capital letters were boldly stylized, deliberate but at the same time, careless. I instinctively put the letter to my nose to smell the paper, his writing, perhaps secretly hoping to catch a small whiff of that soapy scent of his skin. I set the items down on the passenger seat, aware of the absurdity of my actions, and turned off my car light.

I started the ignition and glimpsed a woman in my rear-view mirror walking through the parking lot. I could only see her from the back, and she was so far away, she looked shadowy. She appeared to have long, curly blonde hair and was carrying a messenger bag. She wore a bright red skirt suit, and walked confidently toward the elevator, bouncing along with every step. As soon as I saw her, I realized that the woman reminded me of someone.

All the way home I wracked my brain for an answer to the mystery woman's identity. A gnawing feeling followed me as I fought the rush hour traffic. *Was that woman someone I knew? But how?*

When I arrived at my apartment, I pulled the contract out of the envelope and read through it with a detailed eye, clause by clause. I got to the salary and my eyes bulged out.

He was offering me a five-year contract, along with a salary that was easily fifty percent more than I was making at Warren's agency. There was an annual bonus of twenty percent of my base salary plus additional compensation for client revenue and a car allowance. I continued to read through, and it looked like there were equity shares available.

I had never seen a contract like this, so I was completely blown away by its magnitude. This was *real* money. I couldn't help but wonder why he was offering this to me when LA was brimming with ad executives who would kill for this role.

There was one clause I didn't understand; it stated that those in executive level grades, fifteen through twenty-five, were expected to source a certain number of clients from either competitive advertising agencies or companies within the executive's portfolio. I wondered what, exactly, that meant. I wished I could call Kat and have her look at it but that was not an option.

I read it over again and there was no job description or position title. It only said Executive Level—Grade Sixteen. I was about ready to give up for the night when I heard my cell phone ringing. I fished it out of my purse and saw the letters CK flashing. I had saved his private cell number into my phone contacts. "Jane Mercer," I greeted him in my professional voice.

"Just the woman I wanted to speak to," he said. I heard a lot of noise in the background, like he was in a crowd. "Are you alone?"

"Yes."

"Good. I just wanted to let you know I did receive your message. I had to fly to San Francisco for the day and just landed back at LAX."

I breathed a sigh of relief. Not only had Simone been telling the truth, but she also did her job by giving her boss the message I had left.

"Welcome back." I smiled into the receiver, picturing him in a dark travel suit, carrying an expensive garment bag, looking elegant.

"Did you miss me?" he asked in that casual, silky voice,

one I had noticed he could turn on and off like a light switch.

"Clearly," I replied. It was so easy to go there with him—way too easy.

"Listen." He was back in his professional mode. "I have reservations at One Pico for Friday. Do you know where it is?"

"Is that the restaurant at Shutters on the Beach?" I felt a spear of excitement in anticipation of being at such a high-end place with Craig.

"That's right. Just give your name to the maître d'. I'll call you if I'm running late."

"Okay." I was smiling inside.

"Oh, and don't forget to bring the contract with you. I'm sure you have questions."

"I actually do have one question that you might be able to answer now," I began, thinking about the odd grade system. "What will my title be?"

"What do you want to be called?"

"Well, I'm director of accounts now. I would love to come in as vice president."

"Done," he replied, like I had asked him for extra sweetener in my coffee.

"You mean I'll be a VP?" I asked, now beside myself with excitement.

"I'll call you Queen Jane if it gets you to come work for me," he responded.

"That's awesome," I blurted out like a true valley girl.

I heard him give a breathy, almost inaudible laugh into the phone. "See you Friday, Ms. Mercer."

I spent the rest of the week dreaming up my outfit and making grooming appointments with one goal in mind: looking perfect. There were so many things to get done and, between work deadlines and other commitments, I really didn't have much time. I needed a manicure, pedicure, roots touched up, a quick visit to Dr. Feelgood, and most importantly, the right outfit to be seen in public with the one and only Craig Keller.

On Thursday night, I sped to Neiman Marcus after

work and headed straight for the designer collections area. I could spare no expense here, and I needed something that was glamorous but not too showy, fun yet tailored and elegant. I found the perfect dress. It was by Marc Jacobs, a midnight blue lightweight wool with a soft velvet collar. A bow was tied at the throat, and right underneath was an open keyhole that closed right between my breasts. It had long, puffy bell sleeves and a snug fit at the waist and hips, with a slight flare at the hem. It came to right above my knees. It was so beautiful and magical, I just had to have it.

I thought about shoes and, given the dress was more than nine hundred dollars, there was no way I could afford new shoes to go with it. I wondered whether I could get away with the Gucci boots twice in one week. I instinctively knew the answer was no, so I ventured to the shoe salon. After all, with the kind of numbers Craig Keller was throwing around, I would be able to pay it off the first week on the job, along with all the other debt I'd accumulated. Plus, this was my chance to impress him, to show that I could hold my own, at his level, in any public situation. I found another pair of boots, this time black suede Christian Louboutins. They cost more than my car, but the effect of the bright red soles, peeking out as I walked away from him, would be both dramatic and impressive.

I was about to leave the store, and something made me stop at the fine lingerie counter. I spotted a beautiful black bra and panties set by La Perla. The bra was sheer, with a tiny pink rose embroidered in the center and on each strap. There was a tiny, matching thong. I glanced at the price tag and almost gasped. The set was almost half of what the dress cost.

"Would you like a fitting room?" said a voice behind me. I spun around and saw the sales rep peering at me with a playful grin. She was easily in her fifties and was wearing a smart cream shift dress. "That's a gorgeous set."

"Oh, I don't know," I said, feeling a stab of embarrassment. *Why would I even be considering such expensive, sexy lingerie?* It's not like Craig would see it anyway. But I might feel more confident knowing my lingerie was as elegant as the dress.

Two hours and three thousand dollars later, I was back at my apartment, finding a space in my closet to put the new treasures.

FRIDAY MORNING IN THE office, Anna passed me in the hallway, her rapacious smirk in full effect. Something made me turn to watch her walk. It dawned on me that her gait resembled the woman I had seen in the Keller Whitman parking garage, but Anna's hair was short, straight and brown, like it always was. For the rest of the afternoon, I wondered whether I was imagining things. The whole thing just didn't make sense.

I left work early because I had booked a Brazilian bikini wax at the local salon. If I were to don such exquisite lingerie, I wanted everything it touched to be smooth and groomed to perfection.

I arrived at Shutters on the Beach a little before 7:30. I took an Uber thinking that my red Jetta just wasn't up to par for a place like Shutters. The Uber driver dropped me in the porte cochere. I strolled through the lobby, eyeing my surroundings with delight. I adored this hotel, a luxury inn right on the beach near the Santa Monica Pier. I had never actually stayed there, but I had passed through many times on walks along the beach path. It was stylish, yet low key, much like Craig's personality.

I found One Pico Restaurant and caught a glimpse of myself in a full-length mirror. I almost didn't recognize me. I looked like a glamorous movie star. I had teased my hair a bit at the crown and wore it long and straight. My eye makeup was heavier than usual, and I wore a subtle shade of pink lipstick that looked exquisite with the midnight blue dress. As I swanned across the gleaming hardwood floors, every man's head turned. I felt some inexorable surge of power growing within me. *This is what it feels like to be beautiful and confident.*

I approached the maître d', whose nametag read 'Oscar'. "I'm Jane Mercer, here to meet Craig Keller."

As soon as he heard Craig's name, he ushered me to the side of the podium so the people behind me could not overhear. "Ms. Mercer," he muttered in a clandestine manner and pulled an envelope from his suit jacket. "This is for you."

Visibly perplexed, I accepted the envelope. I wondered whether Craig had stood me up. There was a small note card inside the envelope, along with a room key. The note read 'Seamus Heaney, room seven hundred.' *What?* My eyes darted quizzically at the maître d', who was still standing there watching me. He leaned over and said in a whisper, "Mr. Keller would like you to meet him upstairs."

My eyes watered, and my legs trembled. I turned and headed toward the hotel elevators but then stopped short. *What exactly was going on?* It was now 7:45 and I was breaking into a sweat. I loosened my collar a bit because the velvet suddenly felt too warm around my neck. I retreated to the lobby, confused. Finally, I pulled my phone out of my bag and dialed Craig's cell number, which went straight to voicemail.

"Hi, you've reached the voicemail of Craig Keller, managing partner at Keller Whitman Group," said a voice I recognized as Simone's. I disconnected immediately. Scanning the lobby, I watched the well-heeled businessmen in suits with beautiful women on their arms, milling about, and felt like I was into something deep now—something shadowy and unfamiliar—something beyond my control. And, as though under an intoxicating spell, I floated toward the hotel elevator.

M Y TEETH SANK INTO my lower lip as I ascended to the seventh floor. The top-floor room, which was obviously a suite, was far from the elevator. I knocked at the door and waited, heart racing, clutching my handbag. After a couple of minutes, I knocked again but there was still no answer. I took the room key out of the envelope and slid it over the door sensor. The green light blinked, and I cautiously opened the door, peering in before crossing the threshold.

"Hello?" I called as I ventured into the suite, which was stunning. It overlooked the crashing waves of Santa Monica beach. The French doors to the outside veranda were open and a fireplace was lit. A long table displayed a line of chafing dishes and platters, bottles of wine and other alcohol. No one was there.

I glanced at my watch … 7:55. I wasn't sure what to do with myself. I contemplated fleeing the scene but could not bring myself to go just yet. I thought back to my last conversation with Craig. He said he would call me if he was going to be late. I started to worry that something might have happened. *Why wouldn't he have called me?*

I paced the floor for a couple of minutes and then made

the decision to bolt. Just as I was about to open the door to escape, Craig Keller burst in. I saw his face and my anxiety dissipated. He looked so attractive in a black light-wool suit with a green and navy tie, obviously having just come from work. He was smiling that warm, welcoming smile that melted me every time.

"Ms. Mercer—you made it." He seemed pleased.

"You had me worried there for a minute," I said, watching as he shut and locked the door behind him.

"My apologies. I had sort of an emergency at the office and was stuck on a conference call that lasted forever." As he said this, he gave me the once over, pausing at my boots, amusement and approval melding together in his gaze.

For someone who was dealing with a work crisis, he looked thoroughly unaffected. And, for someone who had unsuspectingly lured a potential employee up to a private hotel room to discuss work business, he was shameless.

"I thought it would be best for us to meet here, where there's no chance of running into anyone we know." It was as though he were reading my thoughts. He advanced toward the open French doors. "We can have the contract discussion, you know, privately."

I considered it and, he did have a good point. I would die if I ran into Jeffrey and his wife or, even worse, Warren. Craig Keller was so clever.

"Shall we step outside to chat?" he suggested as he grabbed a bottle of Perrier water and two goblets.

There were two chairs and a table out on the balcony, as well as a chaise lounge with a terry cloth-covered cushion over it. Craig carefully poured the sparkling water into the two goblets and handed one to me. I sipped it to make sure it was truly just Perrier and found, with relief, that it was.

"Ms. Mercer, I think we should get all the tedious details out of the way, so we can enjoy our night properly," he proposed.

If by tedious details, he meant my future, I was more than a little concerned.

"Did you bring the contract?" he asked, giving me his

slow blink and shifting his long legs.

I pulled it out of my handbag, along with a pen and notepad. "Do you have a copy?"

He shook his head. "I know what's in it." I detected the instant return of professional Craig Keller.

"Let's see." I scanned the items I highlighted. It was getting dark, so I had to use my smartphone as a flashlight. "I don't necessarily understand what this clause means … you know … about bringing clients to the agency."

"That's standard when you're coming from another company at your level," he replied. "Whether it's another agency or corporation, we require you to take others along. Otherwise, why would we invest so much money in you on the front end? I like to think of it as collateral."

"You mean, I need to steal clients from Warren?"

He nodded and gave me the slow blink. "You're okay with that, right?"

I thought about the fact that I was fleeing Warren's agency because of a client who was blackmailing me to sleep with him, and he was asking me to take one with me. I wouldn't even know where to start.

"I'm not sure," I said doubtfully. "I don't want to hurt Warren—he's been good to me." I was growing more and more uncomfortable.

"Then why are you here?" His voice had become razor sharp, and his eyes tapered slightly at the corners.

My internal dialogue was rambling: *Oh, please, Craig, you know exactly why I'm here. It's because you have an intense power over me, like heroin, and all I need every day to keep from going insane is to see you or hear your voice just once.* I shivered at the chilly ocean air and hugged my arms around my body.

"Are you cold?" he asked, standing immediately and taking off his suit jacket. I watched him stretch his arms back to remove the jacket and the silhouette of his amazing body was outlined in the moonlight. It wasn't fair—he was not even mortal. He slid the jacket around my shoulders and sat back down across from me. "Is that better?"

"Yes, thank you." I immediately sniffed the soapy scent

that permeated his jacket, which had been draped over his body all day. The contract seemed superfluous because all I could see were flashbacks from the art library.

"Let me help you with this," he said, moving his chair closer. "This is business. It's not always pretty. And, if Warren were such a saint, you'd be talking to him right now, not me."

"I understand all that." I was trying to find his eyes in the darkness. It was way past sundown, and the only illumination was trembling from the dim porch lights and the inside of the suite. I needed, at that moment, to look into his eyes—to understand that he was being genuine. But his eyes appeared murky and dark, the opposite of the jade color I saw in broad daylight.

"But?" he asked.

"But I don't even know the first thing about stealing a client," I confessed, feeling foolish and naïve.

"I'm sure you'll be a quick study," he said with all the shrewdness of a businessman at the top of his game in a huge city like Los Angeles. "I'll mentor you."

I lowered my eyes to the contract in silence, assessing what he really wanted me to do.

"Jane—please spare me the agony of deliberation. Sign the contract." He was so direct, it was unsettling. He put the pen in my hand and held it over the signature line. "Pull the trigger. You won't be sorry, I promise."

At that moment, he had me. I put the contract down on the table between us and signed away. "Here you go," I said, handing it to him. A mixture of fear and relief filled my body. Although no one held a gun to my head, I couldn't shake the feeling that I had been coerced.

"That-a-girl." He accepted the contract. "May I?" He gestured at my pen. I handed it to him, and he signed his brilliant, bold signature and dated it. I watched his hands and noticed he was not wearing his wedding ring.

"I'll have a copy of the signed, executed document delivered wherever you want on Monday. Now, Ms. Mercer, let's go inside and have dinner. A little celebration is in order."

Once inside, he placed the contract in his briefcase and

led me toward an already-set table with three tealight candles and a bud vase holding a single white rose. I handed him his jacket and he hung it assiduously on the back of his chair. He then put together a communal plate of food from the One Pico restaurant kitchen and placed it between us. Once I smelled the aroma of food, I became famished.

The restaurant had sent us their specialties: pan-seared calamari, salmon tartare and tortellini in basil and tomato sauce. "May I serve you?" he asked, taking one of the small plates and elegantly arranging food for me.

I accepted the plate and ate carefully, making sure I did not spill anything on my resplendent Marc Jacobs dress. Craig, of course, was an expert at eating without spilling a drop on his impeccable shirt.

I wasn't sure what to talk about during dinner and the silence made me uncomfortable. Oddly, Craig seemed fine with it. I decided to ask him a question to stimulate a conversation. "Did you have a nice trip to San Francisco?" I asked, before cautiously biting into a piece of tortellini, and chewing it thoroughly with my mouth closed.

"It was fine," he replied. "My parents live there—it's where I grew up."

"Oh?" I answered, knowing damned well that's where he grew up after so much cyberstalking. "That must have been a great city to grow up in. Do you have brothers and sisters?"

His demeanor immediately changed as though I'd said something horrifying. He paused, set his knife and fork down gently, took a sip of Perrier, and then stared down at his plate, avoiding eye contact. "I had a brother. He died in an accident when I was seventeen."

"Oh my god," I blurted. "I'm so sorry. I didn't mean to …" my voice faded as I tried to think of something to say. "That had to have been awful."

He said nothing, but his eyes had a faraway quality—almost as though someone had pulled a veil over them. After a full minute of silence, he spoke. "Where did you grow up?"

"Suburban Long Beach," I responded, sick that I'd brought up something which obviously had a deep impact on Craig. I never had siblings, but I couldn't imagine losing one at such a young age. I was aching to ask more about his family, and I wondered why his brother's death was not in any of the articles I'd pulled online about the Kellers.

Craig did not say much during the entire dinner. It's almost like I'd killed the conversation as soon as I reminded him of his dead brother. After dinner, Craig served dessert, which was a delicate-looking crème brûlée for us to share.

He handed me a spoon and we both cracked the hard surface of the crisp brûlée shell and tucked into the creamy custard beneath. I watched his mouth deftly maneuver around his spoon.

When we were finished eating, he cleared the plates and placed four large pillows in front of the crackling fireplace. Then, he lay down on his side with the pillows under him, head propped by his hand, and he patted the pillow next to him for me to join.

I was taken aback but tried to hide it. I looked around, not knowing what to do. The dress I had on was not exactly made for sitting on the floor.

Craig smiled reassuringly and patted the pillow again. "Come on, Jane, let's relax. It's been a long week." I awkwardly sat down next to him on the pillows with my tall boots tucked under me. To still appear ladylike, I smoothed my dress so that it fanned around my body. Craig moved closer. "Why don't you tell me what you *like*."

I was still not used to his non-sequiturs, which always propelled us into an intensely personal conversation, but only when *he* was ready to have one. And after the whole dead brother dialogue, I felt tongue tied.

"*Like?*" I asked. "You mean, do I *like* cats, romance novels and snowboarding?" As soon as the comment escaped my lips, I realized how silly it sounded.

He laughed. "Ms. Mercer. What am I going to do with you?" With that, he got to his feet and took a bottle of Casa Noble tequila from the bar, along with two shot glasses. Then, he flipped on the suite's sound system and the soft trip hop music of late-nineties Massive Attack seeped seductively from the speakers. "I think we're in need of a little truth serum here," he announced, pouring two shots, and placing them on the coffee table. He went back to the table and expertly placed lime wedges on a dessert plate, pouring a little well of salt in the middle.

Here we go. There was no way I was going to stand a chance here. "While we're on truth serum," I boldly ventured, "Who's Seamus Heaney?"

He smiled with a slow blink, settled back down on the pillows, and faced me. "You don't know who Seamus Heaney is? Ms. Mercer, your upbringing is showing."

"What's that supposed to mean?" I felt like I had just been insulted.

"He's a poet," he replied laughing. "An Irish Nobel Laureate and the only reason I made that comment is that you obviously didn't grow up in an Irish family."

Nor a literary one. "So, what is that—some sort of alias you use?"

Instead of answering me, he delicately licked his hand between the thumb and forefinger, applied salt and motioned for me to do the same. I mimicked what I saw him do. Then, he picked up the two shots, handed me one, and toasted, "To Seamus Heaney."

"To Seamus Heaney," I repeated, and we licked the salt off our hands and shot down the liquor, followed by the ceremonial chewing of the lime wedges. He immediately poured two more, and we shot those down as well.

"Now," he said, taking my hand and pulling me closer to him. We were at this point both laying on our sides, facing each other, lips dangerously close. "Tell me what you *like*."

The heavenly soap smell was again in my nostrils and the tequila was going to my head. The rhythmic beat of the sensual music in the background made me feel like I was in someone else's body, acting a part I had rehearsed for my whole life—only this time, it was real. "I like—*you*," I uttered dreamily.

"Now, we're getting somewhere," he said, pulling the velvet tie at my throat so that my dress came apart and he could see at least the outline of my clavicles, the tops of my breasts. I did nothing to stop him.

He pulled me toward him and pressed his lips against mine firmly; I opened my mouth to him and felt his body pushing against mine. I could barely fathom what was happening. I briefly recalled the night I was stretched out on my couch naked, with an open magazine containing his image lying against my breasts. This was no magazine—it was the actual man.

He withdrew for a second and began kissing my face— my forehead, cheeks, chin, neck. His mouth touched mine again and I felt his tongue, he exhaled as I inhaled—we were breathing the same air. Then, unexpectedly, he bit me on the cheek, and I flinched. "How about *that*?" he whispered. "Do you like that?"

I didn't answer, stunned that he made that move. He advanced again and bit me on the neck, lighter this time, like he wanted to make sure he didn't leave a mark. "And that?" he asked.

I pushed him back by his broad shoulders for a moment but felt the weight of his body pinning me down. When he turned his eyes to mine, they looked pale green again and his lashes shone in the firelight as he blinked softly. He smiled his dazzling smile revealing those perfect white teeth. "Say yes," he breathed, brushing the hair off my face. I felt his hand run down my neck and onto my shoulder, the pressure of his fingers kneading into it before further sliding down my arm. When his hand brushed across my breasts, an electric current pulsed through me. "Say it," he repeated with his mouth close to my ear. I felt his hot breath moistening my earlobe. "I want to hear you say *yes*."

That was it. There was no going back. I was about to be intimate with Craig Keller and didn't care about the repercussions. All logic went out the window as soon as he touched me. "Yes," I responded, now breathless. "Yes, yes."

And before I knew it, Craig grabbed me by the front of my expensive new dress and pulled me toward him, roughly tearing the dress in half down the front to my belly button.

"My dress," I gasped, retreating to assess the damage, unable to contain my shock and exasperation. "You tore it!"

"Shhh." He pulled me toward him again with the ripped edges. "I'll replace it." I fell silent and obeyed, remembering he could afford to buy the whole store. When the dress was sufficiently torn to shreds and tossed to the other side of the hotel room, I sat in my black La Perla lingerie with the boots still on. I leaned down to unzip one of the boots, but he stopped me.

"Leave them on," he ordered. I looked up at him for his next command. "Stand up. I want to look at you."

I did exactly what I was told and stood before him, while he lay on the floor underneath me, watching intently. There I stood while Craig Keller physically and emotionally pried me apart. My father's disparaging words flooded my mind. I felt my fingers trembling, wondering if he would find fault with my body, compare me to the perfect models he was used to seeing, and then leave me in disgust. He did the opposite. He let out a soft, barely audible whistle, got to his feet, and lowered his eyes to meet mine. I thought my heart might stop. He undid his silk tie and slid it off his neck. He then took each end of the tie and lassoed me, pulling me toward him. I stumbled a bit. "Ms. Mercer, you're a work of art."

And to every woman, this should be a happy ending. That Craig Keller would utter these words was an undeniable victory. For me, all it did was make me wonder if I would measure up. *What was he expecting me to do?* I came from the school of thought that sex was either doing it or not. There were no varying degrees of being good or bad in bed. My lack of experience manifested itself in anxiety.

I watched Craig Keller unbutton his shirt, and undo his French cuffs, dropping his diamond-studded platinum cufflinks into his pants pocket. Then he removed his shirt, unbuckled his belt, and unzipped his trousers. I was in awe that I was about to see him, completely *naked*. His body was cut in all the right places. I tried not to stare but it was unavoidable. And, before I knew it, we were on the bed and he was kissing me, hungrily. He paused to whisper in my ear, "I'm going to consume you—I hope you're ready."

What followed was what I could only describe as rough and painful. My body was his blank canvas—the brushes, his perfect set of teeth, which he used to plant an unrelenting series of bites all over my otherwise unscathed, fair-skinned body. I allowed him to bite into every muscle, every ligament. I let him crush his teeth into my bones. And he did, over and over. I had fully lost track of time until Craig finally slid off me to look at his watch.

"Do you have to go?" I asked, fearfully. We hadn't said a word to each other the entire time. The only gap in our frenetic sexual encounter had been when Craig reached for his trousers a couple of times to pull a condom out of his pocket and unfurl it in the candlelight while I tried, unsuccessfully, to look away.

"I'm afraid so." His voice was even and clear as though we were discussing a business plan. "You relax for a few minutes."

I spun on my side toward the digital clock, which had tipped over on its side. It was close to 11 p.m. Craig went into the bathroom and shut the door. I heard the shower running. Sure, I thought, he needs to cleanse himself of my scent, so he can go home to his wife. I lay there, motionless, as I listened to him shower and towel himself off. When he emerged from the bathroom, he dressed swiftly and methodically.

Once he was fully dressed, he sat on a nearby chair to put on his shoes. He seemed to have a strange obsession with the shoelaces on his black leather oxfords. He kept comparing the laces from either side to ensure they were even; then pulling the crossed laces on the tongue of each shoe to one side or another, depending on which lace was shorter. Then he preoccupied himself with the actual tying of the laces, carefully making sure the bows were even and perfect. He did this at least three times on each shoe before he seemed satisfied that everything was symmetrical.

I just watched from the bed in sadness. He was going to leave me here, in this strange hotel, alone, with only the memory of him and the magical dress that had been ripped up and now lay in the corner, in a crumpled heap. I still had the boots on.

He sauntered over to me, sat on the edge of the bed, and stroked my hair. "Was that what you expected?"

I cleared my throat, sat up, and pulled the sheets up to my neck.

He searched my face. "Oh, come on, Jane. Don't tell me you never thought about what it would be like with me."

I felt my face redden. *How would he know how many times I thought about being with him?* It was almost as though he had some crazy intuition and could see right into my soul.

He took the edge of the sheet, which was clutched in my hands and yanked it down to my waist. He cupped his hands around each of my breasts, gazing at them, like they were his personal property. He then edged the sheet down my thighs and his eyes lowered. He leaned over and whispered in my ear. "Tell me how badly you wanted this. And then I'll go."

You know damned well I've wanted this more than anything I've ever wanted in my life. But my heart will shatter into a million pieces as soon as you walk out the door. Please don't leave. I can't handle being alone right now. I don't even know what's happened here. Tell me, are we having an affair now? Are we working together? Are we doing both? I bolted upright and scrambled to get off the bed.

"What are you doing?" he asked, watching with amused curiosity.

"Getting the hell out of here," I answered, wandering around, naked in my boots, trying to find the pieces of the clothes he had ripped to shreds.

"Don't be silly," he said calmly as I frantically searched for my Marc Jacobs dress, located it, pulled it over my head and attempted to tie the ripped pieces so it would hold together enough for me to be in public. My expensive La Perla set was nowhere in sight. I found my purse and dug through it for a safety pin.

"Hey—take it easy, Jane." He grabbed my hand and

pulled me toward him. "Why don't you stay and sleep here? You can use the spa all day tomorrow—lay by the pool. I'll take care of everything."

"I don't want anything from you, *Seamus Heaney*," I burst out, eyes welling up.

A hardened look passed over his face for a split second while he took a deep breath and licked his lips. "Ms. Mercer, please understand what we have here," he said carefully. "This can be a mutually beneficial arrangement." As those last words were spoken, his look became one of caution, as though he were evaluating whether I was going to be too much trouble—whether what had just taken place was worth what he might be risking. After a few minutes of silence, he put his hand underneath my chin, lifting it slightly, and looked into my eyes. "Jane, you can choose to stay here or leave a few minutes after I go. I'll send a car to drop you off at your home if you'd like. Or you can sleep here and get up when you feel like it. Spoil yourself. You deserve it."

Why? Because I'm fresh and new to you? What happens when you tire of me? Will you toss me aside when I'm used up the way you tossed aside my new dress, torn and unwanted? Suddenly, the thought of who I had just slept with, and the enormity of what saying 'no' to someone like him would entail, overcame me. I was on a bumpy emotional thrill ride—vacillating by the minute—hopelessly wedged between sadness and elation, trepidation, and desire. And the longer I looked at his perfectly handsome face and listened to his mesmerizing voice, the more I wanted to please him. In fact, there was nothing—*nothing* I wouldn't do for him now.

"Jane," he repeated. "Will you please stay and get some sleep?"

I nodded finally. "Okay." I forced a smile with watery eyes.

The tension on his face immediately disappeared and he smiled, kissing me tenderly on the forehead. "Good night, beautiful. Sleep tight."

I just stood there, in my crudely pinned-together rags,

on frozen, unmovable legs, and watched him walk away. The door creaked shut behind him and I remained where I was for a few minutes, staring at the door.

I then meandered about the room and surveyed the remnants of Craig everywhere—the used condoms on the floor and the empty shot glasses. The now repugnant warm odors of food wafted from the dining table where we had eaten only a couple of hours earlier. The fireplace was reduced to embers and the candles had burned out.

I imagined him pulling up in the Bentley convertible to his mansion in Bel Air, where his wife and children awaited. He would be full of excuses about late night conference calls and work deadlines. He would kiss his wife, like he did every night, and she would never know where his mouth had been just a short time before he saw her. Maybe he would look in on his two children, already asleep, hugging their teddy bears and dreaming of how Daddy might take them to the beach, or to a sporting event or amusement park the next day. Daddy would always be the strong, remarkable Craig Keller, managing partner of the leading ad agency in their home city—a city with a population of ten million—the City of Angels. He would always be their hero.

I wandered to the empty bed where the sheets were strewn about and wrinkled, the bedspread thrown on the floor, and I lay on my stomach, put my head on the pillow, my chest suddenly heaving with uncontrollable sobs ... sobs only I would hear.

Sixteen

A LOUD KNOCK AT THE door jolted me out of my sleep and filled me with a sense of panic. The digital clock read 9:37 a.m. I supposed it was housekeeping there to throw me out. I realized I had nothing but my underwear (I had located the La Perla bra hanging from the bedroom chandelier and the matching thong stretched across a wall sconce), shredded dress, and boots to wear home. But it was now daylight, and I would be doing the infamous *walk of shame* to get an Uber ride to my apartment.

The knock was louder this time and I heard someone call out, "Room Service."

Hands shaking, I tightened the belt on the hotel robe, which I had slept in, made sure I was fully covered, and hastened my way to the door, opening it a crack and peering out.

A middle-aged Hispanic woman greeted me warmly. "Mrs. Heaney, may I come in, please?" She was wheeling a cart and carrying a large shopping bag emblazoned with the hotel logo. "I have breakfast for you."

I bit my lip. "Actually, I didn't order anything and I'm going to be heading out very soon."

A puzzled look darkened her face for a moment. "Mrs. Heaney, we don't have you and your husband checking out until Sunday at noon."

I wasn't sure what was happening. "Um, sure, yes, of course." I pulled the door open and stood aside to let her in.

"Would you like your breakfast outside on the veranda?"

I didn't answer as she ambled to the French doors and gently swung them open. She turned to me. "Why don't I set things up outside, so you can enjoy your breakfast in the fresh air while I clear these trays and straighten things up?"

"Okay, that's fine." I nodded reluctantly. I really wanted to get out as soon as possible so the dishonor of leaving the hotel in the ripped outfit would be less impactful. At this point, most of the hotel guests would be either having breakfast or walking on the beach.

I watched as the woman set the tray outside on the coffee table, the same one that had cradled the Keller Whitman contract when I signed my life away. I sighed. So much had happened in the past twelve hours. As soon as she was finished, she came in and gestured for me to go outside, "Now you enjoy, Mrs. Heaney."

Mrs. Heaney. *What a travesty.* I went out, plunked down on the same chair I sat in last night and examined the tray. There was a coffee pot, cream, sugar, and a covered silver platter. I could hear the woman inside clearing plates.

The shopping bag had been placed on the chaise lounge. After pouring myself coffee, I opened the bag. It was full of all kinds of things. I quickly emptied its contents onto the chaise and dug through them. There was a stack of neatly folded clothes, with a ribbon tied around to hold them together. There was also a pair of sandals, a two-piece swimsuit, baseball hat with the hotel's beach chair emblem, sunscreen, and a pair of sunglasses. They were all from the resort's retail shop. *What is all this?* I continued to sift through, finding bubble bath, a small rubber duck, and cherry-flavored lip balm.

I looked in the bag again and, at the bottom, there was one last item—a book. I pulled it out and viewed the front cover: *Seamus Heaney Selected Poems, 1966-1987.*

I was suddenly dizzy and out of breath. *It was him.* Craig

Keller sent this stuff to me, so I wouldn't leave. I opened the book and a card fell into my lap. The envelope read, "Mrs. Heaney." I tore it open immediately and pulled out a card. There was Craig's bold handwriting: "Thinking of you, beautiful lass." There was no signature. I flipped through the book and noticed a bookmark, stuck between two pages, marking a poem entitled, "Blackberry-Picking."

I leapt up in my robe and did a victory stretch, closed my eyes, and turned my face to the sky, feeling the sun and its warm rays bathe my face. It was going to be a perfect day because Craig Keller was thinking of me and nothing else mattered. I spent so much time outside, drinking coffee, eating breakfast, and basking in the glory of the beautiful things Craig sent, I hadn't noticed the housekeeping staff moving in and out of the suite.

When I ventured back inside, everything was clean and neat. The sheets were changed, and the bed made. The whole place looked as though no one had been in it; the casualties of last night had been removed and cleaned.

I went into the bathroom for a shower. As I twisted the faucet on hot and let the robe fall to the floor, I glimpsed myself in the full-length mirror and gasped.

From my breasts to my thighs, I was covered in bruises—some little, some large, but there they were, speckling my body like I had some sort of skin disease. I turned my back to the mirror, and it was the same. There were only a few areas that were free of the bite marks, which had turned reddish-purple overnight. I examined one exceptionally large bite on my inner thigh that looked like it might be turning blue. Craig's words, *I'm going to consume you. I hope you're ready,* echoed in my mind. I recalled him sucking on my fingers, one at a time, like they were popsicles. A shudder went down my spine.

I stepped into the hot shower and let the water run all over my body for about five minutes. I rubbed a soapy wash-cloth over the bite marks as though they might come off with the soap, but they remained, an obstinate reminder of him, Craig Keller's branding.

After I toweled off and applied lotion to my skin, I laid all the clothes on the bed and located underwear, a pair of shorts and a T-shirt. Surprisingly, they fit perfectly and none of the bruises were visible with clothes on. I wondered if he had planned it that way, and a sense of discomfort emerged at the reality that he might be that calculated.

I went for a walk along the stretch of bike path lacing through Santa Monica to Venice, just wanting to be alone with my thoughts, trying to make sense of everything. When I finished about three miles, I returned to the pier, which was located near the hotel. I grabbed a coffee, and, amid the tchotchke-buying tourists, environmental entertainers, and homeless people, I advanced toward the ocean.

I stared out for miles, listening to the soothing waves crashing softly beneath me as the crusty old fishermen cast lures into the sea. I leaned out as far as I could on the rail and inhaled the sea air. The water right beneath the pier lapped persistently against the wooden pilings, which were stained various shades of green from withstanding decades of shifting tides and the occasional storm.

A sudden cloud of sadness swept over me, and my thoughts went to Derek. I seemed to have alienated my core group of friends in a short time and I wondered how they were all spending their weekend. Likely, none of them were squatting in an expensive resort on the beach after having kinky sex with a rich, married advertising executive. I remembered Marisa admonishing me for hurting Derek and I decided to call him from the beach to make amends.

I sat in the damp sand at the line right before it became wet with ocean, pulled my phone out and dialed his number. I heard ringing and began doodling Craig Keller's name in the sand with a stick I had found.

"What's up?" Derek answered in a distant tone.

"How've you been?"

There was a long pause. "Just busy," he said in the same cold voice.

"Well, I just wanted to call and catch up, that's all."

There was another long pause. "Right. So, you can insult

me again. No thanks."

"Derek, I didn't mean to insult you," I insisted, getting the distinct feeling I shouldn't have called.

"Seriously? You accused me of dating my twenty-three-year-old ex-student. What do you call that?" It sounded like he had been holding back his anger until he had an opportunity to give me a whack.

"I'm sorry, Derek. I just thought you and she were together. It's not an insult. She's beautiful and perfect for you." I thought about Chelsea, who probably, right at this moment, was in ballet class, performing a triple pirouette, landing perfectly into fifth position. I had a hunch Chelsea never broke a sweat, experienced a hangover, or had to cover bruises from last night's roll in the hay with her new boss.

"Um, *hello*, you insinuated I'm gay, Jane, do you remember that? Or did you conveniently forget, like you do about everyone else's feelings?" His voice had raised.

"Derek, listen," I said as I smoothed over the Craig Keller doodle with my foot. I was standing now, pacing along with my feet in the water, which got deeper with every step. "I was in a bad mood, you know, I've had a lot of stress lately."

"Really?" he shot back. "Well, it may interest you to know that a lot of people have stress in their lives, but maybe they don't take it out on their friends." His voice had lowered to a flat, icy timbre I didn't recognize.

"Derek, all I can do is apologize. It'll never happen again." When he said nothing, I switched my tone to syrupy sweet. "There must be some way I can make it up to you."

Not only did Derek not take the bait, but he seemed more disgusted by my attempt to woo him into subservience. "There's nothing, Jane. I know what kind of guys you go after and the fact that you put me in that same category just about kills me."

There was something unyielding in his voice. It wasn't even anger now. It was worse. It was disappointment. I thought about everything that had gone on lately and some profoundly real emotion washed over me. I started to tear up trying to think of something to say that would change his mind. "Derek," I implored, my voice now shaking. "You're wrong. I don't put you into the same category as anyone else. You're better. You know that. I don't know what to say other than I messed up. Can you please … *please* just forgive me?"

After another long pause, he said coldly, "I don't think we should talk for a while."

"You mean, we're no longer friends?"

"You know Jane, you really had me conned. I thought you were cool. I felt like I could tell you anything. Then I found out who you really are—a self-centered little girl who plays with people. And I'm not the only one who thinks that. You've changed and you're just not the kind of person I want in my life."

His words felt like a sharp knife, stabbing me in the stomach over and over. I felt like I was going to suffocate as I staggered further and further into the ocean. The clothes Craig Keller had purchased for me were soaked. I was up to my waist in water and a wave was coming directly at me. I tried to retreat but couldn't breathe.

I stood on my tiptoes and dodged the breaking wave while I pressed the phone close to my ear. "I'm not like that, Derek—you know me—no, seriously, you know the real me. You're acting like I'm evil or something. I'm not like that."

There was silence on the other end. I held the phone straight up to the sky. Another wave propelled me slightly towards the shore as it passed. I felt my body being immediately drawn back by the riptide. When I regained my balance, I put the phone back to my ear. "Derek," I pleaded, now desperate. "Don't do this—please don't."

"I need to hang up now, Jane," he returned. "I wish you the best of luck. I'll only say nice things about you."

The line went dead. I stood there watching the tide rising, clutching the phone, and staring at another huge wave headed straight for me. The water was now up to my shoulders and there was nothing I could do because I was going under. My head slipped under water as the ocean thrashed me towards the shore, phone still clutched in my hand as

I got lost in the merciless tide. Miraculously, I managed to come up for air, coughing, choking, and spitting saltwater out of my mouth. My nose burned with the sting of brine as I paddled with the current to find my way back to shore. When I got there, I stumbled out of the water and lay on my back in the warm sand, clothes saturated and stuck to my body, the useless phone still in my grip. I tried to breathe but I felt hot tears streaming down my face. Derek had disowned me. It was almost unconscionable that Derek cut me off so quickly. I had spats with girlfriends before but nothing like this. Marisa and Kat wouldn't just cut me off … *or would they?* I thought about Derek's words, 'I'm not the only one who thinks that.' *What exactly did he mean? Was my trio of friends out there talking trash about me now? Was I an outsider from my once-inner circle?*

After lying in the sand for what seemed like forever, I realized, with sudden urgency, that I needed to pull myself together and get back to the hotel. I got up, covered in sand and seaweed, and vainly tried to dust myself off. I peered to the north and saw that I had drifted far from Shutters on the Beach while I was in the water. I could barely see the trademark white latticed wooden rails in the distance.

The hotel key and my credit card had remained zipped in my shorts pocket, so I slowly trudged back to the hotel suite and unlocked the door. As soon as I was inside, I stripped off the wet, sandy clothes immediately and threw them outside on the veranda. It was already close to 4 p.m.

I surveyed the room to see what clothes I needed to make a swift exit. Luckily, Craig Keller had left a hooded sweatshirt and a mini skirt, so I would be able to wear dry clothes home. I would use the two-piece swimsuit as underwear. I went to the bathroom and began to run hot water for the bath. I found the bubble bath Craig had left and poured some into the running water.

I waited for the hot water to fill the tub, still obsessing about the Derek situation. Once the tub was full, I lowered myself into the hot, sudsy bath. I sank in deep, so the suds were almost covering my face. The water's warmth felt soothing after the ice-cold Pacific Ocean had tossed me angrily underneath its murky surface. I took several deep breaths and heard the door of the suite swing open.

"Room Service," a man called, the voice familiar.

Fuck! Not again. I rose from the bathtub, suds all over me, reached frantically for a towel from the rack adjacent to the tub, and screamed, "Please don't come in. I'm—indecent!"

As soon as I grabbed hold of a towel and pulled it from the rack, a man entered the bathroom. It was none other than Craig Keller, dressed in a dark olive Adidas track suit with the jacket unzipped enough to expose his tanned and slightly hairy chest. His hair was wind-blown, and his light green eyes sparkled. He looked positively gorgeous in a roughhewn way.

I froze at the sight of him, my heart cartwheeling, then I dropped the towel and slinked down into the tub to hide my bruised body under the sudsy water.

"I'm perfectly aware of your indecency, Ms. Mercer," he said, leaning against the doorframe, eyeing me lazily. "The question," he continued, picking up a green apple from the bowl of fruit on the sink and going back to lean against the doorframe, "is how much more indecent can you be?" He took a large bite from the apple and chewed it thoroughly, not taking his eyes off me for one second.

I stayed underwater, the suds dwindling slightly but still covering my body as I watched Craig continue to take bites of the apple and chew slowly, the muscles in his cheekbones and jawline flexing. I wasn't sure how to respond to his innuendos and was in no mood to play sex games. I just wanted to go home, to have someone tell me everything was going to be okay.

"You're awfully quiet today," he observed, finishing the apple, and casually throwing the core into the bathroom wastebasket. He sat on the bath's wide marble rim, right next to me. He leaned forward, placed his elbows onto his knees, and studied my face. "How's the bath water?" As he said this, he rolled up one sleeve of his jacket, plunged his hand in the water and cleared away the suds so my breasts were plainly in view.

I instinctively crossed my arms over them. "What are you doing?" My voice smacked of anxiety.

He just smiled with those apple-fresh teeth gleaming, eyelashes glossy and seductive. "What am *I* doing?" he replied, gently pulling one of my hands from across my breasts and placing it under the water, directly between my legs. "I have the same question for you," he said as he held it there.

I pulled my hand away as though he had lit it on fire. "I—I'm not into that," I protested, the fear in my voice filling the room like cheap perfume.

"Not into what?" Looking amused, he stood and sauntered out, calling smoothly over his shoulder, "I'll be right back." I heard him go to the living room, flip on the sound system, which was playing a song by Glass Animals: ironically, one of Derek's favorites. I heard him pop open a bottle of champagne and return to the bedroom, the sound of clinking glasses getting closer. He re-entered the bathroom with two full flutes of champagne, placing one glass on the side of the tub and sitting down again next to me in silence, holding the other.

He took a sip of his champagne and set the glass down. His green eyes were fixed intently on me. Then, he picked up the other champagne glass and held it to my lips, tipping it slightly. I obediently swallowed, tasting the bubbly alcohol going down my throat and straight to my head.

"Close your eyes, Jane," he instructed. "Relax and pretend I'm not even here."

As he said this, he leaned into the tub and put his hand over my eyes, gently touching my eyelids closed with his fingertips. Then, he began to massage my shoulders, simultaneously talking to me in his soothing voice.

"Close your eyes, beautiful. Don't think about anything." He alternated massaging my shoulders and giving me measured sips of champagne until I started to feel like I was at his command. He wet a washcloth in the water and lightly moved it across my skin.

He took my hand, once again, and put it under the

water but, this time, he took his hand away immediately, got to his feet, shut the bathroom door, and turned off the light. I felt him sit right back down before me in the dark, the intoxicating smell of his skin in the air. I inhaled, deeply, wanting to keep his scent within me forever.

"You're so sexy," he whispered, "I thought about you all day today. I couldn't wait to get back here to be with you. You know that, right?"

I lost myself in his dulcet tones and the apprehension melted blissfully away. I knew he was watching me in the dark, like a lion, carefully observing and sensing my every move. I felt him get closer, his breath on my mouth, but he didn't kiss me.

The nerves in my lower back tingled, slowly crawling up my spine to the back of my neck and then to my head. I became more breathless with every passing second. Finally, I leaned against the back of the tub and cried out loud, the ecstasy wrapping me in its thrall, as bubbles swirled around, and the rhythmic music reached a lofty crescendo. I opened my eyes, but Craig Keller was not there.

I rose immediately from the water, gasping slightly as my breath slowly returned to normal. The door was open now and the light from the afternoon sun was bleeding through the doorway. He had left a towel where he was sitting, so I wrapped it around my body and jumped out of the tub, nearly slipping, and falling on the slick, wet floor.

I wandered out to the living room, feeling like I was high on something other than champagne and saw him out on the veranda, on his cell phone. The French doors were shut so I couldn't hear what he was saying.

While he was occupied, I located the hotel robe, threw it on, grabbed a comb at the same time and pulled it through my wet hair. I then sat near the French doors and observed him from inside the suite. He appeared confident and swanky as he moved from one side of the veranda to the other in his olive track suit with his tall, lean figure. He continued to sip his champagne when he was not talking with a focused expression. When he finished the conversation, he put his phone in his pants pocket and entered the room, shutting the French doors behind him.

"So, Ms. Mercer, how do you feel?" Astonishingly, he sounded almost punitive.

"Um, great," I responded.

"That's good to hear," he replied coldly, sitting next to me on the couch, but not too close. "You know, I tried to call you earlier. I called the hotel room and then your cell phone several times, but it went directly to voicemail." There was a sharpness in his voice now and I was not clear as to the reason. "I texted you three times with no response," he added.

My thoughts went back to my phone, the ugly conversation with Derek and wrestling with the riptide. "I'm sorry," I said contritely. "My cell phone died."

He cocked an eyebrow at me doubtfully.

"I'm serious," I said, jumping up to locate my phone. I found it and handed it to Craig, whose eyes followed me suspiciously. "You see?" It seemed he still didn't believe me. "I accidentally dropped it in the ocean."

He took the phone and turned it over, pressed his fingers against the screen and, when he was satisfied that it truly didn't work, tossed it on the coffee table. He turned his attention back to me. "What were you doing at the beach?"

I stood before him, like I was on trial. "I just wanted to take a walk," I replied.

"And who said you could do that?" His tone was deadpan.

I felt my eyes water. He patted the couch next to him. "Sit." I took slow, measured steps, and sat down next to him again, being careful not to sit too close. He reached into his pants pocket, pulled out business card and handed it to me. I sat up straight and stared at him.

"What's this?" I looked at him curiously. I examined the business card of a woman named Delcine Bianchi, with the title underneath, Personal Shopper. I gave him a wide-eyed stare. "What's this for?"

"I destroyed your dress," he said. "I have no idea what you paid, but if you call Delcine, she'll meet you wherever you want—take care of whatever you want." Before I could respond, he leaned toward me. "In fact, I want you to go *crazy*."

"I—I'm not comfortable with that," I stammered, horrified at being treated like a prostitute; although, based on my estimation of what Craig might consider 'crazy,' I suspected not a common one.

"Oh, sure you are." He focused his intense gaze on me.

"What do you mean?" I felt my throat tighten.

"Last night." He was not at all amused by my reaction.

"What about last night?" I repeated, feeling my mouth drop open. I stood and moved a few feet away from him. "I came here expecting dinner—a business dinner. You were the one who got a room."

He rose to his feet. "But it was you, my dear, who stayed. You made a choice as soon as you got into that elevator, Jane. *You* made the choice. No one forced you. You could have walked away. But you didn't." I watched his eyes turn from the light jade to a darker color, almost the color of his track suit. His tone was calm and collected, but there was a firm, level finality to it that had me on edge. "Tell me, Ms. Mercer, do you always wear such lingerie underneath your clothes for a *work* dinner? Do you always keep yourself so ..." he paused to lower his gaze before looking me in the eye again ... "Smooth—*all over?*"

I felt my cheeks turn scarlet. He knew I had exhaustively prepared for him—he knew our encounter was premeditated—that I was just waiting for the opportunity. I just wished he wouldn't have said it out loud. I wished he would have let me hold on to a shred of dignity. But he was intent upon humiliating me. A sudden fury gurgled from the depths of my abdomen. I thrust Delcine's business card toward him. "I don't want your money." My voice shook.

His eyebrows raised but he didn't move. He was studying me as though fascinated.

"Take it," I shouted, advancing toward him so I was staring right up into his mercurial green eyes. I knew I was playing with fire now—and I didn't care.

A smile tugged at the corners of his mouth like he was stifling a grin.

"You—you're laughing at me now?" I said, feeling my lower lip jut out. "Right, because I'm so funny—I'm so pathetic to you—so *fucking* desperate." I felt angry tears forming and I turned my head to the side so he wouldn't see.

"Jane," he said with unexpected tenderness. "I'd never laugh at you. You're just very—surprising, I guess." He seemed genuine—almost complimentary in this assessment.

I couldn't stop the tears from coming now—my hands flew up to cover my face. I felt his arms around me now, pulling me close and I inhaled his soapiness again. "Come on, Jane," Craig whispered. "Go shopping—consider it a signing bonus."

I breathed his scent deeply, and my lips were tasting the chest hair that poked out of his track suit jacket. His arms felt warm around me. "Okay, fine," I mumbled, too exhausted now to object. I felt him take the card out of my hand and drop it into my robe pocket.

"Good," he said, ending the conversation and withdrawing. He looked at his watch, which I noticed was an expensive Breguet Marine timepiece, one only someone of great wealth would be able to purchase as a collector, not necessarily to wear on a Saturday afternoon—with a track suit. "I need to run now. You should stay another night, *Mrs. Heaney*," he proposed, eyeing my wet hair, and drawing a lock behind my ear.

I shook my head. "I'll get a taxi home now." The thought of spending another lonely night in this room, as lovely as it was, nauseated me. I realized it was now after 5 p.m. and I had not been home to feed Weezer. He was probably, at this minute, circling his food bowl like I'd abandoned him for good.

Craig promptly looked displeased. *What was he expecting me to do? Stay holed up in this hotel room until Sunday in the event he might show up?*

"I need to feed my cat," I said, hoping I could appeal to his sense of compassion in caring for a helpless animal.

"I'll send a car for you," Craig answered, ignoring my comment, pulling his phone from his pocket, and scrolling through his contacts.

"No, that's okay, really."

"I insist. Go get dressed," he commanded, nodding toward the bedroom.

I followed his orders and went to the bedroom, took the card out of the robe and dropped it in my purse, pushing it in the interior pocket as though I needed to hide it well. I pulled on the swimsuit, miniskirt, and hooded sweatshirt. I covered my head with the baseball cap and stashed the sunglasses in my bag. I found my boots to carry downstairs with me, leaving the ripped dress for the maids to take. I refused to look in the mirror for fear of what I'd see.

When I emerged from the bedroom, Craig was seated on the couch talking on his cell phone, his long legs crossed. When he saw me, he told the person on the other end of the line he had to go and stood. "Ready?" he asked, without smiling.

"I think so." I was hoping for some sign of affection—I felt like we had broken the ice somehow. But he had drawn an invisible line of demarcation between us again.

"I have a car coming for you at six," he said. "It'll meet you in valet. The driver's name is Pierre. I had him swing by my office to get you an agency phone. All you'll need to do is call the phone company when you get home."

"Really?" I perked up. "Thank you so much. You saved me today." I took a few steps toward him so that I was an arm's length away. He remained where he was, stone-faced.

"Are you forgetting anything?" he asked.

My eyes ping-ponged frantically around the room, feeling like this was some sort of a test. I spotted the Seamus Heaney book sitting, untouched, on the coffee table. I grabbed it as fast as I could and dropped it in my bag. I could feel his eyes studying me as I made this move. "I can't forget this evening's reading material," I said with a nervous laugh.

Craig did not smile. "Ms. Mercer," he said without emotion. "Let me give you a piece of advice. You're either in, or you're out. Don't *ever* make me have to find you. I was very busy today, and, when I called and you weren't available, it made me wonder what happened. I'm not the kind of man who likes to *wonder* about anything."

My smile disappeared. "It was an accident. Things happen."

"Listen to me," he said, now pressing forward with his face so close, I could smell him again. His pupils were aglow as he stared down almost ruthlessly into mine, but his voice remained calm. "As soon as you get home, you will call the phone company to connect your phone. When it's connected, you will send me a text, confirming that it was done. Do you understand?"

I nodded, feeling prickles at the nape of my neck.

"Let me hear you say it," he said forcefully, yet still devoid of emotion.

"Yes, I … understand," my voice quavered a little with the last syllable, his towering presence was so intimidating.

"Good," he said flatly, and stepped around me, exiting the suite. There was no kiss goodbye; there was not even a hug. In fact, he didn't touch me at all. He withdrew his affection because he wanted to punish me for crossing him—for going to the ocean without his permission—for not staying another night at the hotel. And he wielded the biggest weapon of all: himself.

So, this was Craig Axel Keller, I thought: an expert in both the boardroom and the bedroom, a manipulator with extraordinary prowess, which he could turn on and off at will. He had full control over me, and he knew it. He set out to do it because he knew I wouldn't dare resist. Kat's ominous words came to mind: 'I hope you avoid him.' *She knows.* She knows something, and it was too unspeakable to share. And it wasn't just a bad business deal. There was something else, something deeper.

Even though it was only 5:45 p.m., I sped out of the room in a panic. I took the service stairs recklessly, two at a time, almost falling in the process because I didn't want to be confined in the elevator. When I got out of the hotel, I considered having the bellman call me a taxi. But I stopped in my tracks, thinking that would send Craig Keller into anger orbit. Plus, I needed the new phone. My body trembled from head to toe.

I waited for Pierre while sitting on a bench outside Shutters on the Beach, my thoughts muddled. I thought about Warren and Jeffrey and, even Philippe, the French thug. They paled in comparison to this shark, whom I had somehow managed both to have sex with and to piss off over the course of twenty-four hours.

I opened my purse, remembering the card sitting in the zipped pouch. I pulled it out and stared at it. Delcine Bianchi, Personal Shopper. She must be at Craig's beck and call. I pictured him calling Delcine and asking for a certain Italian silk tie, or a pair of cufflinks. I thought about what it would be like to have a personal shopper—to *go crazy*, as he had urged—and whether I would regret it in the end. It suddenly struck me that for someone who made such a huge fuss out of declaring himself one who didn't follow rules, he doled out more rules than anyone I'd ever met in my life. I just signed a contract with this guy. *What had I gotten myself into?*

Seventeen

*P*IERRE ARRIVED IN A black limousine on time and with phone in hand. He was a short man with a thick neck and small, shifty eyes. He seemed to be decent, however, a devoted servant to *Mr. Keller,* as he frequently called him. He helped me with my phone, which happened to be the newest version of the iPhone. I asked him to stay and wait with me in the parking lot of my apartment while I connected the new phone, my anxiety mounting from Craig Keller's earlier orders.

As soon as the phone was turned on and the settings working, I sent a text to His Highness: "Phone is working." He did not immediately respond.

I thanked Pierre and scuttled up to my apartment, feeling like I had been away for an eternity. Everything was there, exactly as I had left it Friday night. Weezer was, predictably, perturbed as I opened the cupboard to get his food. After feeding Weez, it occurred to me I had not eaten since breakfast. I scoured the pantry, found a can of tomato soup and began heating it over the stove.

My new phone, which was charging on the kitchen counter, began to light up with phone messages and texts. I must have quite a few, I thought since the phone had been shut down for several hours.

As I sat at the counter eating my soup, I picked up the phone and scrolled through the texts. There were only the three to which Craig Keller had earlier referred. One at 1:17 p.m. said, "Where are you?"; another at 2:10 said, "Why haven't you responded?"; and another at 3:25 said, "On my way."

I sighed deeply and lay my head down on the kitchen counter in regret. From his point of view, it certainly did appear that something had happened to me. There were three missed calls from his phone number, but no voice mail, which made my heart burn with longing. I now wanted to have a recording of his voice—something I could play over and over to remember exactly how he sounded.

I dialed into the voicemail messages and there were several from my grandparents. I played back the messages and heard Grandma's voice: "Hey, Pigeon, I'm making roast chicken and those fried potatoes you like so much. See you at 5:30."

Crap, I thought as I checked the time—already 7:45. With all my misadventures at Shutters on the Beach, I totally forgot I had scheduled dinner with them.

I glanced at my phone nervously but there was still no text response from Craig. I dug through my handbag and pulled out both the Seamus Heaney book and Delcine's business card. I opened the book to the poem Craig had drawn to my attention, "Blackberry-Picking," and read it several times. It was scarcely a romantic Shakespearean sonnet; nor was it light, airy wordplay. It was instead dark and brooding, deeply sexual, with references to picking fresh blackberries that are sweet and taste like wine but end up rotting in the can like sour milk in yesterday's sun. I was hardly an English major but had read some poetry, enough to know there was always a deeper meaning. I recalled his words again: *I'm going to consume you—I hope you're ready*. A feeling of sadness gnawed at me that maybe I was like a ripe blackberry to Craig—one that would rot soon after being picked unless I was devoured right away.

I searched the poem online and found a lot of essays

devoted to this one poem, most of them academic rubbish. I wondered again why he chose this poem. I placed the business card between the leaves of "Blackberry-Picking," closed the book, and put it in my nightstand drawer.

By the time it was 9 p.m. I was exhausted but still didn't want to go to bed. I fidgeted and kept checking my phone for a message from Craig, but he was eerily silent. I sat listlessly until I realized I had been so distracted; I never called my grandparents back. I picked up my new phone, dialed their number and Grandma answered straight away.

"Jane! *Oy Vey*, what's going on? Why didn't you call? We've been worried sick!"

"Grandma, I'm sorry—I had to work and then my cell phone died."

"What is with this work? You said you had to work Friday night and now Saturday? What kind of job is this anyway? Don't they know you're Jewish?"

I had a sudden flashback of me writhing on top of Craig Keller in my stiletto-heeled boots while he ravenously bit into my breasts, and I felt the familiar ambivalence of shame and desire return. "Grandma," I protested, "Please don't make me feel worse than I already do. I had to get a new phone."

She began yelling at Grandpa but not bothering to cover the phone with her hand, "It's Jane. She's all *fercockt* with work again—lost her phone."

"Grandma listen to me. I didn't *lose* my phone. It died. There's a difference." I wondered why I had bothered calling tonight. I could have remained a saintly no-show if I had just gone straight to bed. But then they likely would have sent the police for a wellness check.

"I worked all day to make your favorite meal and now it's going to waste!" she continued. I could hear her cigarette lighter flicking several times, Grandpa complaining in the background, something about why I always put work before family and how my priorities are screwed up.

"Grandma, I'm going to spend Thanksgiving with you and then Chanukah starts soon after. We'll have plenty of time together, I promise."

She sighed into the phone.

"Grandma?"

"All right, have it your way, Jane." She sounded ready to cry. I couldn't stand it when she played the guilt card with me.

"How about if I come over next weekend, okay, Grandma?"

"I'll believe it when I see it," she uttered dolefully before hanging up.

That was it. I slogged to the kitchen, pulled out a bottle of Belvedere vodka from the freezer and poured a shot. It went down so easy, I immediately felt better. After three more, I picked up my phone.

Again, there was nothing from Craig Keller. I cursed him for ignoring me and considered calling him. *What would he do if I called him while he was in bed with his wife?* I pictured him sleeping soundly in his Bel Air mansion, carefree and happily unaware that I was having a drunken meltdown on a Saturday night in Santa Monica.

The vodka was making me hungry, so I picked up the phone again and ordered a pepperoni pizza. I took another shot of vodka and realized, with disgust, that I hadn't changed my clothes since I had been home. I walked unsteadily to my bedroom, shedding one piece of clothing at a time, leaving a trail all the way. Once in the bedroom, stark naked, I examined my body in the full-length mirror and, through the haze of my impaired vision, spied the most hideous of apparitions.

My face was a mask that looked sort of like me but with swollen, blood-shot eyes, body branded with the appalling discolorations courtesy of His Highness, and I became nauseous. I went to the toilet and heaved violently, laid my head down on the toilet seat, and started to cry hysterically. Everything that had happened over the past month started to flow out in the form of tears: lies, deceit, powerlessness, rage, obsession, secrecy. I wept as though the despair would exit my body and leave me at peace.

Later, the incessant buzzing of the intercom brought me back to consciousness. I clumsily picked myself off the floor and staggered to the front door. It was the Domino's Pizza guy with my pepperoni pie.

"Come up," I said in a raspy voice before buzzing him in. I stumbled back to my room, ricocheting off the walls, but managed to find my white fuzzy robe and a twenty-dollar bill.

When I opened the door, the guy glared at me as he handed me the box. "Jesus, lady," he grumbled, "I was out there for like twenty minutes."

"I'm sorry," was all I could eek out. I accepted the pizza, shut and locked the door. I placed the pizza on the kitchen counter and opened the box, realizing I was no longer hungry. I saw my phone sitting there, still charging, and a thread of hope emerged. I grabbed the phone to check messages but there was not one text and not one voicemail.

"I hate you, Craig Keller," I shrieked to the indifferent universe. "I hate you, I hate you, I *hate* you!" I hurled the open box across the room and the pizza flew out, spinning like a frisbee. It smashed into the wall near the front door, cheese and red sauce oozing down over my Big Ben clock, narrowly missing Weez, who scurried to hide under an end table.

I wanted to call Marisa, but it was too late, and I was too drunk. I decided to text her, so she would see it in the morning. "Marisa, I need you" was all I was able to type into my new phone and, since I couldn't see well enough to note autocorrect issues, it could have said "Bring me a chocolate Billy goat," for all I knew.

I turned the phone ringer off and plugged it into its charger. I popped two sleeping pills, washed them down with a glass of wine and teetered to the couch. I was passed out cold until the next day.

Someone was banging at my door and incessantly ringing the doorbell. I wondered if it were the police trying to arrest me. "Jane, open up!" Marisa shouted from outside.

"I'm here, I'm here," I called sleepily as I unlocked and opened the door.

"Oh my god, Jane. It's already one o'clock. I've been calling you for hours. What were you doing?"

"What do you think I was doing?" I growled. She elbowed her way through my apartment, examining everything like she was uncovering a murder case. She scooped up the three-quarters-empty vodka bottle, the shot glass, and the container of sleeping pills.

"Is this Amy Winehouse's flat?" she asked, eyeing the wall with the stuck-on pizza. "Yuck," she said scrunching up her nose in disapproval and then turning her attention to me. "You look like hell. No, you look worse than hell," she said, almost fearfully. "Where were you? No, wait. I want to know *who* you are."

"Which question do you want me to answer first, Marisa?" I muttered, feeling my head pounding like someone leveled a crowbar down hard on it. I lumbered back to the couch, where I had passed out all night, and lay down again.

"Well?" Marisa demanded. "Are you going to tell me what happened last night?"

"Maybe after some coffee," I responded in a gravelly voice.

"Fine," she retorted, spinning around, and marching to the kitchen, emerging five minutes later with a cup of hot coffee and a bottle of Advil. She set both on the coffee table and sat next to me on the couch. "There," she said. "Now start talking."

I took a deep breath and sipped the coffee. I got four Advils out and tried to pop them when Marisa stopped me.

"The adult dose is two of those," she scolded, wagging her finger in front of my nose.

"How about a compromise?" I offered, putting three pills in my mouth, and attempting to swallow them with a large gulp of coffee, burning my tongue and throat, breaking into a coughing fit immediately after. I somehow managed to swallow. The remaining pill fell on the floor and rolled like a marble under the couch.

Marisa just stared at me in disgust—like my condition might be contagious. "Jane, I know something's wrong. You've not been yourself for a while now. Whatever it is, we'll deal with it, but I can't help if you don't talk to me."

"You have to promise—Marisa—promise not to judge me or tell another living soul," I said grimly. "I mean this is more than just a pinky swear—this is a lot bigger."

"Okay, what do you want from me? I cross my heart and hope to die," she said, mocking me by drawing an imaginary cross over her chest with her finger.

"That's not worth much to a Jewish woman but, what I want, Marisa—what I really need—is for you to swear you won't share this with Kat or Derek," I requested with an edge in my voice.

She shot me a look with a Botox-thwarted attempt at furrowed brows. "What are you so worried about?"

"I'm sure you already know this, but Derek cut me loose

yesterday. We're no longer friends. And that's not all. He implied in our last official conversation that you and Kat were pissed at me, too."

Marisa's look went from skepticism to gloom. "I'm sorry, Jane. Yes, I'll admit we've had a few conversations about you but it's not like I was going to drop you as a friend. You and I have history together."

I focused my eyes on Marisa's, trying to assess her trustworthiness. "Fine," I concluded. "Then I have your word?"

She nodded. As I began to slowly unfold the story about Warren and Jeffrey, the lunch with Philippe, Marisa's eyes widened, and her mouth opened several times, like she thought I was making it up. "You promised that?"

"I know, Marisa." I touched my forehead—the Advil had not yet kicked in. "I knew it was so wrong, but Jeffrey and Warren, you know, they put a lot of pressure on me."

Marisa stood and began pacing my apartment, the sound of her high-heeled boots pounding the hardwood floor. She suddenly stopped in front of me. "Is there any way you can go to Warren now? I mean, before that creep returns from Paris?"

"Well, I've not told you everything. There's another major factor at play."

"Like what?" she said. "What haven't you told me?"

"You're going to want to sit down," I said, taking a deep breath as I watched Marisa lower herself on the couch next to me.

"Well?"

"Well, I sort of got, um, involved with … Craig Keller." *There, I said it out loud.*

"What?" Her expression turned from empathy to shock. "What do you mean *involved*? How *involved*? Like, are you going to go work for him? Or did you sleep with him?"

I looked her directly in the eye but said nothing.

"Oh my god, Jane," she screeched, glaring at me, and jolting upright as though she had accidentally backed up against a hot stove burner. "You're having a fling with Craig Keller, aren't you? Oh my god. Of all the girls I would have suspected, it would never have been you."

"What's that supposed to mean?" I demanded, hangover headache throbbing as I stared at her in indignation. "Am I not good enough for him?"

"Oh, Jane, please. Any attractive woman is good enough for him. I get it. I totally get how this happened. I was there when you met him. There was chemistry. I knew you'd fall for him. I guess I just thought you'd be more rational, you know, about who he is. It's not like he hides it or anything."

"Marisa, it gets worse. I signed a contract to go work for him and I need to give Warren notice as soon as I get the executed contract back. It could be as soon as tomorrow."

Marisa got up and paced the floor for a few minutes again, not saying anything. Every now and then, she would turn to me as though she were going to ask a question but instead, would turn and continue pacing, like she was working through something in her head but not ready to share.

"Marisa, please say something already." I hung my head between my knees for a minute to let the nausea pass.

Marisa stopped pacing and turned to me. "Are you in love with him?"

I thought of the constant roller coaster and how Craig never returned my text last night. I then realized I had not checked my phone since the dreaded pizza incident. Despite my throbbing head and acute nausea, I jumped off the couch like I was ready for a sprint and found my phone near the empty wine glass. Still nothing from His Highness.

"What's going on, now?" The suspicion in Marisa's voice was palpable.

I looked up at her and sighed. "I was hoping for a text, that's all."

When she saw the look on my face, she smiled wryly. "It's him, isn't it?"

I shut my eyes and nodded.

"Well, I guess you don't need to answer my last question." She shook her head. "Jane Mercer and Craig Keller, *the* Craig Keller. Man, when you go for it, you really go for broke." Marisa's eyes widened. "Have you talked to Kat? I mean, she could probably share some serious intel on Keller, you know, before you commit to working with him *and* sleeping with him."

"I've tried to talk to Kat a couple of times. She never wants to talk about him," I said. "Besides, it's too late, now."

"Well, in view of how things have taken a turn, maybe you should try again," Marisa advised.

"Look, I'm not ready to tell anyone else about this. Telling you is hard enough. I'm not sure what I'm going to do yet."

Marisa's face was now filled with anxiety, like her best friend had gone over the edge of a steep cliff and she was just standing there, watching me fade to black. "I don't know Jane," she said shaking her head in doubt. "I think you're playing with fire on this one. I would be very, very careful of how you handle that man."

I sighed deeply. "Can we drop the subject for now, Marisa?" I said, my hangover giving way to exhaustion. Then I remembered Delcine's business card in the nightstand, and I perked up slightly. "Do you want to go shopping? I need retail therapy."

"I'll bet you do," Marisa said, giving me the once over and making a face. "You need a shower, too. In the meantime, I'll clean that mess off your wall. You're just inviting roaches, you know—so disgusting!"

I entered my bedroom, shut the door, and pulled the Seamus Heaney book out of my nightstand. I plucked the business card from between its leaves and carefully dialed the number. After one ring, a pleasant woman with a deep voice answered. "Delcine Bianchi, how may I be of service?"

AN HOUR OR SO later, we were headed to Neiman Marcus, the one on Wilshire Boulevard. I had asked Delcine to meet me at the Beverly Hills mecca, not my usual haunt in Santa Monica. I decided not to mention Delcine to Marisa just yet.

Marisa volunteered to drive and, as we became reacquainted with our girl gossip on the ride down, I realized I had not even asked about Marisa's life. "So, how's it going with Drew?" I asked, tentatively, remembering our last conversation about him was not exactly positive.

"Oh fine, I guess," she responded. "I mean, we finally, you know, did it." She looked in the rearview mirror as though she were worried someone may have overheard her.

"You did? How was it?"

"Okay," she replied with a bored expression. "Just okay."

"No details?" I asked, snapping my head in her direction.

"I'll give details about Drew the day you give details about Craig Keller," she said, like she was brokering a deal for a television interview.

I stared down in my lap. "I'd rather not."

"Oh, please, Jane. He's the sexiest man in LA. Can you at least tell me whether he's good? I mean, is all the hype true?"

"What hype?" I asked, turning toward her again with curiosity, recalling his insatiable appetite and incessant biting—the whole consumption thing.

"You know—what everyone says about him," she said tearing her eyes from the road to glance at me. "Supposedly, he's an expert in *certain* areas."

I thought about Craig again, with his controlled conversational probing, aggressiveness, and premeditated sexual games, and a shiver went up my spine. "He's … intense."

"'Intense'," Marisa repeated. "Intense, how? Like, what does he actually *do*? Is he, you know, big?"

I felt my face redden. "Marisa, the man is six foot five. If you're asking me whether it hurt after the third, fourth time, yes. It hurts now to sit in these jeans. Is that enough detail?"

Marisa's jaw dropped as though she were imagining it. "Um, yes, I guess so—that says a lot." She drew in a deep breath and let it out slowly before making a lane change. "With Drew, there was simply no passion. I felt like I was in a porn movie or something, like he was, you know, acting."

"Where is he now?" I thought about the past discussions about his ambivalence toward Marisa and wondered why he decided to finally take the plunge.

"In London. He left Friday and won't be back for

another ten days," she explained.

"Do you miss him?" I thought about Craig and the fact that he still had not responded to my text. *What the hell was he waiting for? Enough with the punishment, already.* I didn't know how Marisa was handling herself so well.

"Of course, I do," she replied. "It's just never about me with him. He just comes and goes as he pleases, calls me occasionally and, you know, I'm so busy that I stopped obsessing over it. Well, sort of."

"I think we can both use the retail therapy today," I remarked with a sigh.

WHEN WE ARRIVED AT Neiman's, we meandered into the cosmetics area, where I was supposed to meet Delcine. I picked up a fragrance by Francis Kurkdjian, and sprayed a tiny bit on my wrist, thinking about how I would explain Delcine's impending arrival to Marisa.

"I've been considering a new fragrance," I started as Marisa picked up a tester bottle and sprayed it into the air.

She grimaced. "Ooh, that's way too strong," she remarked, replacing the bottle on the counter. "You do know how much this stuff costs, right?"

A tall, middle-aged woman dressed in a black pantsuit approached us. She had dark rust-colored hair that hit her around the shoulders, and high-arched, over-plucked eyebrows. Deep frown lines gave her a severe appearance. "Is one of you Jane Mercer?" she asked, looking from Marisa to me and back again.

"I'm Jane," I said, shooting an anxious look at Marisa, who was gazing curiously at the intruder now.

"I'm Delcine," she said, holding her hand out to shake mine. "Where would you like to start?" she asked.

"I was thinking in the shoe salon," I answered.

"Of course," Delcine said with a slight smirk, and immediately turned to lead the way.

Marisa jabbed me in the side with her elbow. "Who's that?"

"She's my personal shopper," I said, lowering my voice.

"Since when do *you* have a personal shopper?"

"I'll explain later," I said just to shut her up.

Marisa and I sat in the shoe salon at Neiman's, surrounded by the loveliest assortment of Louboutins, Manolos, Guccis, and all the other greatest hits. Delcine waltzed around like the conductor, barking orders to the sales representatives. They snapped to attention at the mere sight of Delcine, who had them skittering around like frightened rabbits.

"Marisa," I breathed, admiring myself in the mirror while balancing in five-inch royal blue suede Louboutin pumps. "What do you think of these?"

She was busy buckling a pair of black Gucci patent T-strap heels. "They're fun," she said. "But what are you going to wear them with?"

I shrugged. "I'm sure I'll find something." I settled on the Louboutin pumps, a pair of high-heeled blush-colored Salvatore Ferragamo velvet wedges and navy Prada Mary Jane pumps with bold red, green, and white daisies cut out and appliqued to the toes and heels. They were shoes so frivolous I would never consider buying them under normal circumstances. But today, I felt giddy as I stacked up the boxes and Delcine signaled one of the sales associates. They were now flocking around, wringing their hands with delight that I was ready to make a major purchase.

Marisa, who was only buying the one pair of semi-practical (from a stiletto-wearer's standpoint) Guccis, stared in shock. "You're getting all three pairs?"

I nodded, throwing her a casual grin. She just watched in awe as Delcine confirmed my final selections and handled the purchase behind closed doors.

A sales rep lingered near me. "I don't think I've seen you in here before. "What's your name? Do you have a Neiman's account?"

Remembering I had at least thirty-three-thousand dollars on my Neiman balance and that the account had been frozen after the purchase of the Marc Jacobs dress and

Louboutins at their Santa Monica location, I shook my head. "The name is Jane," I said vaguely, not wanting her to look up my account. "Delcine's handling everything for me today."

Marisa could not keep her mouth shut another minute. "Jane," she whispered, "where did you find that woman and how can you afford all those shoes?"

Delcine returned with a super-sized Neiman Marcus bag and handed it to me, along with the receipt, which totaled $2,978.40. Marisa tried to spy the receipt, which I folded and slipped into my purse quickly. What's next?" she asked with a thin-lipped sneer.

"The designer collections," I said, purposely not answering Marisa's last question. Delcine nodded and marched toward the escalator, gesturing for us to follow.

"You want to buy more stuff?" Marisa asked in disbelief, grabbing her bag, and standing. "Did you come into an inheritance or something?"

"Let's go now and then have an early dinner at Mariposa." I smiled at the thought of the store's signature restaurant, the heavenly popovers with strawberry butter, served with the tiny cup of chicken broth. It was an *amuse-bouche*, the restaurant's well-known brand ritual. I was also thinking that I needed a drink. I was feeling withdrawals after all the liquor I had consumed the night before.

"Jane," Marisa whispered, tugging my elbow, as we trailed behind Delcine, "you still haven't answered my question."

I ignored her as we mounted the escalator, bags in hand, and made our way to the designer collections area, one I often drifted slowly past with wistful longing. I would view all the lovely clothes and fantasize about having them in my possession, trying on one piece and trying to justify the credit card expense. But today was different. Today I had Craig Keller's money, and it was the most incredible feeling.

First, Delcine located the Marc Jacobs dress and I considered whether I wanted to replace it. It had already been worn and torn. And if I ever wore it again, in Craig-the-bodice-ripper's presence or not, it would have somehow lost its luster.

I decided to pass on Marc Jacobs. After all, I could afford much more exclusive brands. I expressed my desires to Delcine, who forged her way straight to where the heavy-hitter couture awaited: Alexander McQueen, Chloe, Dior, Balenciaga, Alaia, Céline … the list went on. Marisa dutifully followed behind us, still bewildered.

Delcine ordered the sales reps to equip me with a private salon fitting room, a glass of pink champagne, and a pair of Jimmy Choos to try on anything that required heels. I immediately gulped down the champagne as though it were water, and requested another, as I disrobed in anticipation of the influx of European fashion.

And Delcine did not disappoint. She sent racks of dresses, skirts, pants, jackets, and blouses. Each time I put on an ensemble, I would waltz out of the fitting area and parade it in front of Marisa, who was now lounging on a large velvet couch, sipping champagne, and leafing through Vogue magazine. With every outfit, she would look up and give me either a thumbs-up, thumbs-down, or a shrug as if to say … *comme ci, comme ça.*

I was having the time of my life luxuriating in the fabrics with all their textures, buttons, and stitching details. I was in absolute heaven. I was accumulating a 'yes' rack as Delcine paraded in and out of the dressing room, hanging more clothes for me and ordering the reps to return all 'no' items to the floor.

At one point, I heard Marisa talking to someone right outside the fitting room area in her boisterous way. "Hey, you," I heard her say loudly to someone who spoke much more softly in response. "Oh my god … what are the odds? How've you been?"

After a few minutes of hearing Marisa conversing with the unknown woman, I heard a sales associate walk a customer to the fitting room right next to mine.

I sat on the lounge chair in my bra, panties, and Jimmy Choo heels, waiting for Delcine to return with more clothes and heard my phone ring. I dug through my purse and saw CK flashing on the phone screen. My heart skipped a beat.

Finally! I answered right away.

"Hello," I said, standing, as though I needed to rise before His Highness, regardless of whether he could see me.

"Where … *are* you?" I heard his luscious voice on the other end. He sounded the way he always did before yesterday, careless and confident.

"I'm in the fitting room at Neiman Marcus in Beverly Hills," I answered, inhaling deeply, like I could catch his scent through the phone. I found, with great relief, no trace of displeasure in his voice now.

"Really," he replied. "So that's where you find all those pretty little things. Is Delcine with you?"

"Yes—she's been amazing."

I could hear him smile into the phone. "Good. I like when you do what I say." There was amusement in his voice. "What are you wearing right now?"

"I'm … between outfits."

"You're alone, then?" he asked.

"What do you think?"

"I think you need to meet me at my office, so you can model your new clothes."

"Right now?" I was standing on the platform with the unforgiving three-way mirror and observing my bruised flesh, which had turned into a rainbow of blue, green, yellow, and purple. I considered the street clothes I had selected for our shopping excursion: a dark green cashmere sweater paired with skinny jeans and black ballerina flats. A vintage Hermès scarf with a tiger print completed my look. Not exactly what I would have prepared for a visit with Craig Keller, but acceptable.

"Yes," he ordered. "Right now."

I breathed into the phone and thought about Marisa waiting outside. I would have to explain why I was going to leave so soon and skip our meal at Mariposa. I was also still in pain from Friday night, not just because of the bruises, but what I had told Marisa was real. I couldn't imagine him entering me again until I had time to heal. But after the events of yesterday, I simply could not say 'no' to Craig again.

"It's four o'clock," Craig pressed. "You'll be here by four-thirty if you leave now. Traffic's not bad for a Sunday afternoon."

"Um ... okay. It's just that my girlfriend's waiting for me outside the fitting room. I'll have to let her know I have something to take care of, you know, to explain why I'm leaving so suddenly."

"You do have something to take care of, Ms. Mercer. See you in a bit." And he hung up.

I was so flustered, I opened the door to my fitting room and wandered out in my lingerie, attempting to locate Delcine, who had disappeared. A woman emerged from the fitting room next to me and, to my dismay, it was Kat, trying on an expensive Céline pale blue wool pants suit.

We just stared at each other for a minute in silence and her eyes lowered to my body and back to my face, a look in her eyes that I couldn't even describe.

"Jane ... hi," she said.

I froze and was silent for what seemed like an eternity.

"I saw Marisa outside and she said you were somewhere in here. How've you been?" She locked her eyes on my face only at this point, like she might turn to stone if she looked below.

"Kat," I replied finally, backing away from her, and feeling my way to my own fitting room. I did not want to physically turn my back and let her see the extra-large bite mark smack on the middle of my right butt cheek. "I had no idea you were here. Let me get dressed and I'll meet you out front." I felt sweat beads forming on the back of my neck.

Before I made it to the fitting room, Delcine came trotting back. "Jane," she called after me. "I'm having them bring the new Spring Chanel collection. It's not even out on the floor yet. *He* would want you to have at least one piece," she added with a devious smile.

Kat raised her eyebrows slightly at Delcine, then gazed at me again, lowering her eyes to my body. She knew my current salary did not support the purchase of even one item from the exclusive Spring Chanel collection. She was probably shocked that I was in this area of the store at all.

"Thank you, Delcine," I blurted in full panic mode, hugging my arms around my body to hide the bruises. "But I need to wrap it up here and get on the road. I'll come back some other time to see the Chanel."

And I backed into the fitting room to dress and get the hell out of there before Kat could question me further. *What was that look on her face?* I knew there were a lot of bruises, but she didn't know how I got them. All of those bruises could have been caused from Saturday's ocean pummeling incident. If I had hit rocks, I'd be a lot worse off.

Marisa was still camped out on the couch reading but looked up as soon as I emerged, now fully dressed in my street clothes.

"Marisa, you know Kat's in there," I exclaimed, eyes wide with tension.

"I know. I saw her before she went in," she replied, looking bewildered as to why I would be bothered by Kat's presence. "Did you guys chat?"

"Not really. Listen, Marisa," I said, lowering my voice so Kat couldn't overhear. "I need your help. I just got a call while I was in the fitting room and I have to leave, *right now*."

"Oh, you mean to meet 'you-know-who?'" she asked. Good old Marisa was savvy enough not to mention his name in public, especially with Kat so close. "Where is he?"

"In his office," I answered. "I need you to play it off in front of Kat, so I can get out of here without questions."

Marisa shook her head. "What are you so afraid of? It's not like she knows anything."

"Please, Marisa? I promise I'll never ask you to do this again." She reluctantly agreed.

Delcine was busy having my 'yes' rack wrapped, and I suspected a steep financial crescendo. When the total was tallied, she proceeded to the couch where Marisa and I sat and handed me the long receipt: $13,534.97.

This time Marisa spotted the total and her jaw dropped. I smiled weakly. "Thank you, Delcine." Marisa's eyes were glued to me like I had gone completely mad. "Marisa, it's the new job, top national agency. I have to look the part."

Before she could answer, Delcine cut in. "What's next?" She was grinning like a jack-O-lantern. I glanced nervously at Marisa again. She was no longer paying attention to Delcine. Instead, she was smiling at Kat, who had just approached us.

"Hey," Marisa greeted Kat, "Did you find anything?"

Kat shook her head. She seemed to be lost in thought. Her eyes met mine. "What did you end up buying?" she asked me.

Delcine hovered like a hawk. "Ms. Mercer will there be anything else today?"

I shook my head.

"I'll have your bags delivered to valet if you don't want to carry them," she responded. "They're quite heavy."

Kat shot me a look again, this time of concern. "Well," she said. "I guess *you* found a few things."

Marisa raised her arm with a flourish, eyed her watch and exclaimed, "Oh, look at the time. I have a live shot at 4 a.m. tomorrow and need to get to bed early. We'd better get out of here now or we'll hit traffic. Jane, have them drop your stuff at valet right away."

I nodded toward Delcine, who was bustling to arrange for the bags to be delivered.

"Kat," I said. "It was great seeing you. We need to catch up soon."

"Yes," she responded quietly, turning to walk in the other direction. "I think we should … at some point." And she was gone.

"Let's get out of here," I told Marisa and we darted down the escalator and out the doors to valet.

Nineteen

After the valet attendants loaded my numerous Neiman's bags into Marisa's black BMW SUV, I plugged Keller Whitman Group's address into my phone. "It's on South Figueroa," I said as Marisa skidded out of the parking lot to Wilshire Boulevard and headed toward the I-10 freeway east, in the direction of downtown.

Craig was right, traffic was shockingly light. Marisa had been silent since we got into the car. "Are we okay?" I asked, apprehensively. "I mean, you're not upset with me, are you?"

Marisa sighed but kept her eye on the road. "I feel like I'm your enabler now," she said, voice tinged with remorse.

"No, Marisa, you're more like an accomplice," I said, "which is far more exciting than an enabler."

"That's just great, Jane. What's up with all those clothes, anyway? The Jane I know is strapped for cash and in debt up to her eyeballs."

"It was a signing bonus," I replied, remembering how Craig had positioned it to me the day before.

"A signing bonus?" she repeated warily. "So that woman is really Craig's personal shopper?"

"What's the big deal?"

"The big deal is he calls you on a Sunday afternoon and

tells you to meet him at his office and you go without a question," Marisa said, abruptly changing three lanes in one move, hitting her signal at the very last minute. This was an expert LA driving maneuver which I wanted to applaud.

"I mean, where was he last night when you were having a breakdown? Do you know how *worried* I was? That guy had no idea what you were going through and surely doesn't give a shit either as long as you show up when he calls."

"So? You just told me Drew isn't exactly prince charming."

"Never mind about Drew. Tell me this," she said, taking her eyes off the road for a second to look at me. "Are you going to just jump whenever he calls on a whim because it fits into *his* schedule? You're not even working for him yet. Is he a control freak? Yes, that's what he is, I'm sure. A guy like that must be a master-puppeteer with his employees ... oh and with his mistresses. Did you ever think you'd be some-one's *mistress*, Jane?"

"I'm finished talking about this for now," I said, sitting back in my seat and stretching my legs. She was flipping back to judgmental Marisa, and I was starting to regret ever having shared my odd predicament with her.

"No, Jane, we're not finished talking about this. You brought me into this mess, and I promised I wouldn't tell a soul. I'll never break that promise, but I can't just sit here and watch you go on a self-destructive binge every time he leaves to attend to his other life—one that will never, *ever* include you. That's not what friendship is about. At least not from where I stand."

"The exit's coming up," I mumbled looking out the win-dow, choosing not to respond to her painful soliloquy. Of course, she was right, and the words sliced through me, a proverbial double-edged sword. On the one hand, I didn't want to hear it and, on the other, I needed her to be my voice of reason, now more than ever.

We drove in tense silence the rest of the way until Marisa pulled up to the Keller Whitman building. "Where shall I park?"

"Just pull into the garage near the building elevator so I

don't have to carry the bags too far."

"You can't carry all those bags alone," she said, while redirecting her car to the parking garage, moving up the ramp into the impossibly steep and circular lot. When we arrived at the elevator, she turned to me. "I'll help you get the bags to the office lobby and then I'll disappear."

"I don't think that's a good idea," I said, shaking my head.

"Jane, it would be unrealistic for you not to have told at least one friend you're going to work for him. Besides, he already met me. He knows we're friends."

"Marisa, it's too soon. Plus, he knows you're a high-profile news reporter. You gave him your card, remember?"

"How will you get home?"

"He'll see to it that I get home safely," I said, smiling suddenly. I needed to convince Marisa that nothing too nefarious was going on. I needed to convince myself. Marisa's expression was like that of a mother saying goodbye to her child on the first day of school.

"Come on, Marisa, lighten up." I now desperately wanted her to return to her old, bossy, funny self. "I'm still *me*," I said, feeling like I was not at all still me.

Marisa silently helped me carry the bags to the elevator bank and, when the last of them had been placed, she turned and just held me close, a hug that could have lasted three days. When she pulled away from me, we looked into each other's eyes and were both in tears.

"Marisa let's not do this, please," I urged, dabbing at my eyes with my fingers. "I'll ruin my mascara and then what will he think?" As I said the last line, I forced out a small giggle.

Marisa smiled and nodded, dabbing her own eyes. "I suppose so, my friend."

I turned to hit the elevator button and, when the door opened, Marisa helped me pull the bags inside. Once they were loaded, I got in, too, and Marisa called after me, "Text me when you get home. I don't care how late it is."

I nodded, blew a kiss to Marisa, and waved as the elevator door closed.

❦

AFTER UNLOADING THE BAGS in the Keller Whitman lobby, I pulled out my phone to text Craig. The usual brightly lit lobby with phones ringing constantly was completely dark and silent. It almost felt haunted. "I'm here," I texted him.

"Come to my office. On a call," he responded immediately.

I ventured down the shadowy, deserted hallway, dragging my bags behind me, and stopped at his door. I looked up at his door plaque that read 'Craig A. Keller,' and my heartbeat began to quicken. My memory drifted back to that first moment I entered his office, before I knew what I know now. I bit my lower lip. I could hear muffled voices coming from inside his office and I was not sure whether I was supposed to knock. I didn't want to interrupt his call. I cautiously turned his doorknob, and it was unlocked so I opened it a crack and poked my head inside.

There was Craig Keller, looking stunning as ever, leaning back in his chair, feet up on the desk with his phone on speaker. There was a woman on the line, speaking as though she were giving a serious marketing presentation. When Craig looked up and saw me, he smiled warmly, waving me to come inside.

I opened the door wider and pulled a few of the shopping bags with me into the lounge area of his office, so I wouldn't interrupt him. After three trips, I had all the bags in his office and shut the door behind me. Craig motioned for me to sit in one of the chairs opposite his desk.

He wore dark wash jeans and a hunter green tartan plaid shirt, unbuttoned and untucked, with a grey T-shirt underneath. His shoes were navy suede loafers that had a beige and black striped sole. They resembled a British brand I'd seen, but I couldn't recall the name. He wore funky black and grey flecked socks. *He never looks like he's trying too hard.*

There were at least six voices on the phone, and I listened intently as they discussed branding for a famous restaurant chain, with forty-eight locations, undergoing an expansion.

Craig remained silent and distracted as he stared into his phone, texting back and forth with someone. It appeared he wasn't even listening to the conversation.

Finally, I heard one of the younger, male voices ask Craig a question directly. "Mr. Keller is this the direction you're looking for regarding campaign strategy?"

Craig pulled his feet down off the desk and leaned into the phone to make a comment. "Honestly, I think you're missing the mark. The point of the rebrand is to build a successful new brand culture, while capitalizing on the equity they've already established. They've lost customer loyalty, but not because the product sucks. It's been the same for thirty years. But in those years, they've had, I don't know, more than fifteen ad campaigns—too many sudden changes in direction create confusion as to who this brand really is. The customers have no trust."

The callers went silent for a moment as though they were not sure how to respond to Craig's comments.

The woman spoke first. "Mr. Keller, can you please expound on that a bit, you know, about how we are to deliver a re-brand without rolling out a different campaign?"

Craig's eyes met mine briefly with a look that said, 'Is she really asking me this?'

"What I'm saying," he said slowly, like he was trying to keep his voice measured, "is that you need to retain the brand elements that have helped these guys stay relevant all these years, create something that's informed by those elements. Shall we review those same elements again? What did the client tell us in the numerous meetings? What did you learn from the research we've been over, ad nauseum?"

Now one of the men spoke. "We learned that the older customers want the old version of the restaurant, but the younger customers think it's tired, not alluring. I think what you're saying is we need to retain the traditional elements while putting a fresh spin on it to attract the younger, more discerning consumers."

"Thank you, Andrew. Your translation skills are remarkable." Craig rolled his eyes.

A few people on the call snickered.

"Craig, I have a thought," said another man's voice, which rang with a strong New York accent and sounded a little older and raspy.

I wondered why some people called him 'Craig' and others called him 'Mr. Keller.' I just watched in awe as Craig steered the call effortlessly, pausing here and there to text something. This group made Warren, Jeffrey, and the rest of the agency seem unsophisticated. These guys were smart and serious about making money. I started to feel like I was way out of my element.

A text chimed on my phone, which was in my purse. I dug it out quickly so that I could turn off the ringer, terrified of interrupting the call. It was from Craig.

"I'm ready for the show to start."

I looked up at him, curiously, and he smiled right at me, as he was making another point to his colleagues.

"That's the only way we'll be able to deliver the new brand powerfully, consistently, and competitively to market," he commented, putting his speaker on mute as soon as he finished speaking. He looked up at me. "Use my bathroom to change. I want to see you in every single item of clothing you brought."

"You mean, while you're on the *phone*?" I asked, wringing my hands.

"I mean, *especially* while I'm on the phone," he said before unmuting again. Someone was asking him for more feedback.

As he spoke, he gestured for me to start moving. I got up and walked to the lounge area where I had placed the bags and began moving them into his spacious bathroom. Once I had all the bags in, I shut the door behind me.

Another text dinged: "Please step out for a second." I opened the bathroom door and stood in front of Craig's desk. He gave me the international drinking signal and pointed to the bar, while he countered another colleague with rational, dominant advertising-speak.

I walked swiftly over to the bar area and went behind it to look for booze. I really needed a drink. I was nervous to model my clothes for His Highness and I figured alcohol would loosen me up. Craig had every type of liquor in his bar. The only champagne he had was Dom Perignon. I knew the stuff went for at least two hundred dollars a bottle. I tentatively pulled a bottle out of his fridge and approached Craig, holding it up and shrugging.

He nodded and gave me the thumbs-up with that striking smile and I suddenly felt at peace. He was so cool sitting there, advising his staff, without even paying close attention. I contrasted him with Warren, who would never explain why an idea was no good. He would just pander to the client and leave us hanging. It was a totally different style and, I had to admit, I liked Craig's management style better than Warren's. It appeared more collaborative and authentic.

I leaned down behind the bar to pop the cork with a hand towel around it, so it wouldn't make too much noise. I located a champagne bucket and filled it with ice.

Then, I poured two flutes and brought them back to Craig, noiselessly placing one flute on his desk as he continued to spar with his team. The conversation was becoming more animated, which thrilled me. I loved watching him in action. I was so impressed. If it were possible, it made me want him even more. I carried my champagne back into the bathroom and closed the door behind me. The question was, which outfit would I change into first? I gulped some champagne to calm my nerves.

I selected ornate evening wear with a Marques Almeida ice pink corset top and slim white brocade pants with large, shiny black grommet buttons lining the sides from the low-slung waist to the bellbottom hems. I paired the outfit with the Ferragamo blush velvet quirky heeled wedge shoes. I was shocked at how sexy I looked in his bathroom lighting.

I checked my makeup and decided to make it heavier. After all, this was a show, and I was Craig Keller's runway model. I leaned into the bathroom mirror to apply darker eyeshadow and noticed Craig's wedding ring in the soap dish yet again. I picked it up and turned it in my fingers, feeling the Celtic etching. I slid it on my right index finger for a minute and held it close to my heart. *Where was Alessandra right now?* I caught myself in the mirror, at that moment, with a glum look on my face.

I received another text from Craig, and I jumped. "Where are you?" It was almost like he knew what was happening in the next room. I returned the ring to the soap dish and took another slug of champagne. I looked in the mirror, applied pink lip gloss and ran my fingers through my long, straight blonde hair, puckering my lips in a pout. This was it, I thought. *Showtime.*

I slowly opened the door and slinked out in my new duds, doing a little model twirl. I listened to Craig's voice on the phone as I breezed in front of his desk, back to him. Finally, I turned to face him and saw the look he was giving me.

He mouthed the words, "Oh my god," shaking his head, those sexy eyes becoming slightly wider.

I smiled, wickedly, and continued my prance, moving near him without getting too close. He understood my game completely, coolly sipping his champagne and occasionally cocking his head to the side, like he was watching an ad shoot unfold before him ... *lights ... camera ... action.*

The champagne helped shed my inhibitions. I was taking on the part of the talent and, like a camera was trailing me, glided to the other side of the room, where the champagne bucket sat. I picked it up, carried it to his desk and gently set it down. I sat provocatively on the edge of his desk, pulled the bottle out and drank from it directly, decadently spilling it onto my face and dampening my hair. When I had taken several large gulps, I wiped my mouth with the back of my hand, smearing the pink lip gloss, and then handed the bottle to Craig. He set it down on his desk, leaned back in his chair and swiveled it from side to side, looking largely unfazed by my uncharacteristically wild performance. He continued with unwavering brilliance to control the phone conversation, but he did not take his eyes off me for one second.

He bit his lip and pointed to the bathroom, mouthing the word, "Next."

I obeyed and returned to the bathroom. The whole scene was surreal but strangely empowering. I put on the next outfit, which I concocted from the jacket of a Saint Laurent navy wool pinstripe suit and tight, skinny jeans with slightly short, frayed hems. I decided not to wear a top, just a black La Perla lace bra under the jacket, with its broad lapels and one button. I buckled up the Prada Mary Jane heels and looked in the mirror again. I fixed my makeup and scanned the overall look, which was the perfect blend of masculine and feminine. Again, I wandered out to where Craig Keller's eyes eagerly awaited.

"Martin," he said into the phone—I remembered that name to be one of the partners, Martin Strong: I had passed his empty office the first night I was here—"you bring up an excellent point. The research identified the overall challenges and opportunities. We know the driving market strategies for regional, mid-range and sit-down restaurant chains during expansion. We have all of that and need to incorporate it into this presentation."

"You're right, Craig," said the raspy-voiced New Yorker. "We need to bring in every shred of that analysis or no one's going to buy the creative."

Craig put the phone on mute again and said to me, smiling, "You're deliciously naughty, Ms. Mercer. I had no idea you were so good at this."

I smiled victoriously and returned to the 'dressing room.'

This went on and on, with outfit after outfit, as the intensity of the conference call climbed, and I made my way to the final ensemble. I was saving it for last because it was so incredible, so Bond-girl hot, it was sure to knock him out.

I got out the royal blue Balenciaga miniskirt and the matching tight sleeveless turtleneck sweater. I unhooked my bra and ditched the panties—no lines to ruin the silhouette—I wanted to look smooth and perfect. I pulled the sweater over my head and the miniskirt on, buttoning and zipping the front. I took out the Christian Louboutin sky-high pumps and slid them onto my feet. I painted on more lip gloss and finished the last of the champagne in one gulp. No, that was not enough. I pulled a tube of mascara from my bag and painted it heavily onto my lashes, rimming the corners of my eyes and smudging them slightly. Craig Keller's wedding ring stared stubbornly up at me until I covered it with my hand. I was ready for the final act.

When I re-entered the office, Craig was still on the phone, stifling a yawn. It was dark outside, and I could see my reflection in the glass of his office windows, illuminated by the light inside.

There, I beheld the most amazing image of myself, a final consummation of who I always wanted to be—breathtaking, pink-lipped, blonde-haired—a baby goddess. I watched, transfixed by my statuesque self as it floated through the office of one of the most powerful men in Los Angeles and I stood before him, triumphant in my self-discovery.

I didn't even pause to look at Craig. I just turned and walked, entranced, to the bar and pulled out another bottle of Dom. I was ignoring him but could feel the pressure of his gaze.

I heard him say to his entourage, "Hey, guys, I'm going to peel off now. I have another call to take." And the line went dead. I stayed, with my back turned to him, attempting to open the champagne bottle and I suddenly felt his grip on my shoulders.

"I don't think you need more of that," he said, spinning me around to face him. "I do think you need something else, though," he continued, eyes fixed on mine. "And what I have in mind is so exclusive, you can't get it anywhere else, no matter how much cash you have stashed up that little skirt of yours."

With that, he dove at me, swept me up, carried me to his desk and set me on top of it. He yanked my skirt up and groped my left breast so roughly, I cried out in pain. His other hand slid between my legs, several of his fingers jamming into me. He pressed his mouth forcibly against mine, his shiny white incisors chewing mercilessly into my lips.

The salty, metallic taste of blood filled my mouth.

At some point, he paused to take off his clothes and get a condom out of his desk drawer. I caught myself wondering why he kept them there. Once the condom was in place, he proceeded to give me an even rougher go around than the night at Shutters on the Beach. I realized, with increasing agony, that the bite marks were still fresh, and he had no qualms about making new ones. He became more brutal with every thrust. My bare ass was sliding on his cold, slippery glass tabletop, and a few papers and files flew to the floor. Gone was any semblance of passion or romance; I could only describe it as a form of assault; the word 'rape' came to mind frequently as he pounded my body, but it couldn't be rape because I not only consented, but I also provoked him for over an hour with my bold fashion show and unabashed cock-teasing serenade. *I deserve this. I deserve to get mauled like this.*

When Craig's eyes fluttered shut, his jaw muscles flexed, and his mouth opened in ecstasy, I realized our session was finally over and he immediately picked up his clothes, went into the bathroom and shut the door. I heard him move the Neiman Marcus bags and all my things, so they were right outside the door. I heard the shower go on and I sat up on his desk, unsteady and weak.

I slid off the desk and shakily stood in my heels. I lost my balance, falling to my knees on the cold marble floor of his office. A painful sensation shot through my legs, and I inhaled slowly while pulling the pumps from my feet. I heard the shower water turn off and Craig step out. The sink water was running, and I heard other sounds of him moving around in the bathroom.

I was still on the floor but knew I needed to get ready to leave. Slowly, I got to my feet and started to pull the bags to the bar area where I might have some privacy while Craig finished eliminating every shred of evidence from his body. While crouching on the floor, I heard his office door open and close, cold air whistling past my body. I instinctively hid behind one of his couches, thinking, in horror, that it could be one of his partners. I waited, ducked down, heart pounding and realized it must have been my imagination. No one else was there.

With my hands trembling and my mind fuzzy, I found my street clothes and began to put myself back together, stepping one foot at a time into my underwear, hooking my bra, pulling on my jeans and sweater, barely keeping my balance. I didn't bother with the scarf. He might get the idea to use strangulation techniques.

When Craig emerged from the bathroom, he looked fresh and attractive, wedding ring returned to his finger. He had magically transformed back into a husband and father. His hair was glossy, his skin clean-shaven and unmarred. He looked as perfect as the moment I first saw him at the Shangri-La.

I longed to go back to that moment and reclaim my innocence—to change the nature of our relationship and stop my dangerous obsession with this man—this unreachable, unattainable person who dominated every thought and dream in my mind, body, and soul. I had blithely plunged into his colorful world without consideration of its inherent darkness. Marisa was right. This was a no-win situation and, if perpetuated, I would always be the loser.

"Don't you want to take a shower?" He eyed me like I was too disheveled to be seen leaving his office premises, even on a Sunday when the building was empty.

"I didn't know that was an option," I said, now barely audible.

He smiled that lazy smile as he approached, putting his arm around me, and leading me to his bathroom. "I think you need to freshen up. As soon as you're finished, I'll call for Pierre to pick you up." As he said this, he shut the bathroom door behind me.

The bathroom was akin to a hotel spa, so there were towels, shampoo, soap, and everything else I would need to clean up. I felt like I was racing against time and pictured Craig outside impatiently glancing at his watch, wanting me to hurry so he could get home before his Sunday dinner got cold. I showered as fast as I could, rubbing the makeup off my face and feeling the sting of cleanser in my eyes. I didn't care. All I could think of was my escape.

I emerged, this time without makeup and my wet hair pulled into a ponytail. He was sitting on the white couch where he originally interviewed me, on his phone texting. While I was in the bathroom, he had carefully folded and packed my new clothes in the shopping bags and they stood waiting, close to his office door. I felt like a dog, being sent to the shelter.

He looked up from his phone. "Feel better?"

I nodded but was afraid to go near him.

"Come over here," he ordered. "I want to talk to you."

I slowly advanced to where he was sitting on the couch and he motioned for me to sit next to him, patting the seat gently and smiling warmly. He had this uncanny ability to act as though everything were under control, and it was the most normal thing in the world for me to have walked around half-naked in front of him during a conference call in his office on a Sunday afternoon before getting nailed on his desk.

When I sat, he took my hand. "That was quite a show, Ms. Mercer." I stared silently down into my lap, unsure of how to respond to this comment. "There's something about you," he continued. "You're not like other women. I mean you get it. You really get me. I'm surprised at how much you get me."

I sat mute as though I were being held captive, desperately thinking of how I could get out of there without having him touch (or bite) me one more time.

"You remind me of someone," he said, expression suddenly somber, I felt him squeeze my hand. "It's your energy; a certain spark you possess." It was the same face he had when I brought up his dead brother.

"And you know what, Ms. Mercer?" he added, letting go of my hand and turning to me. "You're going to be successful here. You know that, right?" His eyes had turned almost translucent jade as he pulled a copy of the signed contract out of his shirt pocket and handed it to me. "Here you go. We're official."

I accepted the signed contract and sat dumbly staring at Craig.

"Well? Aren't you excited?"

"I'm sorry," I blurted, feeling my lower lip crack open where he had bitten it, a droplet of blood trickling into my mouth. "Yes, I just—yes I'm extremely excited. Of course, I am. I can't wait to work here." I had officially become Craig Keller's employee and masochistic sex partner.

"Good, because I need a favor, now that we're official," he deadpanned.

"What's that?" I asked, silently praying he wouldn't want more sex.

"I need a copy of The Henrys' contract."

"Why would you need a copy of their contract?" I asked, mortified.

"That's the client you'll bring to my agency at the start of your employment," he said flatly. "I've had my eye on them for months and am in preliminary discussions with their management. You're already familiar with them and have a relationship, so managing their account should be a no-brainer. Now, I could develop an agreement based on what I know, but it would be helpful, especially given Warren's talent for maximizing client profits, to have their current contract and know exactly what they agreed to when they signed on at his agency. It will help me negotiate the deal to our best advantage."

"But I don't have access to client contract files. I'm fairly sure they're confidential, so I doubt I can get anywhere near them."

"So, you're telling me *no?*" Craig's eyes narrowed slightly.

"Of course, not—I'm just saying I don't have access." My voice had become fraught.

"You'll figure it out. You're very resourceful," he said with a devilish, white-toothed grin. "I have faith in you."

Then, to signify the end of our conversation, he pulled out his phone and called for Pierre to pick me up. When he was off the phone, he stood and took my hand to help me up.

"Now, Ms. Mercer, I'll be expecting that item by no later than Friday."

"I don't know if I can get it to you that soon. It's going to take some research and …"

"If you're going to work for me, 'don't' and 'can't' need to be exorcised from your vocabulary. You're an advertising executive. You should be used to deadlines by now, right?"

I nodded.

"And once you have that contract, you need to give Warren your resignation. Since the holidays are upon us, I'd like you to begin working for me the first week of December."

Boom. Just like that. He gave direct orders, almost as though he had rehearsed this scene. But I knew better. I was seeing inside this man's complicated mind. He was so many things: a Machiavellian businessman, a cold-blooded survivor, an animal in bed, and a strict boss. He worked and played hard, but the bottom line was never far from his view. I wondered whether he cared about anyone. Probably his parents, maybe his kids and, at one time, his wife, although there was no evidence to support that he was loyal to anyone except himself.

Without another word, Craig escorted me to the elevator where he promptly handed me my bags, kissed me on the forehead, and said goodbye.

Twenty

THE RIDE HOME IN the black limo with Pierre was long and tiring, with stop-and-go traffic the entire way. It was way past dark, and I just watched as the freeway signs slowly passed, illuminating my face, one at a time, as we inched along. I ached to call Marisa and run the latest by her, but I didn't want Pierre to overhear. Instead, I pulled my phone out of my bag and saw there was a voicemail waiting from Kat.

Her voice sounded different; it had a subdued quality. "Hi, Jane. This is Kat. I need to talk to you. Can we meet tomorrow? For lunch or dinner? Maybe after work is best. It's just … it's especially important that I talk to you. Um, so let me know. Okay, bye."

I thought back to our encounter at Neiman's and how she acted when she saw me in the dressing room. I know the bruises had to be alarming to anyone, not just Kat, but there was something utterly personal about the way she looked at me, with an air of sadness. I wasn't sure why she so urgently wanted to talk to me, but I was going to hold off until I had a good night's sleep and could think with more clarity.

Back in my apartment, I immediately texted Marisa: "Home safe."

She wasted no time in calling. "Are you okay? How was he? You were there all this time? It's like 9 p.m. I was starting to get worried. What were you guys doing that whole time?"

"You wouldn't believe me if I told you."

"Just tell me you're okay," Marisa said, as though she somehow knew what had gone on in Craig's office for the last couple of hours.

"I'm okay—just really exhausted. I need to go to bed now. Can we talk more tomorrow?"

"At least tell me whether you're going to go work for him."

I had wandered into the bathroom and saw my reflection in the mirror. I did a double take at myself in horror. The bite on my lower lip had turned black, like someone drew a vertical line down the center with a thick Sharpie pen. I quickly flipped off the light, so my face was no longer visible—like doing so would negate what happened in Craig's office— like I could cross myself out. "Marisa, I signed a contract and have the executed document in my possession now," I said sitting on the toilet lid in abject darkness. "There's no turning back."

"Okay, Jane, I know it's your decision, but I sure hope you know what you're doing."

❧

I GOT TO THE office early Monday sick with dread—knowing I was committing unethical business practices in attempting to steal The Henrys' contract. I reluctantly decided to search the cloud first, in the event it was filed there. It was highly unlikely, though, as those files could be accessed by anyone at the agency.

Just as I suspected, the files were not kept there. After hunting around most of the day, I realized there were only creative briefs, copies of ads, photo libraries, and job requests in the cloud. I wondered where in the office I might find a hard copy filed away. There were huge file cabinets in Veronica's office and some smaller ones in Warren's office but that would mean asking one of them to help me locate it, which was, of course, out of the question.

Jeffrey might be my only hope, even though I was petrified to approach him. If I could ask some seemingly innocuous yet targeted questions, there was a possibility he might share information. I pulled a mirror out of my purse to check my face. I wore dark purple lipstick to cover the bite mark, which had grown into a purplish black mass overnight. The memory of my afternoon in Craig's office hovered over me like a dark cloud.

After retouching the lipstick, I hurried to Jeffrey's office and found him slumped over his desk marking up ads. He barely looked up when I approached.

"Hey, Jeffrey," I began cheerfully. "Do you have a minute?"

"Not really," he answered grumpily as I plopped in the chair across from his desk.

"Since I was made lead on the panda account, it would be helpful to have a copy of their contract. Do you know where I could find it?"

"You have the scope of work. You don't need to see the agreement, meaning what the client's paying Warren. He's the only one with access to those documents: he and Veronica."

"Do they keep hard copies or electronic files?" I asked.

He finally looked up from his work. "Only electronic files now, and they're password protected. Why are you asking?"

I felt my hands trembling and I slid them underneath my body. "I'm just curious, what do you mean *now*? Did they keep hard copies at some point?"

"They used to have the account directors keep the hard copies, but when a few people left the company and stole the files along with the clients, Warren changed the policy. Now, are you finished with the interrogation? I need to get these revisions back to the art department."

"Um, sure. Thanks, Jeffrey," I said, scooting away, feeling disgusted inside at being so deceitful.

They used to be with the account directors, which

means whoever had The Henrys' account before Warren changed the policy might still have a hard copy of the contract in a file. That's when it came to me: *Anna.* I wondered how I could get into her office. Maybe after she left for the evening. She never stayed past five. I waited until 5:15 so I could sneak in and go through her files.

I strolled past her office and, sure enough, her door was closed with the lights off, meaning she had left for the day. She hadn't locked the door, so I stole noiselessly into her office, locking the door behind me.

I turned on the light and hauled open her large file cabinet. It creaked like old brittle bones. One of Anna's only positive qualities was that she kept neat and organized files—all were alphabetized and tidy. Great, I thought. *She's going to make this easy for me.* As I ran my fingers over the file tabs, pulling certain ones out to see how far I was in the alphabet, I moved to G-H and there it was. There were three thick file folders inside a hanging file with a tab that read The Henrys. I pulled it out and put it on her desk, fingering through each folder to see what was inside. When I got to the correct file, I saw "Client Agreement" as a tab within a folder with multiple files and my heartbeat quickened. I quickly flipped the folder open. It was completely empty. I went through every paper in each of the files but there was no agreement to be found. *Damn!* It had been removed, probably by Warren or Veronica. I sighed. I was going to have to find another way. *But how?*

I replaced the files and closed Anna's cabinet drawers, peeked out the office door and, when I was sure no one was looking, popped out and closed the door behind me. I hastened back to my office, and when I got there, Jeffrey was waiting, looking agitated. "What's up?" I asked.

"He's on the Warren-Path," he answered. The *Warren-Path* was an inside joke we had about Warren when he was having a bad day and none of us were safe.

"What happened now?"

"He's pissed because we lost a major account to his mortal enemy."

"Which client?" I asked, wondering who, possibly, could be Warren's 'mortal enemy.'

"The Henrys. Evidently Keller Whitman Group's been working on this for months, schmoozing Rita and her husband. I'm sure Rita's infatuated with Keller, like every other woman."

"Really?" I felt my heart rate accelerating. I tried to breathe normally so that Jeffrey would remain ignorant that I was already aware of Craig's plan. In fact, I was now spearheading it, but had no idea Craig would move so quickly. If he had already stolen the client, why did he have me searching for the agreement? Was it some sort of test? I needed to play dumb until I knew the full story. "What did Warren say?"

"He was professional on the phone with their manager from what I could tell. But man, he blew a gasket in my office afterward."

"Wow. I didn't know they were thinking of leaving. Do you know why?" It was all I could do to keep cool in front of Jeffrey.

He shrugged. "Not sure. Sometimes, clients just want a new dance partner. One thing's for sure—if I were Craig Keller, I'd stay out of Warren's way."

"I didn't know they were so competitive."

Jeffrey laughed. "Are you kidding? Those two *hate* each other. You didn't know that?"

"No, I didn't." I was astonished by this revelation. I knew they were miles apart in every possible way, personality-wise, but I didn't realize there was open hostility and a history behind it. Craig never mentioned a feud.

"Oh, they've been at it for years," Jeffrey said. "Warren started his business about ten years before Keller opened his agency. Keller was a bright, young newcomer who started out relatively humble, even though he comes from a well-off family." Jeffrey paused as though he were remembering the whole episode. "He started as a kid copywriter out of college and became Warren's protégé. Warren took Keller under his wing and taught him everything he needed to know to build an ad agency."

I tried to picture Warren mentoring a younger Craig—it was tough to imagine. "What happened to their relationship?" I asked.

Jeffrey pushed his glasses up his nose. "The trouble started a few years later when Keller left to form his own agency. He began going behind Warren's back, stealing clients and employees. You know, both Steve Richards and Martin Strong worked for Warren originally."

I nodded, thinking about the raspy New Yorker's voice on the phone named Martin.

"They were his top account VPs," Jeffrey continued. "Warren had planned to make them partners. Keller got wind of it, swooped in, and offered them each a partnership first." Jeffrey paused and shook his head. "He had a lot of old family money behind him to use as capital."

"Old family money?" I pictured Craig's parents as stuffy conservatives.

"Yeah—you know his brother was killed at age 22—mysterious yacht accident. There were all kinds of rumors that the father's *connections* were involved. They'd love to erase that part of their family history—but too many people know about it."

I recalled the look on Craig's face when I asked about his brother—it was like he had fully shut off. What did Jeffrey mean by connections? "Killed at age 22," I repeated softly. "How sad."

"Yeah, lots of people speculate that's what drove Keller to be so cutthroat—never got over it. That's why Keller's known as 'The Axe' in town—you know, his middle name is Axel."

"Did Warren's partners willingly go with Keller?"

Jeffrey nodded. "Keller had already partnered with Ben Whitman, who was in his college fraternity over at Stanford. Both Richards and Strong joined him at the same time and took a bunch of clients with them—nearly killed Warren's business."

I stared at Jeffrey in shock. "How did Warren recover?"

"He had loyal clients like The Henrys, probably about a

dozen who stood by him. It wasn't like he had to start over, but it was nasty."

"Do Warren and Craig ever speak now?"

"Never. Warren avoids Keller. Sure, they show up at the same fundraisers and events. They're on some of the same boards but they sit far apart and barely acknowledge each other."

"What did you mean that Rita Henry is probably infatuated with Craig?" I asked, trying not to sound too interested in this tidbit.

"Because that's what he does. He uses his looks and money to manipulate people."

I felt my heart sink, but I didn't comment.

"He only recruits attractive millennials—pays them better than any other agency. He impresses them with big offices, money, and himself—they only see his charming side at first. After he hooks them, he demands they steal clients from either the agency they just left or others. Most of them fall under his spell for a few years and then leave. But he has his 'favorites' who stay around."

"Favorites?" I repeated, feeling the bile sloshing around in my stomach. The tuna sandwich I had eaten at lunch seemed to be coming back up.

"Yeah, you know, Jane," Jeffrey looked uncomfortable but continued, "the female employees who think he might leave his wife for them. They stick around inventing fantasies that he's going to get a divorce, marry them, and have a storybook ending. They eventually realize he's using them and they're going nowhere. So, they leave."

"You mean ... he," I gulped, "he has affairs with *all* the women at the agency?" I was growing more sickened with the progression of this story. I don't know how I could have been stupid enough to believe that perhaps I was special. *No, it can't be. He spent so much time with me. He is bringing me in as a vice president and paying me a lot of money, so I am in a different category, aren't I?*

"Don't tell me you've never heard the dirt about him. The man's legendary," Jeffrey quipped. "He's just one of those guys. It's a sickness with him."

"How does he get away with it … I mean … isn't he married?" It felt like someone wrung out my heart like a sopping wet sponge.

"His wife knows he plays around, but she looks the other way like most women married to rich, powerful men."

"But doesn't his reputation precede him in attracting new hires?" I felt my cheeks getting hot. *What had I done by signing a contract with this man? I was just another whore to him, one who would soon be replaced.*

"Oh sure, but he's like a rock star in this industry. Only candidates who are bothered by a sleazy reputation care about it—and those are few and far between. They usually meet with one of the other partners first, like Richards or Strong. If they make the cut, they get to meet the man himself. Most of them live for that day, even if they don't get hired."

A dizzying wave of nausea enveloped me. "Where's Warren now?" I asked, trying to catch my breath.

"He was in his office before I came in to see you. I'd stay clear of him for a while, Jane," Jeffrey said as he exited my office.

My mind was reeling, and I felt unsteady in the wake of hearing the ugly story about Craig. I wondered what he would say if I called him on it. He would likely unspool another thread of lies. But there was no way he could be doling out the kind of money he tempted me with to every employee. He would go broke. Maybe I was in some way special: his most talented new girl-toy. I wondered how he didn't get sued for harassment. The younger women were probably too scared to cross him. Plus, if what Jeffrey said was true … if they all just wanted to have their fifteen minutes with him, they would have something to brag about later. He preyed on the young and insecure. He must have felt like he hit the jackpot with me. I hung my head at my desk in shame.

I checked my phone and there was another message from Kat waiting. "Hi Jane, just following up to see if you want to have dinner tonight. Call me."

There was no way I was going to be able to keep my head cool in front of Kat after hearing so much dirt about Craig. I just wanted to get the hell out of the office and go home before anything else happened.

I texted Kat: "Got your VM. Can't have dinner tonight. Call you later this week."

With that, I gathered my things and took off for home, my mind careening with all the information Jeffrey had imparted. As I drove home, I wondered why Craig went after me. I recalled his words about me not being like other women—that I had a spark that reminded him of someone— *what was that all about?* I thought about the first encounter in his art library, the way he touched me as though I were his possession. Then the night at Shutters on the Beach, where he manhandled me, willing me to stay there like some sort of sex slave. And, of course, there was the erotic afternoon in his office where I modeled fifteen thousand dollars' worth of clothes he had paid for. A shudder ran up my spine. But, as disgraceful a portrait as Jeffrey had painted, there was a side of me that was still unwilling to believe it or to give up on Craig. *Could it be that it was not true?* There were always two sides to every story. Still, I had signed a contract with Craig and was supposed to turn in my resignation to Warren this week. *How could I go through with it?*

ALONE AT HOME IN front of my laptop, I went through personal emails and saw one from Neiman Marcus—a notice about my credit card. Great, I thought, clicking on the email. It was my account statement—must be about my account being overdrawn. Yet another thing to stress me out. I logged in to the account and read the balance. It said $0.00. *What?* I gasped and double-checked to make sure I was seeing right. There was no way. It couldn't be a zero balance. I called the customer service line to check and was connected to the electronic phone tree which confirmed my balance, as of Sunday, was at zero dollars and zero cents.

I thought back to Sunday and it dawned on me. Craig

Keller must have paid my balance after he called me. There was simply no other explanation. *He paid it. He paid it because he cares about me.* And, for that moment, all the negative feedback Jeffrey shared drifted away because this man just spent almost $50,000 on me within twenty-four hours. There's no way he did that for every woman.

With renewed determination, I drafted my resignation letter to Warren and dated it Friday, to coincide with Craig's deadline. It was also the same day Philippe would return and expect me to meet him at Chez Jay.

I went to bed that night with a feeling of satisfaction that I had, in fact, made the right choice, no matter what Jeffrey or Warren thought.

Twenty-One

W HEN I ARRIVED AT work the next morning, Jeffrey was standing by my office door, again, with a concerned look. "You're late. Warren just called an impromptu meeting and we're all supposed to be in the creative department. I've been stalling him because I knew you weren't here yet."

"Sorry—I overslept this morning," I answered, throwing my purse and messenger bag in the office, and grabbing a notepad and pen. "What's it about?"

Jeffrey shrugged. "No clue."

The entire agency was standing in the creative department looking like something bad was about to happen. I saw Warren using Jeffrey's office for a call. He looked serious. The toddlers came over to stand by Jeffrey and me. They looked troubled, so I smiled at them encouragingly.

When Warren came out, he addressed the group. "Folks, we're going to have a little chat about competition today. Do we all know who my agency's competitors are?"

No one spoke.

"Come on, no one here knows who our competitors are?" He scanned the room.

Brooke raised her hand. "Davidson Albright?"

"Thank you, Brooke. Yes, that's one. Who else?"

Johann called out, "Y&R?"

"Yes, Johann."

"How about Keller Whitman Group?" Anna said with a fixed stare at me as the words were expelled from her smug lips.

"Yes, Anna. That's another one." If Warren were impacted by the mention of Keller's agency, he didn't show it.

"The point I'm trying to make here is that there are many agencies out there, large, medium, and small, and they're all our competitors." He turned to look me right in the eye. "Are we the biggest agency? Of course not. Are we the best? That's always subjective, but we sure do churn out a lot of good creative. Do we have the best staff? Absolutely."

The group was at rapt attention now.

"Other agencies notice us. They watch everything we do. They're sizing us up every day, with every campaign launch, with every Addy nomination. They are hoping to see us fail."

Warren was walking around the room now. He addressed an unsuspecting designer who had only been there a few months. Adam was his name. He came from BBDO.

"Do you realize that when you come to work every day and create something, everyone's watching? Do you know that it will only be a matter of time before they find out who you are? They'll want to recruit you. They'll find a way to make it so appealing, you can't say no."

Poor Adam sought out Jeffrey for help. But Warren had already moved on. He had turned his attention to copywriter Cecilia, who had been at Warren Mitchell & Associates for about two years.

He leaned toward her. "Do you know that when you write a tagline or some copy, every top agency is going to read it and wonder from whose clever mind it originated? And believe me, they're envious."

He had now crossed to the front of the room again.

"Every single person in this room has a valuable role here. If you can't excel at my agency, then I don't want you. You're here because you're the best. The agencies you've named all have one thing in common: they employ people I reject or who worked here briefly and simply couldn't cut it. So, they land someplace where the bar is set lower." He cast his eyes to the floor and paused a moment.

"You're probably all wondering why I'm having this meeting today. We lost a long-term client this week to a competitor. We all know The Henrys. Many of you are intimately familiar with them because you've been working on their account for years. They were not always the easiest clients to deal with, but they were loyal and paid us a lot of money."

Warren looked down at the floor again, this time shaking his head, and then continued. Although this didn't seem like a slickly rehearsed speech, it was not out of the ordinary for Warren to speak as though he were being filmed for television. His usual delivery possessed a controlled stiffness that lacked the spontaneity of someone who lived on the edge, someone who wanted you to take what he was saying to heart. Today, however, was different. I don't think there was a person in the room who didn't comprehend the severity of the situation.

"Although we're always prospecting new business, this is a sizable loss to the agency," he said. "Sure, there are clients who become fickle and want something new—happens all the time in this business and we have no control over it."

He stared straight at me for a few moments, and I lowered my eyes. When I looked back at him, he had shifted his gaze to Jeffrey.

"I want each of you to think about how we service every client, how we can refresh our ideas and bring new life to the work no matter how long we've been doing it. I don't want it to just be Jeffrey who's coming to the table with new ideas. He's under pressure because he runs the creative department."

He looked around the room. "We all have ideas; we're all innovative; don't be afraid to speak up to your managers and leaders. My door is always open. Let's continue to raise the bar for our competitors. Let them despise us because they can't be us."

Warren wore a tight-lipped smile as he looked around the room. "Any questions or comments?" he asked.

Again, no one spoke.

"Great, let's get back to work. I need to see all directors and above in the conference room immediately. Please. Thank you."

And he briskly exited the room.

There were only twelve of us directors and VPs combined, and we all quietly headed for the conference room in a straight line like a troop of scouts. Once in the conference room, Jeffrey and I sat next to each other on one side while the others filled up the sides. Tara and Brooke sidled up next to Anna, who took the opposite side of the room, so I could see her conceited grin with clarity.

Jeffrey typed a note on his phone, and I heard my text chime.

"WTF?" it read.

I turned the sound off and typed back. "Has he ever done this before?"

"Not since I've been here."

At that moment, Warren entered and shut the door behind him.

"Guys, this will only take a minute," he said sitting at the head of the table on the side closest to Anna. "I really need your leadership right now. It's come to my attention that competitive agencies are talking to our people and prying for client information. I've also been told they're trying to recruit my staff."

Anna's eyes narrowed at me while I stared blankly back.

"Now, I'm not accusing anyone here of talking to competitive agencies. There's nothing wrong with it and we all have the right to see what's out there," he said giving each of us an equal-length look in the eye, so no one would feel singled out.

I was praying my face was not turning scarlet as I sat there thinking of the resignation letter I had drafted only the night before these surprise meetings with Warren.

"But the reality is, I need to protect the agency's interests and the only way to do that is to start with the people we have here in this room."

At that moment, Veronica popped in with a manila folder in her hand and pulled out a stack of forms. She began handing one to each of us, with a dutiful look on her face, like a schoolmarm carrying out the principal's orders with her naughty classroom full of hooligans.

"What you have in your hand is a non-compete agreement," Warren announced. "I'll give you ample time to read it. Take it home with you tonight and review it with your spouse, friends, lawyer, run it by whomever you want. Regardless, it needs to be signed and returned no later than Friday at 5 p.m. if you are to continue in your current role with the company."

We all started to sift through the paperwork. It looked like a bunch of legal crap. I glanced up at Warren, trying to read him. His demeanor was uncharacteristically grave. His grey eyes were intense and serious.

"If you have questions, you're welcome to approach me individually. That's it." He then stood up and walked hastily out of the conference room. My eyes met Jeffrey's.

"Want lunch?" he asked.

I nodded.

"I'll come by your office at noon."

WE STOLE AWAY TO eat lunch down the street at Fiero's.

"So, what do you think?" I asked Jeffrey as soon as we were seated at a quiet booth.

"You mean with the non-compete? I think it's smart. He's gotten a little loose with that over time, but something had to have pushed him over the edge. I'm not sure what, unless he got wind that Keller was trying to recruit someone at the agency."

We both fell silent as the waitress poured water into our glasses and told us about the specials. As soon as she was gone, I leaned toward Jeffrey. "Yeah, but that stuff with The Henrys: what did he mean by saying someone gave out client information?" I had been worrying about this all morning. Maybe it somehow got back to him that I was talking to Craig. It wasn't like I gave out information, though. I had only snooped in Anna's office for The Henrys' contract. I hadn't taken it.

"Maybe he's just putting out the warning because he's paranoid about losing another client," Jeffrey responded. "Maybe he found out certain people are looking to leave. I really don't know. Warren's cryptic, but he never says anything without an intended message."

"Did you look through the non-compete?" I asked, glancing around the restaurant to make sure no one we knew was there.

"Yeah. I signed one a while back that has long since expired but that was when all that stuff was going on with Keller and the partners. It's standard language."

"Can you translate?" I asked, running my fingers through my hair with a jerking motion.

"Basically, it states that if you leave the agency, you can't work for a competitive agency for a full year, at least not in the state of California."

"Holy crap, Jeffrey that's a big deal." I felt my eyes widen and my mouth drop open.

"Honestly, it's standard, Jane. Why? Are you looking to leave?" He searched my face for some sign that I might be jumping ship.

"No." I quickly replied. "I just haven't been through this before because I've worked for Warren my whole career. No one cared about me having a contract back when I was answering phones."

"Well, you've grown up quite a bit since then, young lady," Jeffrey said with a proud tilt of his head. "I don't think Warren—or any of us for that matter—could live without you now."

"Not true. You're the one he can't live without," I responded. "I'm just another account person. There are a zillion of us in this city." I was trying to downplay my own worth as much as possible so perhaps Jeffrey wouldn't think it a big deal if I left. He didn't take the bait.

Jeffrey shook his head. "No, Jane. You're different. I'm surprised no one's gone after you yet. A competitive agency, that is."

The waitress returned and we ordered lunch, even though I was so stressed out, I couldn't think of food. I just stared at Jeffrey. I wanted to tell him what was going on with Craig Keller, but I had stopped confiding in Jeffrey when the whole mess began with Philippe.

"Jane," he called to me, suddenly tapping his lower lip with his index finger. "You have something there." I realized the lipstick covering my bruise must have worn off.

"Do you think anyone will refuse to sign the non-compete?" I asked, nervously fishing the purple lipstick out of my bag, and dabbing it at the center of my mouth. I glanced at Jeffrey, who was no longer paying attention to my lip issues.

"Probably," he answered. "I'm sure there's someone in the group. It's tough though because, if you don't already have an offer, what are you going to do?"

"That must have been why Warren gave us all such a short deadline to have them signed," I commented, shoulders slouching. "I guess we'll find out soon enough. Friday's in three days."

"Guess so," he replied.

I BROUGHT THE NON-COMPETE home that evening and read through it. Jeffrey was right, it was straightforward. I pulled out my resignation letter, my contract with Keller Whitman Group and the non-compete agreement and lay them side by side on my kitchen counter, like soldiers. I sighed. *Nothing like everything coming to its crisis simultaneously.*

While I pondered the whole fiasco, my phone was ringing. CK flashed on the screen. I felt the same flurry in my stomach and shot of adrenaline at the sight of his initials. He just had that effect on me. "Jane Mercer," I answered.

"Where … *are* you?" he asked in his confident, suggestive

manner, as though blissfully unaware of the uproar he had caused only hours earlier.

"At home," I answered tentatively, not quite sure I was ready to flirt again with the devil himself.

"Guess where I am?" he asked in a teasing manner.

"Um, I don't know."

"I'm at the corner of Lincoln Boulevard and Colorado."

"What are you doing here?" *Why would he be in my neighborhood?*

"I thought we could take a ride together and have a little talk," he said casually.

"You mean … now?" I anxiously scanned my outfit, which consisted of a black vintage Ramones T-shirt, ripped up jeans and red Converse All-Star sneakers. I wasn't even wearing a bra.

"Yes, now." I recognized that resolute tone.

"Okay—I'll be right down." I shoved a mint in my mouth, pulled a comb through my hair, peeked in the mirror, and immediately saw the bruise on my lip. It was still purple. I decided not to cover it, since Craig was the one who made the mark in the first place. I ran out the door to the elevator. When I emerged from the building, I saw Craig's Bentley parked on the opposite side of the street.

When I approached, he got out of the car, walked around to the passenger side, and opened the door for me. Always the gentleman, I thought, ironically. When we were both inside the car, he took off driving. "Where are we going?" I asked.

"Not sure," he said.

I observed his profile as he drove and decided it was absolute perfection. His nose was not too small, nor too large and, paired with a strong chin and jawline, he looked almost regal. I marveled at how someone could be born so naturally good-looking. I again thought about the time he told me his brother died. I wondered what his brother was like—wondered if he looked like Craig. I also remembered how disarmed Craig was when I asked about him—almost as though he was haunted. I considered how that may

have changed Craig forever—his behavior—his mood—
his actions. I wanted to know him—wanted to know
everything.

"How did it go today?" he asked.

"You mean after you turned Warren's agency upside
down? I guess okay, a little unpleasant, but everyone's living
through it."

"How bad is it?" There was an air of gossipy pleasure in
his tone at having an in-house spy to report back about the
building blocks toppling over.

"Pretty bad," I said, feeling suddenly protective and
empathetic towards Warren. *Did Craig just want to gloat
about his victory?*

"It's business, Jane," he remarked. "Were you able to get
a copy of the contract?"

"Not yet. I went through everything including sneaking
around in someone's office," I said sighing.

"So, what you're saying is, it's *not* going to happen,"
he answered, eyes focused on the road. "That's terribly
disappointing."

"What does it matter now?" I felt my cheeks heating
up. "Everyone already knows The Henrys are going to your
agency. Why didn't you give me a heads-up? I thought you'd
wait until after I left."

"I didn't plan it that way. It just, sort of, happened. Rita
couldn't keep her mouth shut and word got back to Warren.
The contract is still in the negotiation stage."

I thought about Jeffrey's supposition that Craig used his
charm to woo Rita Henry and wondered how much of it was
true. I pictured Rita in Craig's office, on the white couch,
sipping vodka and debating the works of Marc Chagall.

"I think the larger point here is that your loyalty still lies
with Warren," he said, tearing his eyes from the road long
enough to eye me suspiciously. "You could get the contract
if you really wanted to."

"Now that we're on the subject, you never told me you
worked for Warren," I pointed out, examining his face for a
trace of emotion. There was none.

"I worked for him, right out of Stanford," he answered. "But that's ancient history."

"So, it doesn't bother you to have taken Warren's biggest account?"

"Why should it? The Henrys weren't happy and wanted new representation. If any of my clients were unhappy, they'd be free to find a new agency. You lose a client; you gain one later. Warren's a big boy and his agency will be fine."

I wasn't sure where it was coming from, but I was feeling more upset by the minute that Craig stole the account and didn't care who it hurt. A lot of employees worked on The Henrys' account, and it would no doubt result in layoffs. I remembered what Jeffrey said about Warren mentoring Craig and helping him along until Craig took all his clients and partners. If it were true, it was unsettlingly heartless. That part scared me. Maybe there was truth to Jeffrey's story about 'The Axe.'

We were now on Pacific Coast Highway, cruising north along the coast. The sunless ocean looked bleak and barely visible.

"Now I think we should change the subject, don't you? You know what I can't get out of my head?" he said with a breathy laugh, green eyes glinting occasionally from oncoming traffic lights. "The vision of you in that short blue skirt, on my desk. You were so incredibly sexy. You drive me crazy. You know that?" His eyes strayed from the road once again to look at me.

My mind went back to the finale of my fashion show when Craig pinned me on his glass desk. The pain and humiliation returned—I didn't comment.

"You're so quiet," he observed.

"It's been a long day." My words were clipped.

"I know what might make you feel better," he said, voice deepening.

I said nothing and stared straight ahead. I was in no mood for his overtures and just couldn't shake the feeling that I was one of hundreds, maybe thousands, of women he had seduced at the office.

Suddenly, Craig slammed on the brakes and turned up a winding road in Pacific Palisades. He found a place to pull off the road, put the vehicle in park and turned to face me.

He put his hand around the back of my neck and pulled me toward him. His hand slid down to the small of my back and he leaned over to kiss me. There was the familiar soapy smell again. I clutched the lapels of his jacket, pulling him even closer, realizing at that moment how obsessed I had become. It made me sick to think I was not the only one he could be kissing and touching this way, to think his energy and focus could be on anyone other than me. My hand fell between his legs, and I ran my fingers along the hardness underneath his suit pants. He withdrew from kissing me long enough to push a button and I felt my seat both sliding down, and undulating. I watched his perfect lips curl in amusement. "You like the massage seat?"

My body was supine now, level with his and the 'massage seat' function was working us both. His hand wandered to the zipper of my jeans. I receded toward the passenger door, as far away as I could get within the confines of his car. "I … can't," I mumbled, burying my face in my hands, and tasting blood from my lip, which had cracked open again. "I just can't right now."

"Why not?"

I remained silent.

He pressed buttons on the control panel, and I felt my body returning to a sitting position, the massage coming to a halt.

Craig shifted his legs, and straightened his jacket lapels, stealing a quick glance in the rear-view mirror to check his reflection. He ran his fingers through his glossy brown hair to smooth it down. *Don't worry, your Highness, you still look perfect.*

We sat in his parked car in complete silence for several minutes before I finally spoke again. "How many women at your office have you been with?" I asked, turning to look him in the eye.

"What kind of question is that?" he responded, looking

taken aback like it was a random query he had never heard.

"I want to know before I come work for you," I answered, tracing my fingers along the console between us, feeling the cold, rectangular metal slats.

"You're not having second thoughts, are you?" he asked, furrowing his brows, as if reading my mind.

"Well," I began slowly. "I just heard a lot of stuff."

"You mean, about me." His eyes lowered as though he knew what was coming.

"Yes," I replied. "I want to know if any of it's true."

He pursed his lips. "Jane, I'm a high-profile person and, yes, people talk. But I've never given you a reason to doubt me, have I?" There was an intensity in his eyes now, like he wanted to make sure I believed him.

I looked away without answering. There were so many reasons to doubt him: he concealed his history with Warren; he only wanted me around for sex or intel on Warren's clients; then, of course, there were the damaging stories about his past. There were plenty of reasons to doubt him.

"Hey, Jane, look at me."

I turned to face him and felt tears in my eyes.

"What's all this?" he said, eyeing me uneasily. "You look so broken."

"I ... I don't want to share you with anyone else," I blurted. "I mean, I know you're married and everything, but I thought I was ..." my voice wavered before trailing off into silence. *What was I trying to say? That I wanted him to be loyal to me outside of his marriage? That sounded crazy even to me.*

Craig turned to face forward and, after sighing deeply, he started the car, made a U-turn onto the street, and began driving towards PCH.

"What's wrong?" I asked with panic in my voice.

He didn't answer, and we stayed mute the entire ride back to my apartment. When we arrived, he stopped the car and flashed me a look. "You know, Jane, if you can't handle this, now's the time to let me know."

"What do you mean?" I asked, terrified I had gone too far with my jealousy.

"Exactly what I said: if you can't handle it, you have an alternative," he stressed in an impassive tone.

"You mean not working for you?"

"That's up to you. You're the one with all the questions. I told you before: you're either in or you're out. I obviously want you in, but not if you can't handle it. And it certainly sounds like you can't handle it."

"I *can* handle it," I implored. "I swear I can. I just … well, the rumors …"

"There will always be rumors. It's up to you to ignore them. Now, what's it going to be? In or out?"

"I'm in, *I'm in*, Craig," I cried with desperation in my voice.

"Are you sure?"

"Yes, I'm sure."

"You don't sound very sure," he replied coldly, getting out of the car, and proceeding to open my door.

I stepped out of the car and studied Craig's face, the lampposts shedding swaths of white light over his handsome face while he leaned over and kissed my forehead. "Sleep tight," he said. He returned to his car and waited until I was in the apartment building before driving away.

I went to bed that night with the remnants of the day churning in my mind, making it nearly impossible to sleep. *Was I in or was I out? To be or not to be?* Of course, I wanted to be in, but being in meant ignoring things that insulted my soul. And could I really ignore them? I still wasn't sure. The thought of Philippe came to mind. If I didn't go with Craig, I would have to deal with Philippe and the other shenanigans at Warren's agency. And now that The Henrys were no longer a client, Warren would be looking to clients like Philippe and Frédéric for the revenue loss. If I stayed, I would be in a situation where I had to do whatever Philippe wanted or risk losing the account and my job.

If I could just manage my feelings for Craig, it would be an easy decision. He was such a mystery. I just wanted to crawl inside him and figure it all out. But no matter how intimate I had been with him he was still a stranger. Maybe that's what attracted me. Maybe being on the edge in the relationship was what I wanted. Whatever my feelings were, I was not ready to let Craig Keller go just yet.

Twenty-Two

B Y THURSDAY MORNING, THERE was an air of tension and stillness at the office, which was highly abnormal, given the usual harried atmosphere. Rather than scurrying through the hallways, standing at each other's office doors, or hovering over the art department, everyone kept to themselves. I didn't know if it was Warren's somber mood from earlier in the week, or if people were still considering their non-compete agreements. Either way, I felt awkward because I hadn't turned mine in yet and was going to turn in my resignation Friday instead.

Even Jeffrey was quiet. I considered wandering down the hall, but I didn't want to run into Warren and risk an awkward conversation. So, I engaged myself in some tedious busy work like opening and closing out jobs, inputting billable hours and researching client issues.

The other thing that bothered me was that Craig had gone eerily dark. I had texted him twice on Wednesday without a response. Today, I tried to call his cell phone, but it went directly to voicemail. He hadn't said anything about going out of town, but I wondered if perhaps he went on a business trip—but I was vibing desertion. It made me anxious that he had ghosted me, especially given the fact that

I was resigning the next day and my livelihood would then be in his hands.

My phone buzzed with a new text message. I snapped it up off my desk thinking it was Craig finally coming up for air, but it was Kat asking about dinner again. She was being so persistent I knew I couldn't hold her off much longer. I wondered what was so urgent that she had to see me in person as opposed to a telephone call.

❦

I RELENTED AND THAT night, Kat and I met at Tar & Roses, a laid-back 'Cal-Med' restaurant on Santa Monica Boulevard. I found her sitting quietly at a booth.

As soon as I approached, she jumped up and hugged and kissed me. I felt her hands gently rub up and down my back, like she was afraid she might be hurting me. When she withdrew from the embrace, her expression was one of relief, like she didn't expect me to show.

We sat and ordered wine, and she just stared at me with this contemplative look, like she wanted to share something but didn't know where to start. "Jane," she began nervously, like we didn't know each other. "You look stressed. Is anything wrong?"

"Work stuff," I responded evasively. "I'm up against it right now, that's all."

We sat in uncomfortable silence until the waitress delivered our wine. I took a huge gulp of Cabernet Sauvignon, like I was drinking Gatorade after a marathon. Kat raised her eyebrows slightly but didn't touch the wine. "Jane, there's something I need to talk to you about."

"Yeah, that's what you said in your message. What's up?"

She took a deep breath. "It's about Craig Keller."

"What about him?" I searched her face for some indication as to why she wanted to talk to me about him now. She had studiously avoided the subject at every turn prior to this moment. I started to wonder if Marisa had broken our confidence and told her what had been going on, about my affair and impending job.

"You're involved with him, aren't you?" she asked candidly.

"Involved?" I repeated, trying to decide which way to go with this line of questioning. *Marisa must have told her out of concern.* "I'm not sure what you're talking about. Involved how?"

"Okay, I'm just going to say it. You're sleeping with him, right?" Kat's blue eyes were glued to mine.

"Now, where would you have gotten that impression, Kat? Just tell me the truth. Who told you that?" I said this with all the astonishment of someone innocent of the accusation.

"Look, Jane, no one told me. No one had to tell me. I just know it. I knew it that day I saw you in the dressing room at Neiman Marcus." She leaned forward, her long blonde hair spilling down the front of her crisp white blouse.

I felt my face flush, but I remained silent in the face of her confrontation.

"Jane, I know what's going on. Those bruises, no, the *bite marks.* I know him, Jane, I know him better than you do."

As she said this, I picked up my glass and took another huge gulp of wine. I had no idea what to say. *How would Kat know about the bruises—how would she know that they were really Craig's bite marks?* Unless he slept with her, too. I felt a ripple of dizziness, almost not wanting to hear what Kat was about to say. I had heard enough gossip about this man, enough to last a lifetime.

"Well, I guess now is as good a time as any to tell you that I've signed a contract and will begin working for his agency in December." In my mind, I was making a preemptive strike. "So, there's nothing more to discuss."

Kat's face turned pale. "Take it back. Tell him you can't work for him. You don't know what you're getting yourself into with that man. You don't know what he's capable of."

"And why are you choosing to have this conversation *now?*" I said angrily. "What's done is done."

"Jane, you don't have to give me details because, God knows, I don't want to hear them. I tried to warn you about him, but you obviously didn't listen." She tossed her blonde hair in indignation.

"That's not fair, Kat—you never told me what he *did*. I kept asking but you were vague. We all have our opinions about people but until you elaborate on what, specifically, he did, how could I have taken it seriously?"

"Oh, come now, Jane, you never told me you were considering a job with him so that's why I was reluctant to give you more information. Believe me, I know how he is, how persuasive he can be. I understand how this happened."

"What are you trying to tell me, Kat?" I picked up my glass and drained it in one gulp. Kat still hadn't touched her wine at all. We glared at each other for a moment in silence, my thoughts swimming.

"Jane," she said quietly. "I need to share some things but I'm asking in advance that you please never, *ever* repeat it to anyone. Do you understand?"

I shrugged. "Of course."

She picked up her glass of wine and took a long sip before beginning her story.

"I met Craig about three years ago. We were both married, and his kids were babies. It started as harmless flirtation at a magazine photo shoot. We were being featured, along with three others, as successful business owners. He approached me, and we just hit it off. He was interested in my business and wanted to do branding work—*gratis*. He was irresistible, you know, tall, handsome, smart, successful. I was enamored of him and, even though this was well before Jack and I started having issues in our relationship, Craig was on my mind all the time."

I felt a twinge of sheer jealousy. Kat was so stunning and elegant; it was no wonder Craig went for her. Then, I imagined the two of them together. They had to have made a striking pair. I felt my heart sinking yet again at the thought that he could be so duplicitous.

"Craig progressed quickly to shameless texts that I found impossible to ignore," Kat continued. "When we'd see each other in public, it was electrifying. There was something in his eyes, it was like there was no one else in the room, no one else on the planet."

Sounds familiar.

She took another sip of wine and continued. "The flirting went on for about three weeks before he made an advance. I was surprised he waited that long. I had no idea how much of a chronic cheater he was. He acted like I was his first affair and I, stupidly, fell for it."

Kat paused again to sip her wine. I watched her silently, growing queasier with every word. I imagined Craig kissing Kat's beautiful mouth—telling her he wanted to consume her—asking if she was ready. "How long did the affair last?" I asked. My voice was small and deflated.

"Almost six months," she said. "While we were sleeping together, he had a whole team working on my brand campaign."

"How did you keep it from Jack?"

"With Jack it was not too tough because I always worked late. I was just cutting into my office time to run around with Craig. What wasn't easy was hiding all the bruises and bite marks. I had to invent excuses about falling and other ridiculous stories to keep Jack at bay. I swore Craig made the marks so I wouldn't be able to have sex with Jack. He would never admit it, but he likes having his women exclusively, regardless of the running around he does himself."

"How did Craig keep it from his wife?" I asked.

"With Craig, it was more difficult because he had small children," she answered. "He would cancel at the last minute a lot and arrange odd hours for us to meet at his office, even suggesting business trips to the same cities so we could be alone and uninterrupted. His schedule was so problematic, he was always being watch-dogged by his wife. He was never available to talk when I needed him. And the less he was available, the more I wanted him."

I thought back on how I had a mental breakdown when he ghosted me for twenty-four hours.

"I was texting him day and night," she said, "knowing he would have to respond sooner or later. I began to resent his wife, even though I knew she was the biggest victim in the whole thing. Have you ever seen her?"

I shook my head. "Not in person."

"Well, she's beautiful. And people went on about how kind and lovely she is, which made me feel even worse."

"How did it end?" I asked, feeling lightheaded from the wine on an empty stomach.

"He stopped answering my texts. He even started turning his phone off at night altogether which made me furious. So, I confronted him in person at his office one day. I told him it was over, but he wouldn't accept it. He told me he loved me and was going to leave his wife, so we could be together. He asked me to divorce Jack."

I couldn't help but feel like someone drove a knife through my heart. Craig told Kat he *loved* her, something he would never *ever* say to me. Kat was just, well, she was Kat.

"At first, I believed him. I mean, I loved him, too, I really did." She had a pained look on her face as though recalling just how much she loved Craig. "I seriously considered leaving Jack but as fate would have it, I discovered something about Craig before I ever made a move."

I just stared at Kat in anticipation. The truth was, it was killing me to hear this story, that Craig and Kat *loved* each other.

"I went to his office late one night without calling first. The lights were still on in the reception area, but no one was there. I went to Craig's office and opened the door without knocking. There he was, leaning against his desk getting a blow job from that French bitch who answers his phones."

"You mean *Simone?*" I could hardly believe my ears.

"Yes, long black hair, right? Looks like someone pisses in her oatmeal every morning? That's the one."

I cupped my hands over my mouth. *What the fuck? No wonder she was so weird and possessive of him. She never gave him the message the first time I called. She purposely called me at the office to make an appointment and had flowers sent there, obviously to get me in trouble and block me from Craig. And when I met him at the office the first time, she had clearly gotten to him before me. That's why his shirt was half-unbuttoned. Disgusting!*

"Oh my god, you can't be serious!" I blurted.

"Oh, I'm totally serious," she responded, pausing to take a drink of wine.

"What did he do when you caught him red-handed?"

"I didn't stay to find out. I ran like crazy out of there and drove home. He called me about ten minutes later. The bastard probably waited until he came first."

"Oh my god," I breathed, feeling further humiliation. He had to have an insatiable appetite to have so much sex with so many women. Or maybe, as Jeffrey said, it really was a sickness with him.

"He tried to act like it was nothing," she explained, blue eyes filled with exasperation. "He wanted me to meet him for a drink. Do you believe that? I told him I never wanted to see him again. Still, he kept insisting I was making a big deal out of nothing. He said she came onto him, and he felt sorry for her—that oral sex wasn't the same as full intercourse."

"Huh?" I gulped.

"I cut him off completely and wouldn't return his calls or texts for several weeks. I still had the professional work going but I sent a letter terminating their services. Do you know what that prick had the nerve to do? He had Simone send me an invoice—for $300,000!"

"Did you pay it?" I could not believe what I was hearing.

"I called him right away and demanded an explanation," she answered. "That's when it got ugly. He reminded me that I had signed a contract and, although the work was supposed to be free of charge, the contract read differently. I signed it without reading it because I trusted him. He threatened to file a lawsuit if I didn't pay him the money. I told him he didn't want to take me to court because it would expose our whole affair and ruin his life. That's when he said there was nothing I could expose because he had already told his wife about me."

"Was he bluffing?" I asked, still more disturbed, thinking about all the money Craig had given me already. *Would he want it back if I dared cross him?*

"Of course, but I didn't know that at the time. I was so scared, and guilt ridden, I broke down and told Jack the truth. I didn't want him to find out some other way. He was devastated but we worked hard to put things back together. Still, I don't think he ever really got over it. I know that's why he ultimately found someone else and left."

So that was it. That was the reason Jack left his dream home and life with Kat behind. It all made sense now. Craig Keller ruined their marriage.

"At the end of the whole mess, Craig relented on the payment for the agency work if I agreed that I didn't have the right to use any of the stuff they had done," Kat said. "I was happy to let it go. I just wanted to get away from him."

"Jesus, Kat," I marveled. "That's one hell of a story."

"So, what are you going to do?" she asked, looking me in the eye.

"I don't know, Kat. I mean ..." I stopped talking to catch my breath.

"Call him tomorrow and tell him you can't go work for him, Jane. Break it off. You're not too far down the path. You can end it now."

I felt tears welling up in my eyes and I tried to control them, but they wouldn't stop. How could I explain to Kat that I had strong feelings for him now, regardless of his past or current reputation?

"I know it hurts," Kat said softly. "He's a charismatic guy, but he's also a monster, and you can still get out of this."

"It's not just about him," I said sniffling. "I have to sign a non-compete tomorrow if I'm going to stay with Warren, which means if I leave, I can't work anywhere unless I relocate to another state. You have no idea how much money I'd be giving up. I mean, I don't have a house in Laurel Canyon, with a pool and a fancy car. I'm just not in the same place as you, Kat. Don't you understand?"

"I do understand, Jane. I'm telling you because I care about you, and no amount of money can make up for his behavior. He'll use you and throw you away." Her eyes were wide, and her lips firmly pressed together.

I thought about Philippe, who would be returning from Paris the next day to make good on his deal with me, yet another beast who wanted to pillage my body for his own pleasure. I explained the situation to Kat, who listened quietly.

"That's blackmail," Kat said. "It's illegal. You should go to Warren."

"Oh, right, Kat. I wish it were that simple. I'm the one who got myself into this mess, not Warren. I'm bound to Craig Keller and, no matter how bad he is, the flipside is infinitely worse."

Kat sighed. "I know how hard this seems, but Warren's a good man. I know a little about him and he's a class act. If you told him the truth, I'm sure he'd want to help. He'd want you to stay working for him. Just think of the long-term benefits, not the short-term money. The money will come. But you'll squander your self-respect and reputation if you make the wrong decision now."

I abruptly stood and grabbed my purse, tears streaming down my cheeks. "I'm sorry, Kat. I need to get out of here. I don't know what I'm going to do but I just can't talk about this anymore."

Kat sat there with this solemn look in her eyes. "I hope you think this through," she said, "and come to the right decision. Remember, it's your life."

Twenty-Three

T HE ENTIRE DRIVE HOME, I was consumed by Kat's
story. I couldn't stop thinking about Kat and Craig
together. It both fascinated and infuriated me to think
that my good friend had been with him in the same way I
had, and that there was nothing exclusive or special about
what he had with me. No wonder he kept condoms at work;
there was likely a revolving door of young women ready to
jump on his desk. I wanted to throw up at the thought of it.
How could I possibly go to work for him now?

At some point on the way home, I realized I hadn't
eaten dinner and, as usual, there was no food at my apartment. I made a quick turn and stopped at Whole Foods on
Santa Monica Boulevard. I hadn't been food shopping for
so long, I didn't know where to start so I decided to go for
basic salad ingredients.

As I trudged down the produce aisle where other late-
night office workers were busy snapping up the last of the
fresh vegetables, I sorted through some picked-over tomatoes, trying to find a ripe one. I picked tomatoes up, felt
them, put them down and moved to another batch. When I
finally spotted a good one, I felt a hand next to me reach and
grab the tomato precisely when I grabbed it. I looked up to

see the jerk who was trying to steal my dinner and let out a gasp. It was Derek.

We stared at each other for a moment and Derek finally spoke. "You can have the tomato," he offered.

"I wouldn't dream of taking your tomato," I responded, stretching my arm, and holding it out to him.

"That's okay, I prefer that you have it." There was a blank expression on his face.

"How've you been?" I thought back to last Saturday at the beach when we had our final conversation—before I dunked my cell phone and was tossed ashore like rotting seaweed.

"Good," he answered, lowering his eyes, like he didn't want to see me. "I take it you're working late these days."

"I am, but what else is new?" I forced a smile, not knowing how to spin this conversation. "Were you at rehearsal tonight?"

He nodded eyes still averted.

"Derek," I began, "this is so awkward. I understand why you're mad at me, but some of the things you said on the phone that day … well, you got things all wrong."

"Jane, I don't think this is a good time." He looked around, embarrassed.

"If not now, when?" I pressed. I could feel myself getting emotionally flustered as I tried to keep my voice in check. *Hadn't I been through enough for one day?* A pregnant woman bumped my cart to get around me and shot me a dirty look.

"Look, Jane," he said carefully, "I don't want a scene. I just stopped to buy food. I didn't expect to see you here."

"Well, that makes two of us," I shot back, but then softened my tone. "Derek, don't you see that it was fate we ran into each other? There's unfinished stuff between us. You can't run away from me forever."

"I can do whatever I want, and I'm not ready to talk to you," he replied, backing his cart away so he could head off in another direction.

I was so flabbergasted, I picked up the tomato in question and hurled it at Derek's back, where it promptly burst into a bright red mess on his black pea coat. "Take your fucking tomato," I yelled after him, drawing shocked stares from a crowd of on-lookers.

He stopped in his tracks and removed his coat to view the damage. He looked up at me and shook his head, disgusted. Then he abandoned his cart and marched towards the store exit.

There. I'm such a bitch, I drove a man out of the grocery store. He would rather go hungry than share the same space with me. I left my cart and chased after him. As soon as I was outside the front entrance, I spotted him at his car. "Derek," I shouted at the top of my lungs. "Please stop."

He slipped into his car and pulled out of the parking lot at reckless speed. It was no use. Derek hated me. I called Marisa in a panic. "You won't believe what just happened," I said breathlessly into the phone. "I just saw Derek at Whole Foods and he literally ran away from me."

"What's the problem now?" she asked, sounding weary.

"Well, I did throw a tomato at him but it's because he can't stand me," I answered, now fuming at Derek's cold shoulder treatment. *Who did he think he was?*

"You threw what at him?" Marisa let out a barely audible chuckle.

"It's not funny. I was … he was … he won't talk to me."

"Calm down, Jane," Marisa said. "Just leave him be."

"I can't calm down. I'm furious." I was feeling all the pressure of my work situation and the many stories about Craig overflowing in the form of anger and outrage. Derek's behavior was the final straw. I was sitting in the car with the motor running, the engine emitting a muffled humming noise.

"He's just hurt, Jane. You *do* know why he's acting like this, don't you?"

"Because he despises me." Someone honked at me to leave the parking space I was occupying.

"No, Jane, the exact opposite. Because he *loves* you. I can't believe you don't see it."

"Oh Marisa, please. He's had plenty of time to make a move."

"Well, maybe his timing was off, but that man has a

thing for you now."

"Marisa, there's no way he has feelings for me other than antipathy, especially now that he has a beautiful, perfect young girlfriend."

"Well, Jane, things aren't always as they seem. The man cares for you. Period."

The same person honked at me again, this time with more impatience. I put the car in reverse and slowly backed out. "Honestly, Marisa, I can't talk about this right now. I have bigger issues to resolve."

"You're the one who called me," she said irritably. "What *bigger* issues?"

I thought about Kat and how she asked me to never repeat her story about Craig. I could not breathe a word to Marisa. "Stressed out about resigning tomorrow," I answered. "I just want to get it over with."

"You're really going through with it?" Marisa asked, her voice shaded in disappointment.

I sighed, pulling up to exit the Whole Foods parking lot. "Yes, I am." The truth was, I was not at all sure. I was not sure of anything anymore.

Marisa was silent on the line for a moment.

"Marisa are you there?"

"Yes, I'm here. I guess I just wish you'd made a different decision is all. But it's your life."

I WENT HOME THAT night thinking about the phrase I'd heard twice that night, from each of my friends. *It's your life.* It was my life, and the decision were mine to make. I couldn't help but think it was like playing a game of *Would you rather?* But instead of Marisa and I snickering about which homely, detestable pig we would rather sleep with, I was weighing options about the worst of possible professional situations. Would I rather work for an agency whose managing partner hooks up with anything that moves, including me? Or would I rather work for an agency whose senior management encourages you to hook up with anyone who doesn't agree with the strategic direction? If the decision were based on pure aesthetics, Craig Keller would be the obvious winner. It was really a toss-up at this point, though, as to which option was more egregious. Still, the money and my deep-seated fear of losing what little footing I had left with Craig was seared into my mind. He just had that effect on me.

I went to bed at 11 p.m., tossing and turning until midnight. Finally, I got up, turned on the light and picked up my phone, which was charging on the nightstand. I decided to text Craig another note just for reassurance. I again wondered why he had not contacted me since our little drive up PCH. His silence worried me. And while I didn't get a response from Craig, I did get a new text from Philippe.

"*Mademoiselle*, I look forward to tomorrow night. *Au revoir.*"

My stomach roiled with disgust. Of course, he had no qualms about texting me at midnight, like *he* was the one I was having an affair with, not Craig.

FRIDAY MORNINGS, UNDER NORMAL circumstances, were usually filled with lighthearted vibes—everyone feeling happy in anticipation of the weekend. But the mood was still marred by the deadline of the non-compete agreements and the sense that any one of us could be leaving the agency soon. My stress was amplified by the thought that I was jumping from the frying pan into the fire with Craig Keller and his storied past.

I arrived around 9 a.m. and pulled up my resignation letter on the computer. I had emailed it to myself the night before thinking I would print it and sign it in the morning.

I decided to read it one more time.

Dear Warren,

Please accept this letter as formal notification that I will be leaving my position as Account Director at Warren Mitchell and Associates, effective two weeks from today's date.

> *Thank you for the opportunities you have provided*
> *during my time with your company. If I may be of any*
> *assistance during this transition, please let me know.*
> *Sincerely,*
> *Jane Mercer*

Brief but professional. I hit print, pulled the letter off the printer, and signed my name. I folded the letter, put it into an envelope and wrote Warren's name on the back. I placed it on my desk and felt a range of emotions—all conflicting. I had planned to give Warren the letter right before lunch and then pack my things in the event he wanted me to leave right away. I hoped he wouldn't ask where I was going but knew that would be his first question. And this move, coinciding with The Henrys' drama, would not help me. I sat for a few more minutes just staring at the wall in my office, a gnawing in my belly wrought by fear and uncertainty.

As a diversion, I ventured down the hall to Jeffrey's office to take the temperature of the creative department. Everyone was busily working, and I walked through quietly so as not to attract attention. Jeffrey's door was ajar, but the lights were off.

That's odd, I thought. Jeffrey held a staff meeting with his direct reports every Friday at 9 a.m. like clockwork. I didn't want to engage the toddlers, but I was too curious to hold back. When I poked my head into Sam's and Johann's cube, they were both sitting there quietly, engrossed in their work. "Hey guys, how's it going?" I asked with a smile. "Is Jeffrey in today?"

"I haven't seen him," Sam replied.

"I'll catch up with him later," I responded, exiting their cube.

I stopped in the ladies' room and just stared in the mirror. *What was I doing?* I thought about everything Kat revealed about Craig, about Jeffrey's story, and the fact that I was willingly going to join the bad guy—I was going to join his *winning* team. *But what did that really mean?* It would mean more of the same seesawing of emotions with Craig—the same level of fear that I was disappointing him—the inability to say no to his outrageous requests. It would mean compromising who I was. Sure, I would have to face Philippe, but maybe Kat was right. Maybe Warren would take my side and help me.

It struck me with incredible force that I had gone down the wrong path with Craig. I watched my eyes water and noted the crack in my lip was still visible. I took a deep breath and left the ladies' room to go tear up my resignation letter.

I returned to my office and caught Anna marching toward me carrying what seemed to be a heavy box. As she approached, I noticed a sneer in place of her usual sickening smile.

"Hello, Anna," I greeted her. "Need some help with that?"

She laughed wickedly. "You're the one who's going to need help. Have fun on the Titanic."

I stared at her as she stomped past me. I followed her out the front door of the office and called after her. "Wait," I yelled. "Where are you going?"

"You'll find out soon enough," she snickered as she opened her car trunk, dropped the box in it and slammed it back down.

I stood there, stunned. *Did Anna just quit or was she fired?* I rushed back to my office and found Veronica in the doorway, looking annoyed. "Oh, there you are," she said in a slightly agitated monotone. "I've been looking all over for you. Where's your non-compete agreement? You're the only one who hasn't turned it in."

I stared at her for a minute, frozen.

"What are you waiting for, Jane?" she asked.

I ignored her question, "What happened with Anna?"

Veronica looked around like she was about to reveal a secret. "Well, it's not public knowledge yet but she just gave notice to Warren. She's going to work for a competitor, so Warren had her walked."

"What?" I asked in disbelief. "Which competitor?"

"Keller Whitman Group," she said in a loud whisper. "They made her a vice president. Now Warren wants to have everyone's non-compete agreements signed and on his desk ASAP."

Veronica didn't wait around to get a response from me. She simply turned and walked away. I stood reeling from Veronica's information. *Anna was going to work for Keller Whitman Group as a VP?* It made no sense. I hurried to my office and picked up the phone, dialing Craig Keller's office number, heart pounding.

Simone answered, "Craig Keller's office, this is Si ..."

"Simone, this is Jane Mercer," I interrupted, "and I need to speak to Craig right away."

"Sorry, but he's in a meeting," she said, snobbishly.

"You need to interrupt. Let him know I need to talk to him."

"I was told only to interrupt him for certain people and you're not on that list," she announced, triumphantly.

"Fine," I said before hanging up. That was it. He wouldn't answer his cell phone. I would have to show up at his office in person. I glanced at my watch. It was 9:30 a.m. I grabbed my bag and hustled out of the office to my car.

I sat in traffic fuming about Craig Keller and his unscrupulous character. *How could he have hired Anna? Was it the same job he offered me? Vice President of Accounts? How could he offer us both the same position? Unless he had always planned to hire Anna but didn't bother to tell me. Or maybe he had us both going at the same time. Maybe he just hadn't decided.* I felt a sharp pain rip through my gut. I imagined Anna sitting on his 'casting couch' getting cozy as he plied her with cocktails and his special brand of sleaze-charm. Maybe she said yes to the late-night Chagall tour. Maybe he made a move on her just like he did with me. The thought of Anna smelling that heavenly soapiness made my face burn. *What could I have possibly been thinking?*

I stormed into the lobby and saw Simone sitting with her typical sullen expression. "I need to see Craig now," I demanded.

"Do you have an appointment?" she asked, in her usual bad-tempered manner. "He's in a meeting."

"I don't care." I glowered back at her, picturing her stringy black-haired head bobbing up and down while she performed fellatio on the managing partner.

"As I said, Mr. Keller's in a meeting, with the partners, and has asked not to be disturbed," she said. "I'll leave a message for him to call later."

But I was no longer listening. I bolted past her desk and marched down to Craig Keller's office, where I burst through the door, disrupting his meeting. There he was, looking composed as always, in a dark grey suit with a lavender tie, at the head of his long conference table, leaning back in a chrome swivel chair, lazily twisting it from side to side as he held court. He raised an eyebrow slightly when he saw me. His partners—all men—turned their heads to see who had the audacity to walk in on their meeting with His Highness.

Craig was the first to speak. "Ms. Mercer. I wasn't expecting you; may I help you?" he asked, rising from his chair, and sauntering over to where I stood at the office entrance.

"I don't need *help*. I need *honesty*," I sputtered, voice shaking.

I heard the partners clear their throats and a couple of them snicker in the background. Craig stared at me with an air of surprise and then amusement.

Simone appeared in the doorway with a troubled look on her face. "I'm sorry, Mr. Keller. She wouldn't leave and then she walked right past me. I'll have her removed by security if you'd like."

Craig's eyes didn't stray from mine as he spoke to Simone, "No, it's fine. I forgot we had an appointment, Jane." Then, he turned to face his partners and said, "Guys, I need a few minutes here. We'll regroup this afternoon. Now, will you please excuse us?"

As Simone and the partners shuffled out of the office, I noticed at least two of the partners give me the once over as they passed. *Pigs, just like their boss.*

As soon as everyone was out the door, Craig shut and locked it. He turned to me and held his hand out, gesturing toward the bar area. "Please sit down."

261

"No thanks. I'll stand," I snapped. "This won't take long."

He bit his lip. "You're so tense. Are you going to tell me what's going on? Like why you would break into my office unannounced? Are you trying to blow our cover? You know, I've trusted you with quite a bit—enough to hurt a lot of people."

"Yes, and you know all about hurting people. It's your specialty," I remarked, thinking about the reprehensible things he did to Kat and Warren.

He took a few steps toward me, close enough for me to inhale his soapy smell, which, at that moment, nauseated me. He settled his arms around my waist and pulled me closer. "Now, Jane, I think you need to relax," he said, lowering his palms to the curve of my ass.

I pushed his hands away. "Do *not* touch me."

"What?" He gave me his most dazzling smile. "Why not?"

"Because I didn't come here to get you off."

"Then why *are* you here? You still haven't told me that." His smile waned slightly.

"You didn't tell me you hired Anna."

He drew in his chin and looked faintly surprised but said nothing.

"She just gave notice, right before I was getting ready to give notice," I said, fuming. "But I decided it was a bad idea to leave Warren for you. It took me a while, but I figured out you're pure poison."

"Now, hold on a minute, Jane," he said, eyeing me cautiously. "That wasn't supposed to happen so fast. I was going to call and let you know I decided to hire Anna. But since you just said you ultimately decided to *stay* with Warren, it's a moot point, isn't it?"

"You screwed me over," I spat. "We had a signed contract. What about that?" I was still trying to wrap my head around the fact that he gave my job away without telling me, that if I had followed through with what he wanted, I could be out of two jobs in one day.

"You know, Jane, you just aren't ready to play in the big

leagues," he said matter-of-factly. "It's painfully obvious."

"But you don't even know Anna. You know nothing about her," I protested.

Then he gave me a look that said something entirely different.

"Oh, so you do know her. Tell me, did she spend a weekend with you at Shutters on the Beach? Did she give you a private fashion show in your office? Tell me the truth, Craig. I want to hear it."

"You need to calm down and lower your voice," he asserted. "This is business. And Anna was aggressive in her approach to getting a job here. She didn't hesitate when I requested The Henrys' contract. In fact, she gave it to me the same day I asked. She's hungrier than you, Jane. That's why I awarded her the job."

"You never said anything about it being a competition. You acted like I was the lead candidate—no, you acted like I was the *only* candidate, and now you're telling me that our contract was never valid?"

"That's what I'm saying, Jane," he answered without emotion. "I was certain it would be a relief for you: no more pressure to make a decision, no more stress about doing something to hurt Warren. I thought you'd be happy."

"I compromised myself to be with you—you and your perverted control-freak bullshit," I screamed at him, now enraged. "You made me do things I never would have done, and why? So, you could add me to your ever-expanding harem?"

"What we did was consensual, Jane—you're a big girl— you could have said no." His eyes were piercing mine now.

"Really?" I threw back. "You mean when you *forced* me on your desk? Could I really have said no?"

His eyes widened. "Careful, Jane. What I think you're saying would be exceptionally difficult to prove."

"We both know exactly what happened." Angry tears were forming, and I couldn't stop them.

Our eyes locked and then he spoke calmly, voice dripping with sarcasm. "Jane, my dear Jane. You're obviously upset right now. But there's no reason to burn a bridge here. So, what I would suggest, before you commit career suicide, is to go home, take a long hot bath and maybe some Midol. And once you've calmed yourself, give me a call so we can discuss this rationally."

"I don't need Midol, you arrogant bastard." Tears were now streaming down my face.

"You know, Jane, you're even more beautiful when you're angry," he commented, green eyes flashing, brows beginning to furrow. "But there's one thing you don't want to see and that's me angry. It's not at all pretty. Now will you please leave my office?" Although his voice was still calm, his eyes had turned a dark shade of exasperation.

I took a step toward him, putting my face right up to his. "You never intended to hire me, did you?"

He took a deep breath and gently pushed me away. "Here's what's going to happen. You're going to turn around and walk out of my office like a professional. Tomorrow, you're going to contact me with an apology and then we'll make arrangements for you to return the signing bonus."

"What?" I was flabbergasted. "You want the money *back*? I ... I don't have it."

"Well, that wasn't very bright of you, was it, Jane? Evidently, you didn't read your contract. I believe the amount is around $45,000 as of today."

The faint trace of a smile pulled at the corners of his mouth. *The bastard was enjoying this.*

"You know I don't have that money. You told me to 'go crazy' with Delcine—and you paid off my credit card. I was in debt, and you took care of it. It was a gift; I didn't ask you to do that. It had nothing to do with my employment and you know it." All I could think is that he was pulling the same stunt he pulled with Kat, demanding money once the relationship ended.

He shrugged indifferently. "Maybe you should ask Warren for the money—that is, if he can keep his agency doors open after losing his biggest client." He then moved swiftly around me to the door, unlocked and opened it for me. He stood there with an unyielding look on his face, one I'd never seen before.

I put my hands to my face and brushed the tears away, took a deep breath and walked briskly past him, refusing to make eye contact as I left. I heard the door close softly behind me as I made my way to the lobby.

Simone was there glaring at me, but I ignored her. Then, something made me stop and face her before I walked out. "I guess you won, didn't you?" I remarked sharply.

"Won what?" she asked looking down her nose at me.

"You *think* you're the winner, anyway," I scoffed. "But as far as I'm concerned, you're the biggest *loser* I've ever met."

"No, you're the loser. You're the one working for an agency that's going down."

"And you're an expert on that topic, aren't you?" I said, gesturing toward Craig's office, the tawdry bacchanal that sat thirty feet away ... before exiting Keller Whitman Group ... for the last time.

Twenty-Four

WHEN I RETURNED TO Warren Mitchell & Associates, it was already after 1 p.m. Traffic coming back from downtown was exceptionally heavy. But I needed the time to decompress after the ugly scene in Craig's office. My anger and hurt flowed out in the form of sobs the entire ride and, by the time I made it to the agency, I was still raw with emotion. It wasn't even the job or the money anymore, it was more about having been maligned, rejected, and torn to shreds by the almighty Craig Keller. And as much as I didn't like to admit it, I was suffering from the grief of a breakup, a full-blown breakup, not just the loss of a career-making job. I never thought it would happen this way, but he really hurt me. I never thought I would feel the stinging pain of losing a man I never even had. Those emotions were eclipsed by the thought that Anna would now have him. I knew it was irrational, but I was outright resentful that she would be the one flush with exhilaration when he called her, touched her, kissed her. I would have done anything to take the rest of the day off to mourn my losses properly—to put on sweatpants, drink two bottles of wine and sob incessantly to Elton John songs—but there was no time. I needed to turn in my non-compete agreement before the end of the day to keep my job. I wondered how much of what Craig said was true about Warren being in trouble with The Henrys having decamped. I would soon find out.

When I entered the agency, I went straight to the ladies' room to fix my makeup, knowing the crying jag had surely made a mess of my face. And I was right. As I wiped dried mascara from my cheeks and applied eyedrops to kill the redness, I received a text from Philippe, who was reconfirming our date for that evening. *Crap!* In my obsessing over the Craig situation, I had momentarily forgotten my original problem, the one that drove me to Craig's agency in the first place. I would now have to meet Philippe as promised or go to Warren like Kat had advised.

Back in the office, I looked around my desk for the resignation letter, but it was missing. My eyes dashed wildly around my office, and I wondered if perhaps I had filed it somewhere and forgotten. I crouched on the floor and felt around under my desk, thinking it may have fallen off. I scoured the wastebasket, but the resignation letter was not there. I was frantic. *Did someone find the letter?* I stood there for a moment, unsure of what to do. I then pulled the non-compete agreement from a file folder, hastily signed it and walked it over to Warren's office.

Veronica was at her desk busily typing away and Warren's office door was open. She looked up at me. "I'm just dropping off my non-compete agreement," I mumbled, voice hoarse from crying.

"Jane, where on earth have you been? I tried to call you several times and it just went to voicemail," she scolded.

After everything I had been through that morning, her chastising had zero effect. I said nothing while gently placing the agreement on her desk.

"Warren wants to see you, young lady. He's not exactly happy that you were out of touch."

Great. Now I had pissed off two managing partners. Maybe Craig would get his wish and Warren would let me go, too.

"Now go on in there," she ordered, pointing her long,

bony finger toward Warren's open office door.

I approached the doorway and saw Jeffrey on the red velvet couch speaking quietly with Warren, who sat across from him in his leather chair. It was Jeffrey who noticed my presence first. "Hey," he said beaming. "I'm glad you're here."

"Come in, Jane," Warren said rising to meet me and, at the same time, calling out to Veronica. "Can we get some glasses, please?"

Veronica promptly brought in three champagne flutes while Warren pulled a bottle of Cristal out of his refrigerator and popped the cork.

"Jane, please sit down. We have some good news," Warren said.

I gave Jeffrey a baffled look and plopped down next to him on the couch.

"We're making some changes to the agency," Warren announced as he gingerly poured champagne into each flute, letting the bubbles tame slightly before continuing to fill them. "I've made Jeffrey a partner."

"Congratulations, Jeffrey," I said, giving him a genuine smile. He nodded happily.

"And, in that process, Jane, I'm making you Vice President of Accounts."

I was unable to hide my astonishment.

"That means all the current account directors will report to you," he confirmed. "The job comes with a thirty percent base salary raise plus a bonus. I'll have Veronica send you the paperwork with the new numbers."

He paused to get my reaction. I was more than a little shocked at the irony of the promotion terms. "What? Really? Thank you, Warren. I'm … just surprised, with losing The Henrys and all." I didn't want to ask the obvious question, which was how Warren could afford to give me such a boost on the financial side.

"Yes, we did lose The Henrys, but we gained an even bigger client, one whose budget is more than twice what The Henrys had. You've heard of Brave Harlots?" Warren gave me a triumphant smile.

I felt my eyes bulge. "Of course." I recalled being introduced to Ewan Blade the first time I met Craig.

"They were with Keller Whitman Group," Jeffrey interjected. "But they wanted something different, and Warren convinced them our agency is a better fit."

Warren nodded. "The band management opted out of renewing their contract with Keller and signed one with us just a little while ago. Their lead guitarist, Ewan Blade, requested that you be their account lead ... said something about interviewing with a well-known reporter from KVLA who touted you as the best AE in the city. In fact, the news is probably reaching our friends over at Keller Whitman Group right about ..." Warren glanced at his watch and then back up at me. "... now."

It wasn't just that Warren had managed to get a client of this magnitude, it was that he managed to steal the client from under Craig Keller's nose. Marisa must have interviewed Ewan Blade and sold him on hiring Warren's agency—and me. I thought back to Craig and our confrontation earlier, thinking he would get an unwelcome interruption twice in one day. I suddenly laughed out loud.

I stood and held out my hand to shake Warren's, but he walked over and gave me a hug instead. When I sat down on the couch, Jeffrey put his arm around my shoulders and gave me a squeeze. "Congratulations, Jane," he said.

"You both deserve it. Cheers!" Warren said with a satisfied grin. We all clinked glasses and drank. I had never seen Warren so happy.

"We've had a few defectors today," Warren added in a less jovial tone.

I nodded, "I know Anna's one. I saw her leaving," I remarked, wincing at the thought of her moving into the huge office that was originally intended for me.

"You're correct," said Warren. My eyes drifted to Jeffrey. I knew better than to press for details. Warren was not one to engage in gossip.

Warren talked about a new direction, how he wanted to be less involved in the creative process so that he could focus on acquiring new business. He was also changing the agency name to Warren Mitchell and Partners, given Jeffrey's new status.

"It's time I stepped out of the day-to-day operations and let you and Jeffrey run things on the creative and account side," he explained.

Jeffrey and I exchanged glances. We talked with Warren for the rest of the afternoon about goals and objectives. At the end of the meeting, Warren commented, "By the way, you're on your own with the panda show. I no longer need to be involved in that account. I'm sure you'll do a fine job of producing the creative."

When he mentioned the pandas, my thoughts immediately jumped to Philippe and our imminent meeting. It was already 5 p.m. Warren dismissed us, and Jeffrey and I walked hurriedly back to his office to reconvene. "I don't believe that just happened," I said.

"Don't be pissed at me, Jane, but I knew about this Wednesday night. Warren called me at the end of the day to tell me his plan."

"What?" No wonder Jeffrey avoided me all day yesterday. It all made sense now. "Did you know Anna was leaving?"

"Yes," he answered. "She got an offer last night and broke the news to Warren this morning. Supposedly, Keller's been talking to her for a long time, waiting for an opportunity to get her over there."

I felt the same pain in my gut but kept a straight face.

"The beauty of this whole thing," Jeffrey continued, "is that Warren master-planned it."

"What do you mean?"

"He hated dealing with Rita Henry and couldn't wait to offload them. They were burning agency hours to the point where we were losing money. Employee morale was at an all-time low because the Henrys were never happy." Jeffrey paused to scratch his head. "Warren was the one who suggested Rita meet Craig months ago when she was appearing at some benefit that Keller's team was attending. He knew Rita would be attracted to Craig and that Craig would use that to get her business."

I shook my head in doubt. "You mean, Warren *wanted* them to leave?"

Jeffrey nodded, "Just like he wanted Anna out of here. You think *that* was a coincidence? Warren knew Anna was the only one with a hard copy of The Henrys' contract and the only one who would share it with Craig. She's never been loyal to Warren."

My mouth jutted open. It was Warren who was the master puppeteer, not Craig. That had to feel like retribution after all Craig had done to unravel Warren in the past.

Jeffrey cracked his knuckles loudly. "While Craig was distracted with The Henrys and effectively asleep at the switch with some of his other clients, Warren used it as an opportunity to move in on Brave Harlots, more as a 'fuck you' to Keller than for any other reason. The money doesn't hurt, though, and with the additional budget, he was able to promote us and not lay off any employees."

I stayed silent, thinking that I almost made the gravest error of my career by leaving Warren, especially for a scoundrel like Craig Keller. Now, all I had to do was find a way to deal with Philippe. I had only a few hours, so I would have to work fast.

I RETURNED TO MY office and began sorting through emails. The first one that popped up was a formal memo from Warren to all employees, announcing the promotion of both Jeffrey and me, and about the incoming client, Brave Harlots. My heart swelled with pride to see my name with the words *Vice President* next to it, earned through hard work and dedication, not by compromising myself to the boss. I wasn't in my office more than five minutes when I heard someone tapping at the door.

"Come in," I called.

It was Brooke, distressed but smiling and doing her best to look contrite. "Hi, Jane. I need to talk to you."

She must be concerned about her future now that I was

her boss. Never in my wildest dreams would I have ever seen ahead to this moment she would be approaching me with trepidation, wondering if I would accept or reject her. I had to admit, it felt fabulous. "What is it?"

She tossed her blonde hair to one side and plunked down in one of the chairs across from my desk. "I guess you're my new boss," she said in a voice that sounded as though she were seething under her smile. "Although I can't say I would have ever called that one. You sure have those men wrapped."

"What's your point, Brooke?"

"Nothing. I just never thought I'd end up reporting to you." Brooke must have noticed the effect her comments were having and tried to change her tone. She squinted her eyes and gave me a fake smile. "Will I be working with you on Brave Harlots?"

I knew it was Brooke's favorite band and that she would be angling to work side-by-side with them. Knowing her, she would get involved and then try to take credit for the success. That's when the brilliant idea came to me. "I haven't decided yet. But I do have another big client I'd like you to jump on immediately," I said, intending the vicious pun.

"Which client?" Brooke's face lit up but was masked with suspicion.

"It's a show from Paris that uses live pandas. They have a *huge* budget. In fact, there's an opportunity for you to meet with the client this very evening."

"I have dinner plans," she said haughtily. "I can't cancel them."

"Well, you don't have an option," I returned. "You'll meet the client at 8 p.m. at Chez Jay. His name is Philippe Barineau. I'll send you the client file, so you can spend the next couple of hours getting up to speed on their show campaign. You'll love it," I added smiling, thinking Philippe was in for a wonderful surprise: beautiful blonde Barbie Brooke, with her perpetual tan and coconutty smell. I noticed she was wearing an especially low-cut blue dress today. *Perfect.* Philippe would think he died and went to SoCal heaven. I guessed as soon as he laid eyes on her, his desire for me would rapidly disintegrate. At least that is what I was hoping.

Brooke scrunched her nose up. "Fine," she fumed, standing, and backing her way out of my office before I could give her any more assignments or infringe on her weekend plans.

"Don't be late," I called as she exited.

❧

ON MY WAY HOME that evening, I called Marisa to explain what happened with Craig, Warren, and Anna. She was on her way to LAX, flying to New York for the Thanksgiving holidays the following week. The first thing I did was thank her for talking me up to Ewan Blade. "Marisa, I don't know how you managed that, but you saved my job."

"It was nothing, Jane. I just told him the truth—how great you are. He must have left Keller for a reason. Maybe he wasn't happy."

"Well, that may be true, but you paved the way."

"Are you going to see Craig Keller again?"

"No," I responded, feeling queasy at his memory.

"Are you okay?" she asked. "I know how infatuated you were."

I sighed. "It hurts but I have no choice. You wouldn't believe how awful he was. He showed his true colors in a matter of minutes." I pictured Craig's cold, unbending stare with his green-black pupils.

"I hate to say it but," Marisa started.

"Yes, I know. You warned me. So did Kat. And I didn't listen."

"At least you're free and clear with a promotion from Warren. See how things in life always work out?"

"Well, I still have one major problem," I said with some hesitation. "You see, Craig said he wants me to pay back the signing bonus he gave me."

There was a pause. "What are you going to do?"

"I don't know because I don't have the money. I mean, I could always return the clothes but that's not the worst of it. He paid off my credit card at Neiman's. I owe him close to fifty thousand dollars."

"Wow! You must be damned good in bed."

"Very funny, Marisa."

"Sorry, but that's a heavy commitment when you hadn't even started working there. Do you think he'll try to hold you to that?" she asked.

"I'm sure he will because it's in the contract I signed. He was beyond angry this morning. I wasn't taking his news quietly and I got him pretty riled up." My thoughts went back to Kat and the money he demanded from her. "There's not much I can do. I just don't have the cash."

"Stall him, at least until I get back from New York," she requested.

"What do you mean?"

"I mean, I may be able to help."

"How are you going to help unless you have fifty Grand to loan me?"

"Stall him as long as you can," she repeated. "I'll be back in a week. If I don't talk to you before, happy Thanksgiving, Jane."

"Happy Thanksgiving, Marisa."

ON THE WAY HOME, I stopped at Bangkok West Thai on Santa Monica Boulevard for takeout. I had my evening planned. Now that I had officially gotten a rejection from Craig Keller, a promotion from Warren, and full authority to ditch the Philippe problem via sticking it to Brooke, there was only one thing I wanted to do. I ordered my favorite comfort foods: hot Thai coconut soup, pad Thai noodles and panang with tofu. My evening was set.

Just as I was rounding the corner to my apartment building, I got a call from Brooke.

"Jane," she said, distraught.

My dashboard clock read 8:19 p.m. "What happened to your meeting with Philippe?"

"That's why I'm calling. I showed up right on time and he was, like, totally pissed that it was me meeting him and not you."

"Did you explain that you would be his Account Director moving forward?"

"Yes, but he didn't care. He told me to get lost and he got up and stormed out of the restaurant. I could swear he had been drinking. The way he looked with those black circles under his eyes—you didn't tell me how gross he is, Jane. He really scared me."

"Did he say anything else?"

"He said he was going to fire our agency."

"I doubt that matters now that we have Brave Harlots," I said.

"Then I guess you have nothing to worry about," she quipped. "Is there anything else you need from me tonight?"

"No. I'll deal with it Monday." I hung up with Brooke as I was pulling into my apartment parking lot, which was totally dark. As soon as I was out of the car, with takeout food bag in hand, I heard someone sneak up behind me.

"*Mademoiselle*," a voice called.

I spun around and saw Philippe charging at me. I gasped. "What are you doing here?" I yelled, spooked that he knew where I lived.

"You double-crossed me," he shouted angrily. My heart raced as I backed away from him in the dark lot. "You should have thought twice about sending that woman when we had a deal."

"We have no deal," I replied coldly. "And you'd better turn around and leave or I'll call the police." I tried to keep the fear out of my voice as he continued to advance toward me.

"Oh no, *mademoiselle*," he snarled, "You will do no such thing. I'm here to settle the score. You're coming with me."

He lunged at me and grabbed my arm, yanking me toward him, dragging me roughly toward his vehicle, which was double parked in the lot near my car. The bag of food was in my free hand, so I flung it as hard as I could at him. The food containers exploded, and, by the grace of God, the hot coconut soup container smashed against Philippe's head and the contents sprayed all over his face and into his eyes.

He screamed in agony with the hot soup running down

his cheeks and neck, and I scampered back to my car, hopped in, and sped out of the parking lot, driving towards—I didn't know where.

I ended up on the freeway going north, still speculating as to where I should go. I longed to call Derek, but I knew he was performing right at that moment and wouldn't take my call even if he weren't. I couldn't go back to my apartment because that's probably where Philippe would wait or show up again later. I couldn't go to Marisa's or Kat's houses because both were out of town for the holiday. It was too late to go to my grandparents. Plus, I didn't want to tell them what happened. They would likely call the police. I knew I should call the police, but I didn't want Warren to find out what had happened between Philippe and me, at least not that way.

I ran through my phone contacts in the car, and I spotted Julian Feldman. I hit dial and he immediately picked up the phone.

"Hello?"

"Julian, it's Jane Mercer."

"Hi, Jane," he sounded pleasant if a bit startled by my call.

"Listen, I know this is crazy, but I need your help. Can I come to your place?"

"Now?"

"Yes, now."

Julian lived near Los Feliz, so it would be a drive from where I was at that point. When I arrived, he answered the door wearing a polo shirt and jeans. At least he had a welcoming smile. "Jane," he said, ushering me in. "What a nice surprise."

"I'm sorry to drop in on you like this but I just had a bad experience with this man and … well, I didn't want to go home."

He looked at me, puzzled. "What happened?"

"It's not so much what happened as what I was afraid might happen." I was trembling.

"You look like you've seen a ghost. Please sit down," he

said while getting a bottle of wine and some goblets.

I looked around his large, well-lit house in Martha Stewart style, his mother's work, no doubt. The décor was traditional enough. Everything matched in pastel shades, pointless objects and trite little bric-a-brac placed in just the right positions, with still life prints hanging on the walls.

"I'll just stay a few minutes, okay?" I knew Julian had no other plans, so I didn't feel bad.

"It's no trouble at all," he called from the kitchen. "I have some food left over from Shabbat. My parents were here earlier for dinner."

He trotted out with a tray of fruit, Challah, and some whitefish salad. I suddenly felt pangs of hunger. I really hadn't had anything in my stomach all day except for a glass of champagne with Warren and Jeffrey. I ate eagerly while Julian sat awkwardly across from me, sipping his Merlot, and watching me like I was some sort of zoo animal.

My phone started to ring again, and Philippe's number was flashing.

"Do you need to answer that?" Julian asked innocently.

"No. It's him. I'm going to shut my phone off for a bit."

Julian scratched his head and squinted at me. "Have you been dating him long?" he queried.

"No. It's not a boyfriend or anything." I was about to tell him it was a client but that sounded too bizarre. "He's a work acquaintance."

"Why don't you just tell him not to call you?" he asked. "There are laws against that type of harassment in the work-place."

"It's not that simple," I answered. There's no way Julian would understand my warped situation with Philippe. In fact, it was clear that Julian wouldn't understand any issue related to my dysfunctional personal life.

"Well, I hope it turns out for you," he concluded. "You know your grandmother invited our family to dinner for Thanksgiving, right?"

I nodded. "I heard. Are you coming?"

"I told my parents to decline because I wasn't sure how

you'd feel about it," Julian said, eyeing me pensively.

I was touched because he was so considerate. This was the type of guy I should be dating, not some dishonest, married pervert like Craig Keller who expressed his misogynistic tendencies by being abusive in bed.

We chatted for another hour or so and, when Julian started yawning and looking at his watch, I realized it was time for me to leave.

"I really have to get going," I said rising from his couch, "Thank you for being there for me. I don't know what I would have done if you hadn't answered the phone." I grabbed my purse, tossed it over my shoulder and headed to the front door.

"Next time, I'll know better," he chuckled, walking me out. "Be safe."

WHEN I ARRIVED HOME, I cautiously entered my apartment. Poor Weez gave me an incriminating stare because I had not fed him on time.

I opened a can of Friskies Buffet and turned my cell phone back on. A flurry of voicemails showed up. They were mostly from Philippe, starting with angry jabs about me leaving him with Brooke at a restaurant and *Wetching* on our deal. His calls then progressed to demanding I answer the phone and threatening to get me fired by dumping our agency.

I turned my cell phone off to avoid more disturbing calls. I just needed to rest. I took a hot shower, got into bed, and fell asleep instantly. I awakened at noon to my silent apartment. It was so quiet, I almost forgot what had occurred the night before. As I brewed coffee, I turned my phone back on and discovered no more messages from Philippe. *Whew.* Maybe he would back down now that he knew I wouldn't take his shit.

JEFFREY AND I HAD scheduled to meet late Saturday afternoon to prepare for casting the Brave Harlots' television spot the following Monday. When I got to the office, he was sitting in the conference room with a slew of zed cards scattered all over the table. They usually contained several photos, height, weight, and measurements so the hiring entity was able to narrow down the pool for a casting call.

"Hey," he greeted me.

"Hey," I said, sitting down across from him, picking up a stack of cards. "What are we looking for?"

"Twenty- and thirty-something men and women of all ethnicities to fill in a crowd scene for the spot," Jeffrey responded. "I was thinking like twenty-five people total, ten principals for the front row and the rest filler. We'll shoot it very tight, so the scene looks full of people."

"I'll take the women, you take the men," I suggested as I began sifting through the cards.

"How was your Friday night?" Jeffrey asked casually.

"Interesting," I responded.

"That bad?"

"Worse," I replied pulling out a photo of a woman with long blonde hair and huge breasts and then tossing it aside into the 'no' pile.

"Well, it couldn't be worse than Philippe Barineau's night," Jeffrey revealed. "Warren just called to tell me he was admitted to the hospital early this morning with severe burns in his eyes."

"What?" I was so frozen with terror I dropped a stack of cards.

"Yeah," Jeffrey continued. "He said it was some sort of accident."

"Did Warren say how the accident happened?" I asked, gulping slowly.

"No, only that it was going to delay the opening of the show indefinitely. Frédéric can't function without Philippe in a managerial role, so they have to move the opening date to sometime next year."

"What does that mean for the agency? I mean, we were working towards a short deadline." I pictured Philippe in a hospital bed cursing me.

Jeffrey shrugged. "I doubt they'll want to keep us on while Philippe's recovering."

"Was Warren upset?"

"Not in the slightest. He's ecstatic about getting Brave Harlots and doesn't seem bothered at all. He even hinted that there may be another heavy-hitter client coming our way."

I wondered why Philippe would not have spilled the beans that I was the one who threw hot soup in his face, causing a major incident that landed him in the hospital and thus changing the course of their show opening in Las Vegas. Maybe he didn't think anyone would believe the story since no one was there to witness it and it was self-defense. Plus, I had threatened to call the police and he was dumb enough to leave a host of recorded messages on my voice-mail which could be used, if needed, to prove my version of the story was accurate.

"Did Warren give you a hint as to who the next big client is?" I decided to redirect the conversation away from the Philippe debacle.

"Not yet, but he hinted it may be another Keller Whitman refugee," he said. "Warren has that man in his cross hairs lately."

"Do you think Keller Whitman Group knows Warren's after their clients?" I asked, tossing another generic blonde into the 'no' pile.

"Not sure," he commented. "But I do know stealing Brave Harlots had to really pinch them hard on the financial side, and if there's one thing that hurts Keller, it's losing money. The man loves money even more than he loves beautiful women—if that's possible."

My thoughts went momentarily back to Craig, and I felt my stomach churn. I was still not over being stung by him, no matter how much I tried to put it out of my mind. I hadn't heard from him since the day before, in his office, but had a feeling he would resurface to collect his signing bonus, especially if he loved money as much as Jeffrey indicated. "Do you suppose they'll steal more of our clients?" I asked, deliberately not responding to the comments about Craig.

"Not if we're doing our jobs," Jeffrey answered. "And speaking of which, what do you think of this guy?" Jeffrey held a card out to me with a man who looked a little like a young Bradley Cooper. I gave him the thumbs-up.

"Let's hope this photo is current and hasn't had too much retouching," he commented, tossing the card in the men's 'yes' pile. It was common for zed cards to be inaccurate, which was why we always followed up with an in-person casting call.

I WENT HOME THAT night feeling encouraged, like I had successfully dodged the biggest bullets in my career so far: Craig Keller and Philippe Barineau. I could now rest up and enjoy the Thanksgiving holiday.

Twenty-Five

THANKSGIVING CAME AND WENT, and, with time off work, I was able to reflect on my life and all the recent events. The ego-crushing grief over Craig Keller still lingered, but his lying, deceiving nature was so blatantly ugly, it overrode any romantic feelings I had left. I mostly felt humiliation at the thought that I could be so gullible. I still, however, lived in fear that he would try to recoup the nearly fifty Grand I owed him. He had, in fact, included a clause in my contract that if the agreement were broken by either party, any monies issued pre-employment would be promptly collected—or something like that.

The other thing still gnawing at me was that Derek had not forgiven me. I longed to text him but my pride and embarrassment over our last run-in prevented me. I wondered if he went back home to Portland for the holiday. As clichéd as it sounded, I pictured him cozy in a cable-knit sweater by the fireplace with his family surrounding him. His sister would be there with her husband and children, and they would all be talking and laughing. I wondered if Derek wanted kids. I knew he would be the perfect parent, easy-going and encouraging yet strict about manners and education, and of course doing the right thing. Derek always did the right thing, which was why his silence hurt so deeply.

Marisa called in the middle of my musing. "Hey, Jane ... what are you up to?"

"Not much ... you still in New York?" I moved to my apartment window and peered out. It was bright, sunny and surprisingly smog-free.

"Yeah, coming back in a few days. How was your Thanksgiving?"

"It was calm. And yours?"

"It was good to get out of LA, but I'm ready to return to the insanity."

"Have you talked to Derek, by chance?" I asked, hoping to hear some tidbit about his life.

"We texted a couple of times," she said evasively. "Did you two finally make up?"

"No," I said in a sad voice.

"Maybe you should reach out again."

"There's no way, Marisa. He made it clear how he feels about me."

"I don't know, Jane," she said, "I get the feeling he'd be more receptive at this point."

When we hung up, an Elton John song was playing in the background: "Your Song," which tugged at my heartstrings. Derek and I had always agreed that lots of popular ballads were too sappy to listen to but Elton John, whose love songs had stood the test of time, was one of the few exceptions. Against my better judgment, I picked up my phone to write him a text.

"Happy holidays, Derek. Wherever you are, I hope you're having fun."

Oh, that sounds too weird coming from the woman who hit him with a flying tomato at Whole Foods. I quickly deleted the message.

Later that night, still consumed with thoughts of Derek, I curled up on the couch in my white fuzzy robe with Weezer and a hot cup of tea. I scrolled through old photos on my phone, going back four years, and pored over the images taken when I first started working for Warren. I pulled up a selfie. It was the old me, with my long auburn hair, my original, unretouched face. I zoomed in and found my eyes—the same beautiful green eyes that I was born with, the face that had been cruelly dismissed by my drunken father as unattractive … the face of the whole person he deemed worthless at such a young, impressionable age.

I put the phone down and went into the bathroom, turned the brightest light on and examined my face—the new one with all its improvements—the refined nose and chin, the plumped-up lips, and the smooth, glowing skin without one wrinkle. But one feature never changed—my green eyes, still clear and bright, pupils burning with the inextinguishable fire of my soul.

"You're beautiful, Jane," I said to my formidable, life-long enemy, the mirror. "You've always been beautiful. You're also smart. And I … love you."

My eyes watered as I watched, for once, with compassion, the beautiful, misguided woman in the reflection as she broke down at the concept that she, no matter what anyone said, could be loved. This woman was a princess in her own unique way, regardless of the standard that society prescribed for every woman—for every little girl—those who would never find true happiness because they would never know how to love themselves.

I put my hands to the mirror as though I could touch my face in the reflection, tracing my fingers over my features and staring, with heart-felt wonder at the woman who stared back at me.

I entered my closet and drew my hand across the tightly bound row of clothes that hung, the expensive fabrics fanning against my fingers as I pulled them along. It was all cloth that made up the fancy window dressing that cloaked my body—the clothes I coveted and obsessively cared for more than I ever cared for myself. And although I was not about to part with any of them, their importance diminished with the realization that they were nothing without the person who wore them … the beautiful woman who brought them to life.

I backed away from the closet and my thoughts returned to Derek, the hurt lingering deep in my heart. He was so good, and I treated him terribly. I didn't love myself, so how could I love anyone else? While I was feverishly chasing after Craig Keller, I managed to abort one of the few close friends I had. Derek hated me and there was no recovering. No matter what Marisa said, he wouldn't speak to me. I had no way to communicate my feelings. I was cut off completely.

My mind wandered to the first connection we had: music. And that's when it came to me. I was going to make him a mixtape. It worked for John Cusack's character in *High Fidelity*, so perhaps it would work for me, too. I would put it on CD because if I sent an electronic playlist, with things as precarious as they were now, Derek might delete it before listening. I would have to physically get it to him.

I had made mixtapes before and there was an art to making a true masterpiece. The trick was to include just the right number of songs relevant to both of us. Not every song had to contain a message to him. It might only create a mood or a feeling. It needed to be both cool and honest, melodic, and meaningful. As I sifted through my song database, my only goal was getting him back into my life.

I put my list together and created the mixtape, settling in to listen and make certain it said exactly what I wanted him to know:

Empty Nest—Silversun Pickups

Pages—White Reaper

Withdrawal—Max Frost

Easy—MISSIO

Sofa King—Royal Otis

Jungle—Tash Sultana

Burning—Yeah Yeah Yeahs

Youth—Glass Animals

Love Is Mystical—Cold War Kids

Cigarette Daydreams—Cage the Elephant
Adios—JAWNY
Everybody's Gotta Learn Sometime—Beck
Your Song—Elton John

It was no longer a mere list of thirteen songs, but an epic … one body of work that represented a full range of emotions. I gave it three full listens before I knew it was perfect and complete.

I tucked it into a card that had nothing on it but an iridescent hummingbird. It was blank inside and I wrote on the envelope, 'Derek.' During lunch one day, I sneaked to his apartment to slide it under his door. When I got there, I knocked just to see if anyone was there. To my surprise, the door opened. It was Antonia, Derek's housekeeper. I had met her several times.

"Hello, Miss Jane," she greeted me.

"Hi, Antonia," I replied awkwardly. I had not considered that I could be busted in the middle of my caper.

"Long time, no see," she said.

"Antonia, I need a big favor," I said, feeling like a stalker. "Will you please put this card on Derek's pillow?"

She took the card and looked at the envelope. "For him?" she asked.

"Yes, Antonia, on his pillow," I repeated, clasping my hands together and pretending to sleep on my side.

"Ah, si, si," she said.

"Gracias, Antonia," I replied, gratefully.

THE NEXT TWO WEEKS flew by, and I had been collecting industry party invitations. One for the biggest of the season had just arrived for the upcoming Saturday night. It was the launch of a hot new clothing line and was to be held at the Roof Garden at the Peninsula Beverly Hills. The prettiest people in LA were going to be at this party. I wasted no time calling Marisa to coordinate.

"Hello? Who is this? It can't be Jane Mercer because

she's too busy for me."

"You haven't called me either," I said with a smile in my voice.

"Where the hell have you been?"

"Under water," I responded. "So much so, I'm growing gills."

"Yeah, me too. The holidays are always the worst for the station—both good news and bad."

"Well, I have a great excuse for us to get dressed up and relieve some stress," I said, excited. Marisa had received the same invitation. What we usually did was each invite a guest, which was always Kat and Derek.

"Do you want to RSVP for Kat or Derek?" Marisa asked.

"I have no problem inviting Kat, but Derek is *no bueno*," I explained, feeling a sad twinge in my stomach that we had still not spoken since 'the tomato incident.' And he had obviously shunned my mixtape which was an unspeakable affront, given our musical bond and the effort that went into it.

"You mean to tell me you two still haven't made up?"

"Marisa, do you have amnesia? I hit him with produce and went street crazy on him in a parking lot. You just can't do that and still expect someone to hang out."

"Why don't you just call and apologize? This has gotten way out of control."

"Oh, what a great idea, Marisa," I grumbled. "I'd never thought of that,"

"Well, you couldn't have been too sincere. Derek's a good guy. There's no way he would reject you. Remember what I said about how he feels about you."

"Seriously, I have apologized to this man over and over," I explained. "I even made him a mixtape and he ignored it. He wants nothing to do with me, so going to a party together is not an option."

"I guess I wanted it to be like old times when it was just the four of us, having a great time," she answered.

"The three of us will have a better time than we ever had with Derek. It's settled," I concluded. "I'll RSVP for one.

You RSVP for two. Done."

Before she could object, I hung up and started considering my party outfit. This event was just the thing I needed to pull me out of my holiday doldrums. I went dark completely after everything that happened Thanksgiving week. I didn't text or call anyone.

I even stopped dreaming about Craig Keller, but I hadn't effectively put him out of my mind because I received a letter from his attorney demanding $44,100. At first, I was uncertain about the number, but realized Craig had backed out the $900 I had spent on the original Marc Jacobs dress that he tore in the hotel room. A lot of good that did me. I had no idea how I was going to handle the situation because I didn't even have a lawyer.

Upon receipt of the letter, I showed it to Marisa in a panic. She tossed it aside and told me not to worry about it, that he was just bluffing. Kat, however, disagreed, based on her own experience. No matter what they said, I had a gut feeling he would never relent, and it made me nervous—*extremely nervous*.

Twenty-Six

MARISA AND I DECIDED we would have a pre-party warmup at Kat's house Saturday night. Kat's divorce was about to be finalized and we were, among other things, celebrating her singleness with a night out at a fabulous party.

I had selected a vintage light wool mini-dress, color-blocked with camel, orange, and white. I paired it with Manolo Blahnik boots in softened winter-white suede. Over the Thanksgiving holiday, I had my hair dyed back to auburn, so I looked like my old self again. I had also halted my visits to Dr. Feelgood, and my face had returned to its 'original' state. I took an extra hour to flat iron my hair, so it was long, shiny, and straight.

When Kat opened the door, she gasped. "Oh my, you look drop-dead gorgeous," She exclaimed as I strutted in.

Marisa was there, and they were already at work on a bottle of champagne. Marisa looked up from her cell phone and her jaw dropped. "Good lord, Jane. No girl stands a chance with you in the room. Do you think that dress is short enough?"

I waved my hand in dismissal.

"You'd better try sitting down in here to make sure,"

Marisa warned.

"We won't be sitting." My voice was filled with mischief. "We'll be working the party."

"Maybe I should re-think my hemline?" Kat said looking at her own outfit. She had on a knee-length black slip dress that draped nicely over her slim figure.

"No way," I said. "You look perfect, but you need some strappy heels."

"Okay Ms. Fashionista," Marisa said, standing up and doing a little turn. "Do you have any helpful tips for me?"

Marisa wore a simple red Diane Von Furstenberg wrap dress. A black camisole peeked out from underneath so she would not show too much cleavage.

"Ditch the camisole," I suggested.

"No way, I'm not showing my boobs at a party where I might run into colleagues."

"You're not going to be on TV, Marisa. Besides, your boobs aren't big enough for you to be so worried."

"Thanks a lot," she said, sighing as she untied the wrap dress, removed the camisole, and re-tied the dress. "There. Do I pass now?"

"Excellent," I confirmed. "Let's get out of here."

WE ARRIVED FASHIONABLY LATE, and the party was just getting into full swing. I spotted a group of young, attractive women, all dressed in black, at a check-in table. They had to be some agency's PR team. Whoever the agency was, their red carpet was one of the coolest things I had ever seen. It was an actual runway with a step and repeat on one side. Sexy models dressed in the designer's fashions escorted guests from one end to the other while the media and party goers ogled whoever was on the carpet at any given moment.

Kat was mortified. "I hope no one can see through my dress," she whispered to us as we approached the carpet.

"You'd better hope they can't see *up* your dress." Marisa pointed at my thigh-high hem while nervously adjusting her wrap dress to hide what little cleavage was showing. "I thought you said I wouldn't be on display tonight?"

"Let them look," I replied haughtily. "Want me to go first?"

Kat and Marisa nodded as I led the way. With poise and confidence, I stepped up to the red carpet with my female model escort and walked the catwalk. She stopped me in front of the *step and repeat* backdrop that was spattered with numerous sponsorship logos, and I felt a shower of paparazzi lights as I posed. A barrage of whistles and cat calls sounded from every direction.

At the end of the carpet, I stepped down and looked back to see how Kat and Marisa were doing. Instead, I saw a couple of celebrities from one of the reality shows. They must have jumped the line because of their fame. I felt someone touch my shoulder and I spun around.

"That was quite an entrance, Ms. Mercer." It was Craig Keller with Anna trailing behind him like a puppy dog. She was wearing a long, curly blonde wig. It dawned on me then that she was indeed the woman in the red suit I saw walking in the parking lot of Craig's building. For whatever reason, she didn't want to go blonde with her real hair, so she opted for a wig—an expensive one by the looks of it. Craig looked as crazy sexy as ever in a houndstooth sport jacket over a white button-down shirt with black jeans and black leather oxfords—laces meticulously tied.

He bowed down to kiss my hand and I smiled serenely.

"You're gorgeous with that hair color," he remarked, giving me a sexually charged stare-down, like nothing unpleasant had ever transpired between us and that his lawyer had not sent me a threatening letter demanding five figures. "I should have hired you as one of the models."

Of course, those were Keller's employees at the carpet entrance. The hot new clothing designer was undoubtedly his client. I saw Anna standing behind Craig, looking upset because he was completely ignoring her. She shot me a jealous glare. I was going to have some fun with this. "Well, I was never really available," I commented, looking him straight in the eye but still smiling.

"The best ones rarely are," he responded. He seemed mesmerized by my presence, which was altogether empowering. "But maybe for the right price?" he teased, focusing those incredible green eyes on mine.

"You can't afford it," I countered.

He smiled. "As far as I recall, you still owe *me* money."

"As far as I recall that money was a small token of your appreciation." I returned his smile. "You know, for *services* rendered."

"If that's the case, then I think you, at the very least, owe me a drink tonight. Come on, Jane, have one drink with me."

Anna was becoming more agitated the longer Craig remained with me.

"I think we've been to that dance before, now, haven't we?" I asked, noticing he was wearing his wedding ring tonight.

"Come on, Jane," he said leaning in to whisper in my ear. "Don't let business ruin what we have." I inhaled the soapy scent again and, while it smelled as magnificent as ever, this time it was different. I was the one in control.

"What we *have*?" I returned with a breathy laugh. "What we *had* was slightly degrading—and now, it's slightly over."

Before he could say anything, Kat was standing next to me. Craig recoiled at the sight of her. I gave her a hug, holding her extra close for a long moment. When I turned back to Craig, he had a perplexed look on his face.

"I didn't know you two were friends," he said, growing visibly uncomfortable, a sight I never thought I'd witness.

"Yeah," said Kat. "It's a small world, isn't it?"

Marisa broke into the conversation. "Mr. Keller! What a wonderful surprise. I didn't think I'd see you so soon after our last meeting," she gloated with a cat-like gleam in her eyes.

For whatever reason, Craig was speechless. He simply nodded at Marisa, turned, and walked away as Anna trailed behind him, looking like someone just kicked her in the teeth.

"Would someone please tell me what just happened?" I asked as soon as they were gone.

"It's called Karma," Marisa replied.

"I've never seen that man back off anyone faster than he backed off you, Marisa," Kat exclaimed. "I mean, he acted like he saw a ghost."

Marisa pulled her cell phone out of her bag and waggled it in the air. "That's because I have him by the balls," she said triumphantly.

"What?" I asked. "What do you mean? What did you do, Marisa?"

Marisa began to fumble with her phone and soon had a video file pulled up. She looked around to make sure no one was near us and hit play. The video was of Craig Keller attacking someone on his office desk. You could only see his face and the upper half of his body because the woman underneath him was obscured and effectively blurred.

I gasped. *Was that me?* "Marisa, how did you get that footage?"

"Don't be pissed at me, Jane, but I couldn't just leave you there that day I gave you a ride to his office. I waited until the right moment and sneaked in and hid behind the bar. When he started in on you, I took the opportunity to record it on my cell phone. Then I brought it to my studio and edited it, so nobody could tell who the girl on the desk was."

"What?" I was exasperated. That must have been Marisa I heard opening and shutting Craig's office door while I hid behind the couch.

"When he sent you that threat letter, I showed up at his office and told him if he didn't drop the lawsuit and leave you alone immediately, I would do an exposé on him and his philandering ways. In fact, you should have seen his face when I threw in the words, 'sexual assault.'"

"What did he say?" I asked, now mortified. It was bad enough Marisa had witnessed Craig and me live, but the fact that she also had it on video was embarrassingly surreal.

Kat just stared at Marisa.

"He called my bluff and said he didn't care what I had, that he would deny everything and threatened to ruin Jane's reputation with Warren. That's when I quickly reminded him that I used to be a tabloid reporter and would make sure the footage went viral if he didn't relent."

"Holy shit, Marisa," I exclaimed, throwing my arms around her. "You saved me!"

"Oh my god, you're so amazing," Kat cried, joining in our group embrace.

"It was nothing," Marisa said quietly. "Now let's go celebrate."

As we melded with the crowd, we stopped and chatted with colleagues we all knew. I guessed everyone had inked this party on their calendar. It was a veritable who's who of the PR, advertising, and entertainment world.

I froze when I spotted Derek and Chelsea, sitting awkwardly together in a VIP cabana. They were drinking red wine and observing the crowd.

"Oh shit," I said aloud. "What are *they* doing here?" Derek didn't have the right connections to get into a party like this, let alone into a VIP cabana.

Kat and Marisa glanced in their direction. "Here's your chance to make things right," said Marisa.

"Let's go somewhere else," I urged.

Kat shook her head. "No, Jane. We're going to talk to him. You don't have to join us, but we're going. Come on, Marisa."

I took a deep breath and grudgingly followed behind them.

Derek immediately stood, smiling, and hugging them. That's when our eyes met. I shrugged and waved as if to say, 'I know this is the last thing either of us wants but we're here so let's roll with it.'

Kat looked back at me, motioning for me to join them. I took a few steps forward until I was right on the periphery of the conversation. It was Chelsea who acknowledged me first by running over and giving me a kiss on the cheek. She wore a navy chiffon dress with muted gold stars all around the bodice and full skirt.

"Hi, Jane," she said in earnest, like I had never thrown an invisible dagger. "I was hoping you'd be here."

"It's good to see you, Chelsea," I lied, thinking this must be the part in Grandma's Elizabeth Kübler-Ross book, "On Death and Dying," when you move to the final stage of acceptance.

"Derek talks about you all the time, about how you love fashion. I mean, look at your stunning outfit tonight," she complimented. "You're breathtaking."

Again, Derek and I locked eyes.

"Thank you, Chelsea," I responded, not knowing where this was leading.

"You see, my sister owns the featured clothing line and I'm helping her get the word out. I actually recommended she hire you, but she already committed to another agency."

"I appreciate you thinking of me," I replied, pulling a business card out of my bag. "If she ever wants to move on, have her give me a call."

"I'm going to run and find her to meet you in person. I'll be right back." And Chelsea flitted away like Tinkerbell.

Derek and I were left staring at each other. "Are you hiding any more tomatoes in that outfit?" he asked, examining me from head to toe with a slight look of amusement.

"Nope, just happy to see you," I answered with a half-smile.

"You know, I was really mad at you," he said.

"Really? I had no idea."

He looked down for a minute and then back up at me, his hazel eyes shining in the evening lights. "To be completely honest, I've missed our talks. I was going to send you the cleaning bill for my jacket as an excuse to discuss the new Killers album or something."

We both laughed, and I wanted to ask what he thought of my mixtape. I couldn't get over that he hadn't responded to it.

"There is such a thing as a phone," I said.

He shrugged.

"Derek," I said gently. "I'm sorry about the way I acted—all the careless, stupid things I said."

He didn't have a chance to answer because Chelsea

returned with her sister in tow. "Jane, please meet my sister, Jordan," she broke in.

An older, heavier version of Chelsea smiled pleasantly and shook my hand. "Chelsea tells me you like clothes," she commented, perusing my attire with an approving smile. "I love your Manolos, and that dress is exquisite."

"Thank you," I replied. "Chelsea's right, I do love fashion."

"Come by my store sometime," she invited, handing me her card. "I'll hook you up."

I could feel Derek's eyes on me. I wanted so badly to just take his hand and run away from there. There were so many things I wanted to tell him, I felt like I was ready to burst.

"We should get going," Chelsea suggested, looking at Derek like a girlfriend who'd had enough socializing for one evening. I thought about them going back to Derek's apartment and making out, and then him leading her into his bedroom for hours of sex. Maybe they would do it with the mixtape I had made for him playing in the background. I felt sick at that thought. I watched closely as they interacted. It was almost difficult to imagine them romantically involved because there was no perceptible chemistry. But that's how Derek was. He acted with discretion. That's one of the things I loved about him most. He had class. I was just grateful to be on speaking terms with him again.

Chelsea got her things, and Derek gave Marisa and Kat each a hug. He then walked over to where I stood. I looked up at him, searching his eyes for some indication of how he felt about me, Chelsea, what the future would hold.

"Are we okay?" he asked.

"Yes, of course we are," I returned, feeling my eyes well up a bit. He leaned over and kissed me tenderly on the cheek, which felt almost heartbreaking.

"I'll be in touch," he said softly, studying my wide-open eyes, which were like that because I was trying to keep them from blinking and emitting tears. "Take care of yourself, Jane."

And they walked away.

"She's a little doll," Marisa observed as we watched

them disappear into the dense crowd, Derek leading Chelsea by the hand.

"Yes, she really is." I sighed.

"Did you and Derek make up?" Kat asked me.

"Yeah," I said, looking away. "Everything's fine."

"Then why do you look so down?" Marisa asked.

"Honestly, I'm not," I said giving her a princess smile. "Let's get another drink."

As we continued to wander through the party crowd, I kept thinking about Derek. He really did seem happy and that was all that mattered. I imagined one day, we would all end up with the right person and we'd be happy for each other. I also realized that our relationships would change at some point, which made me feel a pang of melancholy for what we would lose.

We stayed for one more drink and decided to call it a night. While waiting for my car in valet, I heard my phone chime with a text message.

From the initials CK, it read, "Sure you don't want a drink?"

I looked up and saw Craig leaning against the Bentley in his careless, confident way. When our eyes met, he smiled, and a shudder ran up my spine. I found out the hard way what those perfect white teeth were capable of and had no interest in another encounter.

I watched him for a few seconds, thinking he was indeed the best-looking man I'd ever seen in my life, but Kat was right about one thing: his beauty was only skin-deep. I wanted something more. I wanted to be with someone who would be both kind and devoted to me, someone honest and trustworthy—someone who would love me for who I was. The looks were only icing on the cake. I put my phone in my bag and turned my back completely on Craig. The valet driver was up with my car shortly thereafter. As soon as I was safe inside, I gazed out the window. Craig Keller had gone.

Twenty-Seven

THE WEEK OF CHRISTMAS, Jeffrey and I worked fourteen-hour days managing Brave Harlots. The account was easily the biggest we had ever worked with, and we needed to get every detail right on their ad collateral for their New Year's Eve show at the Staples Center, where they were kicking off their world tour. I was getting frantic hourly calls and updates from Jeffrey. The band constantly wanted to change their digital media to boost advanced ticket sales, even though we all knew they would easily sell out.

Everyone was pushing tight deadlines because the agency was closing Christmas Eve through New Year's Day. Jeffrey and I had to show up at the New Year's Eve show, but we weren't disappointed: the tickets included backstage passes.

On Christmas Eve, Jeffrey entered my office around noon with a bottle of Veuve Clicquot.

"Isn't it a little early for that?" I asked, chuckling.

"One of our vendors sent this to me and I know you like it," he said, presenting it to me like he was a sommelier.

"Nice," I replied. "Where's the rest of the swag?"

"In the creative department. Lots of goodies. You're welcome to come by and scope it out for your family."

"Only if there's a box of White Zin," I chuckled. "You know my grandma's high-end taste."

Warren was now standing in my office doorway. "Hey, you two," he began, "I just wanted to personally give you your holiday bonuses."

I stood as he shook our hands and handed us envelopes. "We've had quite a year," he said, gesturing at the envelopes. "This should show you how much you're appreciated."

I opened my envelope and peeked inside while Warren stood watching me closely. I almost fainted at the amount. It was $44,100. There was also a letter in the envelope, which I pulled out and examined curiously. It was my resignation letter. *Fuck!* I looked up at him in a panic, but he just stood quietly studying me. There was no doubt about it—Warren knew exactly what had gone down with Craig. There was a subtlety in his expression, like I was his wayward daughter—one who had temporarily wandered down the wrong road—but he was here to protect me.

"Thank you, Warren," I uttered, barely holding back tears.

"You're welcome, Jane," was all he said.

❧

As TRADITION DICTATED, I joined Grandma and Grandpa on Christmas Day for 'Chinese food'.

"Jane, tell me what you're up to these days," Grandpa asked over his moo shoo chicken.

"Just working. I don't have a lot to report," I answered before crunching into an egg roll.

"I'm sure you have something to report," Grandma said, winking at me.

I realized she was still stuck on the thought that Julian and I should be dating. "Actually, Grandma, there's no guy in my life right now," I confessed. "And I'm completely fine with it. In fact, I'm not even looking."

"But honey, what happened to Julian?" she asked, visibly wounded.

I sighed. "Julian's not for me, Grandma."

"But why not? He's perfect for you …"

"It's about time I cleared things up," I interrupted. "Julian's a nice man, but I don't want to date him."

"But if he's so nice …" she pressed.

"Barb, lay off," Grandpa ordered crossly. "She doesn't like him and that's that."

I didn't expect Grandpa to come to my defense, especially regarding this subject.

"Whose side are you on?" Grandma asked crabbily.

"I'm on the side that wants our granddaughter to be happy," he responded. "Jane, will you please pass the egg rolls?"

💋

It was New Year's Eve, and I was ready for the Brave Harlots show at Staples Center. I offered two tickets each to both Kat and Marisa, so they could bring dates, but Marisa was doing a live broadcast all night and Kat was spending her evening at home in front of the television with Joyce. Jeffrey was my date because we were technically working the event. Warren was also attending with Caroline. They had front row seats.

I decided on a pair of sleek black velvet jeans and a stunning Anne Fontaine white blouse paired with a leather motorcycle jacket. I topped off the look with diamond stud earrings and strappy metallic heels.

When I got to the Staples Center, the band management ushered me backstage where I found Jeffrey milling around with the toddlers. I half-wondered how the toddlers got in, given the backstage crowd was strictly controlled and only four passes had been distributed for Warren Mitchell and Partners.

"Hey," I said, approaching the group.

"Hey, Jane," the toddlers greeted me in unison. And, as though they could read my mind, Johann added, "Jeffrey sneaked us in under the guise that we were necessary agency staff."

My eyes met Jeffrey's and he put his index finger to his

lips. "Don't tell anyone, but I thought we could reward the guys for their hard work over the holidays."

"Dangermetal's the opening act," Sam announced, looking ebullient. "You know they're my favorite band."

"Somehow, I'm not surprised," I commented while Jeffrey smirked.

Dangermetal had just taken the stage and their music was so loud and so penetrating, the arena walls shook, and the bass beat pounded heavily into my chest. We couldn't hear each other if we tried, which was fine because I was done talking for the night and just wanted to enjoy the experience. I saw Warren walking backstage with the band's manager, and I motioned for the toddlers to make themselves scarce. Warren approached Jeffrey and me and screamed, "Is this what kind of music you guys are into these days?"

"Not me," I screamed back. "Where's Caroline?"

"She's in the front row head-banging," Warren yelled his reply, laughing. "Have fun. Happy New Year!" He exited the backstage area.

When Dangermetal had finished their earsplitting set and they were in between bands, Marisa was calling my cell phone. "You won't believe this shit," she shouted into the phone. "I surprised Drew today at his apartment for a glass of champagne before I went to work for the evening and found him in bed with someone else."

"What?" I asked. "Who is she?"

"Not *she. He,* as in a man!" Marisa sounded as if she wanted to kill someone. "He confessed to me that he's a pansexual."

"What the hell is that?" I asked.

"I had to look it up," she explained. "It's someone who has no sexual boundaries when it comes to gender or age."

"I thought that just meant bi-sexual?"

"No, there's a lot more to it and I really don't want to get into it on the phone."

"Are you okay?"

"I have to be because I'm on camera all night. I can't believe I didn't figure this out sooner. It was so obvious, and

I ignored every red flag."

"You didn't ignore them, you misinterpreted them," I interjected.

"It's me," she muttered now sounding like she might cry. "I have the worst luck with men. That's never going to change."

"Don't think like that, Marisa," I pleaded. "It's New Year's Eve and it's going to be the best year ahead, for all of us. I just know it." I could hear her breathing heavily like she was already crying and didn't want me to know.

"I have to go now," she concluded, voice now quavering. "I'll call you. If we don't talk tomorrow, Happy New Year."

It killed me that Marisa had to go through this, but I always had a notion something weird was going to happen with that guy. He just never seemed interested in her.

I returned to where Jeffrey and the toddlers were standing and joined them in exiting the backstage area to our tenth-row seats. There were twenty-one thousand fans in the audience cheering in anticipation of Brave Harlots taking the stage.

After seventy-five minutes of gritty, fist-pumping heavy metal music, Brave Harlots were ready for the first encore. I had a system of escaping concerts prior to the final encore so that I could get out of the parking lot and on the road before the crowd began filing out. Jeffrey evidently had the same system.

He turned to me after the first encore. "You thinking what I'm thinking?"

"As in let's get the hell out of here?" I asked.

"Peace out," the toddlers chimed in as they scrambled away, Converse All Stars squeaking. Evidently, we all had the same system.

Jeffrey checked his watch. "It's after midnight, Jane. I guess it's already next year," he said giving me a hug.

"Happy New Year, Jeffrey," I replied. "Let's hope it's a calmer one."

"Go home and get that champagne open," he said, smiling.

WHEN I ARRIVED HOME and got into the apartment elevator, I caught a glimpse of my reflection. For the first time, I didn't care what I looked like. All I wanted was a hot bath and a good night's sleep.

Once inside, I quickly changed into my white fuzzy robe and began to draw the bath water. As the water flowed into the tub and I felt the steam rise to my face, I began to relax. *What a year it had been.* I had a hard time believing that I had gotten through it. I wondered whether I would be a different person in the new year, whether I would grow from the hard lessons I'd learned.

After my bath, I put on black silk pajamas and slippers and went to the kitchen to see if there was anything in my fridge. Of course, I knew the answer was nothing. That was a New Year's resolution I would make: keep healthy food in my fridge.

I pulled out the bottle of Veuve Clicquot and gingerly picked off the foil wrapping, untwisting the wire fastener so I could properly uncork the bottle. *Great.* Another lonely New Year's Eve with nothing but alcohol to soothe me into oblivion, where the human condition hurt much less. I poured some champagne into a flute.

"Happy New Year, Weez," I toasted, raising my glass toward the hapless feline as he silently and indifferently darted in the opposite direction.

I was about to gulp down the champagne when I heard someone buzzing my intercom. I checked the clock—1:48 a.m. It had to be some drunk with the wrong apartment number. I sighed and pushed the intercom button.

"Who's there?" I called.

"It's me," was all I heard.

"Me, who?"

"Me, Derek."

What was Derek doing at my door at this hour? I thought back to the last time I saw him, at the party with Chelsea right before Christmas. I wondered what he could possibly want with me in the wee hours of the morning on New Year's Day.

The intercom buzzed again, and I answered, "What?"

"Are you going to let me in?"

I took a deep breath and buzzed him in. When I heard a knock at my door, I opened it slowly and there he was, all dressed up in a tuxedo, looking dapper and handsome. "What are you doing here?" I asked, squinting at him standing in the hallway, his sandy brown hair lit up with flecks of gold from the fluorescent bulbs.

He fidgeted and put his hands in his pants pockets. "May I come in?"

I reluctantly held the door open for him as he crossed the threshold. "Where's Chelsea?" I asked, suspiciously.

"I don't know, probably out with her friends," he answered. "We just finished performing at the Dorothy Chandler Pavilion and I came straight here."

I shut the door behind him and followed him into the living room. His eyes raced around my place as though he were worried that I wasn't alone.

"Well?" I said expectantly. "You still haven't told me what you're doing here at this hour. Are you drunk or something?"

"Of course, not. I need to talk to you, and I didn't want to wait."

"About?" I asked skeptically.

"Can we sit down?" He glanced around my apartment for a chair.

"Um … sure," I responded. There was simply no explanation for why Derek would show up uninvited to my apartment unless he wanted to give me more shit about our previous arguments. I felt like we left it in a good place when we talked at that party, but maybe I was wrong. Maybe he was still angry with me. So much for starting the New Year off on better footing, I thought grimly.

I cleared a stack of *Vogues* off the living room couch and gestured for Derek to take a seat. I sat next to him, suddenly feeling self-conscious in my black pajamas. He couldn't expect me to be dressed at this hour, could he?

"Jane," he started slowly. "This is really uncomfortable, but there's something I need to tell you."

"I'm listening." I could tell he felt awkward. He wouldn't even look me in the eye. Then, a horrendous thought went through my head. Maybe he was here to make a big announcement about his life. Maybe he was here to tell me he was getting married to Chelsea. I wished I hadn't bothered answering the door. "Wait, let me guess—you and Chelsea are engaged—am I right?" I predicted with feigned optimism.

"What?" he asked, looking exasperated. "Now, where would you get that idea? Chelsea and I are just friends and I've told you that over and over. There's nothing between us, Jane. But I'm not here to talk about Chelsea. I want to talk about you."

"What *about* me?" He certainly seemed like he was with Chelsea.

"Did you—I mean are you still …?" he stammered.

"Am I what?" *What did he want from me, anyway?*

"Are you still seeing that guy?" he blurted.

"What guy?"

"That ad agency guy—the one I saw you with a long time ago."

I remained silent while my mind momentarily went back to Craig Keller and our torrid affair. "No," I answered. "That guy was a huge mistake. No, he was more like a disaster, but you predicted that, didn't you?"

Derek didn't respond. He glanced down at his feet nervously and then back up at me. I looked deep into his soulful eyes, and they were glistening with emotion. "Do you still have feelings for him?"

"Derek, what's this about?"

"Jane, this is really difficult because I don't know how you feel about me but I … well, I care about you, and I didn't want to let the year end without telling you."

I thought I was not hearing right. For the longest time, I was certain he hated me.

"I was frustrated, Jane," he said as though reading my thoughts. "I tried to talk to you, but you turned me away. I couldn't stand playing games any longer. I had to let you go. Then I saw you at that party and I melted. I couldn't take my eyes off you. It drove me crazy. I couldn't sleep. Then, I found your CD this morning under my bed. There was no name on the card, but I couldn't get past the first track without knowing who it was from. I swore it was some sort of divine intervention, a sign that I just needed to go to you." He paused for a minute and took a deep breath. "So ... here I am."

I was dumbstruck. I thought back on how I had given the CD to Antonia to put on his pillow. He must have knocked it off without seeing it. I had been agonizing for three weeks and he never even saw it until today.

"Well, Jane?" he said, stealing a sideways glance to look me briefly in the eye.

"Well, what?"

"Would you consider dating me?" he asked, with all the clumsiness and vulnerability of a true gentleman.

I shook my head in disbelief. This was finally going to happen. It was meant to be—*Bashert*—as my grandparents called it. And I genuinely had feelings for Derek. I'd had them since the day we met at that baseball game. I just didn't want to acknowledge it because I never thought Derek felt the same. "Derek, you have no idea how long I've wanted to hear you ask me that," I said looking up at him.

"Does that mean yes?" Derek still looked unsure of himself.

"Of course, it does!"

"But I'm not a wealthy man," he said doubtfully. "I'm just starting out. I don't have an expensive car or a big house—I can't buy you beautiful things. What would I be compared to that guy?"

"You'd be the right choice," I said, trying to figure out whether I was telling the truth. What I think I really meant was the *safe* choice. I smiled and felt my eyes filling with tears as he pulled me close. I laid my head on his shoulder, wondering what I did to deserve the tenderness of this kind, caring man. I recalled navigating the torrential waters of Craig and how comforting it felt to feel Derek's arms around me—to feel protected. I pulled away and looked up at him, nodding through tears.

"Happy New Year, Jane," he said, moving closer and kissing me softly on the lips.

"Happy New Year, Derek," I whispered.

He then pulled the CD I made from his tuxedo jacket pocket and smiled at me.

"You know, I have the perfect soundtrack for right now," he said, standing to locate my CD player. He fiddled with the controls and the sounds of Crowded House's "Private Universe," filled the room. Derek turned to me slowly. "So, Jane," he said as he pulled me to my feet and put his arms around me. "What made you include this song?"

"I'm not sure," I answered, settling my arms around his neck. His body felt warm and strong. "Other than I love Crowded House and that song just reminds me of you, of us."

The intensely personal lyrics of Neil Finn oozed from the stereo as we listened, absorbing the moment in its beauty.

I will run for shelter
Endless summer lift the curse
It feels like nothing matters
In our private universe.

We slow-danced, and I closed my eyes, feeling like we were almost floating above the hardwood floor. My eyes were still closed. Derek lifted my face and his lips touched mine. It was our first kiss, one that felt both familiar and new. I was afraid to let it end—afraid if I did, he might somehow disappear—like the moment might slip away as though it had never existed.

I AWAKENED NEW YEAR'S DAY with a sense of peace to find Derek sleeping beside me—above the covers, still fully dressed in his tux. There is a certain feeling you get when you're with the right person—a sense of safety and belonging, like I was finally home. And for the first time I could remember in all my adult life, I wasn't worried about what was going to happen the next day, how long Derek would stay with me, or what it all meant. I had no desire to look in the mirror or even comb my hair. I knew Derek wanted me for who I was, and that feeling was sublime. All I wanted to do was soak in the moment, so I would never forget it.

Derek and I spent New Year's Day together, cooking, talking, and listening to music. Derek, it turned out, was an excellent chef and, disgusted as he was at the contents of my cupboards and fridge, went to Ralph's in the morning and stocked me up appropriately. It was absolute heaven. We were lost in our own private universe and had no desire to return to the real world.

At dusk Derek and I finally ventured outdoors to have dinner, almost tripping over the LA Times on our way out the door of my apartment building.

"Look, Jane, I guess we missed today's news," Derek said, picking up the paper and handing it to me.

I smiled up at him. "I don't think we missed a thing." I quickly glanced at the frontpage headline, above the fold, which read, "RUSSIAN SEX TRAFFICKERS CAUGHT SMUGGLING DRUGS, ANIMALS."

Underneath the headline were mug shots of Philippe and Frédéric. Philippe's face was terrifically disfigured from the burns I had inflicted, and large dark sunglasses covered his eyes.

"Holy crap," I exclaimed. "I've got to read this!"

The story was a full page that jumped to additional pages. Frédéric and Philippe had been detained by the FBI the previous night for questions regarding sex trafficking, drugs, fraud, and cruelty to animals. The two Russians were posing as Frenchmen in a scheme to traffic minors—the "performers" in the not-yet-launched show, "Le Panda Magnifique." Frédéric's real name was Yegor Golumbovsky, and Philippe's was Alexei Baronov. The 'pandas' were brown bears they had imported from the Pyrenees, painting them to look like pandas each night before the shows in Paris. The FBI was also investigating Philippe for illegally smuggling cocaine and heroin into the U.S.

During the interrogation process, they dug up the checkered and unsavory histories of both Frédéric' and Philippe, who each had more than twenty-five aliases and long criminal rap sheets. They were now facing indictment and deportation back to Russia.

There was a quote from Warren stating, "Warren Mitchell and Partners is no longer affiliated with the suspects involved in this heinous crime and has implemented more comprehensive background checks as we accept new business from foreign countries."

I thought about the night I threw hot soup all over Philippe and how he had tried to get me into his vehicle. "Oh my god," I cried. "One of those freaks hit on me!"

"Who hit on you?" Derek inquired possessively, grabbing the paper out of my hands, and examining it. After reading a few lines of the story and observing the mug shots, he turned to me and said, "How do you even *know* them?"

"It doesn't matter," I groaned. "They were so creepy they made my skin crawl."

"I'll kick their asses back to Russia," Derek threatened, visibly upset.

"Sweetheart," I said lightly, "it sounds like the FBI is taking care of that."

"But I really hate that you had to go through that, with anyone," he stressed, pulling me toward him. "Do you understand how hard it is for me to hear these things?"

This time, when I looked in his eyes, I realized that a slow-paced relationship was exactly what I was looking for—that being with Derek would be the opposite of what I'd read about in romance novels or seen in movies. That stuff was artificial—unrealistic even. What I wanted was exactly what Derek was offering: friendship that would bud like a flower into a romantic relationship. I was in no rush.

At that moment, I knew, in my heart, that everything was going to be all right. In fact, it was going to be better than all right. It was the beginning of something real.

THE END

Playlist

Find "Princess Smile" on Spotify.

"Empty Nest" by Silversun Pickups

"Pages" by White Reaper

"Withdrawal" by Max Frost

"Easy" by MISSIO

"Sofa King" by Royal Otis

"Jungle" by Tash Sultana

"Burning" By Yeah Yeah Yeahs

"Youth" by Glass Animals

"Love Is Mystical" by Cold War Kids

"Cigarette Daydreams" by Cage the Elephant

"Adios" by JAWNY

"Everybody's Gotta Learn Sometime" by Beck

"Your Song" by Elton John

Acknowledgments

Princess Smile is the first manuscript I brought to Don Daniels's critique group within the South Florida Writers Association. I am forever indebted to Don, Lori, and Renee for their patience, candor, and valuable input, which helped me craft and construct this book. When I finished *Princess Smile,* I simply could not say good-bye to its characters, so I created the complete series, *Truth, Lies, and Love in Advertising,* including *Camera Ready* and *For Position Only.*

My talented friend and colleague, Merrell Virgen, photographed each cover with care, creativity, and precision—thank you for always taking my small kernel of a vision and painting it in a way that only you can. My book covers are a constant source of pride.

Thank you to my early readers, and to everyone who has gone above and beyond to help me with these books, whether it be publishing, editing, critiquing, or simply believing in me. You are the reason I have these novels.

Made in the USA
Las Vegas, NV
03 June 2024

90700762R00184